The Mystery of the
Milton Manuscript

The Mystery of the
Milton Manuscript

A NOVEL

BARRY M. LIBIN

URIM PUBLICATIONS
Jerusalem • New York

To Margery,

who appreciates what is
of significance in this world,
and took the time to read,
recommend and most of all,
encourage.

The Mystery of the Milton Manuscript: A Novel
by Barry M. Libin

Copyright © 2014 Barry M. Libin

Typeset by Ariel Walden

Printed in Israel

First Edition

ISBN 978-965-524-158-7
Urim Publications, P.O. Box 52287, Jerusalem 9152102 Israel
www.UrimPublications.com

The Mystery of the
Milton Manuscript

London, January 22, 1667

I have sent you a Poem, more extraordinary for the matter than verse, though the last is not very common. The subject great . . . in the opinion of the impartial learned, not only above all modern addepts in verse, but equal to any of the Ancient Poets. And his blind fate does not barely resemble Homer's fate, but his raptures and fancy brings him upon a nearer parallel. I must confess I have been strangely pleased in a deliberate and repeated reading of him. . . . I can say truly I never read any thing more august.

Sir John Hobart
1667
3rd Baronet

BOOK I

CHAPTER 1

Cambridge, UK, 11:00 PM, January 7

The Cambridgeshire Constabulary patrol car pulled alongside the late model dark shaded Rover parked off a lonely stretch of road not far from the American Military Cemetery in Madingley. Constable James Gossage sipped the last of the tea from his thermos, a final sensation of warmth within before venturing out into the frozen, moonless night. It was late and he had more important duties than hasten lovers from darkened roadsides.

And yet, as he approached the Rover on the gravel-covered surface, he felt an unusual foreboding. Surely he had been on the force long enough to sense the untoward, but this was different, a feeling that sprung from deep inside that touched on uncertainty, or perhaps, even fear.

He directed his light through the driver's window, but the car appeared deserted. Puzzled, he attempted to open the driver's side door but to no avail. He checked for plate number and registration, but if there previously, they were now missing.

Gossage walked behind and flashed his beam along the passenger side, observing a half open door. Cautiously, as if walking a tight rope, he made his way alongside the Rover, trying to avoid the sharp rocky slope that fell precipitously from the road's edge. As he reached the open door, he realized that anyone exiting would have plummeted down the jagged surface. With great care he examined the interior, looking for a means of identification, but the car was clean, unusually clean, even the glove box was void of contents. Something was wrong.

His thoughts shifted to the occupants. This was not a night to remain outside. He peered down the steep incline that seemed to end in a grassy clearing not more than twenty meters below. It was difficult to see and he splayed his light from right to left looking for answers until it reached an amorphous form. Gossage stared at the shape, uncertain, his mind racing, the numbing cold bringing on a host of excuses, until he realized he had no choice.

He began the descent on the frost-covered slope, light in one hand, grabbing for the ice-encased branches with the other. Step by step, he made his way down to the flattened clearing. He paused and took a deep breath, removing a handkerchief from his uniform pocket to wipe droplets of sweat from his forehead. Searching for the image, he directed his light along the terrain, trying to orient himself in a world where silence and darkness ruled. Suddenly there was a rustling from his left. He spun to the side, flashing his beam into the dense woods, instinctively reaching for his nightstick. There it was, his light reflecting off a white paper snagged in the briars, trembling in the wind. He made his way to the clearings edge and focused on the torn sheet captive in its entanglement:

CHRIST'S COLLEGE CAMBRIDGE
presents
THE LADY MARGARET MEMORIAL LECTURE
Secrets of The Milton Manuscript
to be delivered by
PROFESSOR THORNTON LIVINGSTON
Distinguished Chairman of Early English Literature
Hertford College, Oxford
Saturday, January 7, 8:00 PM

Gossage left the sheet untouched and moved away, when, without warning, he stumbled. Heart pounding, he tried to regain his balance but it was too late, and he felt himself falling backward onto the grassy surface. Struggling to his feet, he flashed the light beneath him, the body of a man in dark suit and tie was sprawled on its side, the back of his head covered in blood. He hesitated before placing his finger on the carotid, but the vessel was lifeless. Reaching for his mobile, he called the force headquarters at Hinchingbrooke Park.

"Gossage here. I've got a dead body, male, probably in his sixties, must have taken a fall down the rocks out on Madingley Road . . . Yes sir, I'm inspecting it now."

As he redirected his beam over the fallen figure, fright enveloped him.

"Oh dear mother of god!"

It had been years since the constable last made the sign of the cross.

"Better come straight away. Straight away!"

CHAPTER 2

Cambridge, UK, 8:30 PM, January 7

Keith Jessup turned his attention to the tall, scholarly looking man approaching the podium. He had a full head of white hair and eyes sparkling energy that belied his years. He stood erect and spoke forcefully as the silence of anticipation fell upon the 600 scholars filling Lady Mitchell Hall, the largest and most modern of the lecture theaters at Christ's College at Cambridge. Keith and several other Oxford graduate students had driven to Cambridge early to gain a seat, avoiding being directed to an adjacent theater and its television coverage. The disclosure of the long-disputed Milton Manuscript was to be the most interesting lecture that devotees of Early English Literature would hear in recent years, adding a rare intrigue to literary scholarship, and Keith knew that seats would be hard to come by.

"Welcome, dear friends, to the annual Lady Margaret Memorial Lecture, named after Lady Margaret Beaufort, the mother of Henry VII, who in 1505 founded our beloved Christ's College. In her honor, each year, an individual is selected to receive The Lady Margaret Award for exceptional scholarship in the field of English Literature.

"Tonight our honoree will pay tribute to one of Cambridge's great alumni, John Milton, class of '31," he paused and then wryly added, "1631." The response was a quiet chorus of amusement.

"John Milton remains England's most influential poet, who in 1667 bestowed, although some students prefer 'inflicted,' his masterpiece *Paradise Lost* upon the world."

Keith smiled, recalling his own first attempt in high school to read the massive epic.

"As one of England's greatest political and religious thinkers, Milton was the dominant intellect through an era of unusual socio-political discord."

Keith allowed a subtle smirk to escape, skeptical of the newly required "etiquette" being spoken. He had been forced, early on, to deal with life as it was not as one would like it to be, and he was uncomfortable with those who disregarded the thorns when viewing the roses. *Political correctness had become the reality of the twenty-first century, when a murderer could no longer be called a murderer nor a terrorist a terrorist. Even the pos-*

sibility of offending, regardless of truth or intent, had become punishable. To Keith, it revealed how fear had replaced veracity in the world's priorities. Rather, he would have described England's seventeenth century as it really was: an era when religious and political strife revealed the enmity of sectarianism; when suspicion, bigotry, and fear produced blood-filled mass hysteria. It was a time of hatred and conflict to popery, when Protestants battled Catholics and their "cannibalistic" rituals for corrupting true Christian faith, and a time of revolution and civil war when the English nation nearly imploded from the pangs that accompanied the birth of belief that man was created with certain inalienable rights that no one, not even a king, could deny.

Keith returned his attention to the podium.

"The seventeenth century was the golden age of the printing press, affording opinions to be expressed through poems, cartoons, and pamphlets. If sermonizers tried to persuade those who could only hear, then writers attempted to persuade those who could also read, and John Milton was the most influential of them all."

The speaker paused for a moment. "And who better to pay such tribute than this evening's most distinguished honoree, Professor Thornton Livingston, another of Christ's College's great alumni, class of '65, that is 1965." Again the murmur of laughter was heard.

"Professor Livingston is one of the outstanding Milton scholars of our age and the Distinguished Chairman and Professor of Early English Literature at another great institution within our Motherland, Oxford. At this time, it is my distinct honor to ask Professor Thornton Livingston to ascend the podium to accept his award and discuss one of the most interesting, if not controversial aspects of the Milton legacy, 'Secrets of The Milton Manuscript.' Professor Livingston, if you please."

The speaker extended his hand in welcome, and the appreciative audience rose in boisterous applause. Keith jumped to his feet, his pride swelling and his smile broadened for not only was John Milton his hero, but it was his professor who was being summoned to the stage. The Lady Margaret was the most distinguished recognition, next to the Nobel, that a Milton scholar could receive and scholars had come from all parts of the Kingdom; from Scotland and Wales, London and Leeds, Birmingham, and Sheffield, to honor one of Cambridge's own and to hear one of the most popular and erudite scholars discuss one of the "hot" topics of the day, The Milton Manuscript.

As the applause receded and the audience resumed their seats, the speaker remained alone on stage, seemingly searching the room. Once again he announced, "Professor Livingston, please step up."

Keith scanned the tiered rows below and above. *Where is he?* They had spoken only hours earlier when Livingston was on his way. His professor sounded as excited about the evening as he had ever heard him. As the minutes passed and Livingston did not appear, a sense of urgency ran through him. It had been five years since Keith graduated from Brown University as a Rhodes Scholar to attend Oxford and complete his doctorate studies under Livingston's tutelage. And yet, not once had his mentor been late for an appointment, certainly not for a major event as this evening's, and never when there was an opportunity to discuss his life's passion, the search for the Milton Manuscript. *Where could he be?*

Keith pressed the numbers on his iPhone, letting it ring until he heard a click.

"Professor? It's Keith. Where are –" and then another click. He was certain someone had answered, yet chose not to speak, or couldn't.

"Keith Jessup, please step to the podium." Keith heard his name over the speaker system. He picked up his backpack and walked down the aisle, all eyes observing the tall, lanky young figure in jeans and a loose yellow crew neck sweater making his way forward. Keith checked the time, *thirty minutes late, something was terribly wrong.* As he mounted the steps, he was met by a group of scholars in anxious debate: "What could have happened?!"

The cacophony was silenced by the commanding voice of the speaker. "You must be Keith. I have the police on the phone. What kind of vehicle was he driving?"

Keith thought for a moment, the image of his professor's car coming into focus.

"A late model dark shaded Rover."

*

Hours later, under the cover of darkness, an older man who appeared stronger than his years, entered his home and was attracted to the blinking red light of an answering machine. Without hesitation, he strode across the room and played the waiting message: "It's ova, uncle. I buried it like ya tol me."

The man pressed the erase button, walked into the kitchen and switched on the outside light. Seeing no one about, he stepped out the back door and made his way to an old wooden sandbox. With effort, he knelt onto the frigid ground and moved his hands through the fine particles until he felt what he was looking for. Once again he surveyed the area. Seeing nothing unusual, he lifted out a plain brown paper bag, shook off the clinging sand, and carried it back to the house where he examined the contents. It took only a moment for a smile to appear.

CHAPTER 3

Cambridge, UK, January 9

"Mr. Jessup, the coroner is ready."

Keith had caught an early bus to Cambridge and walked the directions to Shire Hall on Castle Street. He spent a half hour in the white-walled waiting room preparing for what he was about to encounter. Sitting opposite him were parents of twin ten-year-old girls who had been missing for weeks. Last night, the parents were awakened by a call that the bodies of two young girls had been found. Would they come in to identify?

He sat there, feeling the depth of anguish in the mother's cries and her husband's helplessness in trying to console her. *How does one justify the ways of God? How ironic. Wasn't that what "Paradise Lost" was to reveal?* Keith felt their despair, wishing he could ease their pain for he also had met the injustices of life. He felt a tightening in his gut, a response that hadn't presented itself since he was a boy growing up in the blue-collar area of south Akron.

*

"Dad, stop hitting her."

"What did you say?"

"I said stop hitting mom. You're drunk again."

How he hated when his father attacked them without cause, and yet didn't the Bible teach *honor thy father and mother?*

The boy stood between his father and the figure of his mother lying on the floor, her face bloodied from the force of a fist.

"Leave her alone. She didn't do anything."

"You little bastard. Want another whipping?"

"Leave the boy alone."

The older man looked with contempt at the fallen figure. "So you're still taking his side."

He started toward her again but the boy screamed and stood his ground. "No!"

How many times had the boy asked why she didn't leave, but her reply was always the same: "Where am I to go?"

It was that snapping sound of the belt across his body that would rouse the boy from restless sleep. He had the dream many times, each time awakening him in cold sweat in the dead of night. In more ways than one, that belt made an indelible mark on the young man.

He was an only child. His father had worked the huge rubber mills in Akron, a booming town that was part of the great automobile prosperity of mid- and Middle America until Europe's radial tires, with almost three times the tread life, replaced Akron's bias-ply tires. America was unprepared, factories were closed, half the workers lost their jobs, including Keith's father, and there was nothing to replace the loss of an entire industry.

In spite of the boy's efforts, there was no pleasing his father, never words of encouragement, yet he never stopped trying. For young Keith, if success never received praise, failure was surely chastised. He was fourteen when his father died, as much from alcohol as from pneumonia, but it was the snap of that indiscriminate belt that imprinted on the boy a hatred of injustice and an instinctive refusal to allow others to be taken advantage of. It was the only lasting gift from a father to his son – a gift that would become his strength – and his weakness.

*

"Mr. Jessup, this way please."

The sound of his name brought him to his feet. He followed a heavy-set woman in a white lab coat down a sterile looking eggshell tinted corridor lit by fluorescent tubes overhead. To Keith it seemed only fitting that a building that housed the end of life should feel so lifeless.

"I'm Gladys, one of the coroner's officers. Appreciate your coming. Sometimes it's not easy to identify accident cases. I'm going to take you down to the morgue to view the deceased. Have you been to a morgue before?"

Keith was already feeling weak. It was no wonder he had chosen the world of literature over the demands of medicine. He had found it easier to understand the frailties of life rather than deal with them. "No, ma'am."

"Well, some don't find it an easy experience, but the work has to be done. Here in the UK, the coroner's role is to identify the deceased and determine the cause and time of death."

Keith followed the heavy-set woman down the stairs to the lower level. Gladys opened a closet door and gave him a white lab coat, extra-large, a green surgical mask and matching paper booties which he placed over his shoes. "Can't be too careful these days."

She led him into a rectangular room, the cold temperature made him shiver and the smell of formaldehyde added to the queasiness in his stomach. One wall looked like a row of stainless steel refrigerators containing six file-like drawers with extending handles surrounding handwritten names with numbers on identifying paper labels.

"Dr. Bethany, this is Keith Jessup."

A balding middle-aged man whose paled face seemed to reflect the vitality of those he examined turned and spoke in a dry, emotionless manner.

"Mr. Jessup. If you don't mind waiting for a moment I'll bring out the deceased."

The coroner pulled a file from off his desk, glanced through it, and walked to the cabinets, checking the labels with the one on his file. He opened the third cabinet and with a sturdy tug, rolled out a gurney. It reminded Keith of a narrow hospital bed except one whose patient was completely hidden by a sheet. He felt as if he was at the movies, watching but not participating.

"Mr. Jessup, I need to know if you recognize this individual."

Gladys walked along side Keith as Dr. Bethany pulled back the cover revealing the head, arms, and upper torso.

"Jesus!"

"Yes, there does seem to be a resemblance."

Keith felt his head spinning and his legs weaken. Gladys must have felt it also because she tightened her grip on his arm.

Keith just stared.

"Mr. Jessup?"

Keith was startled out of his thoughts. "This was an accident?"

He glanced at his file. "That was the police report. Seems to have been a fall."

"But how?"

"We're not sure."

"Why?"

"We don't know that yet either." The coroner paused. "Can you identify him?"

Keith almost choked on the words. "It's my professor, Thornton Livingston."

"No question?"

"No question."

Keith continued staring even as the doctor recovered the body.

"But his face, his hands, what could have happened?"

They looked at each other. "We're trying to figure that out also."

CHAPTER 4

Office of Professor Foster Sundstrom, Oxford, UK, January 10

"I say, young man, please come in. Excuse my not getting up but the back is out of sorts again."

Keith was still shaken from the week's events when he arrived for his appointment. As he entered, Foster Sundstrom sat behind an old walnut desk fitted with a leather writing surface cluttered with papers.

Keith felt uncomfortable, like a stranger in a strange land. He couldn't remember the last time he had discussed his dissertation with anyone but Livingston. *Organized chaos*, he thought, looking at the stacks of manuscripts lying along the floor's perimeter enclosing a faded reddish-brown Persian rug. *So different from Livingston's meticulous habits.* Ten-foot high, darkly stained wooden bookcases were filled with texts of all sizes and colors. Keith recalled the old saw – *the more disorganized, the better the professor*. Supposedly, good professors would rather spend more time teaching than tidying. Keith thought this professor must be very good.

Foster Sundstrom was the "James Tyne Professor of Miltonian Thought" at Oxford and one of the great authorities on John Milton. He was a short, heavy-set man, with a cherubic face whose reddish cheeks and broad smile reminded Keith of a Frans Hals portrait. His face was partially covered by a beard that had grayed in concert with his full head of hair, and his clipped English accent added to the pleasantness that permeated his demeanor.

Sundstrom waved his arm.

"Please, find yourself a chair."

Keith fitted his tall, broad-shouldered athletic frame into one of two wooden arm chairs set before the desk, the seats covered with a dull green fabric worn thin by years of student meetings.

"I dare say, young man, I'm so sorry about Thornton's passing. I know how close you were to him."

Keith nodded, wiping away the shock of sandy blond hair from before his soft blue eyes. "Yes, sir. He was more than my advisor, he was a friend."

"He spoke most highly of you, like the son he never had."

"Thank you, sir. He really has . . . had been like a father. I learned a great deal from him. I, I will miss him."

"And you are becoming a Milton scholar like he was."

"I doubt that I could achieve that. In many ways Professor Livingston and Milton were similar: fiercely independent, champions of truth, challenging regardless of repercussions, fearless against those who restrict freedom of mind and personal liberty, and never substituting principle for popularity."

Sundstrom was never without his smile, if not on his lips then certainly in his eyes.

"That's quite a tribute."

"And well-deserved."

"I would agree. Thornton Livingston was not afraid to challenge anyone."

Sundstrom paused for a moment before continuing. "As you know, I've been asked to assume his responsibilities while you are completing your dissertation. You should be on your last lap, so to speak."

Keith responded, "Yes, he was reviewing my final draft when . . . . when it happened."

"And your thesis is on *Paradise Lost*. A masterpiece. No one has ever written poetry, whether in form or content, as Milton did in that poem."

"Yes, but I've decided to add another section."

Sundstrom was surprised and looked down at the calendar on his desk. "A little late for that, I'd say. You have less than two weeks."

Keith reached into his green backpack and placed a manila folder on the professor's desk.

"I've already outlined it."

Sundstrom opened the folder entitled "*Paradise Lost – Interpretations and Criticisms*" and skimmed through to the new addition.

"Well, let's see . . . The Milton Manu . . ."

Sundstrom never finished reading the title. Slowly he raised his head and locked his eyes on the young man. To Keith, it seemed like an eternity.

"I want to finish what he started."

"But why?"

For a moment Keith didn't respond, his mind reflecting back to his childhood and the nightmares. "Because I need to know why things happen. If there exists an all-knowing, all-powerful God that determines what happens on His earth, then I need to know why God allows tragedy to occur. Can the Lord be so cruel to innocent people? If God is truly omnipotent, how can we justify what occurs on his earth?"

"Is that what the manuscript is to answer?"

"That is what *Paradise Lost* is to answer, yet it remains shrouded in mystery. It was Professor Livingston's belief that the explanation is to be found in a lost document that Milton himself wrote."

"But didn't he find it? Wasn't that what he was to lecture on last week?"

"I'm not certain what the lecture was to reveal. All I know is that he believed the key to its discovery would be found in one of the editions of *Paradise Lost* published when Milton was still alive. That's why he had me review every 1667 and 1674 edition that we could locate, searching for something unusual, some kind of mark that would lead to where it was hidden."

"And did you find anything?"

"Nothing."

"Perhaps there is nothing to find. You know most scholars refuse to believe there is such a manuscript."

"I'm aware of that, sir, but Professor Livingston did!"

Sundstrom paused for a moment. "Well, ordinarily I would encourage such exploration, but . . . ." His words trailed off as his fingers began a drum roll on the desk, the perennial smile slowly evaporating. Keith sensed the palpable change.

"Something wrong?"

The question was met with silence. With obvious discomfort the professor stood and walked to the window behind his desk.

What could be wrong? Keith knew that for over 300 years scholars have debated the meaning of *Paradise Lost*, yet all that Keith was certain of was that since first published in 1667, of the literally thousands of exegeses, there was no agreement. This, Keith believed, explained why more commentary has been written on *Paradise Lost* than on any other piece of English literature, and why his Professor believed that finding the manuscript was so important. Yet, Sundstrom's reaction made him uneasy.

"So you don't believe that we appreciate the real meaning of *Paradise Lost?*"

"Not yet."

As Sundstrom peered out at the Oxford scape, Keith continued. "That's why Livingston believed that understanding the poem's real meaning would answer one of the greatest questions in English literature. That's what the Manuscript is supposed to answer."

Again Keith paused before adding. "Indeed, what if such a manuscript led to a complete reconsideration of who Milton was, requiring us to revise our opinion of his beliefs?"

Sundstrom appeared in deep thought. "So you wish to carry on his work?"

Keith sat erect in his chair. "I believe he'd want that."

"And what about the rumors?"

"Rumors? What kind of rumors?"

Sundstrom continued peering through the window. "That there may be those who do not wish such a manuscript found?"

Keith was taken by surprise. "Sir?"

Sundstrom turned toward his new student, emphasizing his words. "What if someone did not want that lecture given?"

Keith was stunned. "I have no idea what you're talking about?"

Keith waited for a response. "Professor?"

It was as if Sundstrom was brought back from another world.

"Thornton and I were together at Cambridge. He was a brilliant scholar and a friend."

Keith's memory rewound to the professor with whom he spent so much time. They had a special relationship, one of mutual respect for the knowledge of the elder and the potential of the younger. Together they spent hours attacking and defending Keith's thoughts on Milton's work and the age in which he lived, the seeking of liberty, freedom, truth, and justice and how Milton's life was devoted to it. Livingston wanted him well-prepared for the oral defense of his thesis.

Keith verbalized his thoughts. "I had to identify the body. They say he was found at the bottom of a cliff."

"Yes, the local police are helping with the investigation. They're speaking to those who were close to him here at Oxford."

"They're not even certain how the accident occurred."

Suddenly Sundstrom turned from the window and with a focused intensity looked directly at the young scholar. "Accident?"

CHAPTER 5

New York, January 10

The sun had yet to rise when the continuous ringing tones caused the sleeping figure to be roused in a small neat apartment on the Upper West Side of Manhattan. Slowly a man raised his head and extended his arm, fingers fumbling for the little used cell phone lying on the night stand beside the bed. He sat up, wiping the cobwebs from his eyes.

"Sir?"

"He was warned but he chose not to heed them. A brilliant life wasted for no reason."

It took a moment to recognize the topic. "But the lecture? It was supposed to disclose . . ."

"I read the lecture. I found nothing that wasn't known already. He was a fool to pursue it."

"But I thought he found the . . ."

"He found nothing."

"But supposedly he had information . . ."

"I saw no such information."

"With no disrespect, what if someone else finds what you didn't. Could there be another copy of that lecture lying about? The word was out that he was getting close. Shouldn't we be certain?"

The voice on the other end paused for a moment. "Another copy? Perhaps we should."

"I wish it didn't have to happen that way."

"There was no other way."

CHAPTER 6

Keith Jessup tried to fit the pieces of conversation with Sundstrom into a logical format. *Was Livingston's accident not an accident? But why? And who?* A flash of anger swept through his body and an involuntary fist smashed on his desk, a replay of the conditioned response learned from the early days in South Akron.

*

Office of Professor Foster Sundstrom, January 12

"I trust you reconsidered." Sundstrom motioned for Keith to be seated.

"How can I reconsider when it's difficult to believe that someone would want to prevent one of Milton's works from being made known?"

Sundstrom responded slowly.

"Perhaps there are those who may fear what it would reveal."

Keith's mind was trying to comprehend the reality. "But it's been almost 350 years. I mean, except for the few hundred serious Milton scholars, does anyone really care?"

Sundstrom's response was reflexive.

"Millions care! Never minimize the significance of what Milton wrote; understand that for hundreds of years countless numbers of readers believed and continue to believe that Paradise was as Milton described and their Hell is as Milton taught them – nothingness."

Sundstrom recited the poet's words:

"O dark, dark, dark, amid the blaze of noon,

Irrecoverably dark, total eclipse

Without all hope of day!"

Keith followed the logic. "So you suspect that Christians relate more to the images of their religion than its doctrine?"

"I do. And where are those images of the Father, the Son, Satan, Angels, and Paradise?"

It was a rhetorical question, and Sundstrom continued.

"The fact is *Paradise Lost* long ago became a basic expression of Christendom. If you change the perception of Paradise you change the perception of the Christian Bible. Anytime one tries to alter such a basic tenet they had better be prepared for a reaction."

Sundstrom paused for a moment before continuing, "And what if finding his manuscript does just that?"

"Change their perception of Christianity? I can't believe that . . ."

Sundstrom didn't allow Keith to complete his thought.

"I'll tell you about believing. A man wrote to his minister how he had left the Church years before because he lost all belief in God. The letter began: '*After all these years I was led back to the Lord by John Milton!*' The man had just read *Paradise Lost!* Never forget the power and beauty of its language, and the questions that every man must answer to himself: If the world was created by a just and loving God, then why must the righteous suffer? If man is created in the image of God, then what is that image?"

The words echoed within Keith's ears. Sundstrom continued, "Understand what I am about to say: the greatness of Milton's epic is that it transformed myth into doctrine! Hear me now. Myth into doctrine! Never underestimate the significance of Milton's poem on a world seeking meaning."

The silence that followed allowed Keith time to absorb the ramifications of Sundstrom's words, and yet, there seemed no sense to it, or none that he could perceive. Sundstrom read the frustration on the student's face.

"Before you pursue this Manuscript idea I suggest you speak to someone who knows more about it than I do. He's retired from teaching now, but I saw him last week in Cambridge and he was as sharp as ever."

Sundstrom wrote the information on a card and handed it to Keith. "I'll let him know you will be calling, Professor James Bartholomew at Cambridge."

CHAPTER 7

Cambridge, UK, January 13

The late afternoon train to Cambridge is rarely crowded and Keith took an empty seat next to the window, looking blindly out at the growing darkness, the intermittent lights from homes and parks momentarily illuminating the passing English countryside. His mind wrestled with Sundstrom's warning until, almost reflexively, he reached into his backpack and removed a notebook and pencil and began to sketch the flying images. It was something he had always done when tension needed to be eased, a response learned from his mother as a young boy.

He missed her. As much as his father taught hate, his mother taught love: her love of reading and drawing, and a faith in God that would guide him throughout his life – and he followed in her footsteps. As a boy, Keith was never without a book, as if reading allowed him to escape the world in which he was raised, and his talent with pencils and paper produced sketches that flew him, like Peter Pan, to far away lands of his own creation. As he grew, his drawings often expressed an inner fear, as did his stories. He was withdrawn, but with his teachers' support school itself became a refuge. In high school he was too talented to be disregarded – with students and faculty encouraging him to draw for the *Red and Gray*, the school newspaper, and in his junior year they made him art editor of the yearbook. He remained a loner, preferring to keep his own counsel, or fearful of doing otherwise. In college there had once been a young woman, but that was long over. His mother had always given him the security that someone was there for him, but now that she was gone, there was no one else.

The train pulled into Cambridge Station and Keith returned the pad and pencil into his backpack and stepped outside. It was a cold, crisp evening as he walked the five blocks along Kings Parade, passing the warmly lit interiors of the variety of shops and cafes, the rich Gothic architecture and the throng of Cambridge students walking with their books to and from lectures. *Why am I here? Is there really something to fear in seeking Milton's truth? Wasn't truth the essence of who Milton was? Isn't truth what Livingston taught me to seek?*

*

Professor James Bartholomew lived in the Cheshire Apartments on Trinity Street, not far from the College. Keith stopped at #27, a neat three-story brick house, and used the large brass door knocker to announce his arrival. As the door opened, it took a moment for Keith to recognize who Bartholomew was. The older gentleman stood as tall and straight as he did. He had a full head of white hair and his camel slacks, tweed jacket, and black turtleneck reminded Keith of the natty Professor Higgins that Rex Harrison played in *My Fair Lady*. He wore a slightly mischievous smile and his words were delivered as a Shakespearean actor. Keith recalled hearing them before, a deep and sonorous voice inviting Keith into his study. As Keith took in the room he realized where

Professor Sundstrom learned to organize an office, with the edge of the thinly worn brown Persian carpet holding piles of books and stacks of papers. Bartholomew offered his visitor a cup of steaming tea and Keith settled into the chair in front of the burning fireplace that lent a warm glow to the rich mahogany desk before him.

"Nice to see you again."

Keith tried his best to hide his embarrassment. "And you, sir." Keith paused for a moment. "I didn't realize that you were the speaker who introduced the Lady Margaret Lecture last week."

"No need. I thank you for your help." The older man sat back into his chair. "I was sorry to hear about Thornton's passing."

"Yes, I still can't believe it."

Bartholomew looked closely at Keith, "And I've been told of your interest in continuing his work?"

"I'd like to, but Professor Sundstrom suggested that I speak to you first; he was concerned about someone wishing to prevent such a manuscript from being found."

Bartholomew shifted his weight and remained silent for several moments, continuing to study the student facing him.

"Perhaps it's because *Paradise Lost* is the greatest poetic accomplishment in the English language, not only the supreme epic of the English nation but of all Christendom. The world believes that the poem defends the glory of Christianity and the victory of the Christian God, his Son Jesus and the Holy Spirit over Satan and his forces of evil. Is it so difficult to appreciate that such a perception must be defended from any assault?"

Keith appreciated the sermon but had difficulty with the logic.

Bartholomew paused momentarily and pointed at Keith. "Is it not possible that the manuscript may prove such an assault?"

"I prefer that it proves the truth. Isn't it time we know exactly what the poem means?"

The professor smiled. "Yes, from a scholarly perspective such a manuscript would certainly settle a great deal of debate."

Keith interjected. "Yet you suggest that England and Christendom need to be defended from a document that is 350 years old?"

Suddenly the old man sat forward in his chair. As he looked at Keith, his face reddened and he brought his fist down hard on the desk and raised his voice, as if the energy of youth had been restored. "The Bible is older and a hell of a lot of blood has been shed defending that document!"

This was madness.

Keith felt attacked and responded in kind. "But *Paradise Lost* isn't the Bible!"

"To some it is! If you attack *Paradise Lost*, you are attacking a fundamental Christian belief of God's creation and power, good over evil, reward and punishment. You ask why would anyone defend a document that is so old? I'll tell you why! Because some people believe that certain principles in life must be defended, that's why!"

Keith took a hard swallow. Somehow the conversation had escalated into a debate.

Bartholomew quickly withdrew the scorn on his face. "Well now, I'm glad to see I still get so enthusiastic about such small matters." He settled back into his chair and sipped his tea.

"Perhaps you have heard of the Society of the Cincinnati?"

Keith nodded, "Part of American history."

Bartholomew continued, "Correct. The Society of the Cincinnati is the oldest military society in continuous existence in North America. It was founded in 1783 to preserve the ideals of your Revolutionary War against our mother country and is still active in educating the public about the American Revolution."

The old man continued: "Well, the Society was named after Lucius Quinctius Cincinnatus, who left his farm to accept the office of Roman Consul. When Rome was attacked, the Roman Senate appointed him to assume control of the army. When the war was won, Cincinnatus returned authority to the Senate and resumed his farming. The Society's motto reflects that ethic of selfless service: *Omnia relinquit servare republicam.*"

Keith translated, "He relinquished everything to save the Republic."

"Precisely. The Society's first meeting was held in May 1783 and was chaired by Lieutenant Colonel Alexander Hamilton, and George Washington was elected its first President General. After the war, they continued meeting and when a member died that membership was passed on to the eldest son, following the rules of primogeniture."

Bartholomew rose from his chair and poured more tea for Keith and himself.

"Is there a relationship between Milton and the Society of the Cincinnati?" Keith asked.

The Professor retook his seat. "Not directly, but if you understand their legacy you can understand how collective ideals are passed on from generation to generation."

"Are you suggesting that concealing the Manuscript is a generational ideal?"

The scornful look appeared momentarily. "You came here wanting to know if there was someone wishing to prevent a manuscript from being found. I'm merely giving you the reasoning of why people do such things."

Keith's frustration was building. "With all due respect, I came here wanting to know if someone didn't want my professor to give his lecture, not a history lesson."

"A history lesson is what you need! Did not the Church murder millions who didn't believe in a Christian God? Don't you remember how your Ku Klux Klan espoused White Supremacy as a reason to hang blacks? Do not holocausts occur because of some heinous belief?"

Again his fist came down hard on the desk. "Like it or not, tradition is never outmoded!"

Keith fought back. "But truth seems to be! Livingston was searching for truth, and truth, above all, is what scholars must seek."

Bartholomew's voice was delivered as if on stage. "Scholars must seek truth, but defenders must defend!"

Keith felt attacked and fired back. "But we're speaking of murder!"

"If that's what it takes! Especially for those committed individuals who wish to preserve ideas that have been handed down from generation to generation. Do they not have a responsibility to previous generations to defend it, and any attempt to discredit it with false accusations must be destroyed?"

"Even if that accusation comes from Milton himself?"

The old man stood erect, as if orating before the Parthenon. "Especially if from Milton himself! If Milton is the creator, he alone has the power to destroy it. What if the Milton Manuscript discloses something so frightening that its defenders believe it must never be revealed?"

Bartholomew almost stopped in mid-sentence and sat down. To Keith it was as if the old man realized he had said too much, but his words kept reverberating in Keith's head. . . . *what if the Manuscript discloses something so frightening . . . what could that be?*

The room went silent. They had engaged in war and it was time for each side to retreat to their lines. Finally Keith responded.

"Then the only way to know is to find a copy of his last lecture!"

Bartholomew sat staring at the student trying to control himself.

Finally he rose from his chair. The meeting was over. As the professor walked Keith to the front door, he quietly added. "I suggest you think carefully before you decide to carry on. You have no idea what you're getting into."

"It sounds like the honor of God and country."

"That's precisely what it is."

*

He did think carefully, very carefully. *What was in Livingston's speech that could cause such furor?* It had been difficult to believe that his professor died in quest of a manuscript, but now he wasn't so certain. *Perhaps they were right – perhaps it was best to not get involved, after all, why add controversy when all I need is to complete my dissertation.* And yet, the thought that his professor had been murdered made him relive his own past. His father had taught him well. When there were innocent victims, he felt their pain; their abuse was his past relived. Wasn't it Milton who wrote *"I am a part of all that I have met"*?

By the time he returned to Oxford Rail Station, he knew that he, like Milton, would seek the truth regardless of consequences. He would find the lecture Livingston never gave.

CHAPTER 8

Oxford, UK, January 13

The stars glittered and the moon complemented the street lamps as Keith began the 25-minute walk that saved him the six-pound taxi fare. He had a lot to think about as he crossed over the small Hythe Bridge, passing the Said Business School on his left. Could the lecture truly contain something that could cause such fear? Almost absentmindedly he quickened his pace as he made his way onto George and down Broad and Hollwell to St. Cross Road. He realized that in all the time the two of them spent together, Livingston never discussed the Manuscript. Even the times that Keith had raised the topic, Livingston avoided responding. It was the only subject that he refused to engage in, as if it best that Keith knew nothing about his professor's personal quest. More than once Keith had the feeling that Livingston was trying to protect him from a source of danger. As he made a right turn onto Manor Road, the sight of several English graduate students suspended his thoughts.

"Better hurry, John started closing the building."

Keith smiled at his colleagues. "Thanks, just have to check on something."

The St. Cross Building, completed in 1965, was a large contemporary structure made up of three connecting cubes of varying sizes. Keith had always admired the architecture, recalling how it utilized Le Corbusier's five points of modern design, with form dictated by the internal arrangement of the cubes placed at different levels, ingeniously interlocking with each other. The result was a building of massive brick cubes interposed with narrow vertical strips of plate glass windows framed in metal.

As Keith entered the large central common area where the three cubes intersected he sensed something awry. The automatic timer had already begun to turn off the building's lighting, with only the hallways remaining lit, and soon even they would begin to diminish to low energy voltage. Keith smiled at the thought that the world was turning green. But where was John? The security guard always manned the sign-in desk at the entrance to the rotunda until midnight when the building would be locked for the night. Even if he was away from his station, he would never leave the door unlocked. Rather, faculty and students would wait at the door for him to open it for their exit. Keith thought of the number of times that John had to knock on his office door to remind him of quitting time. He checked his watch – it was 11:45, he didn't have much time.

Keith quickly walked into the medium-sized cube that housed the English Faculty Library and offices and hurried along the dimly lit hallway, realizing that the offices on either side must have already emptied. He passed Sundstrom's darkened room and continued through the corridor, his footsteps the only sounds, as it echoed from the walls, until he reached the familiar entrance. Keith hadn't been in Livingston's office since his death and he hesitated before inserting the key, as if holding out the hope that his professor would greet him when he unlocked the door.

Except it wasn't locked. *How was that possible?* Cautious, he opened the solid oak door and entered the outer room where he often met with undergraduate students. But things were not as when he had last left. Books and papers were strewn about the floor. *What could have happened?* He looked across the room and saw a light through the slightly open door that separated the outer room from Livingston's private office. His heart began to beat forcibly and his muscles tightened in response to the unknown as he heard papers being shuffled and sounds of desk drawers being forced opened and thrown shut.

"It ain't ere, Clive. Nutin ere about no manuscript, no copy of no lecture, no laptop. I betta call im."

Keith heard the words and quickly realized what was happening. Whoever was here had come for the same purpose as he had. He strained to hear what was being said.

"It's me . . . No, lecture, nuthin. Yes, sir. I'll wait fer y'call."

Then he heard a second voice. "What did he say?"

"E sez we betta get out and e'll call in a few days. E says we ave to keep lookin."

"You didn't mention the guard."

There was a cruel laugh. "Sorry bout that. Guess I forgot."

"I don't like leaving the place like this."

"Ew cares? They don't know ew did it. We better get the ell outta ere."

It was too late to leave. Keith needed a place to hide and accustoming his eyes to the dim light, spotted the desk in the rear corner. He moved as quickly and silently as he could, but as he crouched behind the desk, he rubbed against a book perched on its edge; the silence broken as it fell to the floor.

"Wat was that?"

The men opened the door and scanned a flash around the room. Keith compacted his body as the light swung over.

"Don't see no one. Betta get out fore someone does come."

As the men opened the outer door, Keith peered from behind the side of the desk, the hall lamp illuminating the figures. The first man to leave was tall and wiry and Keith noticed a deep scar running down his cheek. The second, without warning, suddenly turned back, as if searching for something, something he heard, a sound that didn't belong. He looked directly in Keith's direction. Keith froze, afraid to move, afraid to breathe, his eyes focused on the intruder. If he had to, he would defend himself. The man reached for his belt and removed a gun. Keith was certain he was seen, and then, just as suddenly, the man grinned and disappeared.

Keith took a deep breath, stood up and made his way into Livingston's office. Nothing remained on the shelves or in the desk drawers. Whatever they were looking for wasn't to be found. Keith gave a cursory inspection but discovered nothing – no laptop, no lecture. He picked up the phone and called campus security to report the intrusion without leaving his name. He walked to the door and looked back for the last time, still hoping it was all an illusion. As he closed the door, he recalled what the intruder on the phone had said: *They have to keep looking. But where?* As he approached the security post, John was still absent. *What did they mean by not mentioning the guard?* He needed to know who they were. He walked behind the desk to check what names had signed in that he did not recognize. That's when he saw the red coagulating liquid that had seeped under the closet door. He opened it, fearful of what he would find. Inside, crumbled to the floor, he recognized John, lying in his own pool of blood, his neck almost severed. He picked up the phone and dialed the operator.

"Someone's been murdered at St. Cross."

He exited the building, terror and anger permeating his being, his mind's eye picturing the intruder looking directly at him. It was as if he had seen evil itself, a hulk of a man with a hideous smile, his head covered in blazing red hair.

*

London, UK, January 14

A woman's voice answered the cell phone that had fallen on the floor. "Yeah, ooz callin?"

"I'm inquiring after Abaddon, is he there?"

"Abaddon, yeah, old on and I'll fetch im." The woman in the second floor flat in London's East End tossed the phone on the bed, opened the window overlooking the street and called down.

"Abaddon, somebody's on yur mobile phun – betta get yur arse up here. Sounds awful proper." She walked back to the phone "E'll be right up, guvna."

Abaddon. No one had ever heard of anyone being called Abaddon, certainly not the kids at school. Not only was his name different, he looked different, a huge body with a rodent's elongated head, squinting eyes that appeared through slit like openings in his orbits. He had one flaring upper front tooth and the other had been knocked out and never replaced, leaving a large gap when he smiled. The irony was that he was a fraternal twin and his brother had a normal appearance and was a model student. But Abaddon was always mixed up in something shady.

His days in school were spent less in learning than in fighting those who made fun of him, a history personally recorded on his scarred flesh. He got by doing odd jobs, or when that was in short supply, theft.

Abaddon labored up the stairs and entered the flat. The huge man's face had scars crisscrossing through his scaly reddish complexion and redder hair. As he lumbered into the room he gave a nasty look at the woman. "Didn't I tell ya neva to ansa me damn phun."

"Then keep it wit ya. I ain't gonna led it keep ringin."

A cigarette drooped from the corner of his mouth and he quickly removed it. He sat upright on the bed, took a deep breath and picked up the phone.

"Uncle?"

"Hello, Abaddon. I thought I told you no one else is to have access to this phone."

"Yeah, sorry. Won't appen agin." Abaddon paused for a moment, worried that he had messed up. "Did somethin go bad?"

"No, you did as instructed, I'm sure the force you applied was necessary. I'm proud of you."

Abaddon's eyes lit up, "I try me best."

"I know you do and that's why I have another job for you."

"Yer wan me ta keep lookin, is thad it?"

"Precisely. It's important that we find it. I'll leave instructions and the reimbursement for your efforts in the same place as last time."

"Glad to oblige. I'll tyke gud care of it."

"I know you will."

As he hung up, Abaddon took a long drag on his cigarette and slowly let the smoke stream out into the room. He rubbed the butt into the ashtray and a large smile appeared, revealing the missing incisor. He walked into the small kitchen where the woman was washing a sink full of dirty dishes.

"Forget makin dinna, let's go celebrate. I got pounds comin me way."

CHAPTER 9

Oxford, UK, January 14

The knocks on his door interrupted Keith's writing. Two officers from the Thames Valley Police entered the room.

"Keith Jessup? We have an order to search your room."

"Search my room, why?"

"It appears you were the last person to see Professor Livingston alive."

"What are you talking about?"

As the police went through the papers on his desk, Keith started forward.

"Stay where you are!"

"I need those papers!"

The officer repeated the warning. "Stay where you are."

Keith felt his privacy invaded, but controlled his instinct to strike back.

"This your laptop?"

"Yeah."

"Come with us. The Deputy Chief Constable wants a word with you."

It took the two officers thirty minutes to deliver Keith to police headquarters at Oxford Road, Kidlington in Oxfordshire. As he looked out at the rolling hills of the winter's countryside from the rear seat of the command's new Vauxhall Astra, thoughts rushed in like torrents of rain, thoughts of yesterday's visit to Bartholomew, the break-in at Livingston's office, John's murder, and now this. The whirling fears were interrupted as the squad car came to a stop in front of central headquarters. Entering the building, he noticed the Latin inscription over the door: *Sit pax in valle tamesis*, "Let there be Peace in the Thames Valley." Keith thought that based on recent events, there hadn't been peace in the Valley for a long time.

He was ushered into the small office of Deputy Chief Constable Constance Bathgate. Files were neatly piled on her desk and freshly picked yellow flowers were swimming in a glass vase half filled with clear water on the filing cabinet behind. Connie, as she was called, was a tall, willowy woman about fifty. Her dark hair was cut just above the collar of her clean uniform. Her demeanor and her speech suggested she had few interests that would take priority over her job as Deputy Chief Constable. She placed his laptop on her desk.

"Mr. Jessup, thanks for coming. I understand there was a little misunderstanding with my officers in your flat and I want to apologize for that. This is a high profile case and we've been working round the clock with the Cambridge police to complete an investigation on the murder of Professor Thornton Livingston."

Keith felt his hands tightening on the arm rests. "So he was murdered?"

"That's what we believe we're dealing with."

"You're sure."

"As best as we can say. And I understand you were the last person to have spoken to him."

"That's true. But I had nothing to do with . . ." His voice trailed off, never completing the sentence.

"His murder?" She regarded him as if x-raying his soul. "No, I don't think you did. But we were hoping you might be able to add something to what we already know. Would there be any reason why someone would want to kill the professor?"

"He was a professor. He delivered lectures, not drugs."

The Deputy Chief Constable heard his anger. "Perhaps something that might be – well – out of the ordinary?"

What wasn't out of the ordinary about an extraordinary man. "I'm not certain how much more I can add. The last time I spoke to him he was on his way to give the lecture at Cambridge. Nothing was wrong. If anything, he was looking forward to receiving his honor."

"So nothing to add?"

"Not that I know of." He felt pangs of pressure building within his chest. *So Sundstrom and Bartholomew were right!*

The Deputy Chief Constable, seeming almost relieved, glanced at her watch. "Well then, I appreciate your time but we just wanted to complete the investigation before we send in our final report."

"Did you find the lecture?"

The Deputy Chief Constable, startled by the question, stared at Keith for a moment then glanced at her notes.

"He was identified by a torn cover sheet announcing the program."

Keith persisted. "But the lecture, did you find it?"

The Deputy Chief Constable again eyed the student and rechecked her notes. "No, no lecture was found at the scene. Was there something unusual about it?"

Like someone wanting to prevent it from being delivered? She'll probably think the whole thing absurd. But what if . . .

"Perhaps there was."

Connie Bathgate looked at the young man sitting opposite her. "Unusual?"

"It's possible, especially since there was a murder of a security guard and a break-in at his office."

"Yes, we're investigating those incidents."

Connie sat back in her chair, and Keith realized she was trying to connect the dots – a lecture, a murder, and a break-in. He got the feeling she wished she had never called him, seeing the Livingston death had occurred outside her jurisdiction.

"Would you like to tell me about it?"

Keith realized he shouldn't have brought it up. He just wanted to get out, breathe fresh air, and think. This was no time to begin a lecture on sixteenth- and seventeenth-century English history.

"Mr. Jessup!"

Her command snapped Keith back to her question. "It's really not important."

"That's something I'll have to decide."

Keith realized how tense he was, an ingrained response when people tell him what to do. He tried to relax, realizing she was only doing her job. "Where should I begin?"

"Why not from the beginning?"

"That's quite a ways back."

"How far back?"

"1534?"

Keith figured she thought he was joking, but her face didn't crack a smile.

"Fine, if you have something to say, I'm here to listen."

Keith took a deep breath, tried to relax, and began.

"Well then, in 1534 King Henry VIII asked the Catholic Pope Clement VII to annul the marriage to his wife, Catherine of Aragon, so that he could marry his mistress, Anne Boleyn."

Connie interjected. "Oh, yes, something about a son."

"Correct. The need to have an heir to the throne. When the Pope refused the annulment, Henry grew so irate that he took it upon himself to annul the marriage. That took some careful planning. First, he renounced Roman Catholicism and its Papal authority, then he removed England from Rome's religious rule and established the Church of England, making himself its head, and then, under his authority, dissolved the marriage."

Connie seemed impressed. "My goodness, he did all that in one year?

I must inform our Prime Minister. The poor fellow hasn't done anything in four. Perhaps dear King Henry didn't have to deal with Parliament."

Keith forced a smile. "Actually, he did, though it was just the beginning of Parliament's quest for more power. But it was also the beginning of the Protestant Reformation, provoked by Luther's Ninety-Five Thesis in 1517, denouncing the traditions and leadership of the Roman Catholic Church, especially its Pope. It hit Europe like a bomb, and in England this widespread tide for Catholic reformation demanded that Henry's new Anglican Church go further in ridding itself of its remaining Catholic practices. For the next 150 years there ensued a battle between a popish Anglican Church and those demanding a complete break from its remaining Catholic roots."

Again she eyed her watch, impatiently.

"Perhaps you could add some speed; it appears we have another 500 years to go."

"Well, Professor Livingston believed that John Milton had written an explanation as to the underlying meaning of *Paradise Lost*."

The Deputy Chief Constable picked up a pencil and began tapping the eraser end on her yellow note pad.

"Wait a moment, you just jumped from the Anglican Church to the poem. I assume there is a relationship?"

Keith realized the difficulty.

"Let me explain. The story, as you remember, comes from the Bible."

She turned the pencil over as if ready to begin taking notes.

"Why don't you review it anyway, in brief."

"Of course." Keith began. "The poem begins with Satan in Hell calling a council of the fallen angels in their new council hall called Pandemonium, to discuss defeating God after failing in their first attempt. Satan volunteers to fly up to the newly formed world and see what Adam is all about. With some difficulty he goes through Hell's Gates guarded by Sin and Death, and, as directed by Chaos, flies to Eden. He is struck by the perfect beauty of Adam and Eve, but overhears that they are not to eat from the Tree of Knowledge. Satan uses this information to seduce Eve, and after Adam and Eve fall asleep, Satan whispers into Eve's ear, tempting her in a dream. When Eve awakens she tells Adam her dream and he comforts her, following which they begin their daily work in the Garden. God sends the angel Raphael to warn Adam of Satan's presence, but at night, Satan returns to Paradise and enters the sleeping body of the serpent. In the morning, as they prepare to tend the garden, Eve suggests that she and Adam divide their labors and work separately to allow them to get more done. Adam is fearful of Eve being alone, but she insists until he agrees. The serpent finds Eve, flatters her, and convinces her that his wisdom and speech come from the fruit of the Tree of Knowledge. With cunning, he persuades her to eat the forbidden fruit, and soon she tempts Adam to eat of it also. Immediately Adam and Eve discover their nakedness and experience guilt, accusing each other of being the transgressor. They are condemned to banishment and, as the poem ends, the angel Michael takes them by the hand and leads them out of Paradise, never again to return."

Keith paused. "And that's the story."

Connie looked up. "So what's the problem?"

"Nothing, except that the poem is supposed to justify the ways of God to man and no one is certain what those ways are. That's why Professor Livingston believed that Milton wrote the true explanation in a separate manuscript. That's what his lecture was to be about."

"And where's the manuscript?"

"We don't know."

Connie was fast reaching her endpoint. "And how does this relate to the professor?"

Keith continued, realizing he was now heading into cloudy territory. "Because some scholars believe that the Manuscript contains information that is so explosive to certain God-fearing people that they are preventing the Manuscript from being disclosed."

Connie sat back, thinking about her afternoon schedule. "That's it?"

"Yes, ma'am, that's it."

"So you think God-fearing people caused the Professor's death?"

"It's possible."

"Murdered him?"

"Yes, ma'am."

"But if they're God-fearing . . ." The Deputy Chief Constable decided not to go there.

"And when was this Manuscript supposedly written?"

"While he was writing *Paradise Lost*, around 1650 or so."

"So after 350 years, you're saying we've got ourselves a conspiracy."

"It's one scenario."

"And scholars take this seriously?"

"Some do, but most do not believe there is such a Manuscript."

Connie's first thought was, *our taxes fund this kind of research?*

"Mr. Jessup, I want to thank you for spending time with us today. I think that's all we need to know." She stood up from her chair. "By the way, aren't you preparing to defend your doctoral thesis?"

"Yes, ma'am, next week."

Connie picked up the laptop and gave it to him. "Then you'll need this."

Almost as an afterthought she removed from the file a small business card and a photograph. She showed the card to Keith.

"By the way, do you recognize this? It was found near the scene of the accident."

Keith looked at the typeface: "*Stigmata.*"

"No ma'am. I mean I know what it means, but I don't know what this card is about."

Connie placed the card back into its file. "Well then, it's probably the name of some Italian restaurant." She then handed him the photograph.

"What about this?" Keith looked at a picture of washed out red lettering: PALPAB OBSCS.

"The coroner took this."

He hadn't seen it before. "What is it?"

"We're not sure, but it's a close-up of Professor Livingston's left hand. It seems he was trying to write something at the time of his death."

"PALPAB OBSCS. I have no idea." Keith's mind was searching for some logic. *What was he trying to say?* "I helped identify the body, but the whole scene was a blur. I noticed something on his hands, but not anything like this."

"Perhaps the blood had already been removed."

As two officers entered the room to return Keith to Oxford, the Deputy Chief Constable asked a final question. "Would there be any reason why the Professor was found with punctures on his extremities?"

Again he flashed back to the dead body. "Is that what happened to his hands?"

"It appears so."

"Maybe that's where the stigmata comes in – although that doesn't make much sense."

"That's what we're thinking."

Keith was anxious to leave, but as he stood up he asked a last question. "What about his face?"

Connie looked at him. Keith repeated.

"I remember seeing something. What was it?"

"We're not certain, like we're not certain about what any of this means. His cheeks seemed to be marked on each side. The coroner believes the letters *S* and *L* were branded into his flesh."

CHAPTER 10

Oxford, UK, January 21

On the morning he was to defend his thesis, Keith walked along the path that led from his apartment, his eyes trained more on a journal article than on his direction, when he was startled to hear his name called.

"Keith Jessup?"

Keith looked up to find a well-dressed man in scarf, cashmere topcoat, and the finest Christys' black Homburg approaching him with a rich black leather briefcase in hand.

"My name is Colin Cuttermill, I'm a solicitor in London of the firm Twinings and Whitcomb and represent Professor Thornton Livingston's estate. Unfortunately, it is my responsibility to carry out the Professor's wishes following his ill-timed death."

Keith put the journal down and regarded the man. "Yes, sir. How can I help you?"

"Actually, it appears that I may be of assistance to you. You see, Professor Livingston never married and had no heirs, but he was also the only son of a well-to-do banker in London. In case of his demise, he left instructions for certain provisions to be carried out in the distribution of assets to various charities, organizations – and you."

Keith was taken by surprise. "Me?"

Cuttermill continued, "That is correct, sir. I was instructed to deliver to you a note should he not be able to attend the defense of your thesis, which I believe is to take place this afternoon. He was very proud of you. There is only one stipulation: that you must maintain complete confidentiality regarding this transaction."

Cuttermill placed his hand into his briefcase and withdrew a large manila envelope.

"Should you have any questions, I have enclosed my business card. If you ever need anything, do not hesitate to call. I will be sending you communications during the year to keep you advised of your situation. And sir, I wish you the best this afternoon."

With that, Cuttermill bowed slightly, turned and walked away.

Keith watched as he made his exit, not certain how to respond. He placed the envelope into his back pack, walked back to his apartment, and sat down at his desk. When he opened the envelope, he found it contained a legal-sized typewritten sheet and a small envelope with his name on it written in his Professor's script. It was the first time he had seen the handwriting since Livingston's death and, curious, ran the sharp edge of a letter opener along the envelope's crease and removed the contents. Inside was a neatly written note on Livingston's personal linen stationery.

> Keith,
>
> If you receive this, it will mean that I will not be with you on your special day. I will miss your keen mind, thoughtful insights, and your courage not to shy from battle. You have been a special student, colleague, and friend and it made these last years the most exciting and worthwhile of my career.
>
> I have asked Mr. Cuttermill to inform you of a small gift that I hope you can use in your future pursuits. Perhaps you will even explore finding the Manuscript. If so, please remember that Stigmata is more than you have been taught, and the journey more difficult than you realize. But if truth is sought and justice served, the reward will be great.
>
> May Milton's genius and strength be with you,
>
> Thornton

Keith felt vulnerable, as if caught in a cold wind without a coat. *"Stigmata," that word again. What could make Livingston think he might not be here today?* He removed the second letter, typed on stationery engraved with the name Twinings and Whitcomb, Solicitors.

> TO: Keith Jessup, PhD
>
> Deposited into an interest bearing account at Barclays Bank under your name is the sum of fifty thousand pounds Sterling (approximately $80,000 US).

To a young scholar in school all his life, whose mother had made just enough to make ends meet, it was an unfamiliar gift. As he put the notes back into the envelope, he reread Livingston's last lines.

Perhaps you will even explore finding the Manuscript. If so, please remember that Stigmata is more than you have been taught, and the journey more difficult than you realize. But if truth is sought and justice served, the reward will be great.

Keith thought to himself. *Truth and justice, that's all Livingston wished for. Perhaps, someday, I can give him that.*

CHAPTER 11

Oxford, UK, January 21

It was a typical winter day, with the English countryside bending to the harsh winds arriving from the sea as Keith walked to Radcliffe Square off High Street. Oxford, the oldest university city in England, was founded in the twelfth century. Located about 50 miles west of London on the Rivers Thames and Cherwell, it, like its rival Cambridge, had no multiple acres of green lawns nor expansive fields, its campus consisting of about thirty separate colleges and related buildings. It was difficult for Keith not to think about the morning's events as he walked past the Exam Schools on High Street and approached Broad. It was the view of the great Bodleian Library that brought him back to the thesis he was about to defend. It had been over five years since Keith first opened the Library's huge bronze doors engraved with the coats-of-arms of Oxford colleges and stepped into the world of medieval England. To Keith, it was one of life's unforgettable moments, like his first big league ball game, not knowing what to absorb first, the players or the park. He had recognized the original building built in the 1300s from textbook photographs and salvaged in 1598 by the contributions of Sir Thomas Bodley. It was Bodley who suggested establishing the first Legal Deposit to protect authors, what today we call copyrights, where one copy of every publication was to be deposited in the library. To this day the Bodleian, or the "Bod" as the students call it, receives a copy of each book, newspaper, and periodical published in Great Britain.

He was accompanied by a security guard to the rear entrance of the Library's Lecture Hall, the original hall where, for over 400 years, candidates for Divinity degrees presented their theses in Latin to moderators. Keith looked out at the empty wooden pews, once again unable to rid himself of the morning meeting with Colin Cuttermill. Suddenly, like a clarion call, the huge bronze doors opened, summoning him back to the task at hand. To Keith, its rusty noise of centuries recalled Milton's description of the gates of Hell being opened by Satan's daughter, Sin, allowing him to escape up to earth: w*ith impetuous recoil and jarring sound Th' infernal doors, and on their hinges grate Harsh thunder, that the lowest bottom shook Of Erebus.*

Within moments the crowd began to file through the security check point, filling the seats as they awaited the start of his presentation. Keith sadly shook his head, *What has become of a world that needs security to allow a fifth-year graduate student of Early English Literature to defend his PhD thesis on the meaning of John Milton's* Paradise Lost? But threats had been received and these days threats had to be taken seriously. And yet, why? The topic seemed benign enough, interpreting *Paradise Lost* was always rich fodder for a graduate student to dig into. But once Keith decided to include a section explaining the Milton Manuscript and its proximity to the death of the popular Professor Livingston, word spread quickly. *The Cherwell*, Oxford's student newspaper, had used it as its front page story, hailing it as *"bringing critical scholarship to our historically sedate college,"* and when unfounded rumor fostered speculation that the Milton Manuscript had been found, fascination became contention.

*

Sundstrom entered the small back room where Keith was reviewing his notes, carrying a package about the size of a shoe box colorfully gift-wrapped. "Sorry to interrupt, but I found this outside the door, your name's on it. Looks like you have a secret admirer. Want me to open it?"

Keith glanced at the gift and smiled. "Absolutely. I can use some admiration."

Sundstrom removed the packaging, uncovered the box and found a holiday greeting card with Santa on his sleigh full of gifts. "Well, belated Christmas greetings." As Sundstrom removed the card his head jerked back, dropping the box on the floor.

"Something the matter?" Keith bent down to pick up the box and saw the reason for Sundstrom's reaction. The box contained a mouse with its head sliced off. He placed the box on a small table, calmly took the card from Sundstrom's trembling hands and read the message out loud.

"Of Man's first disobedience, and the fruit of that forbidden tree whose mortal taste Brought death into the world, and all our woe."
Do not tamper with *Paradise Lost* – leave its meaning to its readers – a manuscript is not needed to understand its greatness.

He paused before responding. "The opening lines to *Paradise Lost*. Is this the controversy you were concerned about?"

Keith read the fright in the professor's eyes, as if it confirmed his worst fears surrounding the revelation of the Manuscript. Sundstrom tried to regain his composure. It wasn't so much the shock of what he had seen, but the realization that he had allowed a special young scholar to become involved. He had tried to dissuade him, but perhaps he should have done more. He had often been told by his colleagues that his only failing as a teacher was that he cared too much. It had only been two weeks since they had met, but in that time he had grown to admire the young man. Every day, for hours that went far into the evening, they reviewed material that the examiners might ask, until Sundstrom was satisfied that there was nothing remaining to review.

"I'm afraid I was taken by surprise. I'll never get used to these Oxford pranks."

Sundstrom put his hand on his student's shoulder, trying his best to smile.

"Just remember what Milton would say about controversy."

Keith knew what Milton would say: to hell with anyone who wants to prevent my right to express what I wish.

There was a knock on the door. It was time. Sundstrom looked up, "You're on. Godspeed!"

Keith took a deep breath. Had he made a mistake? Should he have avoided the topic as Sundstrom had suggested? He took a final look at the box with death inside: Keith Jessup, like John Milton, would never allow himself to be bullied. He had sworn long ago that that would never happen again.

*

He walked to the dais as the audience settled into their seats and looked at the three examiners seated in the first row behind a table, his thesis spread before them. For the moment his mind reflected on what he had just seen, and recalled Bartholomew's description of *Paradise Lost* as the defender of Christendom: *For God and Country? How tragic that the world continued to take the battle for the soul so seriously. How ironic, that belief in a god that was to bring peace to earth and good will to man would cause more death and despair than any other tragedy in human history. Perhaps the love and forgiveness that religion embraced was no longer applicable – indeed, perhaps religion was no longer applicable – perhaps political dogma had taken over body and spirit.*

Keith acknowledged his examiners sitting in the front row and began reciting the opening lines of the poem, pausing to allow the verses to be fully absorbed by his listeners – the same lines found on the card he had just received.

> *Of Man's First Disobedience, and the Fruit*
> *Of that Forbidden Tree, whose mortal taste*
> *Brought Death into the World, and all our woe.*

"Thus begins the most famous twenty-six lines in all of English Literature and 'man's first disobedience,' his original sin, resulting in his ejection from Paradise. *Paradise Lost*, first and foremost, tells the story of the beginning of man on earth and his banishment from the good life. And yet, what does the poem *really* mean? Why was it written? To justify the ways of God to man? But where in the poem can we find that justification? I suggest that Milton left those answers elsewhere for us to find."

Sundstrom listened to his student as Keith's confidence grew.

"Was *Man's Disobedience* Eve's eating the forbidden fruit of the Tree of Knowledge in the Garden of Eden? Was *Death into the World* and *all our woe* the result of Adam and Eve's banishment from Eden resulting in man having to toil for his daily bread, women suffer the pain of bringing children into the world, and humanity given the sentence of mortality? Do we really think that the most brilliant man in England, whose eyes blinded by disease, would reiterate the simple Bible story of Adam and Eve?"

Keith searched the faces of the examiners before him. "Or was it something else? Is it a story of God's experiment with man's free will? Was the Tree of Knowledge, which allowed man to differentiate right from wrong Milton's own quest for freedom? Wasn't it Milton who wrote 'Give me the liberty to know, to utter, and to argue freely according to conscience, above all liberties?' Is it possible that the Tree's placement in the center of the Garden with the warning never to be tasted, really a description of how church and king tried to prevent man from acquiring knowledge? Was man's disobedience Milton's own disobedience because he refused to be stifled by the limits of freedom that these institutions imposed, shackling all Englishmen? Isn't that what *brought death into the world and all our woe*? Could it be that Satan's great Hall in Hell, Pandemonium, was merely a description of St. Peter's Cathedral in Rome, the center of Catholicism, a place and a religion that Milton detested?"

Keith paused, surveying his audience, surprised to see Bartholomew sitting directly behind the examiners and several rows behind was Deputy Chief Constable Constance Bathgate.

"We've all been taught that *Paradise Lost* is the sine qua non of Christianity, the epitome of our Christian faith. And yet, is it? Was the poem really created by Milton, the orthodox Christian, as the world has been led to believe? Or has the world misunderstood who Milton was?"

Keith seemed to focus on Bartholomew, as if offering a challenge. He paused and quietly asked, "Who among you can answer these questions with surety? Only Milton. That is why I believe the Milton Manuscript exists and why it must be found."

"Perhaps there is nothing to find!"

The challenge had been accepted. If anyone in the audience had not been paying attention they were now. Even the most senior scholars in the hall could not remember the last time oral exams were disrupted by a non-examiner, albeit a renowned professor emeritus from Cambridge. All eyes turned to Bartholomew who was standing directly behind the examiners, pointing his finger at Keith.

Bartholomew spoke to the examiners who had now turned in their seats to look at him.

"The world hasn't misunderstood Milton, but this young man has! There's too much serious research that needs to be done rather than waste our time searching for imagined texts and ill-conceived concepts that those before have surely put to rest. Why must our young scholars insist on seeking out the sensational in everything these days? Why the need for a Manuscript when the meaning of the poem is obvious? Would the great Milton really waste his time trying to explain what needs no explanation? You have been taught that Milton and his poem is the epitome of the Christian faith – and so it is!"

Keith tried to control his anger. "So you think Milton's poem is the epitome of the Christian faith and Milton was the model of such faith? With all due respect, the Church would never label Milton the ideal

Christian. It is Milton who holds the clergy up to ridicule for their abuse of their positions, condemning their widespread greed, hypocrisy, and sexual immorality. He demands that Christians put their faith not in the Church or their leaders, but in God alone. Is it not Milton who demands that Scripture must be the ultimate authority and Bible, not Bishops, is where a true Christian must find his morality? And finally, sir, if the meaning of the poem is so obvious, then tell me how Milton justifies why an all-powerful, all-knowing God tolerates a world of imperfection? How can Satan exist? How can Adam and Eve sin? If God is omnipotent, as Christianity exults, if He is of perfect goodness, then why evil? Unless, of course, He is not omnipotent, in which case, he is no longer God."

Keith paused for the moment, and shifted his attention from Bartholomew to the examiners.

"That is what Milton tells us in line twenty-six that his poem is to explain, and yet no one appears to have found that explanation. Except for Milton. If you want to know the thoughts of one of the most brilliant men in English history then find the Milton Manuscript."

Not a sound was heard. Was Keith suggesting that Milton was questioning God's power or even existence? Even Bartholomew remained standing in position without a response, keeping his eyes on the student who dared to challenge one of the century's most brilliant Milton scholars. Finally, he took his seat. For those who looked closely they might have detected a subtle smile pass through his lips, a smile of respect yet concern. *The young man knew his Milton.*

"So, Mr. Jessup, until this manuscript is found, we will not know the poem's real meaning?"

The silence was broken by an examiner from Oxford's Department of Early English Literature, and Keith redirected his attention.

"That is my thesis. Milton's genius camouflaged his meaning so deeply within its verse that not only was it not understood then, but remains so today. Why else would more scholars and students study Milton than any other literary personage, with the possible exception of Shakespeare? Why has more analysis been written on his poem than any other in the world's literature? Isn't it because they are all trying to solve the same puzzle: who is Milton and what is his poem about?"

CHAPTER 12

Oxford, UK, January 22

Sundstrom's office was surrounded, as usual, with organizational clutter when he met with the newly awarded PhD student. He poured two glasses of champagne and raised his glass in toast.

"Keith, congratulations, or may I be the first to say Dr. Jessup. I must say you raised some difficult questions, ones that may force our Milton scholars to reevaluate their teaching."

Keith smiled. "I didn't realize Dr. Bartholomew would be there. He had the same reaction when I visited him in Cambridge."

"Dr. Bartholomew is the Godfather of Milton specialists. He's probably trained half of us and takes the education of future generations of Milton scholars very seriously, sometimes, it seems, too seriously. Well, hopefully that's the end to it. No more Manuscript to get involved with – time to start a new life. What will you do?"

"I'm hoping to find an opportunity in the States. I'm waiting to hear about several teaching jobs."

"What about a teaching position here at Oxford? The department could use you."

"That's a wonderful offer, but it's time to get back home."

"Any particular reason? Someone waiting?"

Keith smiled. "No. I have no family. My parents passed away. There was one young lady that I got to know in college, but that seems like ages ago. I just think it's time to start a new life somewhere."

Sundstrom leaned back in his chair. "If that's the case, you'll be surprised to learn that Bartholomew himself called to say how impressed he was with the originality and courage of your thesis. He mentioned that if you were returning to the States you might consider a position with Niles Janeway at the International Milton Society in New York. Niles graduated Cambridge several years behind me and is its executive director. Bartholomew contacted him regarding your work, in fact, he had a copy of your thesis emailed to him."

Keith was surprised at the unsolicited recommendation. He was well aware of the International Milton Society, as every Milton scholar was. The Society could be traced back to 1767 with its objective to preserve Milton's legacy and tradition by encouraging the pursuit of scholarly work. Through its *Quarterly Journal*, the Society published original articles on Milton and other early English writers and maintained a unique library of Early English Literature.

"That's quite an offer."

"One you should seriously consider. I'm only sorry Thornton isn't here to participate in your success." Keith had the same thought.

Sundstrom removed a small gift box from his desk, "This is for you."

It was unexpected. "That's most kind. I don't know what to say, except thank you."

Keith carefully opened the small box and removed what appeared to be two small identical ink stamps, the kind you use to endorse the back of a personal check, but their heads were minuscule. He turned to Sundstrom in a questioning mode.

"It's especially for a Milton scholar. It's a press. Why don't you try it?"

Keith placed the head of one stamp onto a piece of paper and gently pressed.

"I don't see anything."

Sundstrom smiled. "Precisely. It's a Xerox developed process called MicroText. It can only be read under high magnification, similar to the microscopic words hidden in the design of credit cards to prevent forgeries. They tell me those imaging fonts are 100th of an inch high."

Keith nodded. "Like the dots next to Andrew Jackson's right shoulder on US twenty-dollar bills, the ones that read 'The United States of America 20 USA 20 USA.'"

Sundstrom continued, "Same idea. I call these texts *Paradise Lost*, because its words have been lost from sight, just as Milton's eyes lost their sight, never to see his Paradise. I had the first letter graphic copied from an early edition of *Paradise Lost*, but only by putting the two stamps together can you understand Milton's verse. He chanted the words from memory:

> *Earth trembled from her entrails, as again*
> *In pangs, and Nature gave a second groan;*

Keith smiled and joined Sundstrom in completing the verse:

> *Sky loured, and, muttering thunder, some sad drops*
> *Wept at completing of the mortal sin Original*

The student looked at the professor: "Yes, Milton's description of how the earth shook following Adam and Eve's disobeying God's commandment."

Sundstrom gave him a fatherly smile. "May you never have to face an act as catastrophic as original sin."

"I would hope not."

"And do me one favor. Should you ever decide to take up the search for the Manuscript, promise you'll speak to me first."

"Then you should know there is one thing I need to do before I leave."

Sundstrom looked at Keith suspiciously. "And what is that?"

"Find the speech that Livingston never gave."

CHAPTER 13

Oxford, UK, January 22

"Cuttermill, here."

Keith recalled the voice of Thornton Livingston's barrister.

"Mr. Cuttermill, my name is Keith Jessup, I was a student of Professor Livingston's."

"Of course, is it Dr. Jessup by now?"

Keith smiled, Cuttermill didn't forget a thing. "Yes, sir, it is."

"Well, then, I must congratulate you. And will you be returning to the States?"

"I've been offered an opportunity to work at the Milton Society in New York."

"Well that certainly keeps you in your specialty."

"I was wondering if you could arrange for me and a friend to go to Dr. Livingston's home. I'm looking for his last lecture."

"I see. Well, I'll be out there later today, if you can make it. I'm in the midst of disposing of his estate and the house is being readied for market."

"We can be there."

"Do you know where he lives?"

"Yes, sir, Norham Road. I've been there several times."

"Then I'll meet you in two hours."

*

Abaddon received the directions on his cell and with Clive in the car began the drive into Central North Oxford.

"Where we going?"

Abaddon took the cigarette out of his mouth. "Norham Road."

"Same job?"

"Yeah, but this time we've got to find it or make sure it ain't there."

His uncle was clear about that, and Abaddon owed everything to his uncle. His brother's life was easy, but his was the hard one. They blamed it on a difficult delivery, one where his head was positioned sideways as it came out of the womb and the forceps had placed too much pressure on the temporal bones. The son that came out afterward had smooth sailing, but Abaddon would suffer eternally with the cranial-facial distortion and ruddy complexion that children laughed at and adults feared. He hated when his twin acted so superior. It's true that his brother may have been smarter in school, but he didn't have the courage that he had, nor the dedication that he showed to the one person who gave him something to live for. *If it wan't fer uncle I'd be livin in a gutta somewhere. But uncle knew I was good fer somethin – e's the one who trusted me with jobs – importan jobs – and when e told me neva to tell anyone, e knew I neva would.* To be associated with such a great man gave Abaddon the feeling that he, too, was important. He knew that to carry out his uncle's mission was an honor and privilege. He had not failed him yet. He would not fail him today.

*

The black over silver 1999 Ford Ranger Diesel XLT Thunder pickup truck proceeded south on the Banbury Road and just beyond Park Town turned left onto Norham.

Clive broke the silence. "Pretty ritzy area."

The large red-haired man didn't respond, but stared for the moment at the twisted scar cutting through Clive's cheek. It looked like a corkscrew, and, in fact, Abaddon was there when it happened. Clive had just returned from serving two tours as a Royal Marine at Camp Bastion, a large British-run base in the desert in southern Afghanistan, and Abaddon took him out to celebrate. They were playing cards and drinking with some fellows they had just met when one of the players accused Clive of cheating and picked the wine opener up from the table and drove it into Clive's cheek. Clive just flinched, put his hand to his cheek, and looked at the blood gushing out. Abaddon watched as Clive calmly stood up and pressed a cloth against his cheek to stop the bleeding. Then, with one lightening move, he smashed the wine bottle against the edge of the table with his other hand and dug the jagged edges of the glass deep into the carotid vessel passing through his attacker's neck. While the fellow was writhing on the floor, Clive told Abaddon to pick up their winnings. The man had stopped breathing before they were out the door. From then on, whenever Uncle had work for Abaddon to do, he wanted Clive with him.

Abaddon slowed the truck, the cigarette remaining strangled between his lips as he looked for the house. Norham Manor is one of the most desirable parts of historic North Oxford, and the large manicured lawns of the estates that met the road via long driveways attested to the fact.

Abaddon eased the pickup to a crawl as he reached number 137 on the right side. It was a large old three-story red brick house set back on beautifully landscaped land with a variety of trees, shrubs, borders, and box hedging.

"It's ere."

They parked a few hundred feet past the home and walked back.

"Don't see no cars. Betta make sure nobody's round."

Abaddon opened the porch door to the entrance way and rang the bell. He heard nothing from inside and looked through the glass window of the heavy wooden door into a spacious hall. He rang twice more but still no response.

"Seems nobody's ome."

They walked around to a paved terrace in the back where a deep bay window and large paned glass doors faced south, overlooking a garden. Abaddon peeked through. "Don't see no one. Any alarms?"

Clive examined the back doors and checked the adjacent windows.

"No sign of security. It's a piece of cake."

Abaddon took a small hooked instrument and gripped the lock connecting the two doors. Within moments there was a click and the lock sprung. They opened the door which led into a dining room and waited for a moment. No alarm.

"Let's go."

They made their way through the house and after a quick look decided to focus their attention in a large library with high ceilings and a large stone fireplace.

"Someone's been workin ere. I smell cleanin fluid."

The room was surrounded by bookshelves and in the center of the room was an oversized mahogany Chippendale-style writing desk with a burgundy leather-top inset with gold tooling and frieze drawers.

"Wow – what a desk!"

Clive gave him a warning look. "Forget what it looks like, check what's inside."

They spent their time looking through the desk drawers, bookcases, and piles of magazines and newspapers, but after an hour of searching they gave up.

Abaddon picked up his cell and pressed the call button. "Nuthin ere."

. . . . "No, no computer, no lecture, nutin." Abaddon listened for a moment. "Yes, sir."

He slipped his cell into his coat pocket and glanced at Clive.

"He wants to make sure its ain't ere."

CHAPTER 14

Oxford, UK, January 22

Sundstrom met Keith and they drove south on the Banbury Road until they passed Park Town. As they turned left into Norham Road, they were met by police preventing cars from entering. Sundstrom parked and they proceeded by foot along the road lined by crowds of people fixated by heavy dark smoke rising skyward and two large fire engine pump ladders further down the street. They looked at each other and quickened their pace until they reached a cordoned off area in front of Livingston's home. Huge flames flickered upward as fire fighters surrounded the house, shooting torrents of water from cannons connected by long hoses to the fire engines.

Keith found Cuttermill by the side of the road.

"Oh, this is terrible, Dr. Jessup. We were about ready to sell the house."

"Does anyone know how it happened?"

"They think it might have to do with the combustible agents that the cleaning people used."

Keith nodded as he watched the flames.

"Guess I'll never know what was in that lecture."

Sundstrom gave a half-smile. "Perhaps it's better that way."

*

The loud sound of an unmuffled engine alarmed Keith. He turned to see a black and silver pickup truck coming from down the street, slowly weaving between the bystanders gathered in front of the burning home, its horn blowing intermittently. As if drawn by a magnet, Keith stared at the pickup and saw the laughing face of the driver peering out at the blaze before driving away. A flash went through Keith's memory, he had seen the driver before, an image he would never forget. It was the hideous face of evil burning with blazing red hair.

*

New York, January 22

The overseas call had already been placed long before Dr. Keith Jessup boarded British Airways flight 317 to return to the United States.

"Yes, sir."

"I want him watched."

"Yes, sir."

"He believes that Milton has written a manuscript."

"Has he started looking?"

"He was seen at the fire."

"Was he warned?"

"There must always be a warning. I hope he will take it more seriously than the others."

"I understand."

"You know what to do?"

"As instructed."

"Keep me informed."

"As always."

CHAPTER 15

New York, January 27

Keith entered the International Milton Society headquarters, a narrow four-story brownstone building on 25th Street between Fifth and Sixth Avenues. Niles Janeway expected the visit.

"Dr. Jessup, you've come highly recommended. I don't remember

Professor Bartholomew ever being so enthusiastic about someone joining us."

Janeway was a pleasant chap in his mid-fifties, describing himself as a
"gentleman" bachelor. He was taller than average, slight of build, with
pale complexion, thinning straw-colored hair, and light blue eyes speck-
led with gray. He walked with a slightly forward bent, reminding Keith
of what Dickens's Uriah Heep must have looked like. At Cambridge, he
majored in English Literature and although not a scholar's scholar, he
graduated with a respectable "Gentleman's grade." Being responsible
for the Milton Society was a perfect profession for Janeway. With little
drama and few demands, he oversaw Society business in a serviceable
manner. His knowledge of English Literature was adequate, but he
preferred relying on others for scholarly decisions. Janeway had one
other attribute that made him supremely eligible for this position – his
father was the previous executive director, as was his grandfather who,
in turn, had inherited it from his father. Indeed, guardianship of the
Milton Legacy could be traced back in Janeway's family tree to the very
beginning of the Society.

"We are prepared to offer you a position as assistant editor for the
Milton Society *Quarterly*. And to be honest, the sooner you're available
the better. I'm tired of writing editorials."

*

He was available. Keith rented a small two-bedroom apartment on
the fourth floor of a six-story brick building in Queens overlooking a
large tree-filled park with benches, basketball courts, and picnic areas.
Janeway immediately assigned him to help with an exhibit celebrating
Milton's life at the New York Public Library, evaluating various materials for inclusion. Keith wrote the press release.

THE REVOLUTIONARY LIFE AND CONTINUING
INFLUENCE OF JOHN MILTON: POET, INTELLECTUAL,
AND RELIGIOUS AND POLITICAL RADICAL:

The New York Public Library in coordination with the International Milton Society celebrates the four hundredth birthday of
the seventeenth-century poet John Milton, whose renown and
genius challenges that of Shakespeare. The retrospective investi-
gates Milton's life and development, including his mastery of the

biblical languages, Homer's Greek and Vergil's Latin. Milton, who still remains one of the greatest intellects in Western thought, was familiar with the major literary artists writing in the vernacular European languages from Dante onwards. Included among the selections is a 1660 proclamation from King Charles II banning two of Milton's most scathing political writings.

CHAPTER 16

New York, February 1

Keith glanced at the business card: Pierre et Fils. Conservation and Restorers of Fine Art and Documents, 998 Madison Avenue, NY, NY 10021 – Kate Harrigan.

It was a busy morning in the offices of Pierre et Fils. The Frick Museum had a deadline for the restoration of a seventeenth-century Ruisdael landscape that had been damaged and a series of Daumier drawings from its permanent collection that was beginning to mildew. Pierre et Fils was a firm with impeccable credentials that art dealers around the world trusted to authenticate artistic provenance and upon which sophisticated collectors depended to frame their investments.

Keith entered from the 77th Street entrance, just off Madison Avenue, and was met by security. He signed in, showed a picture ID, and disclosed with whom he had an appointment. The guard, who looked like an oversized fullback for the football Giants, checked his computer screen.

"I don't see your name on the list. You sure you've got an appointment?"

"I believe arrangements were made yesterday with a Ms. Harrigan." The security guard eyed him suspiciously.

"It's about a piece for an exhibition at the New York Public Library." The guard appraised the visitor and picked up the phone.

"Hey, Roland down at Security. There's a Keith Jessup down here who wants to see Kate. Says he's here from the New York Public Library . . . something about an exhibition . . . Yeah, I know, I told him . . . yeah, I'll wait." Roland tapped his pencil against the desk waiting for the answer.

"Yeah, Jessup, *J E S S U P*, Keith Jessup . . . Really? She will? OK, thanks." Roland hung up the phone and looked at Keith with a new-found respect.

"Ms. Harrigan's not here, but someone else will see you. Second floor, room 203."

Keith took the elevator and quietly knocked on the door.

From inside he heard a woman's voice. "Come in."

Keith slowly opened the door.

"Mr. Jessup, I presume?"

Keith adjusted his eyes to the bright sunshine streaming in from the window, trying to determine where the voice came from.

Joanne Farnsworth was seated in the cubicle at the far end of the room and took a quick glance away from her desktop computer, casually responding to the man at the door.

"Yes. I'm here to examine a piece for the John Milton exhibition. The owner told us you may be finished restoring it – *The Temptation and Fall of Eve* that William Blake illustrated for *Paradise Lost*."

"Yes, I'll be right with you."

Joanne went back to her screen, smiling with anticipation as her fingers slid across the keyboard.

"Ah, yes, they're here. The Blake illustration is from a series of twelve plates, one for each of the books in the poem."

"Yes, commissioned by Blake's patron in 1808, a Thomas Butts."

Joanne got up from her desk and walked toward the entrance, trying to conceal a smile.

"So you're a scholar, Mr. Jessup – shouldn't it be Dr. Jessup by now?"

He had to look twice. "Joanne?" Keith was amazed. "What are you doing here?"

"I've worked here for four years. I believe that was after the last time we were together or, if I recall, the last time you weren't too busy."

Keith had recalled those years often. Joanne had grown up in Boston, her father was a prominent Boston attorney who had passed away when she was a senior in high school and her mother was a social worker. She was an honor student at the Briar School, one of the elite private schools in Boston. Her passion was art and she chose the Rhode Island School of Design in Providence to further her studies.

"It wasn't like that at all. I didn't want to bring you into a relationship when I knew I would have to spend all my time with my studies. I didn't want you to be disappointed that I couldn't be with you as much as you deserved. I just thought it better for both of us if we were just friends."

"Well, you certainly didn't give me the chance to decide what I deserved."

Keith knew he had hurt her, but the truth was he was afraid to make lasting relationships. He had seen what happens at close range his entire childhood. It was a fear that was difficult to overcome, so he avoided them. There were advantages to non-committals.

They had been introduced at the beginning of his senior year and he took her for coffee at the local Dunkin' Donuts. She was intrigued, initially by the fact that she had never gone out on a first date to Dunkin' Donuts – at least it could have been Starbucks. But what really piqued her interest was his unabashed honesty; he simply told her that he couldn't afford to take her to a nicer place and hoped she didn't mind. She found him to be intelligent, soft-spoken, carefully choosing his words before responding. She thought he had a kind of rugged handsomeness, sandy hair that he kept too long, a set jaw and broad shoulders within his six-foot plus frame. But it was something in his blue eyes that attracted her, something that bespoke of feelings that were protectively concealed.

"And you're at the Milton Society?"

"Just started."

Keith had also been intrigued. Most of the women he had gone out with were more interested in themselves. It wasn't that they weren't attractive; it was just that they didn't have similar interests, often believing that "soul" was invented by James Brown. But as he sipped his coffee with an occasional glance from behind his cup, he had the feeling she was different. He sensed her inner peace and self-confidence and when he looked, he couldn't help but notice how beautiful she was, with long blond hair, blue eyes, and pug nose. Except for his mother, he never met anyone so stable, with such a moral sense of right and wrong, and she was able to draw what was in him out. Their first conversation lasted well into the night until even Dunkin' Donuts had a closing time. It didn't matter the topic, they probably hit them all: art, literature, hopes, ambitions, even fears. He probably spoke more that night than in his previous three years at school.

"Well, it's great to see you again. Your Blake is on the seventh floor restoration section. I don't think it's done yet, but you can take a look. I texted them. They're expecting you."

Keith knew he had to ask. "Is it still Joanne Farnsworth?"

A quiet smile appeared. "It is. And you?"

He matched her mischief. "Dullsville. Nothing's changed."

He stopped before leaving her office. "One last favor. Do you have some paper and pencils I can borrow? If I can't have the original, I'd like to at least draw it."

"Still the artist?" Joanne walked over to one of the large cabinets in the room. "Here, take my sketch pad and pencils, if you promise to return them."

The sound of her voice had him recall their times together. After a few meetings over coffee her crosstown visits to Brown became more regular and their feelings for each other grew. He looked forward to studying with her, sharing a calmness that had never been part of his vocabulary. The relationship went deeper than with anyone he had ever met until the fear of letting out what was inside proved too great to overcome his attraction. It was so hard to trust, and so he walked, but it left a hollow within that no amount of devoted scholarship was able to fill.

"Thanks, I'll get them back to you in an hour or two." He smiled and walked out.

Joanne watched him leave and let her mind wander for a few moments before returning to her screen. Something about him had always captured her interest. It still did.

*

She couldn't wait. She found him on the seventh floor at one of the desks sketching Blake's colored drawing of *The Temptation and Fall of Eve* that was on a small easel in front of him. She watched from a distance as his pencils seamlessly knew where to move, but somehow he sensed she was there. Without taking his eyes off the Blake, he quietly addressed her: "Sorry I've taken so long, but its beauty is breathtaking when you study it up close."

Keith continued to work. "I'm almost done."

"May I look?"

"Give me two minutes." And within two minutes, he signed his name, removed the page, and returned her sketch pad. She looked at the drawing, astounded to see how close it was to the original. The subject was the Tree of Knowledge, its earthly branches full of apples tinted reddish-orange, and a nude Eve standing under it. The Serpent was wrapped around her body, his mouth holding an apple while Eve was taking a bite from it. Behind the tree stood Adam, seemingly dreaming as he looked up at its branches, not aware of, or perhaps, not concerned about Eve and her relationship with the Serpent.

"You're an even better artist than I remember."

Keith turned his eyes from the drawing to Joanne.

"Not as good as Blake – so simple yet so powerful, so provocative and so, so seductive."

Their eyes met for a moment before Joanne's turned back to his drawing.

"You've captured it."

Keith smiled. "Thanks." He handed the sketch to her. "For you."

CHAPTER 17

New York, February 8

He was startled by the notice. *Was this true?*

Professor Stanton Reynolds of the University at Ghent will be presenting "The Disclosure of the Milton Manuscript" at Columbia University, February 12. Please mark your calendars.

Stanton Reynolds had found the Manuscript? Reynolds had lectured at Oxford and Keith had read several of his papers. Reynolds was a serious scholar. That would not only validate Professor Livingston's belief that the manuscript existed, but would also prove that concerns of any conspiracy were greatly exaggerated. Keith marked the date. He would not miss the lecture nor, did it appear from the number of emails the Society received, would many others.

*

The cell phone that rang in the small apartment on Manhattan's West Side was quickly answered.

"Yes, sir."

"There's a lecture scheduled."

"I never thought he would give it."

"He was warned."

"I was certain he would realize the risk he was taking."

"The naïveté in the name of scholarship is amazing."

"Quite so."

"Haven't they learned that revising history has a price?"

"I suppose not."

"Arrangements are being made as we speak. You will be kept informed."

*

New York, February 8

British Airways flight 232 had taken off from London's Heathrow Airport on its regular non-stop flight to New York's JFK. Sitting in business class, Abaddon paged through the girlie magazines he bought at the airport. He had a job to do, the kind of job he preferred – *do it however you want, as long as it gets done.* As the plane landed, he was greeted by a bystander waiting at the entry gate.

"Hello, A-bad-don, haven't seen you in a long time."

Abaddon looked at his twin with disdain. He hated the name, especially the way his brother pronounced it. It was his father's fury that inscribed that life sentence. Abaddon, the word itself meant The Destroyer, from the Hebrew for a place of destruction. To others, Abaddon was the name of the destroying angel. He remembered how his father would viciously repeat the verse from Revelation 9:11 to him without end: *"And they had as king over them the angel of the bottomless pit, whose name in Hebrew is Abaddon."* "That's you, Abaddon, the angel of the bottomless pit."

Was it his fault that his mother died following his delivery? Yet the father would never forget nor forgive the son for killing his wife.

"Uncle is keeping me busy."

"So I hear."

The twin looked at his brother wondering how it could be possible for two boys, born moments apart could, like the biblical Jacob and Esau, be so different.

"I've arranged a hotel room for you. Try and stay unnoticed, or at least sober. Nothing can go wrong."

A big toothless smile appeared. "Nothin ain't ever goin wrong."

*

New York, February 12

The handwritten sign held by the large red-headed Limo driver read: "Dr. Stanton Reynolds." The professor arrived on schedule at JFK's International arrival terminal, and with only a small carry on and a briefcase, walked directly toward the street exit looking for his driver.

"I'm Dr. Reynolds, you must be Lars."

"Sorry chap, but Lars ad an emergincy so I'm ere to take ya where ya wanna go. The name's James."

The hulking man grinned, thinking how the emergency was the two hundred dollar bills that Lars received in exchange for the sign and the passenger. "Where ya stayin?"

Stanton looked at his cell phone.

"I need to go directly to Columbia University, 116th Street and Broadway."

"We'll find it." Abaddon took the man's bag and led him out to the rented Town Car parked across from the terminal.

"Just one bag?"

"Yes, quick trip, in and out."

Abaddon smiled to himself and placed the handbag in the trunk.

"Ready, Professa?"

As he pulled away from the curb, he made a sudden stop, almost hitting the policeman approaching him.

"You're in a no parking zone."

He forgot about the cops patrolling the area. As he lowered his hand, he felt the hard outline of the Ruger .380 revolver in his jacket pocket. Quickly he grabbed a tissue from the box on the passenger seat, wiping the perspiration forming on his forehead. *Stay calm, there can be no mistakes, no callin attention to meself.*

"Sorry, mate. I was worried this tourist was gettin lost and I ad to go fetch im."

The cop looked at Abaddon and his passenger and checked the date on the car's registration.

"Fine, don't let it happen again."

Abaddon let out a deep breath and slowly pulled into the moving lane, exiting the airport and taking the Van Wyck to the Grand Central Parkway. He had practiced the route the last few days, staying within the speed limit and continuously checking his rear-view mirror. Thirty-five minutes later he left the Major Deegan and crossed the Madison Avenue Bridge.

Stanton looked up from his reading, saw the signs for Columbia and placed his papers back into his briefcase. Abaddon made a left onto Amsterdam Avenue, but instead of driving straight down to 116th Street and over to Broadway, he made a left at 123rd Street onto Morningside Drive and into a secluded section of Morningside Park. He pulled the rented Town Car over to the right curb, put on the blinking red lights and turned off the ignition. As he exited the car he placed his hand into his jacket pocket and opened the rear door. "This is where ya get out, Professa."

CHAPTER 18

Columbia University, February 12

The lecture with Stanton Reynolds was scheduled for 8:00 PM in the Roone Arledge Auditorium in Lerner Hall, and there promised to be a large turnout. The possibility that the Manuscript had been found had attracted intense interest, no one more so than Keith. It was 7:30 when Keith took his seat and by 7:45 the hall was already full. By 8:00 it was standing room only when Professor Henry Schreiber of Columbia's Department of English Literature approached the lectern to introduce the speaker.

"Tonight we are privileged to learn the true thoughts hidden within the mind of John Milton when he wrote *Paradise Lost*. It has been a long wait."

Keith thought so also. Finally he would hear, in Milton's own words, *how to justify the ways of God to man*.

It never happened. At 8:15 the program chairman alerted the guests of a delay, and at 8:45 he announced that due to a situation beyond his control there would be no presentation. Professor Reynolds was nowhere to be found.

*

International Milton Society Office, February 13

By the time Keith arrived at work the next morning, emails had already flooded the Society's computers. The mystery of Reynolds's disappearance had grown. Neither the University nor his family had heard from him. The last time his wife had seen her husband was when she dropped him off at the Gent-St-Pieters Station to catch the train to Brussels Airport. The NYPD confirmed that he was on the 10:05 AM American Airlines nonstop flight 171 to JFK, but had no further information on a missing person fitting his description – and no logical explanation was forthcoming. Had he cancelled the lecture for personal reasons?

Keith's colleagues presented a number of possibilities – a personal emergency had occurred, perhaps illness, perhaps a family situation, perhaps he never found the Manuscript, perhaps the announcement of the Manuscript and his absence were mere coincidence . . . perhaps, but Keith wondered if it was more. Conversations from the past came to mind: *Did you ever consider that if the Manuscript was found, whoever finds it would be prevented from disclosing its contents? What was the reason again? – oh, yes, God and country.*

A momentary shudder ran through.

CHAPTER 19

International Milton Society Office, February 13

Niles Janeway walked in with a large FedEx package.

"For you, from a London address."

Keith smiled. He enjoyed Janeway's camaraderie. "Yeah, a secret admirer."

Janeway laughed and laid the package on Keith's desk and walked out. "Give her my best."

Keith read the return ID on the FedEx delivery notice: *Cuttermill, London.*

*

Queens, New York

When Keith arrived at his apartment, he opened the package and found a letter with Cuttermill's name embossed on it:

Dear Dr. Jessup,
I trust this note finds you in good health. Enclosed is a package that Dr. Livingston directed you to receive should anything happen to him. Please pardon the delay, but he gave it to our staff about a week prior to his demise and it was stored in our vault. It also contains information about a lecture that the Professor was scheduled to deliver. Please inform me in a timely fashion should you wish to pursue.

Truly yours,
Colin Cuttermill

Surprised, Keith unwrapped the boxed package which contained a short note from Livingston, an old three-ring notebook and two long tubes enclosed at each end.

He read the note:

Dear Keith,

Enclosed are two drawings that I thought you might enjoy, given your artistic talent. They were given to me by a young American artist who was visiting Oxford some twenty years ago. I offered to let him stay in my home while he was here and, in return, he gave me these drawings. They've remained unopened and I thought you may find them of interest. Sorry, I didn't have time to frame them, but perhaps you could do that for me.

I have also enclosed my personal notebook that you may choose to read and have taken the liberty to include you in an honor I received. Please let Cuttermill know of your interest.

Keith glanced at the two tubes and opened their ends, gently teasing out their contents. As he spread out the rolled papers it revealed two complex colored pencil drawings filled with various shapes of different sizes hanging in space. Keith admired the sketches, especially the intricacy of design. He placed them back into their tubes and set it on his closet shelf before glancing through Livingston's notebook. The notebook was filled with an assortment of old papers, handwritten notes, and several newer entries. He put them back into his desk draw. *Someday I'll read through them.*

Keith opened the third item. It was a copy of a letter from Livingston to a Dr. Ressler.

Dr. Philip Ressler,
Chairman
Tanzer Lecture Symposium

Dear Philip,

I am honored to have received your invitation to deliver the annual Tanzer Lecture at Harvard College. I graciously accept with but one caveat. Should, for any reason, I not be able to make the presentation, I would ask that my associate, Dr. Keith Jessup, accept the honor. There could be no other scholar more qualified to make this most interesting presentation titled "Secrets of The Milton Manuscript."

Sincerely,
Thornton Livingston, PhD

Keith's first thought was: *Livingston was honored with the Tanzer? Wow! To have two major honors in the same year is an amazing achievement.* His second was: *What was Livingston thinking? I have no idea what the contents of the Milton Manuscript are!*

BOOK II

CHAPTER 20

Jeff Moss crossed First Avenue at 30th Street, weaving between the oncoming traffic. The area was one of the main meccas of medicine in the city, home to NYU's Medical and Dental Schools, the School of Nursing, Bellevue Hospital, University Hospital, and the Manhattan VA. He entered the building marked 520 First Avenue, The Milton Halpern Office of Forensic Medicine, climbed the half-dozen steps, and passed through the glass doors. He was greeted by security and walked down the straight hall, entering the third door on the right. The sign read – Chief Medical Examiner.

The middle-aged woman looked up and smiled. "Good morning, Dr. Moss. Dr. Galvin is expecting you."

It had been two years since Jeff left Metropolitan Hospital as Director of Surgery, but after a dozen years of a grueling schedule the 45-year-old realized he needed a different calling. Jeff looked around at his boss's office decorated in the harsh reality of city budget cuts with steel chairs covered with green padding in the finest minimalist tradition. Jeff figured it had to be the original furniture that came when the building was built in the late fifties. It was Stan Galvin who had recruited him for the ME's office. Stan had been a classmate of Jeff's at Harvard Medical School and certainly the brightest student in the class. He was probably ten years older than Jeff, earning a PhD in pathology prior to receiving his medical degree and eventually being named Professor of Forensic Pathology at the State University. When the Medical Examiner's office was criticized for endless backlogs in completing autopsy reports and cutting corners in analyzing and submitting results in drug cases, the Mayor appointed Stan the new ME. It was not an easy job. There had been over 55,000 deaths in New York City the previous year and the ME was responsible for investigating any case where death occurred from violence, suicide, accident, poison, infectious complications, or where an individual in apparent good health died suddenly. Stan set up standards for autopsy procedures and lab workers performance, put in rigorous safeguards, and attracted a top staff, like Jeff, even as he continued to evaluate his own cases.

"Hey, I didn't know the boss got in so early?"

Stan sat back in his chair and smiled at Jeff.

"Just trying to keep even with these 'John Does.'"

Jeff knew that the ME's office didn't have the resources to give them the attention they need. They probably received a dozen a month, mostly addicts, and most get buried in Potters Field without a name. Whatever paperwork there is, is placed onto the stack of "dead" files, mostly sent in with the same request from the New York City Police Department: "Can the ME's office help with identification?"

Jeff looked at the file Stan was holding. "Anything special?"

"I'm not sure. Very little decomposition has occurred since the body was found, mainly because of the cold weather. It's Tom Davis's case. He estimates death took place not more than ten days ago. The deceased was dressed in a well-tailored European suit with an empty briefcase found nearby that had a blood stain that matched the victim. That's not the usual scenario, especially with no identification and no fingerprint match. Anyway, Tom wanted another opinion and I thought you might take a look."

As Jeff glanced at the file, he seemed surprised. The 26th was not a frequent source of cases. Located in Upper Manhattan, it's bounded on the west by the Hudson River and Henry Hudson Parkway and extends north to Harlem. As home to Columbia University and its rapid expansion, the area had undergone considerable gentrification, resulting in a population mix of students and locals. The decrease in crime that followed was not only from the population change, but also due to the priority that the city's mayors gave to safety. Over the past eighteen years, the annual number of murders in the 26th decreased from 15 to 2, and burglary from 807 to 57. He opened the file and read the report:

"Victim male, found in brush in remote area of Morningside Park; Trauma to cranium and cervical spine; extremity and facial lacerations consistent with fall. Cause of death: fractured skull; probable cause: accidental fall. Unusual bilateral markings on skin inferior to orbits, external to the zygomatic arches as well as contusions of all extremities. No identification present; an empty briefcase found at scene. Local kids taking a shortcut home from ball game in park found body."

Jeff put the file back on the desk. "Not the usual scenario."

"Want to give it a try?"

Jeff glanced at the report and nodded. "Why not."

"Good." Stan handed the file and the bagged briefcase to Jeff. "Let Tom know what you come up with."

*

Jeff opened the file. Blood analysis, skull x-rays, and photographs were present. The briefcase was in a plastic bag with an orange "evidence" sticker on it. The photographs showed the body lying face down on the ground in a small grassy area surrounded by rough terrain filled with shrubs, trees, and rocks. No identification was found and all pockets were empty. The report indicated that the briefcase was discovered in the brush about ten yards from the body with the flap open. Methodically, Jeff reviewed each of the items. The lab analysis revealed the blood type as "B positive," matching the blood on the briefcase. X-rays indicated a large fracture and anterior displacement of the occipital bone into the foramen magnum rupturing the vertebral arteries passing through it. *Could a simple fall result in force of such magnitude to cause so much trauma?* Jeff didn't think likely. Rather, he deduced, that a massive force must have been delivered from behind, forcing the victim to fall forward.

He evaluated the photographic images taken at autopsy and recognized definite contusions to the extremities and under both orbits. Again the injuries did not appear to relate to the force applied and he placed the photos under a high power lens.

Something strange about the facial injuries, he thought to himself. *These lesions are too symmetrical to be from a fall – in fact, even the injuries to the arms and legs appear too symmetrical.* Jeff reviewed the photos and the physical description when the body was found. Even the autopsy report appeared unusual. It suggested that several of the lesions had been induced post-mortem. How was that possible? After careful consideration Jeff wrote down his diagnosis: death by trauma with miscellaneous lesions induced post-mortem. This was not an accident: this was homicide and a very strange one at that.

He put on a pair of latex gloves and opened the plastic bag covering the briefcase. The exposed leather was stained and weather beaten, but deeper down the case appeared new and made of expensive calfskin. He looked inside the case, searching each of the separate folios, but someone must have emptied whatever was of value. *Who was this fellow?* Jeff placed the x-rays on his view box and reached for his own briefcase, unzipping the small pocket that held his pen. Suddenly he paused, picked up the victim's briefcase, and methodically reexamined it. He hadn't noticed, but did this briefcase contain a similar hidden pocket? He wondered if the overworked staff had missed something. Taking an examination light from his desk, he observed a narrow thin slit at the base of the case. Using tweezers, he separated the leather face and refocused the light. A dark piece of paper, the size of a business card, was inside the tight pocket. Carefully he removed the item and examined what appeared to be an image of a man dressed in seventeenth-century clothing. On the back of the picture was written a name: *John Milton.*

CHAPTER 21

International Milton Society Office, February 22

"I'm Dr. Davis with the Medical Examiner's office. I have an appointment to meet with one of your Milton specialists."

The Milton Society administrator ushered Tom into Keith's office.

"I thought you might help us." Tom showed Keith the image of the engraving Jeff had found in the John Doe briefcase. "The name John Milton is written on the back. Do you have any idea what this is?"

Keith recognized the image immediately – the artist was the same William Blake whose work he copied at Joanne's office.

"This is a photograph of one of a series of engravings that William Blake made between 1803 and 1808. Blake was a British poet, painter, and engraver who illustrated and printed his own books and this was part of his 'Milton: A Poem in Two Books, to Justify the Ways of God to Men.'"

Keith was surprised at the coincidence. *To justify the ways of God to men. The statement keeps reappearing.*

Tom continued, "The medical examiner's office is investigating a death. We found a briefcase near the body and this picture was the only information we could find."

Tom picked up the photograph and placed it back into its file. "Because he was dressed in a suit, we thought he might be attending a lecture or professional meeting. Would you know anything about it?

"A death? I'm afraid not."

"The man was wearing a suit that appears to be found only in Europe. His body was found in a park not far from Columbia University."

Keith looked up: "Europe? Columbia? When?"

"We're fairly certain it was within the past two weeks."

Keith sat down at his desk. "How did you say he died?"

Tom realized that Keith's tone had changed. "I didn't, but it's possible that he was murdered."

Keith swallowed hard. "Murdered?" As Keith tried to piece together the information he searched his top drawer for a recent issue of the Quarterly. Reaching into the drawer he removed the publication. "Can this help?"

Tom scanned the announcement.

Professor Stanton Reynolds of the University at Ghent will be presenting "The Disclosure of the Milton Manuscript" at Columbia University, February 12.

Keith continued, "Professor Reynolds never made it to the meeting and neither colleagues nor family have heard from his since." Keith realized the significance of the death. "Why was he murdered?"

"It appears to be a random robbery. Anything of value had been taken. All that was left was the empty briefcase."

Keith spoke hurriedly. "Are you sure there was nothing else in it?"

Tom was surprised at the interest. "It was empty, except for the picture. Should something else have been in it?"

"No, just wondering."

"If I showed you a few photographs, would you be able to identify him?"

"Perhaps."

Tom took out the photos and placed them on the desk. As Keith looked through the medical examiner's prints he paused at a close-up of the cadaver. Immediately his stomach churned, as if he wanted to vomit. The sickness wasn't so much from the condition of the cadaver, but what had happened to the hands and ankles and his examination of the high magnification photos of the face. He had seen it before.

Tom observed Keith's response. "The marks on the face appear to be burned into each cheek. We're not certain what it is. One seems to be an *S* and the other an *L*."

Keith's anger flared inside. His face turned to stone and his fists and jaws clenched. Tom tried speaking to him, but there was no response.

"Dr. Jessup, I think you should come with me – we need to talk."

*

Stan Galvin closed the door to his office. "Dr. Davis reported that you may have some information on a case we've been following."

Keith couldn't get the photos of Reynolds out of his mind. *The same marks as described on Livingston!*

"It's him."

Stan looked at Tom and then back at Keith. "I'm sorry?"

"The photos, they're of Professor Reynolds. What did they do to him?"

"Stigmata, Dr. Jessup. Someone inflicted these injuries after Reynolds was killed."

The word hit Keith like a blow to the head.

"Stigmata? You mean the bodily marks or contusions that correspond to the wounds that Jesus received at the crucifixion? But why?"

Stan continued, "That we don't know, but you're right about Stigmata. The wounds of the hands and feet are similar to four of the five wounds of Jesus."

Keith looked at Stan. "You've seen this before?"

"It's the first time I've actually seen the lesions, but there have been reports of individuals developing them without obvious trauma. I've seen a drawing of St. Francis, who was, I believe, the first to report developing such injuries. It's suggested they result from those who have such a deep faith that they wish to undergo the same pain that Jesus underwent on the cross."

Tom brought over a cup of water and Keith drank it.

Stan asked the last question. "Is there anything else you can tell us?"

Keith slowly stood up, his knees almost buckling under him. "I don't think there's anything more to tell."

Stan waited for Keith to walk out of the office. "He knows more."

Tom nodded. He picked up the cup that Keith drank from and placed it into a specimen bag. "I think so too."

*

Keith barely made it out to First Avenue. He crossed the street and sat down on a low concrete wall outside of the Kips Bay Apartments and took several deep breaths. *Stigmata, the letters S and L – just as on Livingston – Why? What did it mean?*

CHAPTER 22

Queens, New York, February 22

Keith was exhausted. He lay down on his bed and fell into a deep sleep, only to awaken hours later with a start. He couldn't get the pictures of Reynolds out of his mind. Almost mechanically he walked into the den and removed Livingston's notebook from the closet shelf, sat down and began to read. Some of the pages were old scribbles of ideas that Livingston had made throughout the years trying to understand what Milton's poem was trying to say; others were copies of his published essays. As he continued to read through, he came upon a newly printed one. His heart raced as he read the title:

THE LADY MARGARET MEMORIAL LECTURE
Secrets of The Milton Manuscript
to be delivered by
PROFESSOR THORNTON LIVINGSTON
Distinguished Chairman of Early English Literature
Hertford College, Oxford
Saturday, January 7, 8:00 PM

It was the lecture he never gave! Keith removed the pages from the binder and began to read. *Was there really something here that could lead to murder?* But as he read the text he could find nothing. Livingston explained how he became frustrated in not being able to understand the deeper meaning of *Paradise Lost* and after careful analyses of other scholarly attempts realized that no one had a full grasp of Milton's verse. As a result, he concluded that Milton, who always made his meanings clear, must have written a definitive explanation that for some reason had never been found.

Keith sat at his desk and slowly closed the book. Livingston was correct, Milton always made his meaning clear, and if his readers didn't understand, then he wrote a simple explanation. *Isn't that what he did for the second edition of* Paradise Lost? *When the readers complained to the*

publisher that the poem was too difficult to follow, Milton wrote a simple sum-
mary introducing each of the twelve books. And yet, Livingston's lecture was
all hypotheses, nothing concrete. As he picked up the notebook, a small
sheet of paper fell to the floor. He placed the notebook back on the
desk and picked up the paper. On it was a small note in his professor's
hand with the words "must check" and then a series of names, the first
of which was not fully legible. Was it E. Goodfriend or Goodfried? He
wasn't sure. Then came "D. Skinner, W. Morgan, Milton, Manuscript?
accidents? conspiracy? 1678?"

Keith looked up for a moment. Who were these people? Did they
have a relationship to the lost manuscript? He made a copy, returned the
sheet to the notebook and placed it back on the shelf. Did Livingston
ever follow up on these names?

He thought back to his first meeting with Cuttermill and the original
note from Livingston. He opened the desk drawer and removed it from
the Manuscript file and reread the last paragraph.

I have asked Mr. Cuttermill to inform you of a small gift that I
hope you can use in your future pursuits. Perhaps you will even explore finding the Manuscript. If so, please remember that Stigmata
is more than you have been taught, and the journey more difficult
than you realize. But if truth is sought and justice served, the reward will be great.

Keith placed the letter back into its file and closed the desk drawer. Now
he understood what his professor was asking, and giving the Tanzer lecture was only the final scene. Not only was he to seek the contents of the
Manuscript, but to serve justice on those who were preventing its being
found. *Livingston wants his murderers identified and justice delivered.* He
sat at his desk for a long time, reflecting on the office break-in, arson,
murders – these people stopped at nothing. How was he to carry out
Livingston's request?

*

New York, February 23

"Is everything OK?"

Joanne looked at Keith wondering why he wanted to meet her. She
hadn't heard from him since he came to her office for the Blake. It had

sounded important and they had a history. They sipped their coffees at a small table in a crowded deli filled with the shouts of rushing waiters barking orders for soups and sandwiches, the clatter of cups meeting saucers, stirring spoons, and the buzz of thirty different stories being told across tables.

"I was at the medical examiner's office and had to identify someone I knew, someone who had been murdered."

Joanne's smile disappeared. "That must have been terrible."

"It was."

She waited before responding. "Are you alright?"

"I'm not sure."

He paused before continuing, "What would you do if a friend needed your help, knowing that it could include a degree of danger?"

"I suppose it would depend on how good a friend."

"Yes, I suppose it would." He took a thoughtful sip of his coffee and when he placed the cup down she added. "And how much danger."

"Yes, how much danger."

Joanne looked away, as if the answers were found elsewhere in the room. Finally she turned back.

"Are you in some kind of trouble?"

He played with the table knife, realizing that was the question he himself had to confront. "I'm afraid I could be, or will be."

"Is there anything I can do?"

"You're doing it. I needed someone to speak to and all I could think of was you."

Joanne was surprised. "Don't you have anyone else to confide in?"

He wished he could say yes, but he knew it wasn't true. Could he really tell her – could he trust her with his deepest thoughts that his father had taught him to hide. He turned his coffee cup around in circles, wanting to emote the hidden hurt. Finally he let out a deep breath.

"Not since my mom. My professor at Oxford was a good friend but it was never like speaking to her. I could talk to her about anything. It was a terrible ending."

"I remember. Leukemia. You were a senior in college. That was a terrible time."

"And you helped me through it. So I suppose there's really no one else I ever really could speak to." He twirled the cup again and then looked into her eyes.

"Except for you."

He noticed the blush but said nothing. She observed the change – he had let her in for the first time. She sensed the stirrings inside her and marveled how the embers of an old love, or was it friendship, could remain alive for so long. Perhaps Plato was correct about soul mates when he described how Zeus feared the power of humans so he split them in half at birth and only when they find their other half would they find peace.

A long silence followed. Instinctively, he reached for her hand and she gave it to him.

"There's something I have to do – somewhere I have to go."

"Will you be away for long?"

"Not this trip, but the journey will be." As he paid the tab, his face relaxed into a smile.

"Someday I'd like to tell you about it."

She returned the smile. "I'm a good listener."

"I know. You always were."

*

They said their goodbyes and walked their separate ways. As Keith walked down the street, he realized what he would do, had to do. He pressed the contact number on his cell phone and waited for the pickup.

"Cuttermill, here."

"Mr. Cuttermill, this is Keith Jessup in New York. Would it be possible to meet with you? I need to discuss the Tanzer lecture."

He then called the Milton Society office. "I need a few days to myself."

CHAPTER 23

London, UK, February 24

He found Abacus House at Thirty-Three Gutter Lane in London. The offices of Twinings and Whitcomb, Litigation Solicitors, were as stately as the firm's name suggested. A long list of partners were presented on the large glass entry doors that led to a distinguished mahogany-paneled reception room with green carpet so plush that Keith assumed it had to be mowed every week.

"Are you certain about this?" Cuttermill sounded concerned.

"Yes, sir."

"But this will mean undertaking great risks. You don't have to do this."

Keith sat forward in one of the soft black leather Gothic chairs across from Cuttermill's desk.

"I'm aware of that. But at some point there must be payback. I couldn't live with myself if I didn't at least try."

"But you would be announcing it at a lecture before the most distinguished scholars."

"What better way to honor Dr. Livingston's name and the ideals he stood for. No sir, I want to do it, and show his murderers that nothing can stop the pursuit of truth."

"You're going to need help."

"Mr. Cuttermill, unfortunately asking for help has not been my strong suit. I'm afraid I'll have to do this by myself."

Cuttermill sat back pensively in his chair.

"It's just that the hourglass has already been turned."

"Sir?"

Cuttermill glanced at a paper on his desk. "The Tanzer Lecture is to be given on June 22."

Keith was taken by surprise. He had never even thought about when the lecture was to be given. "But that's less than four months from now!"

Cuttermill saw the reality settling in. "I'm afraid the date is fixed. Once you accept, there's no turning back. Not only will you be receiving the invitation, but the rest of the world will also be receiving theirs. If you give that lecture, you will have to know what's in that Manuscript."

Keith walked to the large window overlooking Cheapside Street with a view of the heart of London and St. Paul towering in the distance. *St. Paul, where Milton went to school.*

The solicitor remained patiently for a response. Finally Keith turned to face him.

"I need to do it."

Cuttermill looked at him closely. "Are you certain, young man?"

"Yes, sir."

The solicitor waited for a change in mind, but it never came. "Then it's settled?"

"It's settled."

Cuttermill went to his desk and made a note.

"You will need funding. I am placing an additional 25,000 pounds

into your account. If you need more you let me know. As before, this
conversation is to be kept confidential."

Keith was surprised. "Yes, and thank you."

Cuttermill walked over to Keith and put his hand on his shoulder.

"No, thank you. I can see why the Professor was so fond of you. You
are a man of honor and courage. I wish there were more like you."

"Let's talk about it in 119 days."

*

Oxford, UK, February 24

Keith rented a car for the drive to Oxford and parked on Manor Road,
not far from the St. Cross Building where Livingston's office was broken
into and John was murdered. He would do this. *The only way to face
a bully was to stand up to him.* It had only been weeks since he left the
school, but New York was a world away and the passing time seemed
like an eternity.

Keith smiled as he entered Sundstrom's office – it was still organized
chaos, only now he thought the stacks of papers were even higher.
Certainly his professor appeared the same, aside from the possible addition of a pound or two to his already rotund figure.

Sundstrom threw him a bear hug and held it for a few moments.
Keith tried to control it, but his eyes glistened. Not a word was said, but
Keith understood why it was there: if only his father would have held
him like this, just once.

"Well, old chap, so good to see you. I knew you couldn't stay away."

"Thank you, sir. It's good to be back."

Sundstrom sat behind his desk and signaled for his guest to be seated.

As Keith looked around the room, his eyes settled on a worn rectangular mahogany table placed next to his chair.

"I see you redecorated."

Sundstrom laughed.

"So you noticed. Actually, it was left out on the walk and I presumed
it more serviceable between my two chairs than in the refuse."

Sundstrom paused for a moment: "Are you here to accept the teaching job?"

Keith gave a half-smile. "Let's discuss it after I find the Manuscript."

Sundstrom turned serious for the moment. "So you've decided?"

"I owe it to him."

"And you're convinced there's a Manuscript?"

"More than ever."

Sundstrom was afraid this would happen.

"Is completing Livingston's work the only reason?"

Keith knew he would be asked.

"No, it's more than that. I don't like when people take advantage of others."

Sundstrom took a deep breath.

"So it's not just finding the meaning of the poem."

Keith thought for a moment.

"Not anymore. It's become personal – almost instinctive, I guess I can't tolerate injustice."

"So something bad happened."

Keith looked at his professor. "I saw Reynolds's body."

Sundstrom swallowed hard. "I wasn't aware."

"It hasn't been made public. He and Livingston were murdered in the same horrible way. I'm convinced it's by the same people who don't want the Manuscript found."

Sundstrom remained deep in thought. It wasn't just the revelation of the murder, which seemingly affirmed the scattered rumors of conspiracy over the years, but the realization that he would not be able to dissuade Keith from the now very real dangers of seeking the Manuscript. At last, Sundstrom rose from his chair and walked to an old wooden clothing tree in the corner of the room and reached for his overcoat. *Sometimes when you hit what seems an impenetrable wall it may be best to navigate around it.*

"What say a breath of fresh air?"

*

They walked in silence along the banks of the Thames, the fallen leaves of burnt umber, shades from the past season, now quilted into the earth's blanket. The day was surprisingly sunny for Oxford in February, and the temperature a pleasant 7° Centigrade or, as Keith figured, 45° Fahrenheit. Sundstrom, now and then, would take a piece of bread from his pocket and toss it into the flowing waters where little bubbles disclosed where the roach and perch and barbel spun to the surface to snare their floured prey. They followed the current, professor and student held in their own thoughts, surrounded by the gurgling of the river as it flowed between the rocks that appeared above its surface.

"They stole a good man's freedom. It's as Milton said: *None can love freedom heartily, but good men; the rest love not freedom, but license.*"

Sundstrom locked his eyes on his companion.

"But seeking freedom almost cost Milton his life."

Keith weighed the teacher's words.

"As it did Livingston and Reynolds."

"And what about yours?"

"I try not to think about that."

As they continued, Keith looked at the long drooping branches arched just above them, a canopy for their path. At that moment, a flock of blackbirds let out a cacophonous chorus that seemed to echo a warning. A mother duck with her ducklings swam along, stretching their necks to reach Sundstrom's bread crumbs. Sundstrom came to a halt.

"How can I help?"

Keith looked at him, not fully understanding the comment.

"You already are."

"No, I can do more. Like you, injustice is not one of my favorite behaviors. Let's find this damn manuscript. We find the manuscript and those bastards will come to us."

Sundstrom noticed Keith's hesitation.

"Come on now chap, in spite of my being slightly out of shape, I can assure you I can handle myself. Now where do we start?"

"That's what I'm trying to figure out."

CHAPTER 24

New York, February 27

It was a perfect Saturday afternoon without a cloud in the sky and temperatures nearing sixty degrees, a sure sign of global warming. Central Park was bathed in sunlight, full of children taking advantage of winter's spring, playing ball, swinging in the playground or skateboarding under the watchful eyes of parents in conversation. Young couples lay lazily on blankets and older ones were reading the *New York Times* on park benches – all to escape the hustle of big city streets. Keith and Joanne walked along the still waters of Turtle Pond, deep within the park's 800 acres.

"How was your trip?"

"OK. I've decided to help my friend. He's been looking for a Manuscript that Milton wrote and must have hidden."

"Why would he hide it?"

"I suppose he didn't want anyone to read it. The English Revolution was a pretty rough time, especially for Milton, and he was a very independent thinker."

Joanne tried to recall her history. "That was Cromwell, right? Mid-seventeenth century?"

"Sixteen-forty-nine to be exact. Cromwell and his Puritan army executed King Charles I, the first time a king was sentenced to the gallows, and Milton was center stage in defending the legal right of the people to commit regicide."

"I thought Cromwell failed. Wasn't there a restoration?"

"Actually, Cromwell died and his son couldn't hold on. By 1660 the Revolution was over and the dead King's son, Charles II, was restored to power."

Joanne remembered. "And wanted revenge."

"Not Charles as much as certain others, the worst being William Prynne, who charged that Milton was a traitor. Milton, blind and alone, was put on a death list, thrown into prison, awaiting the hangman."

"That's sure sounds like enough reason to hide independent thoughts."

"Somehow he was released, but it didn't stop him from writing."

"Reminds me of Samson, a blind hero refusing to give up."

Keith added. "Milton's final poem was about Samson. *Samson Agonistes*."

"So he compared himself to Samson, who blind and in chains had to wait for his hair to grow before he could defeat the Philistines."

"Yes, as Milton had to wait to take down his enemies, the kings and churches who he believed denied man's liberty. Samson's genius was his patience to regain his strength as I think Milton's was the patience to hide his manuscript until a new generation would accept it and be willing to destroy his enemies."

"Are you saying Milton defied God and country?"

Keith thought back to the first time he had heard that. "Some people believe that."

They walked along the winding paths that led around the man-made pond that Olmsted and Vaux designed in 1858. Every now and then they would stop to point out the turtles sunning themselves on the rocks along the water's edge.

Joanne returned to the subject. "Did he hide anything else? I mean, perhaps that was his thing, writing what he didn't want others to see and hiding them until someone else could find them."

Keith thought for a moment. "Actually he did. I hadn't really thought about it. It's called *The Christian Doctrine*. Milton had written it in Latin, *De Doctrina Christiana*, but it wasn't found until 1823, a full 148 years after Milton's death."

It was getting late and Keith walked her back to her apartment on the Upper West Side.

"In fact, Milton dictated the *De Doctrina* and *Paradise Lost* at the same time."

Joanne picked up the thought. "So if *The Christian Doctrine* was hidden, is it possible that the Manuscript you're looking for is hidden in the same place?"

Keith's face lit up. "I suppose it's possible. I'd have to go back and research it, but it might be worth a shot. Understand the fate of *De Doctrina* – to understand the fate of the Milton Manuscript. I knew you were a genius!"

She smiled. "So you finally recognize who I am."

He stood at her door and gave her a gentle kiss on her cheek. It had been a long time since his lips felt her softness.

"Thanks for the day. I really enjoyed it."

She looked up into his eyes.

"So did I."

*

New York, February 28

The more he thought about Joanne's comment the more he realized how significant it could be. *De Doctrina Christiana* was a massive work, 750 pages long and only translated twice from Milton's original Latin as: *A Treatise on Christian Doctrine, Compiled from the Holy Scriptures Alone.*

Keith went to the Society Library, removed the copy of *De Doctrina Christiana* and read Milton's introduction:

"To all the Churches of Christ and to All in any part of the world who profess the Christian faith." Milton then explained how he began "an earnest study of the Old and New Testaments in their original languages. . . . believing it incumbent upon each individual to do so . . .

[allowing me] to explore and think out my religious beliefs for myself by
my own exertions."

"What do you have there?"

Keith turned to see Janeway looking over his shoulder. "*The Christian
Doctrine*. Amazing how Milton could write this entire book while blind.
Look at this, it's filled with exact translations from the original Latin
and Hebrew and his commentaries on it, and he dictated it all from
memory."

"I haven't looked at that since Cambridge days."

"What a job. Milton no longer trusted how others interpreted
Christianity, so from then on he would check everything himself. He
went back to the original sources, all from memory, and aligned it with
the actual words of scripture. He then compared every Christian belief, every tradition, every church statute to the original biblical text. As
he puts it, *to explore and think out my religious beliefs for myself*. In other
words, Milton's *Christian Doctrine* explained his personal theology, even
as it differed from what the Church presented. Milton, in effect, sought
truth in Christianity as originally professed."

Janeway looked at the page Keith had read from. "All I remember is
heresy. That's why there are scholars who refuse to believe that Milton
wrote this."

"But is it because he disagreed with the official Church canon they
pray to or their idealistic perception of a Milton they have come to idol-
ize?"

"Maybe both."

With that Janeway patted Keith on the back and walked out of the
Library.

Keith sat there. Is that what this is all about? Trying to protect the
great name of Milton from writing blasphemy or trying to protect the
religion that he was attacking . . or both?

He recalled Bartholomew's argument:

Paradise Lost is the greatest poetic achievement in the English language . . . the world believes that the poem upholds the greatness
of Christianity and the victory of the Christian God over Satan and
his forces of evil. Is it so difficult to appreciate that such a perception must be defended from any assault? . . . If you attack *Paradise
Lost*, then you are attacking a fundamental Christian belief of God's
creation and power, good over evil, reward and punishment.

Keith needed direct evidence, but all he had was the possibility that the Manuscript and *The Christian Doctrine* were somehow connected.

CHAPTER 25

New York, March 2, 112 days

The days were passing and Keith began to mark them, realizing time would be his enemy. He had given his word that he would deliver one of the most prestigious lectures in the United States on Milton – and only sixteen weeks remained. There was no turning back. If he was to find the Manuscript, he needed information and quickly. He had to follow up on the *De Doctrina* relationship.

He left a message on Sundstrom's cell. It was Sundstrom and his colleagues who had pieced together the detailed handwriting analysis and forensic evidence to prove that Milton authored *De Doctrina*. Sundstrom returned the call within the hour.

Keith spoke right to the issue. "How was Milton's *De Doctrina* found?"

"That took ten years of historical sleuthing to figure out, so you better get yourself comfortable. It's quite a story and I need to start at the beginning."

Sundstrom began.

"By 1651 Milton was already blind and anything written he had to dictate to an amanuenses. Milton chose a Jeremie Picard who had previously helped Milton write documents, and from January of 1658 through May of 1660 he put into writing Milton's dictation. We established through handwriting analysis that a Daniel Skinner, whose father was a merchant, somehow received the *De Doctrina* after Milton's death. How the young Skinner got a hold of it, we're not certain, but perhaps he talked Milton's family into giving it to him by promising them a financial return."

"And what did Skinner do with it?"

"He tried to have it published, but it was censored as being too anti-Christian."

"So what happened?"

"In 1675, a year after Milton's death, we found documents that revealed that Daniel Skinner gave the unpublished *Doctrina* to a Symon Heere, a Dutch shipping captain. Heere was to deliver them to Daniel

Elsevier, who headed the Elzevir publishing house in Amsterdam."

Again Keith interrupted. "So he tried to get it published outside of England?"

"He had no choice."

"This Elzevir isn't the same Elsevier Publishing Company that publishes today?"

"One and the same, although now it specializes in science and health with writers from Jules Verne to Stephen Hawking. The original name was Elzevir and it was founded in 1580. At that time Amsterdam was the publishing capital of the world and Elzevir was the major publisher of classical scholarship not only for England but all of Europe. That's why Skinner sent it there; he assumed they would be eager to publish an unknown work by the great and recently deceased John Milton. He also assumed they would pay very well."

Sundstrom continued, "Well, Elsevier read through the manuscript and was also concerned about its anti-Church views so he sent it to Professor Phillippus van Limborch for an opinion. We found a letter written years later in which Limborch states 'that a publisher had given him a System of Theology by Milton to advise whether he should print it.' But Limborch advised against it because of its critical views which he felt bordered on heresy."

Keith interjected. "So Elsevier never published it."

"Correct."

"But someone did."

The older man responded. "That's the amazing part. It wasn't published until 1825, after it was found stored away in the Old Paper State Office Building."

Keith thought for a moment. "What happened then?"

"It caused an uproar. Milton's views of Christianity diverged widely from the Anglican and Protestant Churches. Scholars and theologians tried to counter Milton's arguments, but that proved difficult since Milton based his *Doctrina* completely on original biblical texts."

"And then"?

"It became a major debate. The Unitarians loved it, but Bishop Thomas Burgess led a crusade to deny that Milton had ever written it and the Methodist Magazine and the Christian Spectator agreed."

"I guess they couldn't believe that the great Milton would entertain anti-Christian views. It seems as if they were trying to protect him."

Sundstrom responded. "Or stop him. Few cared if a less formidable individual attacked the Anglicans, but if Milton criticized them, every-one took notice."

"So first the *Doctrina* was hidden to prevent its being published, and when it was published they tried to establish a 'cover up' – denying Milton's authorship."

Sundstrom added. "All we know for sure was that the work was found in a bundle of state papers written by Milton while he served as Secretary of Foreign Tongues under Cromwell. But there are still scholars today trying to prove that Milton never wrote it. Ask Bartholomew, he doesn't believe Milton authored it, but neither Bartholomew nor any other de-nier has suggested who else could have."

Keith thought, if you can't attack the message, attack the messenger.

CHAPTER 26

New York, March 3, 111 days

Daniel Skinner. He was riding the subway when it flashed into his mind: Daniel Skinner! Wasn't that one of the names Livingston had written in his note? "Check E. Good something, then, D. Skinner, W. Morgan, Milton, Manuscript? accidents? Conspiracy, 1678?" And hadn't Sundstrom mentioned Skinner's name as involved with *The Christian Doctrine*?! What about the others?

Keith hurried to the office and used the search engine to check the names. First, Morgan. Could there be a relationship to Milton? Keith was surprised at what he found. A William Morgan was presumed mur-dered in 1826 in upstate New York following the announcement that he was to publish a manuscript exposing secrets of the Freemasons. The murder occurred shortly after the publication of *The Christian Doctrine* in Boston in 1825. Was there a fear that Morgan had somehow come into possession of the Manuscript? Certainly the connection between the Freemasons and Milton was well-known, many believing that Milton was a Mason, as were many of the most brilliant and creative men at the time. But the key to the hatred of the Masons was, like Milton, their support of Cromwell, and it put them under constant attack by support-ers of the king and Anglican Church. *Were the "secrets" that Morgan was to publish about the Masons merely a code word for the Manuscript? Was his murder to prevent its publication?*

Keith marked it as a possible and went to the next name on Livingston's list: E. Goodfriend? Keith checked but came up with nothing. Was that why Livingston placed a question mark next to it? He tried an assortment of names, no Goodfry, no Goodfround, no Godfriend, until the search engine asked if he meant Godfrey! Keith couldn't believe he hadn't thought of it: *Of course! 1678 – Livingston had written the date – that must be it! It wasn't Goodfriend or Goodfry but Godfrey, Sir Edmund Godfrey!* – the associations came pouring from his memory: *Murder! The Popish Plot! One of the great mysteries in English history.* Was it possible? Had Livingston forgotten or misunderstood the actual name? No one had ever suggested a relationship between Godfrey and Milton, especially since Milton had died in 1674, four years before Godfrey's murder. What could the relationship be?

*

Keith searched online for information on the Popish Plot and found documents revealing that on October 17, 1678, the corpse of Sir Edmund Berry Godfrey, a Westminster Justice of the Peace, member of Parliament, and a strong supporter of Protestantism, was discovered in a ditch near Primrose Hill. He had been stabbed with his own sword and reportedly strangled. It was concluded that the death of Sir Godfrey was part of "The Popish Plot."

The Plot was initiated two months previously, on August 11, when Titus Oates, an associate of Dr. Israel Tonge, testified that he discovered a document within the wainscot panels of the gallery of the extremely anti-Catholic physician Sir Richard Barker. The document accused the Roman Catholic Church of a plot, overseen by the Pope, to assassinate King Charles II. It named nearly one hundred Jesuits and their supporters as involved in carrying out the scheme. King Charles thought the entire affair rather absurd and refused to take it seriously until rumors of the plan spread and anti-Catholic sentiment heated to the point that Charles had to investigate. On September 6, Oates was brought before the magistrate, Sir Edmund Godfrey, to swear an oath prior to his testimony before the king. Oates testified that he was present at a *Jesuit* meeting at the White Horse Tavern in the *Strand in London* on April 24, 1678, to discuss the assassination of *Charles II.* On September 28, Oates named over 500 Jesuits and Catholic nobles, including the queen's physician, of planning to assassinate the king.

Keith stopped reading for the moment. He couldn't imagine how

Oates could have named so many Catholics as being part of the plot until he recalled America's Red Scare, the Communist witch hunts of the early 1950s led by Senator Joseph McCarthy. That case also resulted in a large number of prominent Americans being accused of subversive activity against the United States, dramatically recreated in the 1962 film, *Manchurian Candidate*. In it, Lawrence Harvey, the McCarthy persona, was asked how many Communists were actually in the senate. The McCarthy persona apparently had never thought about such a question, but in front of reporters he searched for an answer. Keith would never forget how the camera focused on the label of the bottle of Heinz Ketchup on the table directly in front of Harvey who then declared: *there were 57 card-carrying Communists in the US Senate!*

Keith continued his reading: But the seeds of fear and prejudice had been sewn, and the finding of Sir Godfrey's body on October 17, assumed to be by Catholics, sent the Protestant population into an uproar, resulting in the execution of fifteen Catholics. England, especially London, had succumbed to mass hysteria.

The question for Keith was how the death of Sir Godfrey related to the Milton Manuscript? Keith reviewed the available post-mortem records which indicated that Godfrey had died "two or three days prior to being found; that the magistrate's breast looked black, as if he had been beaten, with severe head, neck, and facial injuries." The report indicated that "there were several stab wounds," but it was the facial injuries that drew Keith's attention: a small mark present on each cheek, seemingly burned into the skin. Was it possible that the one on the left was similar to the letter *S* and the one on the right similar to the letter *L*? The wounds were determined to have occurred after death!

Keith stood and walked to the window overlooking Seventh Avenue. It was not unusually warm in his office, but the beads of perspiration found on his forehead were not from the external temperature – it was from the knowledge that the post-mortem findings of Sir Edmund Berry Godfrey in 1678 were the same as those found on the bodies of Professors Thornton Livingston and Stanton Reynolds over 300 years later!

Keith could only think of one thing – conspiracy!

*

March 3, 111 days

But was it possible? Could a conspiracy last so many generations? Keith reviewed the few assignments that he had been given by Livingston regarding the manuscript. All that he really knew was that his professor believed that the "key" to finding the manuscript would be found in one of the early editions of the poem. As a graduate student, he and Livingston searched as many of the 1667 and 1674 editions as they could find, but neither Keith nor any other scholar ever reported finding that key. But perhaps there remained an edition published before Milton's death in 1674 that they had not found. If so, where could it be? He redoubled his efforts, checking sites that specialized in early edition sales of seventeenth-century English Literature. Finally he found one of interest.

He saw it online:

> For immediate sale: A second edition of John Milton's poem, *Paradise Lost*. Offered from the Samuel Hartlib Collection by The University of Sheffield, consisting of correspondence that Hartlib had with the greatest writers, philosophers, and scientists of the age. This is the first publication where Milton divided the ten books into twelve, a format utilized by Virgil's Aeneid. This octavo version, published July 1674, includes the final changes before Milton died 8 November 1674. Condition: Very Good – tight binding, very skillfully *rebacked* with the original spines laid down; Top of pages are red, light corner bumping; previous owner sticker on inside cover, several spots on the edge of the pages. Available for view, March 5–10.

He reread the essential words: *The Samuel Hartlib Collection! Final changes! Skillfully rebacked!* Keith outlined the logic: First, *Samuel Hartlib* – it was well known that the Hartlib Collection remained hidden until 1933 when its trove of letters, essays, and manuscripts were discovered in an old attic in London. Second, *Final changes.* What final changes? What was different about this copy than all others? Third, *rebacked.* Why would it need to be rebacked if it lay undisturbed for 300 years? If this copy of *Paradise Lost* had the answers, he needed to find out.

CHAPTER 27

Sheffield, UK, March 5, 109 days

Sheffield, named for the River Sheaf, which runs through it, is one of England's eight largest cities with a population of over half a million. In the nineteenth century it was famous for its excellence in steel production and the Sheffield name and especially Sheffield knives remain known throughout the world. Built on rolling hillsides, its open green spaces had given birth to over two million trees, a claim that Sheffield touts as more per person than any other city in Europe.

Keith had the feeling he wasn't alone. As he walked through the gate at the Doncaster Sheffield Airport, he sensed he was being followed. He walked into the main passenger lounge and stopped by a water fountain, checking the area as he took a drink. Was that him? A large man wearing a blue baseball cap pulled forward hiding his face. Keith had to know for sure. He walked quickly into a restroom and slowly washed his hands, his eyes fixed on the mirror in front of him with a view of whoever entered. When he saw no one, he walked to a news stand and thumbed through a paperback, glancing around inconspicuously to see if he was being watched. If someone had been following him, he wasn't there now.

Sundstrom had driven the 150 miles north from Oxford on the M1 Motorway and met Keith at the arrival gate. He greeted him with a hug and led Keith back to his old Ford. Even for Britain it was an unusually frigid afternoon, with a cold north wind gnawing at Keith's marrow.

"You certainly didn't give me much notice. Are you on some kind of deadline?"

Keith smiled. *Was Foster psychic?* "Sorry, sort of an emergency."

"So you've come for business?"

"I did, but I need two things," Keith said, putting his hands over the car's heating vent, "and the first is a hot cup of coffee."

"And the second?"

"I'll tell you after I get the first." Keith reviewed with Sundstrom the results of his investigation into the murdered Edmund Godfrey and the post-mortem findings.

Sundstrom was amazed.

"But Godfrey's death is what incited the hysteria of the Popish Plot!

Everyone assumed he was the first one on the list to be killed by the Catholics because he was the magistrate on the case. What could this have to do with a conspiracy that killed Livingston and Reynolds?"

They rode in silence until Sundstrom reached the City Center and eased the pedal. He drove down Pitt Street and parked across from #18, the Red Deer Tavern, not far from the university. They entered and Sundstrom asked for two hot coffees. By the time they settled into a booth on the side of the room, the steaming mugs were served, along with a basket of fresh hot sunflower baps.

"What are you looking for?"

Keith wrapped his hands around the mug and sipped the brew. "There's an early edition of *Paradise Lost* for sale, and it may contain a clue as to where the Manuscript is. If it's not what I need, I can always donate it to the Milton Library."

"I see. Janeway's lucky to have you on board."

"I like working with him, so I guess we're both lucky."

"The last time I saw you, you were as poor as a country church mouse. Did some rich uncle leave you his fortune?"

"Something like that."

As they drank their coffee, a black over silver 1999 Ford Ranger Diesel XLT Thunder pickup truck eased its way down Pitt Street and parked a block from the Red Deer Tavern. Three men exited the double cab, checked Sundstrom's Ford, and made their way to the Red Deer. One of them, a large man wearing a blue cap with red hair spilling out from under it, looked through the front window. "They're here."

Abaddon, Clive, and a well-built blond-haired man entered and walked through to an empty table in the rear. They ordered three local Easy Rider Ales on tap and kept their conversation to a whisper. Sundstrom gave no attention to their arrival.

"So you think this edition of *Paradise Lost* will tell us where the Manuscript is?"

Keith casually glanced at the three men without apparent recognition, and continued speaking to Sundstrom. "I hope it tells us much more."

Sundstrom bit into another bun. "How so?"

"For one, where did Milton learn about the ways of God?"

Sundstrom thought for a moment. "Why, from Christian theology, where else? All great Milton scholars agree that *Paradise Lost* is based on Pauline theology, where the Law of Moses no longer leads to salvation. Paul taught that salvation can only be found through faith in Jesus – the

Trinity – God. It's what *Paradise Lost* is about – it's our fundamental Christian poem."

Keith was quick to respond. "Yes, that is what we have been taught, that Milton believed that Mosaic Law was replaced by a New Testament, one based on love not law."

Sundstrom interjected: "And why not? After all, doesn't Paul insist that Adam couldn't even keep the only commandment that God gave him: *Do not eat from the tree in the center of the garden.* To Paul, the Law of Moses could never prevent man from sin – it was too difficult to follow."

Keith let a small smile escape. "I guess Paul didn't have much faith in man."

Sundstrom returned the smile. "That was the point, wasn't it? The only way man could purge himself from sin was to replace faith in man with faith in Jesus."

"No great show of support for man's capabilities."

Sundstrom raised his eyebrows and nodded. "But perhaps a realistic one. Of course Paul had a clever argument against the hopelessness of Mosaic Law: that the Hebrew Bible demanded that unless you performed every detail of every law, it is as if you performed none."

Keith shook his head. "He got that from James ii.10: *Whoever keeps the whole law, and yet offends in one point, is guilty of all.*"

Sundstrom laughed quietly. "Sort of how kids look at their parents. If they're not perfect then they're all bad."

Keith allowed a sarcastic smile, "True, but scholars have it wrong. Milton never agreed with Paul. Certainly he didn't believe in the Trinity and he didn't believe that James meant that one sin meant you violated all 613 commandments found in the Hebrew Bible, only those sins emanating from Original Sin. If you commit one transgression, then you may find you have committed others, but not all. Paul took it out of context."

"Are you questioning whether it's a Christian poem?"

"I'm only saying that based on his *Christian Doctrine*, I'm not sure what kind of Christianity Milton believed in. And he wrote that at the same time he was writing *Paradise Lost*."

"Careful, boy. You're treading on hallowed ground."

"Isn't that what scholars are trained to do: Look at everything with objectivity – to a scholar nothing can be hallowed."

Sundstrom sat back with a satisfied look on his face. "I needed the reminder. It appears as if you're becoming the teacher and I the student."

Keith took a final drink, paid the tab, and with a grin added. "Wasn't it da Vinci who said, *poor is the pupil who does not surpass his master?*"

As the scholars exited, the three men in the rear room put down their mugs, threw some coins onto the table, and followed them out.

*

Sundstrom drove along Pitt Street toward the university, turned the Ford onto Leavygreave Road and then onto Bolsover where he pulled into a parking lot adjacent to the Library. The two men left the car and walked to the Western Bank Library steps. Sundstrom, ever the teacher, continued the conversation as if in a Socratic dialogue with his students.

"You're saying Milton disagreed with Paul's interpretation of Jesus's teaching?"

"Paul was the publicist, Milton the religious scholar. It was Milton who argued that to be a good Christian meant to live a life of good deeds as defined in scripture, not on Paul's interpretations. Milton declared that a good Christian should study the Bible and find his own answers."

"So Milton wanted Christians to interpret Scripture for themselves?"

Keith nodded. "Yes. To Milton, faith without knowledge is memory without understanding."

"Now you're sounding like the great rabbis."

"Well, I suppose that's who Jesus was . . ." Keith stopped at the library entrance doors before finishing the sentence and looked at his teacher inquisitively:

"What if *Paradise Lost* wasn't based on Christian tenets? What if Milton could only justify the ways of God by learning from the rabbis?"

Sundstrom looked at him as if he was crossing into Hades. "I'd say that alone could cause a conspiracy."

It was like a light went on. "What did you say?"

"I said if it was ever disclosed that *Paradise Lost* was not a Christian poem it would be enough to cause a conspiracy."

CHAPTER 28

Sheffield, UK, March 5, 109 days

The Western Bank Library was a sleek modern glass tower that rose high above its academic surroundings. Keith and Sundstrom walked through the marble-floored lobby and crossed to the young man at the information desk, asking for the Special Collections and Archives Department. Keith informed him that they had an appointment with a Ms. Elvira Throckmorton and showed their identifications. A uniformed security guard led them to a fifth-level office where Miss Throckmorton greeted them.

"Dr. Jessup, we've been expecting you." Throckmorton was a tall, thin, middle-aged woman with graying hair cut short, and horn-rimmed glasses that hung from her neck by a silver chain. Keith thought she looked like Popeye's girlfriend, Olive Oyl.

The security guard accompanied them to a private room where Throckmorton carefully placed the 1674 edition of *Paradise Lost* on the table. Keith took several minutes to examine it, especially the binding. The book was in excellent condition and Keith asked if there had been much interest in its sale.

"Actually, we thought there would be more. We have another interested party arriving shortly, but outside of a few inquiries, no other appointments."

"Then I'll purchase it."

Throckmorton was surprised. "Really? Why that's wonderful. We weren't certain that it would sell at this price."

"There's one further detail I need you to help me with – a complete history of this book, when and how you received it and who had access to it since it was in the Library's possession."

Throckmorton thought for a moment. "I think that's possible. I'll need a little time to put that together. If you could give me an address."

Keith gave her his card. "Send it to the office."

They finalized the arrangements and Keith handed her a check from Barclays Bank. Throckmorton left the room to confirm the account and returned within a few minutes with the bank's affirmation, placing the book in a cardboard package.

Sundstrom was amazed. "That's it. You spend five minutes looking at the book and you buy it for 15,000 American dollars?"

Keith laughed. "Hey, I liked the cover." He looked at his watch. "And I have a plane to catch."

*

Clive and the well-built man with blond hair who was wearing a trench coat over his suit were in conversation while Abaddon paced nervously in the Library's lobby, keeping his eyes on the elevator doors. It wasn't long before he recognized Keith and Sundstrom exiting.

"That's them."

The man in the trench coat didn't seem concerned. "I'm here to inspect the book. If they don't have it, there's nothing to gain by following them. I'll need a good hour to check it out."

Ten minutes later the man in the trench coat reappeared. "You better call. They bought the book and took it with them."

Abaddon pressed the numbers on his cell phone. "Uncle, they were ere and took the book."

If one was standing nearby, they would have heard a raised voice over the cell phone. As Abaddon listened, drops of sweat moistened the red scaly skin that covered his face. Finally he put the phone back into his pocket. "E's real angry and wants that book, now!"

By the time the men raced outside Sundstrom was already pulling out of the lot. Abaddon got behind the wheel of the pickup and the others piled in.

"Which way?"

Clive pointed behind them and Abaddon U-turned the pickup. Sundstrom was already at the end of Western Bank and getting on A57, the Sheffield Parkway. The man in the trench coat pointed to his right and the pickup raced down the local street until they reached the A57.

"He's got to be going to the airport. Follow him."

Far ahead they made out Sundstrom's Ford getting onto the three-lane M1 highway. The pickup entered the M1 and Abaddon floored the pedal trying to make up the distance.

Sundstrom looked into the rear view mirror and saw the speeding pickup.

"There's a crazy driver about to pass us."

As Keith looked to his right he saw red hair flying out from under the blue hat and the men inside looking at them.

"That's the fellow who broke into Livingston's office, the same one leaving the fire at Livingston's home. You better lose them, they're trouble."

"What do they want?"

Keith realized the danger that they were in. "They want me and what I just bought."

Sundstrom pushed the pedal to the floor, weaving between cars to stay ahead of the pickup, but as fast as Sundstrom went, the pickup stayed close behind. Soon the signs for the airport came into view and Sundstrom exited, forced to slow down as he entered the airport road. Suddenly the pickup hit the rear of the Ford, pushing the car forward and Sundstrom and Keith thrust into a whiplash motion. The pickup pulled up along the Ford's side, slamming into Keith's door, forcing the Ford to swerve onto the grass median. The grass was soaked from the evening rain, and the car began to skid until Sundstrom managed to regain control and drove back onto the airport road. Again Abaddon's truck pulled along side and once more rammed the Ford off the road. This time Sundstrom had difficulty in controlling the car as it was forced toward a steep incline that dropped to the highway below. Sundstrom tried braking, but the wet earth couldn't prevent the car from slipping. Abaddon slowed the pickup and watched with amusement as Sundstrom tried to turn out of the skid. As the Ford slipped down the embankment, Sundstrom attempted to turn the wheels into the hill – finally the tread held and the car came to a stop facing at forty-five degrees to the top of the hill. Sundstrom tried to position the car horizontal to the incline, coaxing the vehicle along the hill toward the airport road. Abaddon saw the Ford moving parallel to the hilltop and floored his truck straight down, aiming to hit the Ford broadside. Sundstrom saw it coming and eased his foot onto the accelerator, trying to prevent the tires from spinning yet trying to avoid the pickup heading straight for them. Abaddon's pickup gained speed as it charged down the hill toward the Ford. Sundstrom felt the rear wheels start to spin and then hit a dry spot, gaining traction, and shooting forward. It was too late to avoid a collision, but the pickup only hit the rear corner of the Ford, rotating it up the hill. Abaddon had no such luck, his pickup hurtled down the hill toward the highway out of control. Abaddon pumped the brakes, the wheels stopped rotating, but the car kept sliding until it reached a rocky ledge that hurtled it into the air where it landed on its side and rolled over several times until it came to rest on the edge of the highway. The last view that Sundstrom and Keith had was the three men crawling out of the overturned vehicle.

Sundstrom pulled up next to the departure entrance. He and Keith looked at each other, the fear draining from their bodies. They said their goodbyes, but Keith couldn't get the events out of his mind. *Something was terribly wrong. Somehow, someone knew about the Sheffield trip. But how? And who?*

CHAPTER 29

Keith tried to put the trip behind him, but it was as if his mind had been dialed to a different cognizance. Even his walking to work made him aware of who was following him or who might be waiting for him. He tried to remind himself that he was back in New York, what happened in Europe couldn't happen here. *But that didn't help Stanton Reynolds.*

He settled in behind his desk, looking at the mail, trying to get his thoughts back to working on the Society's publication.

"How was the trip?"

Keith was startled. He looked up to find Janeway at the door.

"The trip? I think it worked out. I mean I found a 1674 edition of *Paradise Lost.*"

"Anything special?"

"Don't know yet."

"Do you have a moment?" Janeway walked in and closed the door behind him. As he sat down, Keith noticed how strained he looked.

"We have some problems. To put it up front: the Society has run out of money."

Keith was taken by surprise. "I had no idea."

"Oh, it's my fault, I admit. With everything going on, I haven't kept tight enough controls on the checkbook. The truth is the Society had been losing membership over the past few years. I've said nothing about it, thinking it would recover. We've had similar periods before, but this time it hasn't improved."

"What's happened?"

"Mainly the economy and Google and the internet. Donors have cancelled or reduced their pledges, and scholars no longer need to utilize the Society for information that can be retrieved online. With our membership dues being several hundred dollars and use of the Society's Library practically limited to those who live in the New York area, our financial losses have become significant. The fact is, unless we're able to raise three to four million dollars in the next few months, we'll either be forced to downsize our operations or close."

Keith was dismayed. "Anything I can do?"

Janeway tried to smile. "Aside from payroll and rent, the *Quarterly*

Journal is our society's major expense. I'm afraid we'll need to econo-mize."

Keith thought for a moment. "I'm sure we can do something."

Janeway almost had tears in his eyes. "We must. I have a responsi-bility to the leaders of this society who came before me, including my father and grandfather. I can't be the one to fail."

For the next hour they went over potential budgetary cuts and ways to increase revenue. Janeway was truly fearful that the Society would go under and kept repeating how, after 200 years, the organization would end on his watch.

Suddenly Janeway's cell went off. "Hello . . . . Oh, yes, . . . ah, abso-lutely. I'll get to it right away."

Janeway got up. "Something's come up and I need to go out for the rest of the day. I'll see you tomorrow."

Keith wondered what could be so important. For the moment, Janeway's problem replaced what had happened in Sheffield. He ordered in a sandwich and spent the next hour going through the mail which covered his desk, but his mind soon returned to the recent events. He was tired and needed a break. He would take the rest of the day off. This Manuscript business was getting to him. He had fifteen weeks left to make it happen.

*

He smiled when he heard her voice over his cell, a feeling of safety amid the war he found himself in. "Joanne?"

She would take off a few hours early and they would take the subway out to Queens, go for a walk in the park across from his apartment, and be together. Dinner would be at a new Sushi restaurant he found off of Northern Boulevard. He didn't realize how much he had missed her, how much he needed to speak to someone, someone he could trust.

The subway rolled on in its monotony of rhythm, crowded with every nationality and color that humanity had to offer. They found two seats in one of the cars, the ride affording them the opportunity to be thrown against each other as the train rounded the curves.

"I was worried about you."

He smiled. "Thanks. I'm still in one piece." Then he grew serious. "But barely."

They didn't speak for a while as the train made its stops to let off its riders.

"So there was a problem."

"Yeah . . . ," and then he smiled, "but I bought a great edition of *Paradise Lost*."

They got off at the Flushing stop and walked to his apartment.

*

The door was ajar. Had he forgotten to close it? He walked in but found nothing out of the ordinary. It was only when he reached the den that he saw the shambles.

"What the hell?! I've been robbed."

"Keith? You OK?"

She followed him into the room. Desk drawers were thrown open, files and papers were strewn about and books were thrown off the shelves lying in heaps over each other on the floor. They went into the bedroom, but the major damage was to his personal work area. *What had happened?* Keith checked the apartment. The flat screen TV was still there, the audio equipment wasn't touched, not even the few dollars that he kept near the kitchen sink had been taken. They began to gather up the papers, putting files back into the desk drawers and books onto the shelves. He walked to the closet and checked the shelf. Livingston's notebook was gone! The last lecture was gone! *This wasn't a random break-in. This had to do with the Manuscript.*

"What are these?"

Keith turned to see Joanne picking up two tubes on the floor of the closet. *It was the only thing left of Livingston's that hadn't been taken.*

"Drawings. They were a gift from my professor and I'm supposed to get them framed. They belong on the shelf."

Joanne put them back. "Why don't you bring them in. We do pretty good framing."

"Yeah, some day."

They restored order, but his head was aching. He felt violated.

"What about this? It was on the floor." She handed him an unaddressed white envelope. What he read made him sit down.

TO: Keith Jessup.
You had been advised not to pursue the Manuscript for health reasons. We hope your trip to Sheffield was for other purposes. That was a great deal of money you spent on an old edition of *Paradise Lost*. We certainly hope it was worth it.

So they found him. *How did they know? He had told no one where he was going, that's why he worked alone.* Anger was building up. He crumbled the letter and threw it toward the basket next to his desk and slammed his fist against the pillowed chair.

"Damn!"

She never saw him like this. He walked out of the room while she finished the cleanup, picking up the crumbled paper he threw in anger.

"*Health reasons.*" She read the words as she was placing it into the basket. She stopped to read the message, and not certain what it meant, put it into her pocket. *Was he not feeling well?* This was not the time to ask, but she made a mental note to do so when he had calmed down. He came out sipping a beer trying to release the tension inside and flopped down on the couch.

"You better call the police."

Keith shook his head. "There's nothing to report. The only thing missing is an old notebook."

She remained silent and sat next to him. "Does this have something to do with your trip?"

"I'm afraid so."

"You said someday you'd tell me about it."

He looked at her, realizing she was with someone who, like Milton, was on a death list.

"I think the less you know about this the better."

CHAPTER 30

New York, March 8, 106 days

He couldn't sleep. A million thoughts sped through his head. *Who are they? Why Livingston's notebook? What else were they looking for?* And with fifteen weeks left to the Tanzer he no longer had Livingston's lecture as a backup. Two weeks had gone by and no progress had been made.

But the threat only increased his determination. He arose early, had breakfast at a nearby McDonald's and took the subway in, reaching his office a good hour before the 9:00 staff would arrive. He took a ring of keys out of his pocket, selected one, and walked to the far end of the hall, stopping in front of a locked room marked SPECIAL EDITION BOOKS AND MANUSCRIPTS. He placed the key into its matching counter and opened the door. The room was windowless, dark, cool and dry, and he could hear the hum of the controlled air-filtration system. In it were a half a dozen tall bookcases partially filled with old or only-edition volumes. He walked past the stack marked *sixteenth century*, with its collection of English Renaissance and major Elizabethan writers – Marlowe, Marvell, Shakespeare, and Sidney, and passed the *seventeenth century* metaphysical poets – Donne, Herbert, and those covering the Restoration period and Age of Reason – Pope, Dryden, Swift, Johnson, Boswell, and Pepys; he continued past the large collection of poems and essays by Milton where the early editions of *Paradise Lost* were stored. Finally, he came to the section titled "Miscellaneous" and knelt down to the bottom shelf and found the volume by Jessup, "Thesis – Interpretations of *Paradise Lost* with Reference to The Milton Manuscript." He looked at it only briefly, for his focus was on the 1674 edition that remained next to it, exactly where he had placed it the previous morning. He left it untouched, locked the door and walked into the Library. *As long as it was safe.*

*

He needed to know more about *De Doctrina*. He began to question how it was found in a stack of papers in the Old State Paper Office building. *It didn't seem plausible that Milton had hid it there. But who did? And if so, could the Manuscript be where the* De Doctrina *was found?* Sundstrom reported that *De Doctrina* was discovered by a Robert Lemon in 1823 and all the references simply reiterated Sundstrom's information. Finally, he logged on to the only search tool he hadn't yet used – *Gentleman's Magazine.*

Gentleman's Magazine had been England's most successful monthly publication in the eighteenth century. It was founded by Edward Cave in 1731 and within a few years was selling up to 10,000 copies, continuing publication in various formats until 1907. Keith had once used its death notices to follow up on a question of authorship and it provided the needed information. He logged on to a computer and searched the name Robert Lemon.

"Robert Lemon" (1800–1867), archivist; son of Robert Lemon (1779–1835). Employed under his father in the state paper office. The son of Mr. *Robert Lemon*, Chief Clerk of the Record Office in the Tower of London . . . . first employed in the business of his profession at the Tower by his father . . ." So there was a father and a son.

Keith then searched the *Gentlemen's Magazine* for Robert Lemon, Sr.:

"2'ld Jan. 1818, Mr. *Lemon Sr.* was appointed Deputy Keeper. The state papers were deposited in two separate buildings, the office formerly in Scotland Yard and lately in Great George Street, in a long gallery over the Treasury passage. In this gallery, a vast quantity of papers, of the highest value, was in the utmost confusion, and buried under accumulated dust and cobwebs. To cleanse this Augean stable, Mr. Lemon set earnestly to work, at the beginning of the year 1823; and it was in this receptacle that the manuscript was discovered of Milton's *long* lost work *De Doctrina Christiana.* . . . At the end of 1823 it was entrusted to the Rev. C. Sumner, now *Bishop* of Winchester, for publication and presented to King George the Fourth."

Keith could picture *De Doctrina* just lying there, in a dusty forgotten room, untouched. He needed to know how?

"Working overtime?"

Keith looked up from the screen to see Janeway standing beside him. He smiled. "Hey, Niles. Still reading up on *De Doctrina.*"

Keith noticed Janeway's smile evaporating for a moment. "Checking anything special?"

"No, just trying to figure why such a good book was hidden for so long."

Janeway spoke slowly. "It doesn't matter. Milton didn't write it. By the way, did you learn anything from that 1674 edition you purchased?"

"Nothing yet. If I don't find what I need I'll just donate it to the Society like the others."

Janeway patted him on the back and walked away. At the same time, the administrator carried in a plain white sealed envelope with a typewritten address to *Dr. Keith Jessup* and handed it to him.

"This was left under the door. Your name's on it."

Keith took one look at it and a hint of fear went through him. *Now what?* Slowly he opened the envelope and read the typed note:

Be aware that the disappearance of Professor Reynolds was most unfortunate. His quest for the Milton Manuscript was such a poor choice. He, like you, was advised as such, yet he failed to heed Milton's opening warning.

Of Man's First Disobedience, and the Fruit
Of that Forbidden Tree, whose mortal taste
Brought Death into the World, and all our woe.

Do not make this your last disobedience. Learn from his mistake.
Stay away from the Manuscript.

Keith put the note down, sat back and stared at nothing. This was different. No one had ever mentioned Reynolds's name before. Roughing up
his home was one thing – but this was admitting to murder. He tried to
turn his attention back to the screen, but all he could see were puncture
marks and the letters *S* and *L*. He couldn't get the pictures of Reynolds
out of his mind. He couldn't stop thinking that he was next.

*

He had to get out. He put on his coat, told his assistant he had a meeting
and slowly walked up Broadway. His head was down and his mind in a
whirl. What was he to do? What could he do? As he walked, he felt a
threat greater than anything he had experienced before. He kept moving, mindlessly. Was someone following him? He turned but couldn't
be sure. He stared into the windows at Macy's, already decorated with
bright spring flowers of every possible color and the newest spring
styles, but all he saw was the reflection of a defeated man. It had been a
long time since Keith Jessup needed to strike out, and he didn't know
where to begin. *This damn Manuscript, how important was it? But he had
given his word.*

 And then he was certain. He saw the reflection in a camera store window, one of the many with a "going out of business" sign on Seventh
Avenue; a husky man with blond hair. Quickly he turned and walked up
to 38th Street then east toward Sixth. He made a sudden stop in front
of a store window filled with rolls of fabrics and took a quick glance behind him. The man with blond hair was taken by surprise and abruptly
stepped into another of the endless fabric-filled storefronts on the block,
but it was too late. Keith recognized him, not more than twenty yards
away and he began to zigzag between the slowly moving delivery trucks
until he reached the sidewalk on the other side. As he looked back, he
saw the man speaking on his cell, attempting to cross the street through
the traffic. Keith walked as fast as he could, turned uptown on Sixth
Avenue, walked into a Burger King and out the side door, crossed Sixth
and entered Bryant Park. He found a bench in a shaded area partially
hidden behind several trees, not far from a group of tourists taking pictures. For the first time he realized how cold a morning it was, and he
drew his coat tighter around him, pulling up the collar around his face.

He saw no one. He found a *New York Post* left on a nearby bench and cautiously held it up, scanning both the sports page and the park at the same time. He forced a smile when he realized how the Knicks, with another loss, were probably in worse shape than he was. Comfortable that whoever was following him was nowhere to be seen, he stood up, again checking the environs. Two women were in conversation drinking steaming coffee on the next bench. In front of him, a young couple, lovers for sure and probably visitors to the city, sat next to each other pointing out the skyline. They glanced at him as he walked by. It was surreal. Were they moving or was he? It was like being on a carousel, but who was going around? He left the park entrance and walked east on 40th to Fifth. Was someone really following? As he looked up he became aware of the majestic building before him, the New York Public Library. He needed a place to sit and think and be left alone.

The New York Public Library's imposing structure was built on a two-block section of Fifth Avenue between 40th and 42nd Streets. Although the cornerstone was laid in May 1902, the project wasn't completed for nine years. When it opened in 1911 the Beaux-Arts design was the largest marble structure up to that time in the United States.

Keith walked up the steps rising between the two famous stone lions guarding the entrance. How appropriate, Keith thought, that the lions were nicknamed "Patience" and "Fortitude" by Mayor Fiorello LaGuardia, to help the citizens of New York survive the Great Depression. Patience was on his left and Fortitude on his right. Keith wondered which side he needed more. As he walked into the massive entrance portico with its beautiful classical detail, he could feel a sense of purpose once more in his gait. He passed the guard at the door and, with a quick glance behind, climbed the stairs to the main reading room and felt the comfort of inconspicuousness within the cavernous room. At 78 feet wide, 297 feet long, and 52 feet high, he was safe. Who would notice him sitting among others in a football field-sized room? Surrounding him were thousands of reference books on open shelves along the floor and balcony levels. The room was lit by massive windows, once illuminated by grand chandeliers and now by small desk lamps. He walked to the far side of the room and sat down on one of the sturdy wooden chairs placed in front of one of the hundreds of wood tables with brass lamps and took a deep breath. He needed time. Things were coming at him quickly, too quickly. *Sundstrom was right: You won't have to find them, they'll find you.* The only problem seemed to be they always knew where he was.

CHAPTER 31

New York Public Library, March 8, 106 days

"Dr. Jessup?"

Keith jumped at the tap on his shoulder and abruptly turned his head. "Yes."

It was the man with blond hair, dressed in a well-tailored suit. He was bigger than he realized, not as tall as Keith, but broader, like a professional wrestler. He had seen him before, at the Red Deer Tavern in Sheffield.

"Dr. Jessup, we've spent a great deal of time trying to find you. If you have a moment, someone would like to speak to you. Perhaps we can go outside the reading room."

As they walked out, a second man, tall and wiry with a deep scar across his cheek joined them.

"An important gentleman, a scholar like yourself, would like a few minutes with you. There's an empty room down the hall that we can use."

Keith looked around. One man was on each side of him as they walked. "Please, Dr. Jessup, the gentleman only wishes to speak to you, but I can assure you it would be in your best interests to join us."

A thousand thoughts ran through his mind, but he had little choice. The three walked to a room at the far end of the hall and closed the door. The well-built man picked up his cell and made a call. "He's here." He removed a cell phone from his jacket, handed it to Keith and began to walk out. "Dr. Jessup, you'll be receiving a call on the cell I just gave you. The cell has never been used, completely void of all information. It will be disposed of when you have completed the call, so it has no value. We will be outside the door."

Within a moment Keith could feel the vibration of the phone. He raised its cover, searching for a number. It only read "out of area."

"Hello."

"Dr. Jessup. I'm pleased that we have the opportunity to speak."

Keith's jaw muscles clenched. He tried to make out the voice, certain he had heard it before, but where?

"Who is this?"

"That is insignificant. What is significant is that you understand the consequences of your actions. I am merely calling to be assured that you received your warning. You see, there must always be a warning and sometimes envelopes can be lost. We do not want to cause you harm, but sometimes harm is necessary if the response is not as we wish."

"What do you want?"

"That you keep away from the Manuscript."

"Why?"

"Because it must remain as it is – unknown."

"At the expense of good people's lives? What could be that important?"

"Tradition, Dr. Jessup, history, the responsibilities of a generation. The defense of God and country. Some of us take such old-fashioned notions seriously. Milton and *Paradise Lost* are part of that responsibility, passing to its millions of readers what they believe are God's ways and a guide to life, one that we are not yet ready to relinquish."

Keith's anger was rising. He recalled Bartholomew once telling him the same thing.

"But that's not what Milton or his poem was about. Milton sought freedom, not to be limited by tradition or convention. Freedom to pray as you wish, without the ceremony and self-servicing doctrines that church hierarchy imposes on its members, preaching that their laws came directly from God. Freedom to speak as you wish, without big brother watching over you. If Milton was alive today he would be as critical of the world now as he was then, maybe more so. Today's governments have become like the church in Milton's time, stifling individual freedoms, collecting money for self-enrichment, grasping for power to satisfy egos through wars that have no end, all at the expense of its citizens. Hasn't the world learned what Milton wrote so long ago: *For what can war but endless war still breed?* Individuals will be responsible for themselves when they are left to be responsible. The human spirit does not want to be handed everything. The Lord took that gift away from us when we were exiled from Eden. You want to know what God wants? Reread your Milton. God sent us out of the Garden to work our fields, experience pain, and be productive. Don't you remember? Didn't you finish the poem?"

Keith came to an abrupt end and took a deep breath.

The voice on the other end responded. "Well put. You are one of the few that understands our dear Mr. Milton. But that is the reason that the Manuscript must be left alone. The masses understand the story of

Paradise Lost on its most superficial level – perhaps the word '*pshat*' means something to you – in Hebrew it means interpreting something at its simplest, most obvious level. That is how we wish to leave it – no commentary – no explanation – just the story of Adam, Eve, and the Serpent – a true drama that begs to become one of your Hollywood movies." Keith was trying to control his anger. "But you're denying everything that Milton lived for – freedom. How much clearer could he be: '*No man who knows aught, can be so stupid to deny that all men naturally were born free.*'"

The voice continued: "Look around you, my friend. I believe the world has learned the consequences of excessive freedom. Freedom must come in small doses, tradition, steps fought for over time, carried out with discretion. Until then we must maintain, what did de Tocqueville call it? ah yes, *democratic despotism.*"

"And you think that only the few are capable of making decisions as to what knowledge should be available to the people?"

The voice paused for a moment. "Dr. Jessup, I will tell you the one decision that we are certain of: if the Milton Manuscript presents what Milton really believed, it could be most disturbing."

"Citizens must make up their own minds."

The voice continued: "Be that as it may, we will not let our link in the chain that began hundreds of years ago break. Not on our watch! The real Milton is not a man for our age or any other."

"And who is the real Milton?"

The voice on the other end responded. "That, Dr. Jessup, you and no one else will ever know."

Keith smashed his fist on a table. "If you couldn't prevent *The Christian Doctrine* from being revealed, how will you prevent the finding of the Manuscript?"

"Quite simply. We have been watching you, Dr. Jessup. Either you forget the Manuscript or you or your friend, Joanne, is it? . . . will become another statistic."

Keith's mind shut down for the moment. *Did he say Joanne?* He shouted into the phone. "You leave her out of this!"

The voice remained calm in response. "Only if you stay out of this."

The call came to an end, the last words vibrating in his ears. Slowly Keith stood up as the door opened and the two men entered. "Thank you, Dr. Jessup, we hope you found that helpful." They took the cell phone clenched in his hand. "You're free to go."

CHAPTER 32

New York, March 8, 106 days

"Hey, where've you been? I tried your cell all afternoon but there was no answer."

"Sorry." Keith was still trembling and holding a menu he could not see. They threatened her. It was no longer about him. "I was in a meeting."

Joanne studied him. She felt something was wrong. "Anything unusual?

Keith didn't know how to respond. Should he tell her? How could he. It was best she not be involved, didn't want her to worry – never thought it would come to this.

"No, nothing major, just a lot of work right now. You?"

"Same. A special order came in."

He tried to focus. "That's great."

"Except the client wants it done by Monday for a charity event she's hosting. I'll have to work late Friday night."

A shudder went through his body. "Friday night? Who's going to be with you?"

"No one, the building should be pretty much empty. Just security downstairs."

"I don't like your being by yourself."

"Why? There's nothing to worry about. I've done it many times."

"Then I'll stay with you."

"What?" She looked at him with surprise. "You want to stay while I'm working. Forget it; I'll never get anything done."

Keith thought for a moment. "I insist."

"What are you talking about?"

"Hey, I've got nothing to do Friday night and if I'm your friend then at least let me drop you off at the door and pick you up when you're through."

"Fine, on one condition. You bring in those drawings you wanted framed."

He was relieved. He didn't want her to be alone. "OK. You win. When?"

She smiled. "First thing Monday morning. And by the way, are you always going to worry about me like this?"

He smiled and thought to himself. *I hope so.*

She had asked if anything was wrong. What was he to say? *There was more at stake now than simply responding to injustice. It now involved a friend, his best friend.* He tried to understand his anger and he became aware that something within him had changed – without his realizing it he now understood that she had become more than a best friend.

*

He tried to focus on work, but the threat was too real and the close-up photographs of Reynolds's permeated his mind. *What kind of animals could behave with such disdain for the miracle of life?* He pictured the peculiar branded letters, burned into the flesh of each victim. *Why? To add to the degradation of the victim? And why did they choose an S and an L? For what?* Without thought he kept writing the letters on a pad, *S L, S, L,* and then, in an instant, his mind exploded, like an emergency alarm resounding in his brain. He looked down at the written letters. *No! It couldn't be! It was 1633, so long ago! S! L! Why didn't I think of this before? William Prynne, the lawyer, the religious zealot, member of Parliament, condemner of anyone who introduced innovation into England's way of life. William Prynne, the firebrand, Milton's sworn enemy, who fought Milton's liberal views on divorce, wanted Milton hanged for treason because he supported the execution of Charles I. William Prynne, who's fiery words and radical letters led him to be tried and declared guilty of sedition and libel, imprisoned in the Tower of London, his ears removed in the pillory and whose cheeks were branded with the letters S, L, signifying "seditious libeller." The brilliant William Prynne who laughed at his prosecutor, Archbishop Laud, and renamed the S and L "stigmata laudis," the "sign of praise." Yes, that was what S and L meant. William Prynne! The man with no ears! The "sign of Laud"! –"stigmata laudis" – Stigmata!* Again that word! It had been a long time since unadulterated fear entered Keith's being: *these people were mad!*

CHAPTER 33

New York, March 10, 104 days

At 10:00, Monday morning, Keith entered the Pierre et Fils building. He and the two tubes were checked at security and escorted by a young woman to Joanne's office.

"So you finally brought them." She looked at the tubes. "Shall we take a look?"

Keith needed the change of subject – and just seeing her helped ease his mind from recent events.

She removed the drawings, spread them on the work bench and studied them for several minutes.

Joanne seemed surprised. "Where did you get these?"

Keith recounted how Livingston had been given the two drawings by a young American artist visiting Oxford some twenty years ago.

She continued to study them, paying careful attention to the scribbled signature in the bottom right corner.

Keith looked at her. "Something wrong? Livingston didn't remember the artist's name and I can't make it out."

"They're Braniffs and not just studies, finished pieces. I believe you have something very special. Jeremy Braniff is one of the hottest names in the contemporary art market."

You mean good news! "I'm amazed." He hadn't heard good news in a while.

Joanne smiled. "You should be. We just finished framing a large collection of Braniffs. Based on those valuations, each of these could be worth between one to two million dollars, and The Museum of Modern Art just paid eighteen million for his big Solaris painting in acrylic."

Keith gave a long slow whistle. "Should I start celebrating?"

"I better ask Kate to give me a second opinion on this to be sure. She really is the expert on this. But, if you ask me, you are looking at geometric abstraction as its best."

Keith studied the drawing. "Geometric abstraction? Don't know much about it."

"It's a school of modern art that Braniff founded, or really refounded in the 1980s. It sprang from the Abstract Expression movement that began in the 1930s in the midst of the Great Depression and the height of the Socialist movement in America. Before that, American artists like Thomas Hart Benton and Grant Wood were more concerned with social realism, depicting America's problems rather than artistic style. But a group of New York artists, like Pollock, Brooks, Ernst, and de Kooning broke with the mainstream and expressed an art of rebellion, anarchy, even nihilism. The times, as Dylan would later sing about the Sixties, were a changing then also; the world, led by their dictators had become violent and these artists expressed their terror. Among them was a lesser-known group, artists like George Morris, Joaquin Torres-Garcia and Alice Trumbull Mason, who called their work geometric abstraction. Their paintings lay dormant until Braniff reinvented their work, and influenced by the action painting of Pollock, combined linear and non-linear elements into a gestalt of shapes and colors. In deference to those who went before him, Braniff called his work 'neo-geometric abstraction' or as his wealthy collectors dubbed it, 'neo-geos.'"

Keith thought about the prices that Joanne had mentioned. "What makes Braniff worth eighteen million?"

"Like anything, it's timing. He's clear, defined, and succinct in his approach, and I think that's the age we're living in. People are tired of clutter and politics, and want patterns honest and simplified, whether it's their life, their music, or their art."

"Sounds very Miltonese."

"Perhaps every age strives for that in their lives. Unfortunately, Braniff was killed in a car crash several years ago. That's another reason why his works, even these studies, have become valuable. There's limited supply."

He pointed to the Braniff. "I suppose I could always draw one."

Joanne smiled. "Like the first day you came up here. I never told you, but after you left, the restoration team took a look at it and thought you removed the original."

"Yeah, who would know?"

Joanne smiled. "All you'd have to do is buy the same materials that Braniff used, a premium grade, lightweight, acid free parchment type of paper, probably a number 41. These were all done on 47.5X60 cm. sized paper."

Keith clapped his hands: "Nothing to it."

*

Keith opened the envelope placed on his desk. It was the invitation to give the Tanzer. *How could I have agreed to this? And now the threats.* If they were only against him, he would fight, but now he was no longer the only one to consider. He looked at the invite again.

Harvard College
Cambridge, Massachusetts 02138

Dr. Keith Jessup
The International Milton Society
New York, New York 10017

Dear Dr. Jessup,
The Tanzer Foundation and Harvard College are pleased to confirm your invitation to deliver the annual Tanzer Lecture at Harvard College: Please contact Dr. Philip Ressler, Chairman, Tanzer Lecture Symposium by email at pressler@Harvard.edu.

We look forward with great anticipation to your joining us on June 22.

*

Janeway handed back the invitation. "Well, I guess you've made it, old chap. Milton scholars may not get the Nobel but the Tanzer's major. Major, my boy. This calls for a celebration."

Janeway disappeared into his office and returned with a bottle of champagne. He popped the cork and raised a toast. "To Keith Jessup, may you continue to have success in all you do."

"Thanks, Niles, it's an incredible honor, but I don't deserve it."

Janeway interrupted. "Nonsense. No one works harder than you. And think of the prestige this brings our Society? We need something to turn this around."

Janeway sipped the champagne and turned to Keith. "By the way, what did they ask you to lecture on?"

Keith looked at Janeway, "The Milton Manuscript."

Niles removed the glass from his lips. "But Niles, I'm not going to give it. I'm finished with this Manuscript business."

CHAPTER 34

New York, March 12, 102 days

It didn't take long for Kate Harrigan to offer Joanne her opinion on the Braniffs. They had worked together ever since Joanne joined the firm, and were not just colleagues but friends. She had grown up on Manhattan's West Side, and received her PhD in art history from Columbia University where she still lectured on occasion. As she had thought, there was no written record of Keith's drawings in any catalogue, but the ownership and origin were as clear as the scribbled signature. Of that there was no dispute.

Joanne looked at the drawings. "I'm going to ask Carlos if I can use his materials to frame these myself. He already framed a Christmas gift I bought for my mom so I don't want to bother him again, but, it would be a great gift and I think Keith will be surprised."

Kate smiled. "Nice gift. Sure sounds like he's more than a good friend."

Joanne blushed at the thought. "He used to be."

*

The overseas call came to the seldom used cell phone in the small tidy apartment on the Upper West Side of Manhattan:

"Yes, sir."

"Have you corrected the problem?"

"Not yet."

"You have put us in a very serious situation."

"I realize that, sir."

"I want it corrected, and I don't care how you do it."

"Yes, sir."

"You have lost a great deal."

"I'm aware of that."

"Then take care of it,"

"Yes, sir."

"One more thing. What's happening with our young friend?"

"I don't believe we have a problem. In fact, I recently received information that should resolve both problems at the same time."

"Excellent."

*

Queens, New York, March 20, 94 Days

Keith's cell rang. "It's Joanne. I'll be there in a few minutes."

Keith changed into jeans and a sweatshirt and went down to meet her. She was holding a large flat brown package by its handle.

"What is it?"

"A surprise."

Keith carried it into the den and carefully opened the brown paper wrapping. Under it was a strong, heavy cardboard box with the name "Pierre et Fils" printed on it. As he removed the wrapping a card fell out.

"For Keith. Enjoy. Love, Joanne."

Inside the box were two colored pencil drawings framed in a modern chrome finish. He placed them side by side on the table and studied them. They were not scenes, classically speaking, such as a portrait or a landscape, with easily identified objects in a cohesive pattern. Instead, it was a series of pencil colored, geometric shapes, seemingly placed randomly on the paper. They were the Braniffs that he had brought to Joanne's office, but now framed. "I did them myself, so if you don't like them I can redo them. What do you think?"

"They're beautiful. Thank you."

He kissed her gently on her forehead and sat down, turning away as he felt the moisture in his eyes. It had been a long time since he had let someone else in.

"I wanted to surprise you."

He wiped his hand across his eyes and turned back to her. "You sure did."

While he was looking at the framed pieces, Joanne noticed the invitation on the small table. "What's the Tanzer Lecture?"

He looked over. "Oh, some lecture that Harvard sponsors each year. They ask someone in the field of English Literature to present a talk on a particular subject."

"And this year"

"Secrets of The Milton Manuscript. They asked my professor to give it, but he suggested they ask me"

"Isn't that the work that Milton hid?"

"Yeah."

"You mean you found it?"

"Not yet."

"Seems like quite an honor."

Keith called in from the kitchen. "I'm not going to give it."

"What do you mean?"

He walked in with two Heinekens. "I don't know. I've been spending too much time on it and I'm not getting anywhere. I'm going to start to look at some other areas of interest."

She looked at him suspiciously. "That doesn't sound like the Keith Jessup I know. You're a scholar, and you seek answers. It's a part of you. How could you be happy if you give that up? One of the things I love about you is that you've always been true to yourself. Don't let that change."

She was correct, of course, but he was willing to put it all aside to protect her, not that he could tell her. But as she spoke so clearly about what and who he was, he became certain of what he felt: he loved her, and perhaps, how much he always loved her.

CHAPTER 35

Queens, New York, March 20, 94 days

The plain white, sealed envelope addressed to "Keith Jessup" was under his door. *I thought this was over. You've won.* He withdrew the note.

Dr. Jessup.
Thank you for your cooperation. There is one last item before our business is complete. You received two framed drawings yesterday. We would like you to remove the drawings from the frames, place them into artist tubes and deliver them this Sunday to an address of which you will be advised.
You have our word as gentlemen that our business is over.

It was as if a knife had been plunged into his heart. The art? *They knew about that also?*

*

March 21, 93 days

It was Saturday morning and ordinarily he would have slept, but not today. Keith got out of bed, washed his face, threw on some clothes, and made his way to the kitchen. Joanne had mentioned that her mother was arriving from Boston and he was invited to meet them Sunday at the Waldorf for brunch.

But brunch was the last thing on his mind. The new instructions had changed everything. The deep emotions within him, recalling the years he and his mother were being attacked were all consuming. He had learned that a bully may harm you physically but you cannot allow it to penetrate your soul.

He needed to get out – clear his mind – figure out what to do. Milton had said, *He who reigns within himself and rules his passions, desires and fears, is more than a King*. Keith was aware of his limitations: he could not and would not aspire to kingship.

He took the stairs and walked out into a sun-filled day that, by noon would celebrate the Vernal Equinox. Keith took it as a sign that a profound event was about to occur.

His thoughts were preoccupied with Joanne. *What she had said struck a deep chord. "You're a scholar, and you seek truth. It's a part of you. How could you be happy if you give that up? One of the things I love about you is that you have always been true to yourself. Don't let that change."*

He jogged past a schoolyard where some kids were playing ball. Perhaps someday he would be a father – but different from the one he had. Yesterday's note kept rebounding in his mind. It had to be dealt with. He turned, jogged home and opened the desk draw – once again reading the last demand: *Deliver the package on Sunday and it would be all over*. Would it? Business with murderers? How could I be sure they wouldn't be back for more? He was reminded of what Milton wrote in Book I of *Paradise Lost*: *Who overcomes By force, hath overcome but half his foe*. Keith's other half demanded retribution.

He knew Joanne was right. Could he truly be happy if he wasn't true to himself? She understood, perhaps better than he, what that meant. You're a scholar, and you seek truth. It's a part of you.

As he placed the letter back into the desk drawer he noticed the MicroText gift that Sundstrom had given him on his last day of academic life. It was Milton's description of how the earth shook following Adam and Eve's disobeying God's commandment.

He walked into the dining area and sat down, aware of the framed Braniffs that Joanne had placed on the table. It was her gift to him, just as the drawings were a gift from Livingston. They had already taken Livingston's life, his home, everything he ever worked for – and now they wanted Keith to return his tokens of friendship?

I would have traded the manuscript for peace, but how can I when it means betraying two of the people I hold most dear.

This time he could not rationalize the threat away – they could never be trusted – the anger stirred within him. He wanted battle, but he wanted Joanne safe.

He looked at the Braniffs glowing in the sun, the beautiful metal frames reflecting the rays that poured through the eastern window, almost blinding him. They began to absorb him, filling his field of vision. He couldn't turn from them, drawn like a moth to flame. The longer he stared, the more intense the colored geometric shapes and intersecting lines burst from the paper to blur his mind.

He noted the time: 12:08 – the moment of the spring equinox, the vernal point, the moment that the center of the sun lies in the same plane as the earth's equator. He recalled the Latin name, *aequus*, meaning equal and *nox*, meaning night. It was the moment in time when the day and night are of equal length, the start of spring, a time of Easter and Passover. A time of rebirth. A time of renewal. A time to begin again.

He knew what he had to do. As Milton wrote in Book III. "Die he, or justice must." Like Milton, Keith could not allow justice to die. He couldn't give it up. Somehow he would find that manuscript, he would give that lecture, and he would survive!

The cost would be huge, more than he thought he could ever pay in this world, but at least, she would be safe. He understood, more than ever, why Milton wrote *Paradise Lost*. They had both been pushed to the point of losing everything they had gained, Milton, his revolution and Keith, what he held most dear. Like Milton, he would have to leave Paradise but, perhaps, a new world could be found. At the end of the rainbow, a new beginning, the vernal Equinox.

CHAPTER 36

Queens, New York, March 21, 93 days

Keith no longer focused on the Braniffs. All his mind could see was the Tree in the center of Paradise, that compulsive draw of temptation and deceit. As he sat there, Milton's description of Eve being seduced by Satan, cried out:

> *A goodly tree far distant to behold,*
> *Loaden with fruit of fairest colours mixed,*
> *Ruddy and gold. I nearer drew to gaze;*
> *. . . . . . . To satisfy the sharp desire I had*
> *Of tasting those fair apples, I resolved*
> *Not to defer; hunger and thirst at once,*
> *Powerful persuaders, quickened at the scent*
> *Of that alluring fruit, urged me so keen*
> *Amid the tree, now got, where plenty hung*
> *Tempting so nigh, to pluck and eat my fill*
> *I spared not, for such pleasure . . . .*

Keith equivocated, as did Eve: He thought, surely temptation is far from the act. What harm is inquiry?

> *But say, where grows the tree?*
> *From hence how far? . . .*
> *And the Tempter smiles:*
> *Empress, the way is ready, and not long – . . .*
> *I can bring thee thither soon.*

What harm is there to look, to plan? thought Keith.

> *Lead, then, said Eve.*
> *So glistered the dire Snake, and into fraud*
> *Led Eve, our credulous mother, to the Tree*
> *Of Prohibition, root of all our woe;*

But, like Eve, Keith drew back, . . .

> *To whom this Eve, yet sinless: Of the fruit*
> *Of each tree in the garden we may eat;*
> *But of the fruit of this fair tree, amidst*
> *The garden, God hath said, "Ye shall not eat*
> *Thereof, nor shall ye touch it, lest ye die."*

But temptation, once inside, is difficult to remove. How our minds rationalize the Tempter's logic to satisfy our desires:

For such a petty trespass, and not praise
. . . will God incense his ire
Rather your dauntless virtue . . .

Keith's logic, like Eve's, was blinded:
  What fear I, then? . . .

Here grows the cure of all, this fruit divine,
Fair to the eye, inviting to the taste,
. . . What hinders, then,
To reach, and feed at once both body and mind?
So saying, her rash hand in evil hour
Forth-reaching to the fruit, she plucked, she eat
Earth felt the wound, and Nature from her seat,
Sighing through all her works, gave signs of woe
That all was lost.

Yes, all was lost. Earth's first sin – and now another. Keith Jessup had reached the end. He would give in to his hatred of injustice. Was it his strength or his weakness? *For those who have been tempted and resisted, they know what miracles are, but far too many of us know it not.*

"*Citius, Altius, Fortius,*" the Olympic theme: to the "*Swifter, Higher, and Stronger go the gold.*"

Keith walked out of his building, recalling how Rudyard Kipling put it: "If you can meet with triumph and disaster and treat those two impostors just the same . . ."

He walked to the art store on Main Street and spoke to the clerk.

"I need several sheets of premium grade, lightweight, acid free, parchment type number 41 paper."

"Not a problem. What size would you like?"

"47.5 × 60 cm. and two plastic protective tubes."

*

There was no need to measure the minutes. Time no longer existed, only the labor to be accomplished. He worked until it was complete. How many hours had gone by? Ten? Twelve? He went to his desk drawer, took out Sundstrom's parting gift, the MicroText presses, and removed their covers. He remembered Sundstrom's wish when he first received it: "*May you never have to face an act as catastrophic as original sin.*"

Carefully he impressed their small heads into the reverse side of the parchment. *The catastrophic act had arrived.*

The call came in as he completed his work. "Mr. Jessup. Someone is downstairs in the lobby. By the time you reach your mailbox you will find final instructions. Follow them."

Keith heard a click and quickly called into the phone. "Hello? Hello?" but all that remained was a dial tone. He slammed the phone on the table, grabbed his coat, ran out of the apartment, and raced down the stairs in time to hear the outer door slam shut. Reaching the lobby, he raced past the mailboxes, and out the door, his eyes trying to adjust to the darkness and his body to the deep cold that had set in. Except for an occasional car, there were few people who had ventured out. He heard quickening footsteps ahead on the walkway that led to the street and started to follow, increasing his pace until he reached the sidewalk. *Was that the messenger?* He looked both ways but heard no sounds nor saw any movement. The figure seemed to have disappeared. Suddenly he made out a light as a car door opened halfway down the block on the other side of the street. He started toward it when he heard the door slam and an engine engage. The car pulled out of its parking space and drove slowly toward him. He waited between two parked SUVs, his anger coiled like a powerful spring, and as the car made its way past, he ran out toward the driver's side and reached for the door handle, trying to open the door. The driver floored the pedal, the engine roared, and Keith was dragged along the asphalt surface as the car sped toward the main thoroughfare. He managed to pull on the handle and the door opened for a moment, and then it was slammed shut. He banged his fist as hard as he could against the driver's window. It shook but didn't break. He looked up only to meet the hideous sight of a scarred beastly face laughing, taunting him like Lucifer in all his evil.

"Cumon, big guy. Let's see how long ya can old on."

As the car gained speed Keith caught a glimpse of the truck.

The ravings of the driver continued. "Hold on, you bloody bastard, hold on!"

The truck was bearing down, its horn blasting. There was no choice. His hands were almost locked on the door handle, but he managed to loosen their grip. Within moments he was thrown to the edge of the road, the truck swerving as it rushed passed. Slowly he got to his feet, and limped back to his building, the pain beginning to enter his body like a rising tide. He was shaking, his hands bleeding and the stain of red seeping through his trousers. Yet, all he could remember was the evil embedded within the scarred face of the driver, a Satan illuminated by the car's interior light – hair like burning embers. He had seen him before – but not like this – it was the man with red hair. He limped back to the lobby and flipped down the front cover of his mailbox and removed the contents. He made his way to the apartment and, as the pain from his legs intensified, tore open the envelope and withdrew the instructions.

TO: Dr. Keith Jessup:
Please deliver the two pieces of art to the concierge at the Grand Hyatt Hotel at Grand Central Terminal, tomorrow, Sunday, precisely at noon.

Keith ran a gentle stream of warm water over his hands and lightly blotted the blood off his legs where the skin had been ripped off its underlying tissue. He took a warm shower, gently dried himself, and gritted his teeth as he poured peroxide over the open wounds before placing on bandages. Slowly he put on fresh clothes and walked back to the den, withdrew a piece of stationery and an envelope from the desk drawer and began writing. He tried to explain everything. He realized it was the second time he had left her. It would be his last. He had no right to ask for her forgiveness. He sealed the note in the envelope, wrote out Joanne's name, and returned to inspect the drawings he had completed. *Yes, whoever you are, I'll give you the Braniffs, but I promise they will be your forbidden fruit which will bring you all your woe. You are taking everything I ever wanted and ever loved. May God damn you to hell for making me leave Paradise.*

As Keith went to bed that night he recalled a line from *Paradise Lost*, one that summed up his new life and Milton's in many ways. *If not Victory, revenge!*

*

New York, March 22, 92 days

It was 11:30 AM when a messenger, holding an envelope and two cylindrical shaped packages, arrived at the corner of 50th Street and Lexington Avenue, walked into the Waldorf Astoria Hotel and entered Oscar's, its upscale restaurant. He looked at the sumptuous brunch buffet before handing an envelope with Joanne's name to the maitre d'. but quickly exited onto Lexington Avenue. As instructed, made his way down to 42nd Street, where he wound his way through the crowds of Sunday tourists and shoppers until he entered the Grand Hyatt Hotel at Grand Central Station. The substitute concierge was expecting him and the packages. Fifteen minutes later a tall, string bean of a teenager, arrived at the same concierge desk and spoke quietly. The concierge excused himself and, in short order, returned with the packages that he handed to the boy, pocketing the hundred dollar bill that the teenager held in his hand. Without a word the boy walked through Grand Central to Lexington and into the Starbucks located two doors away. As he placed the packages on a rear table, he picked up the hundred dollar bill that was handed to him and left. The man at the table tore off the paper wrap, examined the contents and smiled. He took a last sip from his cup of coffee and walked out holding two cylindrical tubes into the crisp, sun-filled day surrounded by the crush of humanity visiting the greatest city in the world and the vitality of a new age. It was spring.

BOOK III

CHAPTER 37

JFK Airport, New York, March 25, 89 days

The tallish, thin, slightly bent man in the black wool overcoat, scarf, and hat was glad to escape the cold that frosted his breath. Winter hadn't realized that spring was scheduled to move it aside. As he entered JFK's International Terminal building, he regarded the crowded walkways, shifting his eyes as he looked for any sign of recognition, any suggestion of being followed. This time he could not fail. At the security check he removed his coat and hat revealing a head of thinning grey hair. He placed his shoes, a black leather case, and two plastic tubes on the conveyor belt to be checked by the scanner.

"Final Boarding for Swiss flight 107, now departing for Zurich at Gate 18." The man slid his passport and boarding pass back into the inside pocket of his suit jacket and entered the wide body plane's coach section. The plane was crowded, and when he arrived at his seat, he realized he would have to squeeze himself between two heavy-set women reading magazines. He snapped open a dozen overhead bins before he found one that would accept his personal items, but the two tubes he kept under the seat in front of him. He swore that, if his mission was successful, he would never fly this way again.

Over the loud speaker the Captain welcomed everyone. "Today's flight to Zurich is non-stop. We are scheduled to be in the air for eight hours and ten minutes, with an estimated arrival time of 10:55, tomorrow morning. If there is any way we can make the trip more enjoyable, please let our flight attendants know."

*

Lucerne, March 25, 89 days

It took no more than an hour for the Swiss Federal Railway to travel the 65 kilometers from Zurich Airport to Lucerne's Central Railroad

Station. Outside the speeding train was a winter fairy tale, with pine tree boughs on the mountain sides weighed low by the freshly fallen snow. Lucerne sits at the north end of the Vierwaldstättersee, one of the busiest waterways in Switzerland and the Hotel Waldstätterhof is situated directly opposite the railway station. It was an easy five-minute walk to either the lake or the center of the city.

As he left the train, skiers were still boarding, hoping to spend the afternoon on the cross-country ski runs along the summits of the Bernese Oberland or, for the more adventurous alpine skiers, at the Brienzer Rothorn – the region's highest peak. He made his way to the hotel, occasionally checking to see if someone was following, then stopping for a moment to watch the skaters on the frozen lake. *Perhaps, some day*, he thought. The hotel had been recommended not only for its ease of access, but precisely because of its quiet, low-key, three-star presence and inexpensive accommodations. It was perfect for those that prefer to remain unnoticed and the Swiss fully understood the need for their guests to remain just that. Again he looked around, then, not seeing anything unusual, crossed the street and entered the hotel lobby. *What a perfect place to relax*, he thought, *if only that was the purpose of my visit.* It was old world European, probably from the turn of the nineteenth century, and while it appeared recently renovated, the crystal chandeliers and dark wood paneling kept the aura of the original nostalgic elegance.

He walked to the front desk, put his bag down and was greeted by the desk clerk.

"Good day, sir." The clerk was a cheerful fellow and obviously well-trained.

"Yes, the name is Remington."

"Welcome, Mr. Remington. We hope you had a pleasant flight. Your room is ready. I see you will be with us for one night. If I may see your passport." The man retrieved it from his jacket pocket and handed it to the clerk, trying to appear disinterested as the clerk reviewed the document.

"Please wait one moment." The clerk disappeared into the back office.

The man looked around. *Was there a problem?* He had been assured that the work was flawless. *What was taking so long?* He felt the perspiration building on the back of his neck. It seemed like hours but it was only minutes before the clerk reappeared with passport and key.

"Have a pleasant stay."

He entered the elevator, exited on the third floor, and opened the door to a room which although Swiss neat, was also Swiss bare. The totality consisted of a bed, small desk, a bureau for clothing, and an arm chair. He placed his suitcase and the two tubes on the bed and looked at his watch. He didn't have much time. He carried the two tubes under his arm, took the elevator down to the lobby, checked one of the tubes into the hotel's safe and exited the hotel door. The street was fairly crowded but he quickly turned to the left and entered the first café he saw.

He approached a waitress. *"Entschuldigen Sie mich, könnten Sie mir bitte erklären, wie man andie Schützenstrasse 57 gelangt?"*

The waitress nodded, pointed in the direction that Remington had been walking.

"Do you speak English?"

The man, surprised, nodded hesitantly.

The waitress replied with a light accent. "Keep going straight and make your second right."

The man thanked her, disappointed that his German pronunciation had identified him as a visitor. As he walked out, he glanced in both directions but saw nothing of concern. He took a deep breath, relaxed the tightness in his shoulders, and slowed his pace. He even took the time to notice how beautiful and yet how small a city Lucerne was. It was packed with tourists and tourist shops, but the man reminded himself that he had other things to do than look at the small shops that lined the streets. Even so, with every shop selling the same souvenirs, it was difficult to forget that this is where William Tell shot an apple with an arrow off his son's head.

The Schützenstrasse was a quiet street lined with small antique and art shops. The man thought that in any other country the street would seem cluttered, but in Switzerland everything is as orderly as their watches. Number 57 was half way down the block on the right side. A small sign hung in the window: *Galerie Auktion Nurbard: Durchführung von Auktionen und Ausstellungen sowie Handel mit Gemälden, Skulpturen und Antiquitäten.* The man quickly translated: "Management of auctions and transactions of paintings, sculptures, and antiques."

He opened the door to the narrow four-story building. As he entered, he pulled his hat lower over his face. He knew what to do: find and avoid the short bursts of red light from some well-placed security camera. A small bell tinkled, announcing his presence. He smiled. *At least it wasn't a cuckoo clock.*

He took one step into the shop and was surprised to find himself in a beautiful gallery with fine paintings hung on walls covered with red wine fabric and overhead spotlights highlighting each painting. Oriental sculpture, much in jade, was displayed on antique tables. Fine furniture was placed throughout the space, and nineteenth century display cases were filled with watches and expensive jewelry. From his place he took all of it in, but the man was more interested in observing the shop's perimeter then its offerings. From across the room a young man in a business suit, sitting behind a desk, looked up and smiled.

"May I help you, sir?"

The man took out a card from his coat pocket and read the name.

"Yes, thank you. I'm looking for a Peter Gerard."

The young man excused himself and soon returned. "He will be here in a moment."

Almost immediately he heard a voice. "I'm Peter Gerard. May I help you?"

The man turned to see a large, thickly built middle-aged gentleman, with a shock of blond hair and a kindly face. He spoke softly and when they exchanged greetings, he noticed how large, yet soft, his hands were. Manual labor was not part of his resume.

"Mr. Gerard, my name is Thomas Remington."

"Ah, Mr. Remington, I've been expecting you." He looked at his watch. "You must be part Swiss. You are very punctual." He pointed to the staircase at the rear of the room. "Perhaps we can go up to my office to speak."

He led the man up the dimly lit stairs to a small office packed with books, photographs, and paintings, and motioned for him to sit down. The man pulled out one of two chairs placed in front of a small, polished antique wooden table. As he sat down, he carefully laid his package on the empty chair, wondering how a large man like Gerard could fit into such a cramped space.

Gerard went over to the small coffee urn on the credenza behind his desk. "I was about to pour myself a latte. Perhaps you would like some after such a long trip."

"Thank you. That would be fine."

Gerard continued, eyeing the tube. "So, Mr. Remington, I see that you brought the piece we discussed."

"That is correct."

The man placed the tube on the desk and carefully opened it, spreading out its contents. Gerard studied the drawing for several minutes.

From his center desk drawer he took out a large reading lens and me-thodically examined several areas, paying special attention to the hand-writing on the bottom right.

"You say this was a gift and you represent the person to whom it was given. Is that correct?" "Yes."

"And the drawing was uncatalogued?"

"That is also correct. The gift was given directly to the person I rep-resent. No one else was involved."

"Yes, that seems to be the case. After we spoke, I did some checking and there's no record of it. But I did place a call to an old friend of mine, a Mr. Rassolo, who represented Braniff up to his death and still represents the Braniff Foundation. He recalled having a conversation quite a few years ago about Braniff giving the two pieces to a friend of his, although Rassolo never actually saw them. It was just before he represented him." Gerard paused. "I must admit it is a wonderful repre-sentation of his work. I never realized he completed his studies to such an extent."

Gerard was about to continue but hesitated, as if recalling something.

"Rassolo was interested as to the reason for the individual selling it."

The man responded confidently. "I really can't answer that. The seller never confided that information to me."

Gerard leaned back in his chair and looked closely at the man, tap-ping his fingers on the carved arms. The man remained silent, keeping his eyes on Gerard.

Finally, Gerard leaned forward, nodded, and smiled. "I congratulate you, sir. This is the finest drawing I've seen from this artist. I will take it."

"Thank you, Mr. Gerard."

"Braniff is in demand here in Europe. There will be a number of parties interested in owning this." Gerard paused. "I believe we agreed on 1.8 million US dollars, is that correct?"

"That is correct."

"And how shall that be paid?"

The man handed a note to Gerard. "I have written out the instruc-tions of payment. I assume they will be satisfactory to you?"

Gerard read over the note. "I see that in addition to wiring the major portion, you require a substantial amount in cash. I note Swiss francs are your preference. No problem, sir. I will take care of it. Perhaps you would like another latte, or prefer to look around the shop and see if there is something you may be interested in. We will need a few extra minutes to handle the cash part of the transaction. It's a little more than we usually keep here."

The man sat back in his chair as Gerard left. He thought how easy this had been. Even so, he felt a slight constriction in his throat. It was about twenty minutes before Gerard returned with the paper work and cash needed to complete the sale.

"Here you are sir, I think you will find everything as you stipulated, including wiring confirmation."

The man took the receipts and an envelope containing the Swiss francs from Gerard and examined the contents. "Thank you. The owner will be most pleased."

As Remington rose, Gerard shook his hand. "Mr. Remington, if you are available tomorrow, I would like to invite you to join me for lunch at my club."

The man responded. "Thank you, but I'm afraid I have another appointment scheduled. Perhaps on my next visit."

As the man walked out, he turned and asked a final question. "Mr. Gerard, I couldn't help but notice that you appear not to have any surveillance equipment here. Is that the usual case?"

Gerard smiled. "Ah, Mr. Remington, you are very observant. Actually, the cameras are undergoing repair and will be reinstalled this evening."

"I just want to be sure that your Braniff will be safe."

As he walked out, he felt much lighter without the package. He put his hand inside his jacket pocket and felt the envelope. A smile appeared on his face. The first half of his business trip was over. He turned in both directions but saw nothing suspicious. His step became more leisurely, and as he walked back to the hotel he even took a few moments to enjoy inspecting the shop windows all filled with statues of William Tell. He thought how he and William had a lot in common. They both took risks and hit the bull's-eye.

*

Zurich, March 26, 88 days

A fresh coat of snow had fallen overnight. As the afternoon train pulled out of the station, the beauty of the bright sun lit up the mountain forests, and the sparkling half frozen streams invited the man to stay longer. But there were miles to go and promises to keep. As he disembarked, his step blended in with those around him, quickly making his way through a crowded Zurich Airport, passport and tube in hand. As he walked he sensed no danger, and a slight smile appeared. It was as if he was anticipating a pot of gold at the end of the rainbow.

"Final Boarding for SWISS Flight 138, now departing for Hong Kong at Terminal 1, Gate 24." The man made his way through security and upon entering the plane, made a left turn, taking a window seat in the exclusive first class section. Even before he had a chance to put his suitcase and the tube under the seat, a pretty stewardess, wearing her dark hair in a bun and looking very fit in her Jean Paul Gaultier designed navy blue uniform was standing over him.

"Good afternoon and welcome to SWISS, sir." She sounded as efficient as she looked. "May I get you something?" He glanced at his watch, it was 10:40 PM. "Not right now, thank you."

Over the loud speaker, the Captain gave the essentials. "This evening's flight to Hong Kong is non-stop and will cover a distance of 9,281 km, or 5,670 miles. We are scheduled to be in the air for eleven hours and forty-five minutes, with an estimated arrival time of 5:25 PM. So sit back and enjoy the flight on our new Airbus A340."

The man took a final glance around, leaned back in the plush wide leather seats, took a deep breath and relaxed. It would be a long flight and he was looking forward to enjoying the First Class amenities. It had cost him nearly $6,000, but now he had money and he was going to make the most of it. He folded his suit jacket, placed it neatly on the empty seat next to him and closed his eyes.

"Ah," the man thought as he fell asleep, "the Swiss have surely learned from their watches what makes a man tick."

CHAPTER 38

Hong Kong, March 27, 87 days

The man looked down as the A340 approached the city, reminding him of the delicate brush strokes of China's art. The aerial scene was filled with soft green hills, steep peaked mountains seemingly floating on sparkling blue waters. The man had done his homework. Hong Kong is located on China's south coast on the Pearl River Delta, bordering Guangdong province in the north and facing the South China Sea to the east, west and south. Its population of nearly seven million made it one of the most densely populated cities in the world. What the man found interesting was that even after Hong Kong became a part of Communist China, it had been allowed to retain the "one country, two systems" policy that provided the self-governing capitalist economy that allowed it to be so successful. He appreciated China's ingenuity. *"Do not repair what is in running order."* Already the Hong Kong Stock Exchange was the sixth largest in the world, with a market capitalization of over three trillion dollars, US, and a valuation of its IPOs next to London's. The plane set down at Hong Kong International Airport and judging from the number of arrivals and departures on the screens and the herds of passengers stampeding through the terminal, he could understand how it was one of the world's busiest airports. But it was also clean and spacious and he saw why it had been voted the world's best. Even getting through customs and out of the terminal to the waiting taxis was relatively hassle free. Of course, having the signs in English was helpful.

There were too many people for him to observe, or hopefully, be observed. No one seemed more interested in him than any of the other thousands of travelers. As the man followed the exit signs, he adjusted his watch to local time and removed a sheet of paper from his suit jacket with Chinese writing. Just in case the driver did not speak English, it instructed the taxi to take him to the Hong Kong Plaza. The hotel was new, located off Wanchai Road, between the Hong Kong Island districts of Wan Chai and Causeway Bay. As he rode through the crowded streets, he realized that the only way for Hong Kong to continue its rapid growth was to build up. No wonder the city had the highest number of skyscrapers in the world, there was no sprawl space. Already the back of his neck was feeling the tension of looking skyward, and it was easy to figure that millions of others in the city felt the same way. He smiled as he thought, *what a great opportunity for a physical therapist.* With thirty-eight of the world's one hundred tallest residential buildings, more people lived or worked in Hong Kong above the 14th floor than anywhere else on earth.

By the time the taxi pulled up to the hotel, it was already 7:00 PM, local time. Quickly two porters ran to greet him, opening the taxi door. The man resisted their taking the tube he was carrying. As he approached the front desk, the clerk welcomed him in excellent English and had him fill out a guest card.

"Ah, Mr. Stratton, I hope you had a pleasant flight. Your room is ready. May I see your passport for a moment, sir?"

As the desk clerk made a copy of his passport, the man took in his surroundings. For the first time, he felt at ease. The hotel was perfect. It had all the comforts that could be desired and was close to his destination. A piano bar and snacks were featured in the lobby lounge, and some familiar tunes made him feel closer to home. At the far end of the lobby, he noticed two large glass doors which opened into a crowded bar. He made a note that it would be his first stop. The clerk returned his passport and the man called Stratton asked to exchange Swiss francs for Hong Kong dollars. It wasn't worth his haggling over exchange rates. The clerk handed the room key to the porter who led him to the glass elevators and up to his seventh floor room. As the porter bowed and left, the man gave him several coins. The room was spacious and neat, with a traditional local look of wood and brass, but still had the required minibar, in-house movies, and marble bathroom. He washed his face, checked the time, and brought the tube to the front desk clerk to keep in the safe, placing the receipt into his pocket. With a new-found confidence, he walked across the lobby and through the glass doors that led into the bar. The place was crowded, but he found a seat at the far end and ordered a Balmoral single malt scotch. The man stayed by himself, spoke to no one, and after a second drink chose to have dinner at the Star Court Chinese Restaurant, one of the six restaurants found in the hotel. He took the elevator up to the thirty-fourth floor and was greeted by a traditionally dressed maitre-d', who ushered him to a table in a quiet corner of the room overlooking Victoria Harbour and the Hong Kong skyline. The dining area was beautifully decorated with warm burl wood panels and raw silk wall coverings in the Oriental style. He remembered what a Chinese friend had once taught him about choosing a Chinese restaurant: *make sure it is well lit and crowded with local Chinese people who bring their children.* Well, it was too late for the children to be up, but the place was certainly crowded with well-dressed international businessmen and what seemed to be a large number of smartly dressed locals. For dinner the waiter recommended any of the dim sum specialties, and he chose the pan-fried turnip cake and for dessert a cold pomelo and sago with mango juice. He was tired, and after paying in cash, took the elevator down to his room. As he placed the key into the door lock, he knew that the alcohol and dinner would assure him of a deep sleep.

*

The alarm sounded at 8:30. Slowly the man awakened and looked around the room, reorienting himself. *Ah, yes, Hong Kong.* He took a long hot shower, put on suit and tie, and took the elevator to the lobby. He finished the complimentary breakfast of coffee and roll in the hotel's café, walked to the front desk and handed the attendant his receipt to the safe. With the tube under his arm he walked out of the hotel and followed the instructions to his destination. As he walked, trying to take in anything unusual, he couldn't help but notice everything was new. As he looked up, he could barely see the tops of the buildings through the haze. He was aware of a faint putrid odor – he would remember never to complain about New York again. As he walked, he passed an open food market with a large variety of fish lying in bowls and jars for sale. The shop was down a busy street, stifled by cars and humans, as if all seven million people were trying to fit on the same street at the same time. It was human gridlock with hawkers constantly approaching to entice him into their shops. Food stores touting shark fin soup saturated the sidewalks, and inside he could see dried shark fins hanging from the ceiling. On either side of the street antique stores were compressed against each other hosting Chinese and Tibetan rugs, Chinese fine art and exotic jewelry displayed in the crowded windows. Finally he saw #20-55. A small sign hung in the window with both Chinese and English letters, "Shin Shen Art Gallery." He stopped quickly and looked behind him. How interesting to feel so compressed by the mass of humanity and yet so free.

A buzzer sounded allowing him to open the door. From the short dark entryway he made out a large room crowded with antique photos, furniture, art, and jewelry. In front, on a narrow table, a fat, bald, laughing Buddha greeted him. He turned from the Buddha and scanned the room, noticing the blinking red dot of a security camera on the left wall. Quickly, he pulled his cap down, as if to hide his face. As he walked from the entryway toward the Buddha, he turned away from the blinking light, but tripped over the single step that rose to the main floor. Clumsily, he fell forward, tightening his grip on the tube in his left arm, while trying to regain his balance, but it was too late. As he threw out his right hand to stop the fall, it hit the corner of the Buddha in front of him, almost knocking it over. Quickly he recovered, looked at his hand, and removed a handkerchief from his pocket, pressing it against his skin. Within moments a young man in a business suit approached.

"May I help you, sir?" His English was perfect. The man, keeping his back to the left side of the room took out a card and read the name.

"I'm looking for Mr. Weiliam Teng."

"One moment sir." He picked up the phone. "He will be here in a moment."

"I'm Weiliam Teng." He spoke softly, "May I help you sir?"

Teng was a short, round, balding man with big round eyes matching the rest of his physique. To the visitor he seemed to share a striking resemblance to the greeting Buddha. He was well-dressed, courteous, and spoke the King's English.

"A pleasure to meet you, Mr. Teng." He gave Teng his card.

"Mr. Stratton, I've been expecting you. I hope you had a pleasant trip?"

The man smiled to himself. "Yes, sir. So far very pleasant."

Teng nodded. "Excellent. Perhaps we might go to my office where we can discuss the matter of mutual interest."

Teng led him toward the back of the building and up a narrow stairway that led to a floor filled with antiques and artifacts. He followed Teng to the front end of the floor, and paused at the entrance to Teng's office, appearing to search the walls. Apparently satisfied with what he saw, or what he didn't, he entered, noticing the marked difference between the crowded shop area and Teng's well-appointed space. A beautiful wooden bookcase, filled with leather-bound books, photographs, and paintings were on the white-painted walls. Teng motioned for his guest to be seated in one of the two teak chairs in front of an elaborate matching desk. The seats were made of black leather and strips of the same leather were draped as arm rests. Teng sat behind the desk in a matching chair and the man sat opposite, gently placing down his package. Teng went over to a small urn located on the credenza behind the chairs.

"I was about to pour some tea. Perhaps you would like some after such a long trip." "Thank you. That would be fine."

"I prefer a fine Chinese tea, Mr. Stratton. Is that your preference also?"

"That would be excellent."

Teng placed a small, delicately decorated porcelain cup in front of his guest. "I'm not certain that you have experienced Shui Xian, an Oolong tea with a most flowery aroma. I believe you will find it most flavorful. It originates from the Ooyee Mountain in the FuJian Province of China. I will give you some to take back with you."

"Thank you."

"Of course, if I may suggest, when you prepare it, heat the water to a temperature of 190 degrees Fahrenheit and allow it to sit for precisely one minute, adding one tablespoon of tea for every six ounces of water. Let it brew for four to five minutes and you will have made the perfect cup."

"I will do that."

Teng continued, "So, Mr. Stratton, getting back to our business, I see that you brought the piece we discussed."

"That is correct." The man placed the tube on the desk and carefully removed its contents, spreading out the drawing. Teng studied it for several minutes. From his center desk drawer he removed a large reading lens and methodically examined it with special attention to the hand writing on the bottom right.

"You say this was a gift and you represent the person to whom it was given, is that correct?"

"Yes."

"And uncatalogued?"

"That is also correct. The gift was given directly to the owner I represent."

"And the work is untitled?"

"Yes."

"And this is the artist's signature?"

"That is Braniff's signature."

"I agree. After we spoke, I did some checking and there's no record of it. But we are speaking about a large amount of money and I do hope that you will forgive my further due diligence on the piece. I called up the dealer who discovered Braniff, which I assume anyone interested in your piece would do."

Stratton nodded his head. "Absolutely, most prudent."

"Yes, well Mr. Rassolo mentioned that indeed two pieces were given to an individual that were never catalogued. He further mentioned that most recently another call was made to him asking the same question." Teng hesitated, and looked at Stratton, as if waiting for a response.

"I have no knowledge of that."

Teng sat back and thought for several moments. "I see. Yes, I'm sure any buyer would be concerned. So this is the second piece?"

Stratton shifted slightly in his chair. "Sir, I can only be certain about this piece."

Teng said nothing, just staring at the drawing and then at his visitor. The man shifted his position again, wondering if Teng could detect how quickly his heart was beating. Finally, Teng broke the silence. "The fact is, that most reputable dealers and auction houses rarely get involved with the time and expense of scientific evaluation of art. A good dealer prefers to prove authenticity by meeting and evaluating the seller and determining whether the history of the piece and the reasons for the sale appear proper. In this case, sir, I believe that I have enough information to be certain this is a new Braniff on the market."

The man said nothing

"Now, Mr. Stratton, about your asking price."

"The price is non-negotiable, sir. I believe we discussed that previously."

Teng took a long look at Stratton before responding. "Yes, I believe we did. I think you arrived at a most opportune time, as there is a growing demand for contemporary artists in the Far East, and Braniff is one of them."

Teng looked down at his desk for a moment before once again training his sight on Stratton. "Well, then, Mr. Stratton, I will take it. I believe, we discussed $1.8 million US dollars, is that correct?"

It took a moment before he realized that Teng would buy the piece. "Ah, yes, that is correct."

"And how shall that be paid?"

The man removed a piece of paper from his inside suit pocket and handed it to Teng. "I've written out the instructions of payment. I assume they are satisfactory?"

Teng read over the note. "No problem, sir. Please give me a few minutes."

The man sat back in his chair, as Teng left. Perhaps he was needlessly worried. Certainly he was getting the asking price but he would have preferred for a smooth, less memorable, discussion. Teng returned with the completed paper work needed to finalize the sale.

"I believe everything is complete, as per your instructions. Here is the receipt for the wire transfer."

The man rose from his chair and shook hands with Teng. As Teng walked him out, the man looked at the Buddha. "Mr. Teng, I'm interested in your Buddha."

"Buddha? What Buddha?"

The man pointed to the statue that welcomed him when he first entered the store.

"This one, isn't this the Laughing Buddha?"

Teng turned to see what the man was pointing to.

"Ah, Mr. Stratton, the West may think he's a Buddha, but he was really a much loved Ch'an monk who wandered about the land with his belly exposed. Over the centuries stories of the miracles that he performed spread throughout China, and he came to be called Pu-tai or Budai, which means "hempen sack," because he always carried a sack full of surprises for children. Eventually, Pu-tai came to symbolize happiness, generosity, and wealth, and a protector of children, the poor, and the weak."

Stratton looked at the statue. "So, rubbing his belly is not good luck?"

Teng laughed. "On the contrary, rubbing Pu-tai's belly brings very good luck."

Stratton smiled and rubbed Pu-tai's belly. "Then I'd like to buy it."

"Pu-tai is not for sale, sir, but it is a gift from me to you."

""I would prefer to purchase it."

"Please, in Hong Kong you cannot refuse a gift when offered."

"Thank you, sir. You are most kind."

"Where shall we send it?"

The man paused for a moment. "I will have to get back to you with an address."

"Of course, sir. You have my card. I will keep Pu-tai safe for you and if there is anything else I can do, I am at your service."

As the man took his leave, he turned to the proprietor. "I believe there is something you can do. The seller would prefer that our discussions be kept private. If someone does appear to be asking, how would you say, too many questions, perhaps you could leave me a message. Here is a number you can call."

"Of course, sir. We businessmen understand the value of discretion."

He felt much lighter without the package under his arm and much wealthier. On the plane back, he smiled as he thought how Pu-tai's good fortune was already rubbing off.

*

New York, April 1, 82 days

The ringing of the cell phone so early on Sunday morning was expected. He had been waiting for the overdue "thank you" for days.

"Good morning."

"Good morning, sir."

"I understand congratulations are in order."

"Thank you. Our task was completed more successfully than I would have imagined."

"Excellent. I knew you would repair the situation. You deposited the funds?"

"Yes, sir."

"Well done."

"I appreciate your confidence."

"And what about that scholarly chap? Is he behaving?"

The answer came slowly. "Yes, sir. I'm sure he is. We have an agreement. He's done all we asked. No need to be concerned."

"Excellent. I'm glad that was taken care of. What's he doing these days?"

There was no answer.

"Are you there? I asked about our friend. What's he doing these days?"

"I'm . . . I'm not certain."

"Not certain?"

"We don't know where he is."

"What!"

"He's disappeared. We haven't seen him in weeks. We've tried, but he's simply melted away. "We're certain that –"

The sentence was never allowed to be completed: "Find him! Once one tastes the forbidden fruit you can never stop!"

"Yes, sir."

BOOK IV

CHAPTER 39

It had been a month since Joanne had last seen Keith. Not a day went by that her mind didn't replay that Sunday morning when they were to meet for brunch. *What could have happened?* She had memorized the letter that was delivered.

> Dear Joanne,
> Forgive me but I am no longer able to keep you safe from all my woe. I will not be joining you today. You spoke about being true to yourself and so I must go to find that truth. I'm afraid it is best that I no longer exist. Be careful of strangers who want to know where I am.
> I love you,
> Keith
>
> > *When I consider how my life is spent,*
> > *Ere half my days in this dark world and wide,*
> > *And that one talent which is death to hide*
> > *Lodged with me useless, through my soul more bent*
> > *To serve therewith my maker*

Joanne reread what she needed to know. *He loves me.*

*

In truth, Keith Jessup no longer existed. In his place a new man appeared, one he called Samuel Hartlib, a bearded scholar with long black hair that had gray streaks and heavy horn-rimmed glasses that hid his soft blue eyes. Samuel Hartlib looked older and walked with a limp. Perhaps most telling was his constant checking of the environs, as if trying to spot danger coming from behind or before his path. But at least he was free to do what had to be done. There was no other way. Keith had gone over it a million times, but if he was to seek the justice that was due, he had no choice. There could no longer be a Keith Jessup. Once the Braniffs were delivered it was as if he had crossed the Rubicon. They would be coming after him. That meant he had to give her up. He owed her that, although it broke his heart, and worse, perhaps hers, but at least she would be safe.

CHAPTER 40

New York, May 7, 46 days

Every morning for fifteen years, M. Francois DeLordet strode down Madison Avenue with briefcase and paper bag and arrived at the Pierre et Fils office promptly at 6:30 AM. He would remove a set of keys from his suit pocket, open and then relock the large thick-plated glass front door. He would then take the stairs to his second floor office, place his briefcase on the credenza behind his desk, transfer the paper bag onto a small round table, and remove a cup of latte. Sitting at his desk, he perused the dispatches that had arrived by overnight courier.

He was in his late fifties, short, square of frame, not an ounce of fat, and slightly balding. But his most remarkable attribute was his incredible energy, bounding up stairs with no use for an elevator. It was rumored that the man never slept, watching over his New York enclave as a father dotes over his child. He received his degree in Fine Arts and Conservation from the Sorbonne and went to the Louvre where he steadily rose through the ranks until named conservator for its Department of Fine Arts. After ten years he decided to open a fine art preservation and restoration shop in New York.

On this particular morning he recognized an envelope from an old friend in Zurich and read the note.

Mon cher Francois,
I hope this finds you in good health. An acquaintance, M. Charles LaMer, recently purchased a Braniff drawing and inquired about its framing. Of course, we have all read of the large series of Braniff studies you completed and I ask if you might take it on. Also, I would appreciate your authenticating the provenance of the piece, based on your Braniff experience.
    Merci,
        Frederick Paz

Within the week, the couriered package arrived. DeLordet opened it and smiled as he studied the Braniff, appreciating the workmanship of the composition and yet thinking how it really wasn't his taste. He had always been more classical, more structured, a life that always exuded order and definition. He returned the study to its packaging and placed it on the credenza. Then, as every morning, he reached into his brief-case, removed *The Wall Street Journal*, *The Financial Times*, *The London Times*, and *Le Monde* and placed them neatly on his desk. He took a sip of latte and began reading.

*

At precisely ten, Joanne arrived for the usual Monday meeting. DeLordet removed the package from his credenza and handed it to her.

"I received this from an old friend. Once you authenticate the artist he would like to have it framed. Will you take care of this?"

She forced a smile. These days they did not come easily. "Of course, sir, let's take a look."

DeLordet sat back in his chair, placed his glasses, which hung by a single cord around his neck, onto his nose, and returned to reading the Times. Joanne unwrapped the package and examined the piece.

"No question, sir, only Braniff does . . . this." Her last words trailed off. She looked at it twice, as if stung by what she had seen. *It was one of Keith's Braniffs! Was this possible?* She examined it again, almost as if he was hidden within the multitude of shapes. *It was his, no question. One of the Braniffs I framed for him.*

"Do you have a lens, sir?"

DeLordet handed her the magnifying lens from his desk and con-tinued his reading. She evaluated the colored pencil drawing in detail, studying every aspect. Slowly, she put the lens back on the desk and tried to regain her composure. Thoughts rushed through her mind like a fast moving waterfall. *What could have happened?* She tried to clear her voice, but it was difficult to speak.

"M. DeLordet, where did your friend receive this?"

DeLordet put down the Journal and handed her the request from Paz. Joanne read it twice, as if hoping to find something that wasn't.

"Any problem?"

Joanne hesitated for a moment, not knowing what to say. "Uh, no sir. No problem. Do you know the circumstances of how he acquired it? Was it purchased here in the States?"

"I believe we can answer all of your questions. Are you sure there is nothing wrong?"

Joanne hesitated. She felt her heart beat – it was the first connection to Keith since he disappeared. "Oh, nothing, but I would be most interested in the circumstances."

"Of course, I'm sure that Frederick would share with us whatever he knows. In fact, why don't we try him right now, it will give me an opportunity to speak to an old friend. Let's see, it's about 4:30 in the afternoon in Zurich."

DeLordet removed a small green book from inside his desk drawer, thumbed through its pages and punched the numbers. Joanne tried to follow DeLordet's side of the conversation.

"Frederick? Francois. . . . *oui*, I received the package. . . . *oui*, I have it here. Should be no problem. . . . Actually, Frederick, I do have a question. How did you come upon this piece? . . . I see . . . So you were not the dealer . . . I see. . . . The purchaser is an old client of yours. . . . When was that? . . . *je comprends* . . . about a month ago from a dealer in Lucerne . . . the dealer said he purchased it from an agent representing the owner . . . uncatalogued . . . received it as a gift directly from the artist . . . *bien* . . . no I think that's all. And Anna, how is she and the children? That's wonderful. . . . *oui*, I will be at the Paris Forum. I look forward to that. Frederick, one more thing. Do you know the purchase price? I see, *merci, mon ami.*"

DeLordet hung up the phone, and looked at Joanne.

"I believe you heard the essentials of the conversation?"

"Yes, thank you. I'll ask Carlos to have it framed by the end of the week." Joanne picked up the Braniff, turned, and slowly walked out.

She didn't know what to think. It was received under the same circumstances as Keith described. *A gift from the artist to Keith's professor, obviously uncatalogued, who gave it to him. What could have happened?*

"By the way. The purchase price was one million eight hundred thousand dollars, US."

She barely made it back to her office, uncertain if there were any tears left to hold back. She tried to maintain control, but the unanswered questions numbed her mind. After the first weeks of his disappearance, her mother convinced her to report it to the police. There was very little to tell them. He had moved out of his apartment and his phone was disconnected. She had no idea where or why, unless it had something to do with a manuscript, but she never heard the full story. All the police could promise was to put out a missing persons alert with a recent photograph and hope he would be noticed.

She sat at her desk dazed from what she had learned. His Braniff appeared from somewhere in Zurich. Did this mean he was in Europe? Had he sold it? Was it stolen? There were so many questions and no answers. She walked to the window and stared out over 77th Street, her tears matching the rain drops.

*

New York, May 10, 43 days

The gentle knock interrupted Joanne's meeting with her associate, Kate Harrigan. "May I speak to you, Ms. Joanne?" Carlos Minoza was the most experienced of the restoration artisans at Pierre et Fils, and known as one of the finest in the world.

"I noticed a faint darkened area on the back of the Braniff from Zurich you asked me to frame. I assumed it was the usual paper stain on the reverse side, but through a lens it may be some type of design. Then again, it may be nothing. I thought I should mention it to you."

Joanne picked up her lens and examined the lightly darkened areas. "There's something here, but if it's not a stain, I would have no idea what it is. It certainly hasn't affected the drawing."

She gave the lens to Kate who inspected the mark. "Did Braniff do this on the back of his other work?"

Carlos thought for a moment. "No, Ms. Kate. We've done two dozen Braniff drawings since I've been here. I've never seen this on his work before."

Joanne glanced at Kate. "Then I don't know what it could be, but I think we all agree that it's a Braniff. Go ahead and finish the framing. I'll sign off on it, show it to Monsieur DeLordet, and we'll send it out to Zurich."

When Carlos had left, Kate glanced at Joanne. "That looked like the Braniff you framed for your friend, the one you asked me to examine. Did he sell it?"

"I wish I knew."

CHAPTER 41

New York, May 14, 39 days

It was early on a quiet Sunday morning in Manhattan when Keith, carrying an old brown leather briefcase and a set of keys, entered the empty office of the International Milton Society. It had been six weeks since he left. He walked through the office and, by habit, checked his old mail slot. At first it appeared empty, but from his height he could see an envelope stuffed well into the back of the opening. The return address was "E. Throckmorton, Western Bank Library, Sheffield." It was post-marked three weeks past. He put the envelope into his jacket pocket and walked directly to a locked room at the far end of the hall marked SPECIAL EDITION BOOKS AND MANUSCRIPTS. He removed a key from his pocket, unlocked the door, and switched on the light. The whirl of the environmental controls was the only sounds heard as he made his way to the rear bookcase and knelt down, retrieving an old text placed next to his thesis. He recalled how he added the portion on the Manuscript at the last minute and smiled. *So that is how it all began.* Within minutes he turned off the light, relocked the doors and walked out into the bright morning sunlight. Inside his briefcase was a copy of a 1674 edition of John Milton's *Paradise Lost*.

*

New York, May 18, 35 days

For days, Keith sat alone in a small, one-room apartment in lower Manhattan, rented to a Samuel Hartlib and paid for in cash. For hours on end, his eyes and mind pored over the 1674 edition. He had little more than a month before the Tanzer Lecture and had found nothing. Nothing that is, until his third reading through the old text when he focused on line 406 of Book II. What was it? Something was different. At first he had skipped right over it, but now he saw it: it was the words *"palpable obscure,"* they were underlined – and in ink! *Why?* He was certain that nothing else was so marked in the entire text of his copy, nor in any text that he had examined. Who would have inked it in? The book hadn't been read for hundreds of years. He wrote the words down – letter by letter – P A L P A B – he stared at the letters, and then realized he had seen them before.

Keith remained motionless until the letters appeared in his mind:
PALPAB OBSCS.

It was the letters seen on the photograph that Deputy Chief Constable Constance Bathgate had shown him disclosing what Livingston had scribbled on his palm at the time of his murder. Somehow Livingston knew.

He went to the small closet and checked his jacket pocket – the envelope was still there. The letterhead read, "University of Sheffield, Western Bank Library, Special Collections and Archives Department, Elvira Throckmorton." With anticipation he withdrew the contents.

Dear Dr. Jessup, (He hadn't heard that name in a long time.)

Enclosed is the history of the 1674 copy of *Paradise Lost* that you had purchased from the Samuel Hartlib Collection here at Sheffield:

Samuel Hartlib was born in Poland about 1600 and moved to England about 1620 where he lived until his death. He was a friend of John Milton who dedicated his Treatise on Education to Hartlib and described him as a "master of innumerable curiosities." After Hartlib's death in March of 1662, the entire collection of papers was purchased by William Viscount Brereton. Brereton was interested in Hartlib's philosophy and, as an observer of Hartlib's circle of intelligentsia, made the acquaintance of Milton. Hartlib's papers consisted of a vast correspondence with the world's greatest intellects of his generation in science, literature, religion, and education. The papers had remained forgotten until 1933, when a cache of documents, seemingly last seen at the end of the seventeenth century, was discovered in a wooden trunk in the offices of a London firm of solicitors. They were acquired by George Turnbull, a lecturer in education here at Sheffield. When Turnbull retired, he took Hartlib's papers with him and when he died his widow had thought of burning them. Fortunately, in May of 1963, they were retrieved by the former Sheffield University librarian who brought them here in the back of his car. How Milton's 1674 edition was part of the collection we are not certain, although it is assumed that Milton personally gave it to Brereton who simply stored it with the rest of his literary collection and passed on when his family sold it.

Our records indicate that since we acquired it there were a number of scholars, notably Charles Webster, that studied the Hartlib papers, but no record of anyone examining the 1674 *Paradise Lost* until most recently. I assume that is because there are so many other copies of the poem available. Only three individuals have been given access to it: Professor Thornton Livingston, on several occasions, his last visit was November 18 of last year. The second, Professor James Bartholomew this past January 15, and the third spent two full days examining it, a Professor Stanton Reynolds.

A momentary chill ran through him, like turning on a cold shower before the warmth was reached. *Had Livingston and Reynolds seen the same* PALPAB OBSCS*? But what was Bartholomew's interest?*

*

PALPAB OBSCS – *what could it mean?* Keith reread the lines surrounding the words *"palpable obscure"*: it told of Satan in Hell, seeking revenge from his recent loss in his battle with God, trying to convince his fallen angels to renew the battle. He called for one of them to fly up to earth and spy out God's newest creations – Adam and Eve.

> *But, first, whom shall we send*
> *In search of this new World? Whom shall we find*
> *Sufficient? Who shall tempt with wandering feet*
> *The dark, unbuttoned, infinite Abyss,*
> *And through* the palpable obscure *find out*
> *His uncouth way, or spread his airy flight,*
> *Upborne with indefatigable wings*
> *Over the vast abrupt, ere he arrive*
> *The happy isle?*

Satan would find no volunteers and had to make the trip from Hell to Earth himself. But could Milton have had a hidden meaning? Keith sat back and reflected: *Scholars had often suggested that Satan is the hero of* Paradise Lost. *If true, could Satan have played the role of Milton, the hero, seeking revenge for all that had been inflicted upon him? Was not Satan's perilous journey from the Gates of Hell to Heaven the same journey that Milton would need to travel to reach a world of true freedom?*

Keith thought of Livingston: was it not also Livingston's journey, evading his adversaries for whom he now sought revenge?

The scholar allowed a knowing smile to appear. He would provide

Livingston with his revenge, and, if he was correct, the first step would be through *the palpable obscure.*

*

He needed air. Keith placed the old book on his desk, took his cane and walked toward the park on the river, the Statue of Liberty in the background. His body ached to jog again, but for now it was no longer possible. The place was empty, except for two kids shooting a basketball while their mothers were sitting nearby gossiping. He found a bench and sat down in the warm rays of the bright spring sun, the words of Milton's poem incessantly flashing through his mind like a banner headline.

"Hey, mista, can you throw the ball over."

Keith's reverie was broken by the boy's shouts.

"Throw back the ball!"

Keith got up and without thought or cane, picked up the ball, dribbled in a few steps, and took a long shot that swished the basket. Surprised at his accuracy, he sat back on the bench, and then realizing what he had done turned to be certain he hadn't been seen.

"Hey, mista, can you do that again?"

Keith looked up to see the face of one of the kids.

"Can you show me how to shoot like that?"

Keith smiled and this time, remembering his cane, limped over to the basket.

"Here, hold this." Keith handed the cane to one of the boys. "It's all in the feel of your fingers on the ball – when you release it, you want the ball to go right where your eyes imagine it to go – so feel the ball in your hands." He took another shot but it clanged off the metal rim.

"I haven't shot in a long time – but if you keep practicing you'll get good."

"Thanks mister. I guess you lost the feel."

That's when it hit him. The feel of the ball – the palpable – the palpable obscure. And what could be more obscure to Milton than his poem, purposely so, to hide his real meaning. Palpate the Obscure – palpate the poem!

Keith limped back to his room and sat down at his desk. He picked up the 1674 edition, staring at the cover when a smile appeared on his lips. He should have thought of it before – yet he hadn't even examined it, though he knew it was a favorite place for concealing secret messages in the seventeenth century. Keith reexamined the book cover. *It wasn't in the poem but on the poem – the cover itself! The book's binding, where hidden messages were sent to avoid the censor or an unsuspecting husband's eye. In fact, hadn't he just read how scholars recently found a secret note from a Lady Margate to her lover, the Duke of Winchester, concealed within a book binding?*

He recalled the original description: Condition: Very Good – tight binding, very skillfully *rebacked* with the original spines laid down. He reviewed the logic: if the book had been out of circulation since published in 1674 – lying untouched – what would be the need for its repair? He examined the rebacked binding and began to palpate the obscure, until his fingertips differentiated between the binding and something within it. With a pair of tweezers, he removed a small piece of paper, gently spread it out and read the inscription – מִקְוֵה יִשְׂרָאֵל. He recognized the language. What was Hebrew doing in the binding of a 1674 edition of *Paradise Lost*? He wasn't sure, but he would find out.

He took a pencil and lightly drew a small key inside the front cover, signifying the end of his search. Livingston had never lived to find it, but he would memorialize this edition to his professor – it would be called *Livingston's Key*. Finally, a break.

CHAPTER 42

New York, May 19, 34 days

The courier had a busy day. It began with his delivery to the Milton Society office of a brown papered boxed package addressed to Niles Janeway. Janeway's administrator asked the courier to wait while she brought him the package. By the time she returned, the courier was gone. No receipt, no signature asked for.

Janeway looked at the package. There was no return address. He proceeded to remove the paper and opened the box. Inside he found a 1674 edition of *Paradise Lost*. He looked through the precious volume and smiled: *So this is what he purchased in Sheffield. He said he would give it to us when he finished with it.*

It was late in the afternoon when the courier reached the offices of Pierre et Fils. He handed a large, thick, cardboard box tied over with cord to the security staff in the lobby. The package was addressed to Joanne Farnsworth. No sender was listed. No receipt and no signature required. By the time security looked up, the courier had disappeared.

BOOK V

CHAPTER 43

The visitor to Yeshiva University was a tall gentleman who walked with a limp and used a cane. To the untrained eye, it would be difficult to determine his precise age with his full beard and long hair, both of which contained streaks of gray. He was dressed in a dark blue suit, looking no different than many of the other men gathered inside the entrance hall of YU in Upper Manhattan except that he wasn't wearing a yarmulke, the traditional Jewish head covering. Rabbi Zevulen Shenken didn't look like the rabbis Keith had seen in pictures. Shenken was in his mid-thirties, not as tall as his visitor, but more trim. He had light brown hair, a neatly shaved beard, wore the traditional head covering, and carried a warm smile. The rabbi ushered the visitor into a neat, modest-sized office on the third floor.

"So, you're the Samuel Hartlib who telephoned." The Rabbi shook the visitor's hand.

"Welcome to Yeshiva University, where we combine Jewish scholarship with science, liberal arts, and continue the 1,500 year tradition of *smicha*, rabbinical ordination."

"That's a lot to teach."

The rabbi smiled. "The students think it's a lot to learn. But I understand you would like some help in your research on John Milton."

"Yes. *Paradise Lost* was written to justify the ways of God to man. I'm trying to determine where Milton learned those ways."

The rabbi smiled. "Shall I do it while standing on one foot?"

Keith returned the smile, appreciating the reference to the great Rabbi Hillel being asked to explain the entire Torah in one sentence. Hillel replied: *What is hateful to you, do not do to your fellow; that is the whole Law: all the rest is interpretation. Now go and study.*

"I found some information that might be helpful and wonder if you knew its source."

Keith took out a sheet of paper and showed it to the rabbi.

"מִקְוֵה יִשְׂרָאֵל, *Mikveh Yisra'el*, Hebrew for the Hope of Israel. It's one of the oldest synagogues in Philadelphia, founded in 1740."

The visitor nodded, "Could it be related to something else?"

The rabbi placed his hand on his chin for a moment. "You mean in reference to John Milton?"

"Yes."

"I'm not certain. Milton is a favorite subject of many rabbis and perhaps one of them would know."

The visitor was perplexed: "Milton was a favorite subject of rabbis?"

The Rabbi reached into his drawer and removed two brochures. "Take a look. This is the schedule of programs that we are giving this semester." He handed one to his visitor. "The seminars on Milton will not begin until next week."

Keith was amazed. He was only looking for a reference, but not this. "You're having an entire symposium on Milton and the Rabbis?"

"We have one every few years. This year we're investigating Milton's use of Hebraic sources."

"I wasn't aware that Milton had such knowledge."

Rabbi Shenken smiled. "Well, that's what we'll find out. We know that Milton had an excellent background in Hebrew, but, as brilliant as he was, the question remains could he have mastered the intricate commentaries that the great rabbis spent a lifetime writing."

Keith thought for a moment. "Where else would Milton have learned it?"

The rabbi responded. "That's the problem. He would have had to find someone to teach him – someone who had mastered the Talmud."

Keith appeared confused. "That would mean Milton had to find a rabbi. But in London in the 1650s?"

The rabbi smiled knowingly. "I see you know your English history."

Keith responded quietly. "Enough to know there were no Jews in England in 1650, and hadn't been any since 1290 when King Edward I expelled them!"

Rabbi Shenken heard the disappointment. "Look, although Milton is one of my areas of interest, one of my teachers, Rabbi Lecht, has put a lifetime of work into understanding him. Rabbi Lecht received his rabbinic ordination here and his doctorate in English Literature at Yale. His concentration was on John Milton."

Keith was amazed. *A rabbi with a doctorate from Yale on John Milton?*

Rabbi Shenken continued, "Most of the time he teaches in Israel, but he comes here on a regular basis. He's the one I call when I have a *shi'ela*."

"You mean a question?"

The rabbi looked a little closer at his visitor. "And you understand Hebrew."

"A little."

"Perhaps, Mr. Hartlib, you would like to attend the symposium as my guest? Rabbi Lecht will be leading it and I think he might be able to answer many of your *shi'elot*."

"That would be most interesting."

The visitor continued to read the schedule of lectures. "You're giving a seminar on Ecclesiastes?"

The rabbi smiled. "That's actually one of my areas of interest. Milton was greatly influenced by Ecclesiastes, or *Kohelet*, as we call King Solomon in Hebrew. He thought it one of the greatest poems ever written. If you haven't read it recently you may wish to review it."

The visitor thanked the rabbi for his help. *So there was a relationship between Milton and the Rabbis!* He marked the date. As he walked out he texted Sundstrom.

"Could Milton have had a rabbi?"

*

New York, May 20, 33 days

Security sent the package to Joanne's office. She was not expecting a delivery and the lack of return address made her suspect. She untied the cord, opened the cardboard box, and removed two pieces of framed art wrapped in heavy brown paper.

What's this? She looked for a note, but there was none. She removed the paper and placed the two pieces side by side on the table. *Was this possible?* She looked at them again, trying to control herself. They were the framed Braniffs she had given Keith! *So he hadn't sold them. But where was he? And if Carlos wasn't framing Keith's Braniff, what was he framing? Could Braniff have made two drawings that looked so similar?*

CHAPTER 44

Yeshiva University, May 24, 29 days

The opening session of the Milton Symposium at YU was fully attended. Keith signed in as Samuel Hartlib and glanced through the informational brochures.

Rabbi Shenken approached with a small black yarmulke. "I thought you may wish to put this on your head."

"Yarmulke? I don't recognize the words."

"They're actually from the Aramaic, *"yerai malka,"* which means "awe of the king."

Keith smiled as he fastened the small head covering to his hair with the Bobbi pin clipped on it. "Thanks, I can use all the help I can get."

Keith continued browsing through the brochure.

"Still trying to understand why an institution of Jewish learning is so interested in John Milton?"

Keith smiled. "You read my mind."

"*Torah Umadda*, Mr. Hartlib, Torah and Knowledge. We try to teach our students both Hebraic tradition and modern learning. If we can combine Jewish tradition and scientific exploration with Jewish ethics, we have prepared the student to live in the modern world as an honest contributing citizen."

Keith realized how Milton would appreciate that the search for God required, without restriction, the seeking of intellectual truth. He placed the brochures into his briefcase. "Milton would have enjoyed being here. He also rejected a religion where blind tradition replaced moral values and scientific inquiry."

The rabbi nodded. "Perhaps that's the problem Milton had with his Christianity. Milton came to realize that moral values required laws. We call them Mosaic laws."

The words brought an immediate reaction. "You believe Milton believed in Mosaic Law?"

"I think we all agree that Milton was a Christian, but one that emphasized both logic and faith. Morality needs guidelines, not just belief. Granted, in his early years Milton seemed to believe that man could exist without a common set of laws. But, I suppose, the failure of the Puritan Revolution made him realize that a society could only exist with common guidelines. Didn't he write that 'Anarchy is the sure consequence of tyranny'; or 'no power that is not limited by laws can ever be protected by them'?"

Keith was impressed at the rabbi's familiarity with the poet.

"We, as Jews, call those guidelines Torah. Torah knowledge and Torah values must be an attitude twenty-four seven, not to be used only when you find it convenient. Isn't that how *Paradise Lost* ends? If I recall, in Book XII, line 225, the angel Michael teaches Adam man's future and the importance of law."

> *In the wide Wilderness, there they shall found*
> *This government, and this great Senate choose*
> *Through the twelve Tribes, to rule by Laws ordaind:*
> *God from the Mount of Sinai, whose gray top*
> *Shall tremble, he descending, will himself*
> *In Thunder Lightning and loud Trumpets sound*
> *Ordaine them Lawes; part such as appertaine*
> *To civil Justice, part religious Rites*
> *Of sacrifice, informing them, by types.*"

The rabbi looked at his watch. "That's enough sermon. My seminar on Ecclesiastes is about to begin."

Keith followed him, thinking of that passage from the last book of the poem. He had never thought of it in those terms. God himself ordained the Laws that regulated government and religion, the Laws brought down from Mount Sinai by Moses. There was no intermediary. Milton the Christian believed in Mosaic Law!"

*

The seminar was held in a brightly lit modern classroom with tables for students to sit in pairs and study together. For centuries Talmudic students have learned with a *chavrusa*, a partner, with whom they discuss ideas and defend their thoughts while studying how the great rabbis analyzed the complex Talmudic tracts. *Learning Talmud is an attitude, a methodology of evaluating any problem in life.*

About forty men were in the room as the rabbi began his discussion.

"*Kohelet* is read during the festival of Sukkot, a time of great joy for the Jewish people. Two weeks before was Rosh Hashanah, when Jews prayed for a happy and healthy new year and then, ten days later, observed Yom

Kippur, asking forgiveness for the sins we committed against God."

"What about the sins against man?" someone asked.

"For that Jewish law dictates that you must go directly to the person you sinned against and ask forgiveness. Asking forgiveness from a rabbi doesn't help you. God doesn't take you out of your responsibility."

Rabbi Shenken continued, "But as happy as the holiday of Sukkot is, Jews know that too much joy may have you forget your obligations to God."

Someone in the audience called out. "That's why we read *Kohelet*, it sobers you up."

There was quite a bit of laughter and Shenken smiled with them. "Yes, reading *Kohelet* requires intellectual and spiritual examination, so there's no time for wild celebration."

Shenken looked around the room. "What does Solomon say in *Kohelet*?"

A man answered in Hebrew and Rabbi Shenken translated. "Yes, Solomon wrote, 'I said to myself, Come, I will experiment with joy and enjoy pleasure. That, too, turned out to be futile. I said of laughter, it is mad! And of joy, what does it accomplish!'" Once we read what the wisest of all men concludes, our thoughts turn more sober."

The rabbi followed up with a question. "Why would Milton have thought so highly of *Kohelet*?"

Keith looked around the room, but no one offered a response.

"Mr. Hartlib, any thoughts?"

Keith hesitated before answering. "From a superficial reading one might see in *Kohelet* only the helplessness of man and the futility of life, but certainly this was not what the Rabbis, nor, I believe, Milton understood. Rather, as they delved into its deeper meaning, they realized that a life lived only for pleasure was the seduction that lost Paradise – but by dedicating one's life to one's Maker, Paradise could be regained."

Rabbi Shenken added, "Yes, and the great Rabbis worried that not only would the unlearned misunderstand *Kohelet*, but those who purposely wished to cause harm would make it appear as if *Kohelet* was, in itself, heretical."

Keith responded. "Interesting how history repeats itself. Milton had the same concerns about his writings. He also had to make decisions about what to include in his poem. He realized that there would always be those who chose to misunderstand, but he concluded that honest people would appreciate the truth of his message. Perhaps that's why

Milton waited for a more understanding generation to appear before some of his works were published."

The rabbi handed out a reprint. "So we see a relationship between the conflict of the Rabbis and that of Milton. For those interested in understanding *Paradise Lost*, I suggest you review this sermon written in the thirteenth century."

Keith remained reading long after the class ended. The sermon was on *Kohelet*, delivered by the great Jewish philosopher Nachmanides, known as the Ramban, just before he left Spain to live in Israel in 1266. In it, the Ramban discussed the three essential elements of King Solomon's book:

That Man should not pursue worldly pleasures, for they are momentary and void of meaning; that only God is eternal and man's place in this world is to complete creation, enjoy the fruits of his labors, but only with the objective of serving God; and third, Why the righteous suffer and the wicked prosper.

To Keith, it was as if it came from the pen of Milton himself. *Kohelet* was teaching man the ways of God, precisely the reason that Milton wrote *Paradise Lost*. Was it possible that Milton patterned *Paradise Lost* on Solomon's *Kohelet*? Once again the visitor realized how close Milton and rabbinic exploration were. *But where did Milton learn this? How could he have studied the depths of Solomon's writing without a rabbi to guide him?*

CHAPTER 45

New York, May 24, 29 days

Joanne sipped her coffee and perused the new issue of *Art World News*. Suddenly, she sat up and drew the magazine closer. Something was wrong, very wrong, she had made a terrible mistake. She should have notified DeLordet immediately. She took a red marker from her desk drawer, circled the article and picked up the phone.

"M. DeLordet, I need to speak to you."

*

Joanne, what is this all about?"

She sat in DeLordet's office, her temples throbbing, not knowing where to begin. "I noticed a small entry that may be a problem."

Joanne handed him the magazine. "It's circled in red."

As he read the outlined article and glanced at the included photograph, she could feel her face flush as the blood rushed to her head.

DeLordet looked up for a moment then read the information out loud:

"May 10. Hong Kong: It has been reported that an unframed Braniff drawing will be offered at auction, at the 12 July, Post-War and Contemporary Art Sale of Sotheby's Hong Kong office. The work was obtained by a private collector in Hong Kong for an undisclosed amount. The untitled work is a newly discovered colored pencil drawing by Braniff of exceptional quality."

DeLordet handed the magazine back to Joanne. "Is there a problem?"

"I've seen this Braniff elsewhere."

Joanne brought him up to date, explaining how her friend received two drawings from his professor who received it as a gift directly from Braniff. When she saw the Zurich Braniff, she assumed her friend had sold it to the dealer there and when she received the two framed drawings she assumed that Braniff had made a second copy of one of the drawings. But now, a second Braniff has appeared which looks the same as her friend's other Braniff.

DeLordet remained silent, placing his elbows on the desk and resting his chin in his palms in contemplation.

"Have you completed framing the Zurich Braniff for Monsieur Le Paz?"

"Yes, sir. Carlos just finished."

"And you think it is an exact replication of your friend's?"

"As far as I can tell."

DeLordet paused for a moment before continuing in his tempered fashion. "Then I believe it best if I notify Frederick that we will need more time to check our sources."

DeLordet rose from his chair and went to the window. "I would have preferred to have known about your friend's Braniff as soon as you received the Zurich drawing. We are fortunate to have avoided an improper authentication, but now we must deal with a different type of problem."

Joanne sat up, "Sir?"

"Forgery. It's doubtful that Braniff made identical copies of two different drawings. I can understand if he made them as studies with different degrees of completion, but not the same. No, Ms. Farnsworth, I'm afraid one or now two or who knows how many fine copies of the Braniffs are being sold in various parts of the world for large sums of money. We are in business to authenticate works of art. If this is a forgery, then we have a responsibility to let LePaz and others know. If the Hong Kong is also a forgery then we are dealing with a major international scandal and the auction house must be told. Remember, *tout le monde* relies upon us to frame authentic works, not forgeries."

"Yes, sir."

DeLordet continued, "I will tell you this. Whoever did this may be a very talented artist, but an amateur in the art scene. We are a small fraternity and a professional would have known that every sale of any major artist is immediately posted around the globe. Perhaps, if these studies were kept in the hands of a private collector, as the Zurich was, then we would never have known. But once it was purchased by a businessman who wanted to flip it for profit, then the entire art world would know about it."

"Yes, sir."

"But that works in our favor. We will find this person. No, let me correct my statement, we must find this person, because when something like this happens it can shake the entire foundation of art sales. The business of art more than anything is trust. When we sell art, we are confirming that it was created by the artist we say it was created by."

DeLordet continued, "What is your friend's name?"

"Keith Jessup."

DeLordet made a note of it. "I would like to meet this Keith Jessup and I would like to examine his Braniffs."

Joanne looked at DeLordet. "His Braniffs are here, but you will not be able to meet him."

DeLordet looked puzzled. "And why is that?"

"Because he's disappeared."

CHAPTER 46

New York, May 25, 28 days

Keith received Sundstrom's text.

RE: Who tutored Milton? Milton's friend, John Aubrey, wrote in his diary that every morning at 4:30, a man who Aubrey did not know arrived at Milton's home to "read the Hebrew Bible" to him for several hours. Aubrey noted that the man would then leave and return at 7:00 for the remainder of the morning.

Keith had forgotten about Aubrey's diary.

*

Yeshiva University, May 25, 28 days

It was the second day of the symposium and Keith settled into his seat. Rabbi Lecht, a tall, bespectacled elderly gentleman, with thinning hair that had turned white and a neatly trimmed matching beard, was introduced. He wore a businessman's dark suit, white shirt, and silver tie under a large black hat. His eyes were blue and sparkled with intensity.

He looked over his audience. "The key question always remains: Are there Hebraic origins to *Paradise Lost*? If so, how did Milton have such knowledge? Could he have read it from the Hebrew books that were available? Was he able to find a tutor, as he did with his other subjects, to teach him the intricacies of the Jewish commentators?"

Rabbi Lecht began his reponsa. The answer lies in the role that anti-Semitism played in Christian Theology since the fourth century and which became pervasive throughout Christendom. This attempt to destroy the parent religion to justify its offspring reached a crescendo during the First Crusade of 1095, when uncontrolled mobs marched through Europe to save the Holy Land for Christianity. Advancing like a tidal wave, they robbed and killed entire Jewish villages, spawning lies and distortions that spread the flames of hatred like wildfires across Europe. In 1120, the Jews of England were fined 222 pounds, a huge sum of money, because a Jew was falsely charged with murder. In 1144 the world's first blood libel was recorded in Norwich, England, blaming Jews for the murder of a Christian boy. There could not have been more than 5,000 Jews in all of England in 1144, and probably less than 200 in Norwich, but ignorance breeds fear which leads to prejudice, intolerance, and finally hatred. It resulted in the mass murder of innocent Jews."

"What happened in Norwich?" a man in the back called out.

Rabbi Lecht looked for the questioner. "I will tell you. On March 20, just before Easter and Passover, the young son of a wealthy farmer was found missing. It was reported that he was last observed entering a Jewish home and two days later his body was found with his head shaved and multiple stab wounds. The boy's mother and the local priest accused the Jews of the murder, declaring it a reenactment of Christ's passion, the Stigmata."

Keith heard the words and shot up straight in his seat. *Stigmata? What did Lecht know about stigmata?*

"Later, Christian maids working in Jewish homes swore they looked through cracks in the door and saw the boy being gagged and tied following a Jewish service. They testified that they saw thorns forced onto his head and nailed onto a cross in the same way that Jesus was crucified. Several days later, the story was further embellished. To the original murder someone declared that the boy was killed because it was Passover and Jews needed the blood of a Christ substitute. Soon, conspiracy was added. Now it was proposed that each year a secret congress of Jews would meet in Spain and selected one community where such a ritual murder would take place. Norwich's year was 1144. Thus began the age-old perversions that Jews, on Passover, would kill a Christian child.

Rabbi Lecht paused for a moment. "It has always puzzled me not only how false the claim is, but how the charge could be made to begin with since the Torah specifically prohibits Jews from ingesting blood or anything mixed with blood. Regardless, it was the first of many pogroms occurring from London to Leningrad, from the eleventh century to the present, culminating in the murder of the six million."

CHAPTER 47

New York, May 25, 28 days

Joanne heard her office phone ring from down the hall. She ran, carrying a package of books and pressed the speaker button as she let the books fall on her desk.

"Hello?"

"Joanne Farnsworth?"

"Who's speaking?" Joanne didn't recognize the voice.

"Ms. Farnsworth, we're associates of your friend, a Dr. Keith Jessup. We have had some difficulty in locating him. Can you please tell us where we can reach him?"

She was about to answer when alarms began ringing, recalling Keith's last letter. *Be careful of strangers who want to know where I am.*

"I'm sorry; I didn't get your name."

There was a pause at the other end. "We're friends of Dr. Livingston, Keith's adviser. Now perhaps you could tell us where he is."

"I have no knowledge of a Keith Jessup."

"Oh, we think you do and we would appreciate your telling us."

Joanne did not answer.

"It will be much easier if you tell us now."

The caller heard her response – a dial tone.

*

May 25, 28 days

Stan Galvin gave Jeff Moss the assignment. "The NYPD inquired if the body of a Dr. Keith Jessup had been received as a John Doe."

Jeff tried to recall the name. "Should I know him?"

"It was Tom Davis's case about the well-dressed man killed near Columbia University? You did a work up."

Jeff nodded. "I remember."

"Keith Jessup was the one who identified the body and seemed to have an inkling as to who did it. This fellow Jessup worked at the Milton Society. Well, he disappeared a couple of months ago and hasn't been heard from since, and I need someone to check it out. And by the way, we have his salivary sample if you need a DNA analysis."

*

New York, May 25, 28 days

Joanne was still shaken by the phone call when Jeff arrived at her office.

"I believe you reported Keith Jessup missing. Have you heard from him?"

"Not directly."

"Not directly?"

"About ten days ago, I received two Braniff drawings that Keith had received as a gift. That's the only connection to Keith that I've had and I don't even know if he sent it."

"So, the only clue as to his whereabouts is the art. What about the return address?"

"There is none. It was delivered by hand and simply left at the front desk. Before security had a chance to speak to him, the messenger had left."

"And the art is here?"

"Yes, in the director's office." Joanne hesitated. "There's one other thing. I received a troubling phone call yesterday."

When she had finished reviewing the call, Jeff realized there was more to the case than following up on a John Doe.

*

Jeff examined the drawings and the packaging they were delivered in. "Is there any way we can identify who sent the drawings?"

"Not that we know of. But they have become a major source of embarrassment for us."

"Meaning?"

DeLordet sat back in his chair. "Forgery. We are trying to determine which of the two drawings is real. And now we were notified of an auction in Hong Kong that includes a Braniff matching the other framed Braniff we have."

Jeff looked at Keith's framed and the Zurich Braniff lying side by side on the table.

DeLordet gave him the lens. "Take a look."

Jeff inspected the two drawings. "I don't know much about art, but they certainly look the same."

DeLordet continued, "So either Braniff made two of the same, which is highly unlikely, or someone else is making them. Furthermore, someone returned the apparent originals to us and we have no idea why."

Jeff looked at Joanne. "Unless Keith is sending a message that he's OK and wanted the art returned for safekeeping."

DeLordet thought for a moment. "True, but someone made copies either with or without his knowledge, and the art is worth a great deal of money. Several million dollars. Perhaps your Mr. Jessup is missing because he is no longer alive or he is involved in the scheme."

Joanne bit her lip, trying not to respond.

"Then why would the art be returned? That's a lot of money to give away. No, I don't think that's the case."

DeLordet answered. "Well, either way, my company is involved."

"Because you must authenticate the artist's work?"

"Exactly, and I'm not sure I can. Am I to report that the Zurich Braniff is a forgery or an original? The slightest inaccuracy on our part could have serious repercussions for us and the art market."

"And you have no way of knowing?"

DeLordet responded. "How? There's no paper trail because Braniff never signed any documentation. All we see is the signature on the drawings. We're not looking at aging these drawings because they are not historical and there are no paint pigments to analyze. What else can I do?"

Once again Jeff inspected the piece. "So you saw nothing unusual?"

"Actually, there might be something." Both men were surprised and looked at Joanne who had turned the Braniffs over. "Our framer mentioned dark spots on the reverse side of the Zurich drawing. Usually it's a paper stain, but under higher magnification he thought there was a pattern of some type. He recently framed a series of a dozen Braniffs. There were no such marks present on any of them."

Jeff took the lens and reexamined it. "So the marks are unusual?"

"It's possible."

Jeff thought for a moment. "Perhaps I can help."

DeLordet looked at him questioningly. "In what way?"

"At the medical examiner's office, we always need to determine identification and causation of the slightest amounts of evidence. This may be such a case."

DeLordet stood up. "What do you have in mind?"

"I need to know everything."

The two of them reviewed the information they had from Zurich and Hong Kong.

Jeff was fascinated. "Look, if this information helps to find this fellow then I'd like to take the drawings back to my lab for a few hours."

"I'm not certain how that can be arranged."

Joanne responded. "What if I stay with the art. We're insured and I'd take responsibility as we do with any pieces we pick up from our clients."

DeLordet agreed. "If you wouldn't mind staying with the drawings while the doctor is examining it that would be perfectly acceptable."

He turned to Jeff. "So you are a doctor detective? Like our Inspector Clouseau, or perhaps more appropriately like our neighbor across the sea, Dr. Sherlock Holmes. Good luck, Dr. Moss, welcome to the world of art."

CHAPTER 48

Yeshiva University, May 25, 28 days

As the afternoon session was to begin, Keith glanced around the room wondering how many were Holocaust survivors or their children. *Even that they are trying to deny. From where does such blind, ignorant hatred come from? For what purpose?* The morning's history of Christianity and anti-Semitism still caused chills in his spine. *So much death and sorrow in the name of the Lord. The truths of the past are not easy to deal with.* Keith reflected back to a thought William Faulkner had written: *the past is never dead; it isn't even past.*

Rabbi Lecht began:

"There's no end to what fear and jealousy can spawn and the lies of the blood libel led to a mass reaction. From 1263 to 1266, England's Jewish communities became victims of large-scale atrocities – robbery, murder – including those in London, Cambridge, Canterbury, Worcester, and Lincoln. This hatred culminated on July 18, 1290 when King Edward I, blaming England's ills on the Jews and having already taxed them to the point of destitution, issued an edict that banished them. It would prove to be the first of many expulsions the Jews suffered during the Middle Ages and also the most complete. By the deadline of November 1, All Saint's Day, England's entire Jewish population was forced to leave whatever possessions they had and flee to France, Germany, Flanders, or anywhere they would be accepted. And this restriction lasted into the 1650s with the execution of Charles I, the acceptance of a more Puritan theology, and the establishment of a Republican form of government under Cromwell. The increased acceptance of Puritan practice, with its increased focus on the Old Testament, resulted in a greater tolerance for Jews and a call for their readmission to England. With Roger Williams and others in support of Jewish admittance and the need for economic revival that Jewish ingenuity could supply, Cromwell offered favorable treatment for Jews to return to England. Even after Cromwell died in 1658, and his son Richard was overturned in 1660, Charles II continued the relaxation of anti-Jewish laws and when a leader was needed to bring Jews back to England, it seemed as if heaven sent a rabbi from Amsterdam to alter history. The rabbi's name was Menasseh Ben Israel."

CHAPTER 49

New York, May 26, 27 days

They unpacked the two Braniffs in the ME's lab as Joanne surveyed the room.

"Looks like Star Trek."

From behind, a voice called out, "It's latest." They turned to see a slim young man of moderate height, mid-twenties, narrow face, with long straight black hair, standing behind them.

"Mikhail, thanks for staying. Joanne will be joining us."

"No problems, Dr. Moss. Nice meet you, Joanne. Sorry to hear bout your friend. But if anyone can find him, it's Dr. Moss."

They shook hands. "So we have art project. No problem. Dr. Moss and me search for details all time. With infrared technique we check for marks or signatures on anything. We even take photomicrograph of different drawing and the computer tell difference."

"You can do that?"

"No problem, that's how we compare handwriting sample, or piece of fiber, or small chips paint. Computer sees every line and tells if same. Here, I show you."

Mikhail took a black camera out of one of the drawers.

"It's PAXCAM USB2 digital microscope camera. It can do almost everything because not just camera but part of powerful computer system with large database. I put one image over another and measure similars and differences."

Joanne was fascinated. "But how do we examine a large piece of art?"

"No problem. We don't need art, just image from camera. Then we analyze image any way we want"

Jeff added, "That means we can overlay the photo of Keith's drawing with the Zurich and the computer will analyze it."

"That's impressive."

"I no longer need actual material, just image."

Joanne smiled. "So reality is no longer of significance, only image."

Mikhail laughed. "Don't tell my girlfriend."

He continued, "Anyway, camera automatically adjusts resolution of image and light available."

Jeff added, "It's like your computer at work. Most captured images are used for documentation, archiving, slide show presentations, written reports, or just email. Those procedures don't need a great deal of resolution."

"Exactly, Dr. Moss, but here want much detail, and that means high resolution. But, more resolution means more memory and that means slower process, so need special set up. Its real name is PAXCAM ARC, a super high-resolution camera that can analyze documents, measurements, and images."

"How much magnification can we get, Mikhail?"

"All way to 20 megapixels!"

"Sounds like you don't need an x-ray."

Mikhail appreciated Joanne's interest. "I can't see under skin, but I see cells on it. Computer makes calibrated measurements from crime scene or forensic images. That's what we do now, measure every line and angle, then software sees if these are same or not."

"Well, let's take a look and see what you guys can find."

"No problem." Mikhail placed the camera onto the stand and turned on its power. "OK, Dr. Moss, all yours."

Jeff gently put the underside of the Zurich Braniff on the table under the stand and slowly "clicked" several images of the "stains" that Carlos had pointed out.

"That's all there is to it. Now we don't need drawing anymore, it's all been saved. Take look at computer screen."

Jeff clicked on the auto focusing. "So far just a slight stain of some type."

Joanne was amazed. "The last time I looked in a microscope you had to look through it."

Mikhail laughed. "Those were long time ago."

They examined several "stains," but found nothing.

Mikhail interrupted. "Dr. Moss, let me switch on infrared capability." Mikhail connected the computer to another type of apparatus. "Now, we increase resolution up to 5 megapixels."

Jeff clicked his mouse.

Joanne exclaimed. "Well, what do we have here?" They all looked at the found image.

Mikhail was surprised. "Wow! Xerox MicroText – cool! Haven't seen that in long time."

Joanne tried reading it. "It looks like some type of old lettering. Can you make it clearer?"

"Go to 10, Dr. Moss."

Jeff clicked two more times. "There we go. Wow! That did it."

 Earth from entrails
Again pangs, Nature a
Groan loured, muttering
Somedrops at of mortal
Original

Jeff read the wording: "O Earth from entrails Again pangs, Nature a Groan loured, muttering Somedrops at of mortal Original."

Jeff was confused. "What is it?"

Joanne shook her head. "I don't know."

Jeff began taking photomicrographs of the image on the computer. "Mark it Exhibit A. Could Braniff have done this on the original drawings given to Keith?"

Methodically they repeated the same steps with Keith's Braniff that Joanne had framed. It was completely blank.

Mikhail was intrigued. "So, whoever copied drawing, add something. Why?"

Jeff nodded. "Perhaps instead of a signature."

Joanne thought about it. "You mean they wanted us to know who did it?"

Mikhail broke the silence. "Possible. Our criminal psychologists call them 'mixed signal' offenders. They believe some part of criminal wants admit crime, but other part doesn't. So they tell us in way that wouldn't be noticed."

"Very interesting."

Mikhail continued, "We had case several years ago where religious man felt guilty for murdering homeless person. Forensic psychologists worked on case and said man had much guilt and needed to confess without letting anyone know he was confessing."

Joanne interjected. "So the confession clears their conscience without the retribution."

Jeff added: "At least not human retribution."

"Yes, Dr. Moss, but psych guys figure individual needed more confessing, so they had police visit all churches and speak to clergy. And it worked. They found individual, matched the DNA and man confessed before trial."

CHAPTER 50

Yeshiva University, May 26, 27 days

As the audience filled the hall, Rabbi Lecht began the final lecture. "Menasseh Ben Israel was born a Marrano, in Madeira, in 1604 and baptized. Marranos were Jews who chose to convert to Catholicism rather than face death by the Spanish Inquisition, yet continued to practice Judaism secretly. Eventually the family escaped to Amsterdam and resumed their Jewish identity, so Menasseh didn't begin formal training in Judaism until he was twelve."

As Rabbi Lecht spoke, Keith observed the similarities between Ben Israel and Milton. Ben Israel proved to be a Talmudic prodigy and by seventeen had already written his first book, *Sefer Berurah*, a Hebrew grammar book. Hartlib recalled how Milton also published a grammar textbook as a young man. Furthermore, like Milton, Ben Israel's knowledge of theology was as vast as his proclivity for language. Ben Israel wrote in Latin, Hebrew, French, Spanish, Portuguese, and English, many of his books being written to educate Christians about Judaism. His *Conciliador*, written in Spanish and Latin, reconciled biblical passages between Jew and Christian and earned him great distinction in the Christian world. Christian nobles and Church officials attended his sermons regularly and by the end of the 1640s, Menasseh Ben Israel was the most recognized Jewish scholar in Europe.

The rabbi continued: "In the year 1648, violent pogroms, often with state approval, arose against Jews throughout Eastern and Central Europe. Entire villages of thousands of Jews were wiped out by marauding Cossacks. To escape, Jews fled west, crowding Amsterdam, one of the few places that accepted them. But Ben Israel, the leading rabbi in Amsterdam, was concerned that the massive Jewish migration into the city would damage Jewish acceptance. To survive, he believed the Jews must find another home and that God had ordained England to be that home. Under Cromwell's rule, England's laws were based on the Old Testament, and Ben Israel and the Puritans believed that the Messiah's appearance was imminent. But they also believed that the Messianic Age could only begin if the dispersion of the Jews was completed to *K'tzeh haAretz*, "the end of the earth," a name used to identify England. In 1655, Ben Israel arrived in England and submitted his petition to Cromwell for the readmission of Jews. The court of law determined that the original exile in 1290 was not the law of the land, but only a personal dictum of King Edward I. This, in effect, allowed Jews to reenter England. As a token of his appreciation for his efforts, Cromwell rewarded Ben Israel with a pension of L100 a year. Menasseh would never live to enjoy it."

*

New York, May 26, 27 days

It was noon when Jeff and Joanne met in DeLordet's office. "Let me enlarge that for you, sir."

 **Earth from entrails Again pangs, Nature a Groan loured, muttering Somedrops at of mortal Original**

"Well, Doctor, you really are a detective. This is very interesting, especially if it wasn't on any of the Braniffs that we had here, just on the Zurich. But is it on the Hong Kong?"

"And another question," Joanne added, "why this symbol and why this text?"

DeLordet took out a pad of paper. "Why don't we take them one at a time? First, in terms of the Hong Kong. If it is a forgery, the auction cannot be allowed to proceed."

"To prove it," Jeff said, "we'd need to examine the Hong Kong the same way we did the Zurich."

"I don't think," Joanne interjected, "that they'd send the piece here."

DeLordet thought for a moment. "Then one of us has to go there!"

DeLordet looked at each of them, waiting for a response.

Finally Joanne spoke up. "I'll go."

Jeff looked at the others. "By yourself. I don't like it. Especially in light of the threat. These people seem for real, and if they are connected to the forgery, they are not going to want to be caught."

"I'll be fine, and I feel responsible for this mess. No one would suspect that I'm anyone but an art investor."

DeLordet remained worried. "The doctor is right. I'm concerned about your safety."

"It's more than the art. This has to do with Keith. Now what do I have to do?"

Jeff saw her determination and looked at DeLordet who shrugged his shoulders.

"Same process that we went through. Pictures will need to be taken of the Hong Kong Braniff and compared to these Braniffs."

Jeff gave her the laptop. "Take this. Our Braniffs are all stored on it. It's got a lot of interesting programs. So if you want to watch movies when you're on the plane you can even view it in slow motion."

Jeff pointed out the program and smiled. "And if you put it on frame by frame one movie will get you all the way to Hong Kong."

He looked at DeLordet. "Give us a few days to make the arrangements. My boss should be able to take care of the lab work if you can get Joanne into Sotheby's."

DeLordet responded. "I'll take care of it. What about the message?"

Joanne repeated the phrase several times. "Something's missing."

Jeff repeated the words. "What is 'mortal Original'?"

Silence filled the room until Joanne spoke. "Could it be Original Sin? If it is, I know someone you can speak to – Dr. James Goodwin at the Union Biblical Seminary."

CHAPTER 51

Yeshiva University, May 26, 27 days

During the break Rabbi Shenken and his guest filled their cups with coffee. "So, Mr. Hartlib, I hope you found the information on Ben Israel of interest."

"Very much so, but if *Paradise Lost* included Talmudic tracts, how did Milton learn Talmud?"

"Rabbi Shenken, your friend asks a perceptive question."

They turned to see Rabbi Lecht standing nearby. Rabbi Shenken quickly made the introductions.

"Scholars have long debated the extent of Milton's knowledge of

Hebrew. For several hundred years prior to Milton, early Christian thinkers had studied with rabbis to understand the Old Testament, yet their knowledge allowed them only to read the Hebrew Bible, not to probe the depths of rabbinic commentaries. But Christian scholars soon found learned Jews to help delve into the intricacies of Talmud and Midrash. Many of these Jewish teachers had been forced to convert to Christianity and the scholars used that training to challenge Jewish beliefs. Throughout Europe, the Church would have Jews debate Christians or converted scholars in front of the local populace, arguing the virtues of their respective beliefs. The effect was that Jews were put on trial and made to respond to ambiguous questions. Regardless of the responses, the outcomes were always the same, with Jews being charged with heresy resulting in huge fines, imprisonment, or even death."

Rabbi Lecht continued: "In fact, the demand to learn Hebrew had grown to the point that by the seventeenth century Hebrew along with Greek and Latin, were the classical languages to be studied by all serious students. But for Milton to have gone beyond this basic ability and use Jewish sources directly would necessitate intricacies in interpretation that even Milton would have found a Herculean task."

"So, Rabbi, now I'm puzzled. If Milton couldn't have understood it by himself, where did he learn it?" Rabbi Shenkin asked.

Rabbi Lecht sipped his coffee. "Perhaps from the Latin translations of the Hebrew."

"I would respectfully disagree," Keith interjected. "Milton would not use secondary sources, regardless of how good the Latin translations were. As we learn from his *Christian Doctrine*, he insisted on only original sources. Milton had to do this by himself."

As the discussion continued, a gathering of attendees began to grow around the three men until finally someone shouted, "Speak louder."

Rabbi Lecht gave Hartlib a gentle smile, and spoke to the growing crowd.

"If everyone will please sit down, perhaps Mr. Hartlib and I will move up to the dais and we might all be able to gain further insights."

The return of the attendees to their seats quickly attracted the remaining scholars and with Hartlib and Lecht standing in front the room once again was filled to capacity.

"Do you have a better suggestion?"

Keith looked around. He had taken great pains to avoid the spotlight for the past months, but now there was no way to avoid it.

"Perhaps I do." The statement brought full attention from those seated in the room.

"Milton had a tutor."

Lecht seemed surprised. "A tutor?"

"Yes, sir. Milton had a rabbi."

Rabbi Lecht paused for a moment. "But who would that be? There were no Jews, let alone rabbis allowed in England since 1290."

You could hear a pin drop in expectation. Keith waited several moments before he answered. "Except for one. Menasseh Ben Israel."

Sounds filled the hall as the scholars discussed the merits of Hartlib's answer.

"Did they know each other?"

All eyes turned to Hartlib. "They were both in London in 1655 when Ben Israel addressed Parliament."

"But who would have introduced them? They came from different worlds."

Again a quiet murmur as all heads turned back to Hartlib.

"Roger Williams. Not only was Williams an old friend of Milton's, but as the great advocate of religious freedom he was a major supporter of Ben Israel's attempt to have Jews allowed back into England."

Keith paused for a moment, realizing the effect of the new information. "And I believe that Milton was already familiar with Ben Israel through reading his book, *De Termino Vitae*, which discussed if the length of one's life is coincidence or predetermined."

Lecht responded thoughtfully. "Certainly they were both interested in the extent of free will, but we would need more evidence."

"I believe I have that evidence."

The room remained silent, wondering who this individual was that seemed to have so many answers.

"Professor Foster Sundstrom of Oxford reported to me that John Aubrey, Milton's close friend, wrote in his diary that every morning at 4:30, an unknown hired man came to Milton's home to read him Hebrew texts. Then, in the afternoon, Milton would dictate to a writer the books he was working on – *The Christian Doctrine* and *Paradise Lost*."

The rabbi put his hand to his chin and stroked his beard. "I'm familiar with Aubrey. He had befriended many of the scientists of his age and was one of the founders of the Royal Society. What else did you learn from Aubrey's diary?"

"That after arriving in the morning, the tutor would spend time with

Milton and then leave after two hours, only to return an hour or so later. That part I don't understand."

A broad smile appeared on Rabbi Lecht's face. "But we do, and that confirms your answer. Every morning Ben Israel had to attend the early morning *Shacharit* prayers held in one of the few remaining Jewish homes, at least until December 1656, when a house was rented for use as the first Jewish synagogue. Next time you're in London, visit the Cunard building on Creechurch Lane. You'll see a plaque that marks the site of that first Sephardic synagogue established on the readmission of Jews to England in 1657."

*

Keith took his seat and Rabbi Lecht continued until concluding the program.

"Menasseh Ben Israel remained in England until 1657. Shortly after his return to Amsterdam, he died, but, as our friend Mr. Hartlib pointed out, by that time Milton was already writing both *Paradise Lost* and *The Christian Doctrine*."

As the audience filed out of the room, Keith made his way to where Shenken and Lecht were in animated conversation.

"Thanks for inviting me. In all my studies I hadn't come across this before."

"That's because most scholars prefer to conform their academic thoughts to their personal beliefs. There's a lot at stake here, Mr. Hartlib."

Keith had heard that before: *Paradise Lost* is a Christian poem. If you attack the poem, you are attacking a fundamental Christian belief of God's creation and power, good over evil, reward and punishment. A defense of church and state.

The rabbi continued, "You remind me of an old friend with whom I spent many hours discussing some of the same ideas that we went over today. I wish I could have put the two of you together."

"And who was that?"

"Professor Thornton Livingston."

*

As the attendees left the room, Keith asked Lecht a final question.

"Rabbi, why Milton? Of all the great men in the history of the world

why did you choose him? Surely the great Jewish rabbis and philoso-
phers had enough to offer to write your thesis on."

Lecht turned his full attention to Keith. "Why? Because Milton was
the greatest defender of all that Judaism has taught this world: justice,
law, tolerance, liberty, the freedom to express one's views regardless of
their orientation, and the duty to defend those precious values regardless of the consequences. It was Milton who said, '*Give me the liberty to
know, to utter, and to argue freely according to conscience, above all liberties.*'"

The rabbi paused for a moment. "Let me tell you a story. It was my
seventh birthday, November 6, 1938. I had five older sisters. We were
living in Berlin where my father was the rabbi of the synagogue, and that
meant I was always treated as someone special – the rabbi's son. But I
also had to be the best student – it was expected of me – and so I learned
every day at the yeshiva and then alone with my father after dinner. He
was wonderful. Tall, strong, and handsome with a long graying beard,
intense blue eyes and a gentle smile. I don't ever remember his losing
his temper – even when I got into trouble – which I often did. He would
teach when you lose your temper you lose your reason. Well, Germany
in the late thirties was a time of great hatred against the Jews and I
remember how the congregants would come to my father to speak about
a man called Hitler. I couldn't understand why this Hitler would hate
me when he didn't even know me. Anyway, that afternoon when I got
home from school my oldest sister, Naomi, brought in the cake and my
other sisters brought in the presents. I was so excited. And then, as they
began to sing 'Happy Birthday' there was a loud banging at the door.
Everyone stopped singing. My parents looked at each other, held hands,
and continued to sing until they finished the song.

"I'll never forget how they held hands – it was so tight their skin
turned white. The banging continued and grew louder and there was
shouting outside. My father went to the front door. The rest of us
peeked out the dining room to see who was banging, and we saw men in
brown uniforms yelling at my father and hitting him with their guns and
dragging him away. My mother ran to the door to stop them, but they
pushed her down and laughed. We ran to the windows as the soldiers
dragged him to their car and threw him inside. All the neighbors saw
what was happening. People walking by, people I grew up with, kids
I played with, Jews and non-Jews stopped to watch yet pretended not
to see. I saw the neighbors across the street pull the shades down, no

one said a word. No one helped. I couldn't understand. He was their rabbi. When they needed him he was always available, no matter when or where. But now it was as if they never knew him.

"We didn't see my father for two days, no one knew what happened, no one wanted to talk about it. And then, on the third day, a car pulled up on the street outside our home and two soldiers with big black boots got out, opened the trunk, and threw a large bundle tied together with rope into the middle of the street. I was sitting on the stoop with my sisters. We didn't know what it was and called my mother.

"She went out and saw the bundle and slowly walked into the street – all the neighbors were watching – she knelt down and hands shaking untied the bundle. Her scream was so loud that I was sure that it reached the heavens. I remember running to her and looking at the bundle she had opened. At first I didn't know what it was, and then I realized it was my father, they had broken his bones to fit him into the sack, stripped him of his clothes, cut off his sacred beard and shaved his hair. Only old Mr. Bernstein came to help us bring my father into the house and my sister ran for the doctor, but there was nothing he could do. I never saw my father, of blessed memory, alive again.

"That night every synagogue in Berlin was burned to the ground, Torah scrolls destroyed by mobs of Germans laughing as if they were at a party. Jewish shops and homes were broken into, the glass windows broken into a million jagged shards. My mother just kept repeating: '*Ich konnte nicht glauben, dass so etwas wirklich passiert*' – 'I can't believe this is actually happening!' By the end of the night, 191 synagogues were burned to the ground and 30,000 Jewish men were pulled out of their homes and sent to concentration camps. In the days that followed, not a word was said, not a sentence of outrage from the world was ever stated."

Rabbi Lecht took a deep breath, as if he had relived the madness. "And so, you ask, why Milton? Because if he was there, the world would have heard outrage, one voice would have been heard above the mobs, challenging the animals who had lost all humanity. Since that night I realized the ally of prejudice is complacency – the danger of not speaking out – the danger of not defeating injustice no matter where it is found, what is called a conspiracy of silence. John Milton was one of those righteous individuals who understood that. Nearly a hundred years later Edmund Burke restated it: '*All that is necessary for the triumph of evil is that good men do nothing.*' John Milton never did nothing."

Only the dulled sounds of the street traffic outside could be heard above the silence of those remaining in the room. Finally Rabbi Lecht turned to his questioner.

"Are you, Mr. Hartlib, also a warrior against injustice?"

"Yes, sir. I believe I am."

"Then you understand the Conspiracy of Silence. As Pastor Martin Niemöller confessed of his own silence as the Nazis rose to power:

> First they came for the communists and I didn't speak out because I wasn't a communist. Then they came for the trade unionists and I didn't speak out because I wasn't a trade unionist. Then they came for the Jews, and I didn't speak out because I wasn't a Jew. Then they came for me and there was no one left to speak out.

*

As he exited the building, he heard his name called. "Mr. Hartlib, I believe this is the information you asked for – the significance of *Mikveh Yisra'el*."

Rabbi Lecht handed him a sheet of paper and smiled knowingly: "Mr. Hartlib, are you, by any chance, a distant relative of Milton's friend, Samuel Hartlib?"

The man called Hartlib held the Rabbi's hand for an instant longer than usual and looked into his eyes: "Rabbi, you are very wise."

As Keith walked out he glanced at the paper the rabbi had given him: "*'Mikveh Yisra'el' is the title of Menasseh Ben Israel's book, The Hope of Israel.*"

BOOK VI

CHAPTER 52

ME's Office, May 28, 25 days

"I have your information."

Jeff looked up to see Stan at the door. "Already?"

"I emailed Dr. Yih-Lin Koo, who heads up the pathology department at the Tianjin Cancer Institute and Hospital in Hong Kong. We get together at least once a year at the International Pathology Conference. He said he'd be glad to help. He's got the lab, the Nikon for the digital analytics and a department full of ace technicians."

"Then I think we're ready. We have a Joanne Farnsworth ready to go."

*

The cell phone rang in the small Manhattan apartment.

"Have you found him?"

"I don't know where he is."

"What about the girl?"

"I asked. She wouldn't answer."

"Then follow her. There are ways of helping people tell you what you need to know. I want Keith Jessup found."

*

New York, May 28, 25 days

It was a warm spring day when DeLordet met Dr. James Goodwin, the Frederick Smyth Professor of Bible and Comparative Religion at the Union Biblical Seminary and Professor of Religion at Columbia. His secretary led him into his office and advised him that he would be in momentarily. Goodwin had written fifteen books and over a hundred articles on the various derivatives of religion.

DeLordet appreciated the setting. It appeared more like a dimly lit chapel than a scholar's office. The room was enclosed with aged wood paneling against which was a rectangular shaped table built with planks of darkly stained wood. The table was probably eighteenth-century English with wooden butterfly swaging used instead of nails. A small reading lamp with a parchment shade, yellowed by years, was positioned on the table along with a number of manuscripts. The door opened and Goodwin walked in.

"Monsieur DeLordet, Joanne mentioned you would be calling. How can I help?"

DeLordet placed the photomicrograph of the image on the table.

 Earth from entrails
Again pangs, Nature a
Groan loured, muttering
Somedrops at of mortal
Original

"Well, this is a puzzle. I don't believe it's from the Bible. The style appears to be Old English. I don't recognize the verse, but something must be missing. I suppose the words mortal and original may be biblically related."

"But from where?"

"I'm not sure, but I have another idea."

Goodwin picked up the phone. "Alice, can you get a hold of Peter Flamm?" Goodwin continued, "Peter is a computer specialist and a brilliant biblical student. In fact, he was involved with deciphering the computer interpretations of the Bible, working on the various algorithms that appear within a chapter."

Five minutes later there was a knock on the door and Goodwin stood up to greet a young man of about twenty-five, heavy set with a cherubic face. He showed Peter the image. "Can you determine where this comes?"

Peter looked at the image for a moment. "I can try word matching with one of the search engines. Can't promise anything."

*

"All arrangements have been made, sir."

DeLordet was back in his office when Kate Harrigan peered into his open door.

"I just spoke with Sotheby's in Hong Kong and they confirmed that

Joanne can examine the Braniff. They also mentioned that they spoke to the owner of the Braniff, a Mr. Teng, and he might be able to meet with her at his shop, the Shin Shen Gallery and discuss who he purchased the drawing from."

As Kate started back to her office, she turned to DeLordet. "She will be OK, won't she sir?"

DeLordet looked up from his desk. "I hope so."

*

Hong Kong, May 28, 25 days

It didn't take more than a few minutes following Sotheby's call that Teng walked up the stairs to his office and fumbled through his desk drawer. Finding a business card he picked up his phone, dialed a number in New York, and left a message.

"Mr. Stratton, this is Teng in Hong Kong. You asked if I would notify you should someone be more than interested in your product. A Joanne Farnsworth from New York's Pierre et Fils will be arriving to inquire about who had sold us the Braniff."

CHAPTER 53

Hong Kong, May 30, 23 days

The trip to Hong Kong on Continental Airlines left Newark Airport at 3:00 PM and arrived the next day at 6:50 PM. Joanne was met at the gate by Peter Chen holding a large sign, "Ms. Joanne Farnsworth." Chen's English was excellent. He explained that he had graduated from Northwestern in Chicago before returning to Hong Kong to work as Dr. Koo's personal assistant at the Tianjin Cancer Institute and Hospital in Hong Kong. He led her to his car for the thirty-minute trip to the hotel.

"So, you are staying at the Bishop Lei International? It's very nice, good location, and very modern. Dr. Koo said you may be spending a few days here and he assigned me as your designated driver."

"That's very kind of Dr. Koo."

"Dr. Koo is very generous man. It's much easier if I take you around the city."

Chen let her off at the hotel entrance. "May I suggest that you check in to your room, unpack, and get a good night's sleep. I'll meet you in the lobby at 9:00."

*

Joanne met Chen as scheduled. He was standing with a slender young man of medium height with a broad contagious smile, jet black hair, deep dark eyes, and carrying a bag over his shoulder.

"Joanne, meet Zao Yang, Dr. Koo's best technician."

"Ms. Joanne, welcome to Hong Kong. Dr. Koo forwarded an email from Dr. Jeffrey Moss as to what we have to do. This camera should take care of all our needs."

They shook hands. "Great. I believe my boss made arrangements for us to meet his contact at Sotheby's."

She handed Chen a piece of paper. "This is their address. Do you know where it is?"

"Yes, it's not far."

As they walked out of the lobby a man sitting in the far corner of the lobby, wearing a dark colored trench coat, lowered his copy of *The Standard*, Hong Kong's daily newspaper, and followed them out. As he walked out of the hotel, the concierge couldn't help but notice the scar that looked like a twisted corkscrew running deep into his cheek.

*

Chen dropped the two of them off at Pacific Place, a dazzling architectural development of office towers, hotels, and shopping center in the Admiralty section of Hong Kong, in the heart of the city. The building was a modern, sleek steel structure that looked more like sculpture than office space. They entered the lobby and gave security their information. Within minutes they were met by a young female assistant who brought them to the thirty-first floor office of Mr. Oni Fujita, the Deputy Chairman of Sotheby's Asia. Joanne spoke with him privately and within minutes Fujita and his assistant escorted the two visitors to a small private viewing room. While the assistant retrieved the Braniff, Fujita explained how Sotheby's was the first auction house established in Hong Kong and was central to the Asian art market.

"With Asia's incredible economic growth, and the new wealth of individual Chinese and Asian entrepreneurs, modern Chinese Art has become aggressively sought after. We see the interest in collecting art increasing, so we are looking forward to the July auction."

"Will the Braniff be in that auction?"

"Oh, yes. The Braniff and several other pieces of Western Contemporary Art. It will be a good test of the interest our new Asian collectors have in this genre. Last year, we sold record numbers to collectors who depend on our assuring them of the finest provenance."

Joanne realized the significance of her trip and the ripple effect of a single pebble causing waves across the sea.

"Would it be possible for me to contact the owner of the Braniff?"

"We have already made arrangements. As you know, Sotheby's policy is not to provide any details of our clients, but, we did speak to the gentleman and he will be expecting you. If you will allow me, I will let him know that you have arrived."

"That would be most appreciated."

Fujita returned to his office as his assistant brought in the Braniff and placed it on an easel for them to examine. Joanne took out photos of Keith's second drawing. By eye, they seemed identical.

Zao took out his Nikon 812D digital camera and within moments took the required images from different perspectives, front and reverse side.

"That's all I need."

"That's it?" Joanne was impressed. "Twenty hours to get here and all you need is twenty seconds?"

The assistant removed the Braniff, and led them back to Fujita's office.

"My client said that if you call this number, he would be glad to arrange a time to meet."

Fujita handed Joanne a card with the client's name and number. They thanked him and went outside to find Chen.

*

At the hotel, Zao took out his computer and connected his Nikon to it, bringing up the image of the back of the Hong Kong Braniff. As he zoomed to the higher power an image appeared.

 trembled her as in and
gave second Sky and
thunder sad Wept
completing the sin

Joanne stared at the symbol.

"The symbol is the same as the Zurich, but the words are different!" Joanne's mind was working quickly. "Can you bring up the Zurich image?"

Zao quickly brought up the other image and placed it next to the Hong Kong. They studied it for several minutes.

Earth from entrails
Again pangs, Nature a
Groan loured, muttering
Somedrops at of mortal
Original

Finally, Joanne spoke. "I still don't know what it means."

Zao tried to focus the image. "But I think it shows that whoever did the Zurich did the Hong Kong."

Joanne nodded. "I agree, but the question remains, would Braniff have done this himself or is this the work of someone else, and, if so, why?"

"The computer can tell us."

Zao began the analysis. First, he brought up from his computer's memory both the Hong Kong Braniff and Keith's Braniff onto the screen. Then he clicked on the analysis program and within moments the outlines of the two Braniffs were superimposed over each other. The program began detailed measurements of pencil strokes, areas of color, pressure, and density. What had appeared to be the same picture, showed under magnified analysis how different they were.

"Take a look." Joanne was pointing at the pencil stroke analysis. "Notice how the pencil stroke on Keith's Braniff shows a darker line on the right of the stroke. But, on the Hong Kong it's darker on the left of the stroke."

Zao then analyzed several other lines drawn on the two pieces.

Joanne saw the difference. "Same thing. Definitely, every line drawn on Keith's Braniff is darker on the right, and the lines on the Hong Kong are darker on the left."

"Now let's compare Keith's to the Zurich." Zao brought up the Zurich and clicked on the analysis program.

"Look, same as the Hong Kong. Darker on the left. I would say that the Hong Kong and the Zurich were done by a different artist than the ones Keith received."

"But why?"

"Because Braniff was right-handed and the second artist was left-handed. You're a lefty. Draw a picture."

Joanne was surprised. "How did you know that?"

Zao smiled. "That's what I'm trained to do. I see the hand you wear your watch, open a candy wrapper, open the car door."

Kate drew a picture on some hotel stationery as Zao explained. "But handwriting analysis has become more scientific and is now a major source of evidence at our office." Then, with a slight grin he added, "We have also learned to be careful with lefties, after all, left in Latin is *sinistre*, or sinister in English."

Kate gave Zao a skeptical look as he took a photo and placed it under low power. Next to it he placed the same line under higher power.

"Notice the difference with magnification of your line."

"Now, let's do an analysis of the line itself." Zao clicked the program.

Joanne was surprised. "I never realized. I guess as I draw with the pencil in my left hand I must put more pressure on the outside, the side my pencil leans to."

"Or, as we say in forensics, you slant to your dominant side." Zao continued, "Now, let's do a color analysis comparing Keith's Braniff with the Zurich."

The two of them studied the color analysis for a few moments.

Zao shook his head. "The colors are not the same."

Because the drawings were done with different pencils."

Zao looked up. "Is that unusual?"

"By itself, it's not conclusive, but in most cases an artist works with what he's used to."

Zao clicked under link. "Now compare the Zurich with the Hong Kong."

Joanne nodded. "Same color spectrum as the Zurich."

"I agree. Whoever did the Zurich used the same pencils for the Hong Kong."

"So, it appears that we have a very fine left-handed artist who copied Keith's Braniff and then coded the work in Old English and a symbol. The question now is, who is this individual and why did he leave a calling card?"

Joanne went online. "I'll email this information to my boss in New York, he's working on finding its source."

"Is that all we need to do?"

Joanne looked at Zao. "Not yet. I need to phone the man who purchased the Hong Kong Braniff."

Joanne picked up the phone and called the number that Fujita had given her. A few words were exchanged and Joanne stopped the call.

"He wants to meet me now."

CHAPTER 54

Hong Kong, May 30, 23 days

Chen and Zao waited in the car as Joanne entered the dimly lit Shin Shen Gallery. Teng's assistant greeted her and brought her upstairs where Teng was in his office on the phone. Seeing the visitor, he cut the call short and rose to greet her. Joanne introduced herself, explaining that she represented Pierre et Fils in New York.

Teng gave a gracious smile. "Yes, Ms. Farnsworth. I've been expecting you. How can I help?"

She explained how she had viewed the Braniff that was going up in auction at Sotheby's and was interested in whom he had purchased the drawing from.

"As I recall the name of the individual was Stratton." He looked at his assistant.

"Is that your recall?"

"Yes, Stratton was the name."

Joanne made a mental note. "Did either of you observe anything special about how he looked or where he was from?"

Teng answered: "I thought he was English, but I don't know where he's living now. We have been waiting for him to send us his address. He was clean-shaven, thinning hair, well-dressed. We did not spend a lot of time together. He told me he was representing the owner who received the drawing as a gift from the artist, which explained why it was uncatalogued. I bought it at a reasonable price and believe that we will get a very competitive bid when it goes up at auction. I can't tell you more than that."

Can't or won't, Joanne thought. She looked at the assistant, but he gave no response. Seeing there was no more to be learned, she thanked them, told them she would be at the Bishop Lei Hotel and left a number where she could be reached.

*

It didn't take long. Joanne was having a drink at the hotel when her cell rang.

"Joanne Farnsworth?"

The call was from Teng's assistant. "Mr. Teng has gone for the day, but I looked through our security tapes on the day Stratton came to our shop. Would you like to see them?"

*

A taxi dropped Joanne off and Teng's assistant welcomed her. "I found the surveillance footage of the gentleman you inquired about. I can't make out his face and the video is not of the finest quality, but I thought you might be interested."

The assistant began the playback while Joanne made a copy on her computer.

"Here is where he enters the shop and here he is speaking to me," the assistant narrated as the video played. "This is where I went to find Mr.

Teng, and there's the two of them speaking. Now they are going up to Teng's office. I don't have that on camera."

Joanne interrupted. "I can't see his face."

"I'm sorry, but this is all we have. It seems he never looked into the security camera the entire time he was here."

Joanne continued her viewing. "And that's him leaving?"

"Yes. That's all we have. Just shadows of his back."

The disappointment was obvious. "Can you play this again, maybe we missed something."

The assistant pressed replay.

Suddenly she pointed to the screen. "Did you see that?! Play it again."

They played it again. "There, something happened. Do you have a slower speed?"

The assistant replied "I can only go a little slower."

"Wait, I think I can." She went to the program that Jeff had shown her and reviewed the replay. "All I see is that when he comes into camera view his hat is pulled over his face. Now I see him raising the package in his left hand."

"Yes," Chen's assistant observed, "but it's blocking his face, as if he is purposely avoiding the camera."

"Yeah, pretty clever. He knew exactly where the camera was."

The playback continued. Joanne pointed her finger at the screen. "Look at that. Did he stumble when he came in?"

The assistant replied, "Maybe he tripped on the step up. I keep telling Mr. Teng to make an incline rather than a step or at least improve the light."

Joanne agreed. "This fellow was so busy shielding his face from the security camera that he never saw the step."

The assistant pointed to the screen. "Yes, but then what happens? Play it again, but go slower."

Joanne went to a frame by frame and her eyes lit up. "Wow, no question."

The assistant nodded. "You're right. He trips on the step, falls forward, and holds onto his package with his left arm."

She replayed the last frames. "And he seems to be throwing out his right arm to break the fall against something." Kate pointed to the screen. "But then what?"

She replayed it. "He's putting his finger to his mouth."

"Yes, and then he takes out a handkerchief and holds it on his finger."

"But we don't have a face. In other words, we have no idea what this person looks like."

The assistant felt badly. "I'm sorry."

Joanne was in thought. "I need to speak to Dr. Moss." She made the call and heard a tired voice on the other side of the world.

"Hey, can't you let a man sleep around here?"

"Sorry."

"I need to get up anyway. How's it going?"

She explained the situation.

"OK, email the part where he trips and we'll go through it together."

It took a few minutes for Jeff to receive the frames.

"Got it." Jeff played the tape.

"Why is he holding the handkerchief to his hand during all these frames? What happened?"

Joanne tried to find an answer. "Because he cut it?"

Jeff studied the frame. "That's what I'm thinking, but on what? It's just a blur."

Jeff played it back, but they couldn't make out the object that cut his hand.

"I'm going to walk over to the entrance and try to retrace his steps."

Joanne went through the exercise. "There's nothing here to cut anything on."

Teng's assistant called out. "Wait, that's where Pu-tai was."

Jeff called out. "What did he say?"

Joanne looked at the assistant questioningly: "Pu-tai? Who's Pu-tai?"

"I mean the Buddha. He must have cut his hand on the Buddha."

"What Buddha?"

"We had a statue of a Buddha here. In fact, Stratton bought it, or to be correct, Mr. Teng gave it to him as a gift for bringing us the drawing. We were going to send it to him, but he hasn't given us an address yet. It's stored in the lower level ready to be sent."

"Jeff, did you hear that?"

"Yes, OK, maybe we don't need to see his face. Here's what I want you to do. Take a look at this Puta – see if you can find any blood from the guy's cut. If there's a problem, have one of the technicians from Dr. Koo's lab come over to examine it. Maybe he can find a remnant. He'll know what to do."

Joanne didn't understand. "OK. I'll see if I can find anything. By the way, what's the tech going to do?"

"DNA. Bring it back to me safely and I'll do the rest. We'll find out who sold these copies."

And, she thought, where I can find Keith.

Joanne turned to the assistant. "He wants me to look at the Buddha."

"Sure, it's in the basement down the hall. Let me just put the cartridge back into the camera."

Joanne walked down the hall, past the steps that led up to Teng's office and toward the rear of the building.

She called out. "Not much lighting here."

"I always tell Teng to improve it but he never does anything about it."

She stopped by a door, opened it, and walked onto a landing. "Is it down here?"

Joanne heard the assistant running down the hall. "Stop. Don't go there!"

Joanne looked down a long dark stairway. "I hope we don't have to go down there?"

"Please, Ms. Joanne. Don't stand there. The landing's OK but some of the steps have some rot – so you must be very careful – big fall."

Joanne backed out of the stairwell and the assistant closed the door.

"I've asked Teng to seal the door permanently, but he says if he did it would be a fire hazard violation. Now we bring everything up and down by the rear elevator."

He continued to the rear and she followed. "You sure you need to see it? Your clothes are going to get very dirty."

Joanne was not ready for this. "Dirty? Now that I think about it, this may not be the best time. Do you mind if I come back in the morning? Anyway, I need to bring someone who can help me look at the Pu-tai."

The assistant hesitated. "I don't think Mr. Teng will let me. I could lose my job if he found out."

Joanne opened her handbag and counted out 200 American dollars from her wallet. "I would appreciate your help. It will only take a few moments. We just want to look at it."

"I don't know. Mr. Teng has an early morning appointment and I can't let him know about this."

Joanne pressed the bills into his hand. "I can get here very early."

The assistant looked at the fistful of dollars. "How early?"

CHAPTER 55

Hong Kong, May 31, 22 days

At ten to five Chen and Zao met Joanne outside the hotel and drove to Teng's shop. It was still dark, and the streets that were so congested during the day were completely empty, except for the calls of stray cats roaming for their daily meal. Bags of garbage, yet to be collected, lined the sidewalks, and the odor of dead fish permeated the air. The only sign of life was a black Mercedes parked several shops down the street.

"If you don't mind, I'll wait in the car."

Zao smiled at his friend. "Get some sleep, Chen. We shouldn't be too long."

Teng's assistant unlocked the door. "Glad you got here." They took off their coats while Teng's assistant relocked the door and disappeared down the hallway. Five minutes later he was carrying a heavy package. Zao cleared a table and wiped it down with a moistened towel from the large bag that he carried and carefully removed the wrapping from the Pu-tai.

"Your Pu-tai is freezing."

"The stone floor of the basement is two levels down where the temperature is always cold."

"That could be helpful." Zao carefully removed the statue from its thick cardboard carton. "Dr. Koo is very concerned about contamination in his lab. Even the slightest misstep could cause errors." Slowly he removed the soft cover cloth enveloping the solid stone and placed it on a nearby table, washed his hands with soap, and dried them thoroughly on towels from his technician's kit. He completed the protocol by putting on a clean lab coat over his street clothes and placing his hands into sterile latex gloves.

The Pu-tai was now standing alone. Zao took out a high intensity flashlight and a 4X magnifying lens and began a visual examination of the entire surface, especially in the area of the Buddha's left arm where Joanne assumed the injury took place.

"We've got something!" Zao pointed to the sharp edge of the Buddha's left shoulder. With the Nikon he began taking images of the statue from all sides, including close-ups of the specific area. He then attached a cable from the Nikon to his computer and transferred the images. Slowly Zao examined the areas, increasing the resolution to 5 megapix.

"There it is, a red stain on the corner of Pu-tai's shoulder. We've got what we came for – a drop of dried blood."

Zao turned to Joanne. "The surface of this stone seems quite non-porous so I'll need to lift the blood off with an adhesive material." While he looked through his kit, he spoke to Teng's assistant.

"It's good that you stored the Buddha in a cool, dark place because sunlight and heat could degrade the specimen."

Joanne was watching as Zao did his work. "How long can the blood be there and still be of value?"

"With proper techniques, we've seen successful analysis after thirty years of storage. Dr. Koo told us that frozen specimens of mitochondrial DNA of bones, teeth, and hair can be analyzed after hundreds and even thousands of years."

*

Hong Kong, May 31, 22 days

The door to the parked Mercedes opened and a man, wearing a dark trench coat walked toward the car standing in front of the Shin Shen Gallery and knocked on the driver's window.

"Who you waiting for?"

Chen opened his eyes from his nap and saw the man at his window. "What?"

"Who you waiting for?"

Chen noticed the large scar down the left side of his face, sort of like a corkscrew in his cheek. He didn't notice the skin-colored latex gloves.

Chen opened the door. "Hi. I'm waiting for some friends. They should be out . . ."

Chen never finished the sentence. The man pulled open Chen's door and without a word silently drew his blade deep across the front of Chen's neck, the blood from the carotids pulsing out as if from a hose, splattering the windshield.

The man slammed the door shut. "Hey, your windshield's dirty. Better turn on the blades."

*

Zao took a piece of fingerprint tape and placed the sticky side down on a clean part of the Pu-tai and transferred it to a piece of plain white typing paper. Then he placed the "lift" into an envelope and marked it as a control. He then duplicated the technique with a new piece of fingerprint tape over the blood stain on the Pu-tai's arm and placed the paper into a separate envelope, sealed and labeled it. He placed both marked envelopes into a small insulated lab container.

Zao flashed a big smile. "That's it, Joanne. All done." He handed the container to her. "Bring this back to New York. As long as you keep it dry and at room temperature on the trip there'll be no harm to the DNA."

*

Teng's assistant heard the knock on the door.

"You expecting anyone?"

Zao brought up his smile, the light reflecting off his white teeth. "Must be my friend Chen. He's been waiting out in the car. Tell him we're almost done."

The assistant opened the door.

"Your friends will be right out."

The man shoved the door open knocking the assistant against some antique lamps that crashed to the floor. Joanne and Zao looked up and saw what was happening. "Call the police."

The intruder ran toward Zao but tripped over the step, sprawling to the floor. The assistant got to his feet, picked up the broken lamp and swung it at the fallen man, but it didn't faze him. He reached into his pocket and pulled out a gun. One shot through the skull and the assistant was down. Zao took out his cell and made the call. The man picked himself off the floor and ran toward Zao who tried to defend himself, but it was no match. The man picked him up and threw him like a rag across the store, crashing into the antiques.

Joanne raced up the stairs into Teng's office, looking back just as the intruder began to follow. She threw a chair down the stairs but the man swept it aside. She picked up a pole lamp and swung it at him just as he reached the top step. He teetered backward for a moment but regained his balance. She had to get away. As she ran toward the rear, her arm struck the electrical circuit box on the wall. Instinctively, she threw open the cover and snapped the switches to the off position. The lights went off and they were in the dark. She had to find a way out. She tried to make her way through to the back but couldn't see, bumping into dark shadows everywhere. Behind, she heard the man stumbling in the dark after her.

"You're making this very difficult. Just tell me where Keith is and what you're doing here and I'll let you go."

Joanne didn't know which way to turn. Dawn was arriving, but there wasn't enough light coming through the windows to see. Then she realized she had a light. She pulled out her cell and turned it on, the glow revealing a hallway that led to the rear of the building. She ran down the hall, but the man must have seen the light. She heard a shot and then another, the bullets hitting the antiques on either side. At the end of the hall, she found a stairway and raced down, slipping on a step and sliding down the staircase. She couldn't stop her fall, the back of her head being thrown against each step, her cell phone lost in the blackness. The man was catching up, she could hear him at the top of the stairs. She felt dizzy, her head aching, and when she tried to stand a pain in her left ankle became excruciating. She placed her hand to the back of her head and felt the wet stickiness of oozing blood. She had to get up. He started down the stairs. She struggled to stand, pulling herself up while holding onto the banister. She tried to walk, but the pain was intolerable. She managed to limp down the hallway, looking back to see that his outline amidst the darkness had reached the bottom of the stairs and coming after her. She couldn't keep going. She put her hand out and felt a doorknob. She could hear him right behind her. She held onto the knob and stepped aside. As he was about to reach her, she swung the door open as hard as she could, slamming it into his face, stunning him. He fell backward, just enough time for her to enter the door. She stood on the landing trying to see in front of her, looking down the stairs. She didn't know what to do or where to go, like an animal caught in a trap and about to die. And then she remembered what the assistant had said about the stairway. She slammed the door shut behind her and moved as far to the side of the landing as possible so as not to be seen. It was pitch black. She stayed still, afraid to move, her hands clenched in her skirt pockets, afraid to inhale, her weight on the good leg. The man opened the door and took a step inside. She heard his breathing, smelled his sweat, not knowing what to do. He tried to make out where she had gone as the morning light began to make its way through the outer windows. Her mind tried to work, but the pain was blocking her other senses, until her fingers felt the coins. As if by reflex, she let the coin drop, meeting the basement floor with an empty ring. The intruder turned his head downward and saw the shadows of the stairway. He hesitated, then began to step down. "Now I got you. And when I find you, you'll not be happy."

She couldn't hold her breath any longer. Slowly she exhaled, the pain in her leg incessant. He had already gone down about eight steps when she was forced to take a deep breath. As she tried to put some weight on the other leg the floor creaked. He stopped to find the sound, turned, and saw her struggling to open the door.

"You bitch!" He charged back up the stairs as she managed to force open the door. Suddenly she heard a snap, like wood splintering, and then a scream that ended in a loud crash. She waited but heard nothing. She leaned against the wall, trying to take the weight off of the bad leg and listening for a sound. There was only silence. Suddenly the lights went on. She accustomed her eyes and looked down the two levels to the basement. Sprawled on the stone floor was a motionless body.

"Joanne, you here?"

It was Zao. *Thank God.* She started to cry, her whole body shaking, unable to gain control. She made her way down the hallway toward the entrance door, holding on to the tables on either side of the hall. "Zao, I'm here."

"You OK?"

"I'm alive."

He realized she was in shock, her head bleeding and an ankle swollen like a balloon and too painful to touch. And then they heard the sirens.

"You better get out. You don't want to get involved with the Hong Kong police and what went on here this morning. I'll tell them what happened. Get to Dr. Koo at Tianjin Hospital."

He almost forgot. "Wait a minute." The sirens were getting closer. He searched the area where they were last standing.

"Found it. Better take this with you. It's the DNA." He gave her the container and helped her on with her coat. She draped her arm around his shoulder as he helped her out the door. She shuttered when they passed Teng's assistant's body lying in a pool of blood. When they reached the street, they saw Chen slumped over the wheel in his car. Zao walked her away from the lifeless figure and continued a short distance down the block.

"That was no robbery. That man was after you. Why?"

Joanne was wondering the same thing.

"You gonna be OK?"

"I guess so."

"Find a taxi and get to Dr. Koo, Tianjin Hospital. I have to go back. I have to see Chen. Remember, Dr. Koo, Tianjin Hospital."

She managed to walk a short distance as the police pulled up to the store. Her final memory was seeing Zao speaking to the police.

BOOK VII

CHAPTER 56

Hong Kong, June 2, 20 days

"How is she?"

Dr. Yih-Lin Koo brought Jeff into his office. "She was lucky. The people who found her said she was lying on the street repeating my name and Tianjin Hospital. When I realized who she was, I called you immediately."

"I caught the next plane to Hong Kong."

"She lost quite a bit of blood, but the x-rays were negative. She's got a pretty bad sprain. Our orthopedists put her in a soft cast. She should be fine in a few weeks."

"What happened?"

"It's a little cloudy, but seems like a robbery. They found the killer. He must have fallen down two levels onto a rough stone floor, his skull was fractured. But I'm afraid I lost my dear Mr. Chen. He has been with me for many years. They also found the shop assistant with a bullet in his head. Forensics told me the place was a bloodbath. At least Mr. Zao and Joanne are still alive."

"I'm so sorry."

"Best to take her home." Koo walked over to a refrigerator. "Better take this." He handed Jeff the container. "The people who found her said she wouldn't let it go until they got her to me. It's your DNA sample."

CHAPTER 57

New York, June 3, 19 Days

Joanne was exhausted. It wasn't just from fatigue but from the narcotics she was taking to control the pain. Kate had stayed with her since DeLordet called to advise her of Joanne's situation. When she finally awoke, it was already noon, and in spite of her condition and Kate's caution she insisted on knowing what had transpired over the past hours. She played back the phone messages that had been left while she was gone, erasing most of them and then she asked for her laptop.

"You sure you're up to this?"

"I'm not sure. All I can remember was dreaming about Keith and trying to find him."

She flipped through her emails until she saw Goodwin's name. He had copied her the email he had sent to DeLordet regarding the origin of the passage written on the back of the Baniffs.

"I think we've solved your puzzle. With the additional words you sent us, Peter simply put every other word together."

Earth trembled from her entrails, as again pangs,
    and Nature gave a second groan;
Sky loured, and, muttering thunder, some sad drops
Wept at completing of the mortal sin Original

"The phrase comes from Book IX of *Paradise Lost*. I suggest you contact the Milton Society here in New York. Dr. Keith Jessup lectures to us each year and is one of the finest Milton scholars in the world. He should be able to tell you what you need to know."

When she saw Keith's name, she only wished it would be that easy. Everything that happened was to find him, but she realized she had gone as far as she could go.

"Kate, I need a big favor. I'm going to be out of commission for a while. How much do you remember about John Milton?"

*

New York, June 3, 19 days

Kate returned to the office and reread Goodwin's email. Keith Jessup! Great. If he's working at the Milton Society, what's he doing on a missing persons list?

She called the Society and heard a voice on the other end, "Milton Society."

"Hello, this is Kate Harrigan. Dr. Goodwin suggested that I call for some information. May I speak to Dr. Keith Jessup?"

"Dr. Jessup? Dr. Jessup hasn't worked here for several months."

"He hasn't? I mean, would you know where he is?"

"I'm sorry, but we have no forwarding information. Perhaps you would like to speak to our executive director, Niles Janeway. He's not in at this time, but I could make an appointment for you."

"Thank you, that would be helpful."

*

ME's Office, June 3, 19 days

Jeff went to the ME's Lab and showed Tom the container with the envelopes. "I've got a blood sample for a DNA analysis. What's the waiting time these days?"

"Could be a week or more. We're swamped with samples, and every other good lab is also."

Jeff knew the statistics. The backlog of cases waiting for DNA analysis around the country was shocking. In spite of hundreds of millions in government grants, the country had made little progress in catching up. Most labs never even qualified for the grants, and if they did, never spent it, at least not for DNA analysis. In New York City, the situation was much better. With Stan in charge, they were able to almost completely reduce the backlog of more than 17,000 sexual assault and homicide cases. But elsewhere in the country over 400,000 open cases remained, many from sexual assaults and many already beyond the statute of limitations. Once that happens the perpetrators could not be prosecuted.

Tom continued, "And I hesitate to schedule you in front of someone on the waiting list. Some politico is just waiting to get his name in the headlines: *Innocent person remains in jail, or murder committed by criminal awaiting arrest because DNA analysis delayed.*"

Jeff looked at his associate. "I get the message."

"When I see it on the schedule, I'll give you a call."

*

"Joanne?"

Joanne clenched her fist around her cell. She couldn't forget the voice.

"What do you want!"

"We tried asking you nicely for the whereabouts of your boyfriend. We even met you in Hong Kong. What you did was a very bad thing. There will be retribution."

Joanne heard the dial tone. She remembered Keith telling her how Milton was put on a death list.

A cold sweat broke out over her body. Now she understood how that must have felt.

CHAPTER 58

New York, June 4, 18 days

Kate was in DeLordet's office speaking to her boss when Jeff walked in.

"Doctor Moss, I'd like you to meet Kate Harrigan. She will be our contact for you on the case while Joanne is recuperating."

Jeff couldn't help but notice her. She was in her early thirties, with long brunette hair worn down, spilling over her shoulders, and her skin was tanned to a golden brown.

DeLordet continued, "So the phrase is from *Paradise Lost, oui*? Very interesting. Tell me, Doctor, what about the Hong Kong DNA?"

"Still waiting for the analysis."

"And Kate, any relationship between the forgery and Milton?"

"Only that Joanne mentioned that both Keith and his professor were Milton specialists. Milton is in this somewhere."

"Did you set up that meeting with the Milton Society?"

Kate nodded. "End of the week."

Jeff added. "And I'm thinking along the lines of the forensic psychologists. If the verses from *Paradise Lost* are really a confession, let's find out who's doing the confessing."

DeLordet stood up. "Yes, and whoever did would have knowledge of today's art scene. Someone who appreciated the value of such a piece."

"And," Jeff added, "would have to know how Keith acquired it."

"Exactly." Kate pointed out. "They have to know the history. I mean if they knew that this was a personal gift that was never recorded or ever seen, then they could make as many copies as they wanted. It becomes that much more difficult to deny its authenticity."

Jeff agreed. "Then who knew the history?"

Kate gave a slight shrug to her shoulders. "I guess we did and Keith and Joanne, but who else?"

DeLordet looked at her. "Give Joanne a call. She may know."

*

New York, June 4, 18 days

There were several rings and then a message.

"This number is no longer in service. If you believe you have the correct number, please dial again." Kate tried several times. There was no mistake. She tried calling Manhattan information but no other number or address was listed.

That's weird. I was with her two days ago.

She called Jeff and they went to Joanne's apartment on the Upper West Side, but no one answered the bell. They rang the superintendent.

"We're looking for Joanne Farnsworth. Do you know where she might be?"

"Moved out yesterday, no forwarding address, no contact number. Real sudden like, so I figure some emergency must have come up because she wasn't in the best of shape. Told me to put everything in storage and left me a check."

They walked out onto Columbus Avenue.

"She couldn't have just disappeared?"

"Keith did."

"But why did she?"

Jeff recalled the telephone threats, the attempted murder in Hong Kong.

"Because she had no choice."

*

June 4, 18 days

Keith completed his research on Menasseh Ben Israel's book *Mikveh Yisra'el*. The question, of course, was why would the name be found in the 1674 edition of *Paradise Lost*? The book, written in 1650, told of the discovery of Israel's Ten Lost Tribes in South America. Ben Israel had brought a copy with him to England in 1655 and dedicated the Latin edition of the book to the English Parliament in hopes they would give Jews permission to resettle in England. *But why would the name be found in a copy of Paradise Lost?* Keith wasn't sure, but he had to start somewhere and he had only eighteen days left. The first question was: *were there any copies of the book to be found after 350 years?*

*

Kate met Niles Janeway at the Milton Society and mentioned that she was referred by Dr. Goodwin.

"Of course. Dr. Jessup lectured at the Seminary several times a year. We offer that service to a number of institutions. Keith was a top Milton scholar and editor of our *Quarterly Review*."

"Was?"

"Unfortunately, several months ago Keith left us and we haven't heard from him since."

"I see." Kate was trying to find the pieces without giving away the puzzle.

Janeway looked at her. "Was there something specific you wished to ask me?"

Kate took out a copy of the verse that was on the back of the Braniffs. "Could you help interpret this verse?"

As Janeway read the verse, Kate added, "I believe it's from the ninth book of Paradise Lost."

"Well," Janeway said as he reached for a copy of *Paradise Lost*, "let's take a look."

> *Earth trembled from her entrails, as again*
> *In pangs, and Nature gave a second groan;*
> *Sky loured, and, muttering thunder, some sad drops*
> *Wept at completing of the mortal sin Original*

"This is how Milton described the world's response when Adam ate the fruit that Eve picked from the Tree of Knowledge, resulting in Original Mortal Sin."

"So the earth trembled in response to Adam's sin."

"Without that sin, we would be living in Paradise, not Manhattan. And look at the three lines before it:

> *She gave him of that fair enticing fruit*
> *Against his better knowledge, not deceived,*
> *But fondly overcome with female charm*

"The meaning remains the same as then. Good men, give in to temptation, for whatever reason, be it a woman's charms as here, or greed, or

Satan himself."

Kate thought about the verse. "So Adam knew exactly what he was doing."

"Milton says it was '*with full knowledge and no deception.*' As they say on Broadway: 'the guy only did it for the gal.' Oh, he knew exactly what he had done, for when God called out his name, didn't Adam try to hide?"

Kate concluded. "So, regardless of fault, it caused the universal fall, and each time someone sins against God's commandments, the world has the same reactions, although we may not be aware of it."

Janeway went to his computer. "That's one interpretation. I have several articles from past Society Quarterly publications that might be of help. After that, if you have further questions, I'll be glad to review them with you."

Janeway returned with a large envelope containing several journals. Kate placed them in her briefcase, thanked Janeway, and took the first taxi she could find back to her office.

CHAPTER 59

New York, June 5, 17 days

DeLordet's concerns that Pierre et Fils was involved in an art forgery had increased. Jeff tried to assure him the investigation was proceeding smoothly.

"The DNA identification of the individual who sold the Hong Kong Braniff is much more accurate than any fingerprint could be. Fingerprinting is, at best, ninety percent accurate. DNA doesn't make mistakes."

DeLordet asked, "Once you have the result, what do you compare it to?"

"We'll check our database to see if there's a match, otherwise, we'll have to wait until we find a suspect that we can match it with."

Kate interjected. "Any chance of my observing that?"

"Shouldn't be a problem."

"What about the Hong Kong video?"

"No help. Whoever it was had their back to the camera the entire time. We see a figure, we see it's a man, and we see his movements. But we have no pictures of his face."

DeLordet was speaking methodically, as if trying to hold in his rarely evoked frustration.

"And, what happened with the Milton quote?"

Kate reported that she had met Niles Janeway at the Milton Society, how the name of Keith Jessup had come up, and how he had suddenly left his position as editor. Kate opened her briefcase and handed him the journals from the Milton Society.

"Janeway explained that the quote describes how the earth shook when the original sin was committed."

DeLordet sat back with his hands under his chin.

"This man is not a professional thief. He may be a talented artist, but when he committed his crime, his earth trembled, and he heard heaven's cry. Whoever executed the crime is a tortured soul. If one can feel pity for a sinner, feel it for him. What could have caused him to do it?"

There was no response.

DeLordet stood up and walked to the window. "Did you get a hold of Joanne?"

"We don't know where she is. She moved."

"Moved?" For the first time that Kate can remember DeLordet raised his voice. "Then find her!"

*

New York, June 5, 17 days

"I don't have any other number."

"Keep looking. There has to be something."

Kate looked through Joanne's resume. "All I can tell you is that her family lived in the Boston area. I have no idea if they still do."

"Then let's find out." Jeff called the ME's office, spoke for a few moments, and hung up. "They'll get right back."

Within five minutes Jeff's cell rang.

"OK, there are four Farnsworth's listed in the Boston area. I don't know which one, but we have to start somewhere."

They made the calls.

"Dead end. No one knows a Joanne Farnsworth. If her parents were living in the Boston area before, they're not there now."

They sat for a moment trying to figure what to do next.

"Wait. That's not her mother's name."

Jeff looked at Kate. "What do you mean?"

"Joanne had Carlos frame a painting for her. She had it sent out for a family Christmas gift. Let's find out where it was sent."

She went into the delivery files prior to the holiday.

"Mr. and Mrs. Kevin McNichols. Right, she had mentioned her mother remarried several years ago."

"What's the address?"

Jeff wrote it down. 816 Jennings Avenue, Swampscott, Massachusetts.

"If I'm correct, Joanne won't be answering any phone calls."

BOOK VII

CHAPTER 60

The sign for "816 Jennings" was attached to the black mailbox of a large white colonial house on a street lined with other such houses. Towering old oaks, swaying willow trees and colorful gardens filled the green acres on which the homes were located. The affluence of the neighborhood was obvious, with landscape and service trucks in every driveway transporting lawn mowers, plumbers, electricians, and dry cleaning deliveries.

Kate and Jeff were met at the door by the housekeeper. The McNichols were not at home, but would be expected in several hours.

Kate took a chance. "When will Joanne be back?"

The woman looked long and hard at the two of them. "Who may I say is calling?"

"Kate Harrigan. I worked with Joanne in New York, and this is Dr. Moss, who helped treat her ankle."

The face relaxed. "Oh, I see. Yes, I believe she went to a doctor's office about that ankle. She should have been back by now."

"Do you mind if we wait for her?"

"That should not be . . ." The housekeeper looked up and pointed to a car coming down the block. "That's her now."

*

"Kate, Jeff, what are you doing here?"

Joanne parked her car in the driveway. Jeff noticed the limp as she walked toward them.

"We need to speak to you. I see you're walking a lot better."

"I'm feeling much better, thanks to you and Dr. Koo. I just saw the orthopedist. He said my ankle should be much better by next week. How did you find me?"

"Kate checked the address where you sent your mother the Christmas gift."

"Clever. I hope no one else thinks of that."

"You left New York in a hurry."

"They called again. Same ones that came after me in Hong Kong. I had no choice – I had to get out. I didn't know what else to do."

Tears welled in her eyes and she reached for a tissue in her pocketbook. Finally, she took a deep breath and a deeper exhalation.

"I'm sorry, but this is really getting to me." She placed the tissue to her eyes and tried to focus. Jeff understood the seriousness of the situation. "You better call the police and explain what's happened. You're probably safe here, but be careful."

"They think I know where Keith is."

"You still haven't heard from him?"

"Not a word."

Jeff asked gently. "Did he leave a note?"

"It doesn't say much."

"Can I see it?"

"Sure. It's inside."

As Joanne walked back to the house Jeff called out. "Joanne, did Keith ever draw?"

As she opened the door she called back. "He's one of the most talented artists I've ever met."

*

Joanne returned with a copy of the letter. "And one more thing. Keith once threw away a note he received. I asked him about it, but he said it was only a joke. I kept it because it didn't seem like a joke."

Jeff slipped Keith's letter into his pocket and read the note:

TO: Keith Jessup.

You had been advised not to pursue the Manuscript for health reasons. We hope your trip to Sheffield was for other purposes. That was a great deal of money you spent on an old edition of *Paradise Lost*. We certainly hope it was worth it.

"Milton again."

Joanne had questions in her eyes. "What does it mean?"

"I'm not sure, but we're going to find out." Jeff put the note down. "Call me if something comes up."

"I will. Thanks. Thanks for being such good friends."

*

On the drive back, Jeff gave the copy of Keith's letter to Kate to read:

Dear Joanne,

Forgive me but I am no longer able to keep you safe from all my woe. I will not be joining you today. You spoke about being true to yourself and so I must go to find that truth. I'm afraid it is best that I no longer exist. Be careful of strangers who want to know where I am.

I love you,

Keith

> *When I consider how my life is spent,*
> *Ere half my days in this dark world and wide,*
> *And that one talent which is death to hide*
> *Lodged with me useless, through my soul more bent*
> *To serve therewith my maker*

Kate folded the letter. "What are we going to do?"

"I need to call the ME's office. Some very intuitive colleagues can get me a DNA analysis of Keith's saliva. Then we're going to review our English Literature."

CHAPTER 61

New York, June 6, 16 days

Janeway led them into the Milton Society library. It was a beautiful room having two levels, with the central area of the ten-foot ceiling above them cut out, giving the classical feel of twenty-feet of height. Rich leather chairs and darkly stained wooden tables were placed around the lower level. The perimeter of both floors were lined to the ceilings with mahogany bookcases neatly filled with the works of masters, and ladders that rolled on casters attached to reach the higher shelves. It was a room for scholars. Janeway explained that the library was only open to Society members and, at times, to students. Through the years, thanks to the largesse of several wealthy individuals, they had invested in a number of rare first editions of the period and now had one of the finest collections of early English literature in the United States.

Kate looked admiringly at the room. "It's a little jewel."

Janeway smiled. "Thank you. We're very proud of what we have accomplished."

"Do you keep all your books here?"

Janeway shook his head. "No. We keep our special edition books and manuscripts in a separate room. It's windowless and made out of double-shell construction with a specially designed computer controlled air-filtration system."

Jeff was impressed. "It must be difficult to preserve them."

"We try. The system maintains the temperature at sixty degrees Fahrenheit and the relative humidity at 45 percent. Perhaps you'd like to see some of our most prized Milton pieces."

Janeway and an assistant returned within minutes, carrying several old but well preserved books.

"These are three of the earliest editions of *Paradise Lost*." Janeway pointed to each of them as he slowly opened to the title page. "This one was published in 1667, the very first edition, with a simple cover. The second one is a 1674 edition, a little more substantial cover. These were the only two published while Milton was alive. And the third is the beautiful 1688 edition that the publisher went all out to sell. Milton probably began formulating the poem in the early 1650s and completed its writing, or at least its dictation, by 1665 when it was submitted to the official licenser for clearance to be published."

Jeff was curious. "You mean books had to have official clearance?"

Janeway nodded. "Absolutely. The government had tight control of all publications to prevent anything critical of the state. But probably due to the revolution in England and especially with London in turmoil, the 1667 book was approved. I don't think the censors interpreted it as being as radical as many of us have."

Jeff was becoming interested. "In what way was a poem about the Garden of Eden radical?"

Janeway looked up, his face becoming serious.

"Dr. Moss, *Paradise Lost* is not just a poem about Adam and Eve. For those who truly understand it, it is a severe criticism of the King, the Anglican Church, Christianity, a brutal attack on Catholicism, and, whatever else might be holy, and, in my opinion, all due to Milton's reaction to the failure of the Puritan Revolution."

Jeff was apologetic. It was almost as if Janeway was personally involved. "I wasn't aware of that. The first edition must be worth quite a bit."

Janeway's smile returned with pride. "Milton didn't think so. We have a copy of the contract that Milton signed with his publisher on April 27, 1667. Milton was paid five pounds for the publishing rights."

Kate looked surprised. "That's all?"

"The publisher was afraid that the government might arrest him, so Milton took what he could get."

Janeway gently closed the cover of the first edition and continued: "*Paradise Lost* was Milton's crowning achievement, and modesty was not one of his traits. Milton wrote in his introduction to the first edition that his poem was intended to go well beyond what Homer or Dante wrote in their epics, and most believe he succeeded. As John Dryden wrote in his poem 'On Milton.'"

Janeway quoted the verse by heart:

> *Three poets, in three distant ages born,*
> *Greece, Italy and England did adorn.*
> *The first in loftiness of thought surpassed;*
> *The next in majesty; in both the last.*
> *The force of nature could no further go;*
> *To make a third, she joined the former two.*

Jeff whistled softly. "So Dryden felt that by putting together the great poets Homer and Dante, it would equal Milton. Now that's special."

Kate gently ran her fingers over the cover of the 1667 edition. "I don't blame you for preserving them so carefully."

"Actually, Kate, the installation of our environmental monitoring system was insisted upon by our last editor, Keith Jessup. In fact, all of these copies of *Paradise Lost* were purchased because of Keith, or I should say, by Keith."

Kate was amazed. "Keith Jessup purchased this for the Society?"

"Well, technically he's loaned them to the Society. While he was here, he attended a number of sales and examined many early editions of Milton's works. I don't know what drove him, but once an early edition was posted for sale on the internet, he would follow up immediately. Of all those evaluated, he only purchased these three."

"Why these?"

Janeway shrugged his shoulders. "I often asked, but he wouldn't say. I'm not sure he knew. Keith was an unusually dedicated and devoted scholar who probably had a better sense of who Milton was than anyone

I know. Sometimes we thought he even was Milton and, I daresay, I think he did also."

Janeway thought for a moment. "We miss him."

They were thinking the same thing.

Jeff and Kate examined the treasures in front of them. Without question the 1688 edition was the most beautiful, and by far, the heaviest. They agreed that each of them would read one of the editions to get a feel for Milton again. As they turned the pages to the opening lines it was like a time machine, transporting them back 350 years to when *Paradise Lost* was written. By the time Jeff finished the 1667 edition, he was tiring. He drank some cold water and tried to regain his energy. He didn't have to wait long. As he opened the cover of the 1674 edition, his body came to attention. He rubbed his eyes, looked again, and tapped Kate's shoulder, and with a little too much emphasis said, "Take a look."

She leaned over to see what he was reading.

PARADISE LOST.

BOOK I.

 F Mans First Disobedience, and the Fruit
Of that Forbidden Tree, whose mortal taste
Brought Death into the World, and all our woe,
With loss of EDEN, *till one greater Man*

"The first letter. It's the same calligraphy as on the back of the Braniff drawings. I didn't see it on the 1688."

Jeff checked. "You're right. Only the 1674 has it."

"I wish we knew a little more about Keith."

Kate picked up the Spring copy of the Milton Society *Quarterly*. "We can read his editorial."

FROM THE EDITOR'S DESK
Paradise Gained and Paradise Lost:

Dear Friends,

What a sincere privilege to be involved in editing your Journal with
the awesome responsibility of carrying on the tradition that began
in 1767, on the one hundredth anniversary of Milton's first publication of *Paradise Lost*. Perhaps, someday, a Milton Manuscript
will be found that will help us understand the mysteries that lie
within Paradise. Someday we will understand how Milton justified
the ways of God to man.

Until next time,
Keith Jessup
Assistant Editor

Their thoughts coincided. It certainly didn't sound as if he was planning
to leave.

"But where is he?"

CHAPTER 62

Yeshiva University, June 7, 15 days

"Mr. Hartlib, good to see you again."

Keith entered Shenken's office. "Rabbi, I've tried to find a first edition
of Ben Israel's book, *Mikveh Yisra'el*, but without success. I was hoping
you could help."

"And Yeshiva University doesn't have a copy?"

"I spoke to your librarian as well as the one at the Jewish Theological
Seminary, but they have no knowledge of any original copies remaining.
I checked the internet and found nothing."

Rabbi Shenken sat back in his desk chair and thought for a moment.
"The only thing I can do is ask Rabbi Lecht."

The rabbi glanced at his watch, checked his small address book and
punched in a number on his cell phone.

"There's a seven-hour difference between New York and Jerusalem.
I'll put us on speaker."

"Shalom, Rabbi. It's Zevulen, in New York."

"Ah, Zevulen, *ma sh'lomcha?*"

"*Baruch HaShem*. I have Mr. Hartlib here and he's looking for Ben Israel's book, *Mikveh Yisra'el*? Do you know if there are any remaining first editions?"

There was a pause. "I don't know for sure. I was never able to find one, but if you could trace the family, it might have been handed down through the generations. I suppose you have to start in Amsterdam." There was a pause on the line . . . . . "Perhaps there's one other possibility, a man named Cyril Reich, a British Scholar and historian who taught at the City University of New York. He passed away a number of years ago, but if you ask around maybe you could find a lead."

Rabbi Shenken penciled the information and passed it to his visitor. "By the way, Mr. Hartlib, if I find out any more information, is there some way that I can reach you?"

The visitor looked up and thought for a moment. "Rabbi, for now that would be impossible."

*

Of the two choices, tracing the genealogy of Menasseh Ben Israel from 1657 or Cyril Reich who taught at CUNY in the 1960s, Keith chose the latter.

The internet quickly told him that Reich had not only taught at CUNY but had even written a book on Ben Israel. He called the school's administrative office to see if they had any further information on Reich. It was suggested he speak to a Professor Martin Braun.

*

New York, June 8, 14 days

Martin Braun had taught at the school for forty years and still gave one seminar each semester. He agreed to meet Keith at the university. He was a short, stocky man in his early seventies with grayish balding hair.

"I remember Cyril very well. I was a student of his in the early sixties and we became friendly. He was a true scholar and wrote a number of history books. He lived for a while here in New York with his family. He has a son Steven, a physician. I believe he was teaching at Albert Einstein Medical School the last time I saw him."

Braun went over to an old brown Rolodex file and began flipping through.

"I haven't spoken to Steven in several years, but let's see what we can come up with."

Braun called the number he had and it was met with an answering machine.

"Steven, Martin Braun here. Hope you've been well. I'm with a Mr. Hartlib who would like to speak with you. I've given him your number."

*

New York, June 8, 14 days

Keith called first thing in the morning and after a few minutes of discussion, Reich invited him to his home on West 78th Street.

It took fifteen minutes to find a parking space on the correct side of the street without fear of being given a hefty New York City ticket. The building was a four-story twenty-foot wide brownstone on a tree lined block not far from the Museum of Natural History. Keith walked up the faded brown cement steps and rang the bell.

Steve Reich was a runner – Keith didn't even have to ask. Thin and of medium height with brown hair and a broad smile, he was the kind of physician with whom you immediately felt comfortable.

Reich put out his hand. "Mr. Hartlib, please come in, Steve Reich."

They walked into the living room, comfortably appointed with a shaggy gray area rug, leather sofa and chair, and filled bookcases lining both sides of the room.

"You were asking about a book written by Menasseh Ben Israel?"

"Yes. He wrote it in Latin in 1650 called *The Hope of Israel, Mikveh Yisra'el* . . . Have you come across it?"

Reich thought for a moment and shook his head. "Not that I recall, but my father accumulated a large collection over the years. While my mother was still alive, we donated most of my father's collection to a university."

Keith looked at the large number of volumes in the bookcases. "What university?"

"The Reich Collection is at Leeds University in the UK. My father was born in London and after fighting in World War I, graduated from the City of London School and read history at Merton College at Oxford, where he received his PhD in modern history. He concentrated his studies in Jewish history."

Keith was fascinated. "I wonder if they have the book I'm looking for?"

Steve went to a desk drawer and removed a thick volume of papers bound in a soft transparent cover.

"Here's a catalogue of what is, or at least, was in the collection. Leeds recently ran into some financial problems and they put some of the material on sale to raise cash. I don't know if the one you're looking for is included."

When Keith browsed through he found 119 pages listing over 800 individual documents dating back to the twelfth century, encompassing Jewish history, prayers, commentaries, marriage contracts, and hundreds of letters between Jewish communities around the world.

"You can take the copy with you and if you contact Leeds I'm sure they'll tell you which of the collection is being sold." Reich thought for a moment. "By the way, if I find anything further, how do I find you?"

Keith looked at Reich as if trying to make up his mind. He realized there had to be a way for him to be contacted. Finally, he wrote down a number. "Please treat this as a doctor-patient relationship."

*

Once Keith was back in his room he began to go through each of the entries to determine if *Mikveh Yisra'el* was included in the collection. Slowly but surely he made his way down the list:

```
#1. Services for Day of Atonement according to the
Italian or Roman rite, 15th century.
  1 volume (135 ff.); 240 × 170mm; 23 lines to a page;
vellum.
  The original velvet binding and boards are kept
with the recently-conserved volume in a custom-made
box covered with brown cloth.


#286. Certificate in Latin issued by the Rector and
Senate of the University of Leiden, Holland, on 31
August 1758 to the Sephardi Jew, Isaac Henriques
Sequeira, conferring upon him the degree of Doctor
of Medicine, signed by five members of the Senate,
including the Academic Rector, the Promoter, and the
Dean of the Faculty of Medicine, with a large red
seal attached.
```

Finally he came to #633.

```
Author     Menasseh Ben Israel, 1604-1657.
Title      Mikveh Yisra'el
           Mikveh Yisra'el, Esto es, Esperança De
           Israel. Obra con suma curiosidad conpuesta
           por Menasseh Ben Israel...Trata del admi-
           rable esparzimiento de los diez Tribus...
Published  En Amsterdam. En la Imprension de Semvel
           Ben Israel Soeiro. Año. 5410 [1650]
```

CHAPTER 63

Leeds, UK, June 10, 12 days

Flight 0178 on British Airways out of JFK brought Keith into London's Heathrow at noon, and then a Jet2.com flew him the 190 miles north-northwest into Leeds Bradford Airport. Sundstrom was waiting at the gate.

"Sorry I'm late. Bad connections."

The professor looked long and hard at the new arrival.

"So, you're the new Samuel Hartlib."

"I am, with a new address and phone number." Keith wrote the number on a piece of paper and Sundstrom entered it into his cell. "I hardly recognized you. That beard makes you look different. I confused you with one of our rock stars."

"They have beards as long as mine?"

"No, you're right. You look more like a rabbi."

"Probably because I've spent quite a bit of time with rabbis."

"And their relationship to *Paradise Lost*?"

"It's proving more important every day."

They walked out of the terminal and toward the low cost parking lot.

"Are you in trouble?"

"Afraid so. Same group who killed Livingston and Reynolds. Same group that came after me the last time I was here."

"And they're still after you."

"Yes, but hopefully now they have no idea where I am. I've dropped out for a while." They walked toward the far lot. "Are you still teaching that course on the influence of early Christianity on English literature?"

"First semester every year for twenty years."

"What do you know about Stigmata?"

Sundstrom was surprised at the question. "Stigmata? Why do you ask?"

Keith stopped walking and grabbed Sundstrom's arm. "Because that's what they did to them."

Sundstrom's eyes widened in bewilderment. "My lord, who are these people?"

As they walked toward the car, Keith pursued his question. "Where does the term come from?"

"Stigmata first appears at the end of Saint Paul's Letter to the Galatians where he says, *I bear on my body the marks of Jesus.*"

Keith pounded his fist into his hand. "Those bastards. They're still murdering in the name of the Lord?"

Sundstrom continued, "Galatians is the ninth book of the New Testament. It's a letter from Paul to the early Christian communities in the Roman province of Galatia, now part of Turkey. In the letter, Paul is responding to an argument between his beliefs and . . ."

Sundstrom paused in midphrase.

"And what?"

Slowly he finished his sentence: "and Mosaic Law."

Sundstrom looked at his friend. "Do you realize we're back to your original thought?"

Keith nodded slowly. "Yes, questioning the interpretation by Milton scholars that *Paradise Lost* is based on Pauline theology, where the Law of Moses no longer leads to salvation."

"Yes, but it's more than that, much more. Hear me out. Apparently Paul visited the pagans of Galatia to spread the gospel and even established several churches in the area, but after he left, those churches disregarded Paul's teaching of faith-based salvation and reverted back to salvation based on Mosaic law."

Keith interjected. "So they rejected Paul's theology?"

"Yes, that's why Paul's letter was written with such anger, accusing the Galatians of turning against his preaching and listening to 'others.'"

"What others?"

"Most believe these 'others' were 'Jewish Christians' who taught that for pagans to belong to the people of God, they must be subject to some or all of Jewish Law. Paul's letter accuses them of observing the Sabbath, the Mosaic Covenant, and especially circumcision which, like Abraham, they believed was God's transmission of that holy covenant."

Keith quickened his pace, his mind spinning with the information until Sundstrom grabbed his arm.

"Will you slow down, I'm trying to get in shape but I'm not yet ready for the Olympics."

Keith complied. "So you're relating the stigmata to the dispute between Mosaic Law and Paulian Theology?"

"That's where it was first used."

Keith stopped, as if in deep thought. "Is that why they recreate stigmata on their victims? To let us know they'll punish anyone who contradicts Paul's theology. Does that mean anyone who would reveal –"

Sundstrom completed the thought. "What *Paradise Lost* is really based on."

Keith looked at his companion: "So the Manuscript must disclose that the poem reveals that the battle between Mosaic Law and Paul is won not by Paul but by Moses and the Law. That would mean that Milton didn't believe that Jesus preached to annul the Law of Moses."

They reached the car and as Sundstrom drove out of the airport, he looked at his colleague.

"I think we just found that *Paradise Lost* is no longer just a Christian poem."

Keith looked at his friend. "You always said that alone could cause a conspiracy."

CHAPTER 64

Leeds, UK, 2:18 PM, June 10, 12 days

They drove in silence reviewing in their minds the significance of their thinking when Sundstrom called out: "Milton sure relied on Moses when it came to divorce!"

Keith was surprised at the intensity of the outburst. "Good point. Milton based his thoughts on marriage and divorce directly from Deuteronomy in the Old Testament."

Sundstrom glanced at his passenger. "He wrote that emotional stress and incompatibility was as sacred a reason for divorce as any other."

Sundstrom almost shouted. "Mental cruelty! That's what they call it today!"

Sundstrom swerved off the road and stopped in front of an old inn. "I need a drink."

Keith had never seen his friend react like this. "Hey, take it easy. I agree with you. Milton argued that since Christ's mission only spoke of moral law, not judicial law, Milton espoused that Mosaic law prevailed. Again he disagreed with Paul."

They sat at a table in the middle of the room, and Keith continued, "Jesus said it quite clearly. He came not to do away with Mosaic law, but to *vindicate them from abusive traditions.* He was a reformer, not a revolutionary."

Sundstrom remained silent, his mind lost to another world. Keith raised his hand to get the waitress's attention. "One on tap and one iced tea."

Sundstrom's fingers played on the table top, finally speaking in a soft, almost confessional voice. "I know Milton's *Doctrine and Discipline of Divorce* by heart. He was way ahead of his time, but he also believed that natural order dictates that the husband was the master and the wife the servant."

Sundstrom paused for a long, serious moment. "It didn't work in my house."

It took a moment for Sundstrom's smile to come back. "I should have realized that when Milton's first wife ran to her father's home soon after the wedding and didn't return for weeks."

Keith smiled. "Sounds like a tough guy to get along with."

The waitress placed the order on the table and Sundstrom took a long drink, then sat back and wrapped his hands around the cold mug.

"But brilliant. Milton dared to ask what few ever asked before: Would you rather have divorce or adultery?"

Keith was beginning to understand where the outburst came from. "So this is from personal experience?"

Sundstrom stiffened. "'Tis a sore subject, me boy, but you're damn right. You see, my wife picked up my copy of *Doctrine and Discipline of Divorce* and turned to the page where Milton wrote *that the chief end God intended in marriage was the cheerful conversation of man with woman.*"

Keith pressed the iced glass to his cheek. "Because he believed that ideal marriage should conform to the classical definition of friendship – more of an intellectual and collegial arrangement."

Sundstrom added. "That was the problem. Milton tried to change marriage from fulfilling physical and reproductive needs to one of cheerful conversation."

Sundstrom, continued, letting his impish smile appear: "And so did my wife – eighteen years ago."

A long silence and Sundstrom's smile waned. He lowered his voice which became serious in tone and he spoke slowly. "I have a son. His name is Richard. He was five when she left and took him away. Moved to the States where her sister lived. I've only seen him once since then. I've tried to reach out, but I guess she wouldn't let it happen. He was a little boy then. He's twenty-three now."

Sundstrom paused and then laughed quietly. "Funny about God's ways. Perhaps some day we will reconnect. I received a letter from him not long ago. He wants to come over and spend some time with me. Amazingly, he's interested in English literature."

Keith saw a side of his friend he never knew about. *To have a son and not see him. It must be like living in continuous pain.* "And you never chose to remarry?"

Sundstrom leaned forward, his smile quietly returning. "I could never get the voice of Oscar Wilde out of my mind. *A second marriage is merely the triumph of hope over experience.*"

"You've got that right, dearie."

The scholars looked up to see the droll face of the waitress peering down at them. They smiled at each other as she handed them the check.

Keith put a few pounds on the table as Sundstrom continued: "Milton's views on divorce caused him to be attacked unmercifully by the Christian churches, and by the man who would become his archenemy, William Prynne."

Prynne, again, Keith thought. *His name keeps coming up.*

Sundstrom kept his smile. "Speak to Bartholomew about Prynne. He's a big fan."

"But Prynne hated Milton. Contradicted him on every issue."

Sundstrom smiled as he turned on the ignition. "Too late for me. I sent my wife Prynne's arguments countering Milton's thinking on divorce, but by the time she read them, if ever, she had already left."

*

They parked in the library's visitor section and walked to the front of the Parkinson Building which houses the Brotherton, Leeds University's main library.

"What are we doing here?"

"Following up on a book I may buy."

"Another one?"

They walked up the steps and were directed into the central catalogue room where they were greeted by one of the administrators.

"Ah, yes Mr. Hartlib, we were expecting you. The room housing the Reich collection is upstairs in our rare book section. I'll take you there. And take one of our Leeds Library bags, we give them to all our readers."

Keith looked at the bag – it was imprinted with a large white "Sshhh . . . !"

They followed the administrator up to the rare book area. *Mikveh Yisra'el Esperanca De Israel, The Hope of Israel,* by Menasseh Ben Israel was waiting for them.

"I believe this is what you were interested in, a first edition published in Latin in 1650." She placed the thin volume on the table in front of Keith. "I also have several later copies of English translations."

As Keith looked at the book, the administrator added. "I must tell you that no one has ever asked for this title, until today."

Keith shot her a hard look. "What do you mean?"

"Someone else called for the same edition. I'm expecting them later."

Sundstrom was surprised. "Who else would be looking for this?"

Keith had a worried look as he looked around the empty room. "Maybe I'm not as alone as I thought."

He looked at the administrator. "What time is their appointment?"

"In about an hour."

The two scholars looked at each other and Keith began examining the book, thumbing through its pages, checking its binding, covers, and frontispiece. He put it down, thought for a moment, then picked it up and slowly looked at it again. Finally, he motioned to the administrator.

"I'm afraid this is not what I'm looking for. Sorry to bother you."

As they stood to leave, the administrator returned holding another book. "Might you be interested in this? It's also a first edition of *Mikveh Yisra'el* but not for sale."

Keith opened the cover to the signature page. He looked twice as if to confirm what he was seeing, then turned to Sundstrom. "Look at this!"

The signature page contained a note under the heading:

PUBLISHING HOUSE OF MENASSEH BEN ISRAEL
Amsterdam
January, 1677

For Daniel Skinner:
Final copy of *De Doctrina Christiana* as requested and under separate cover return of edited and deleted pages; enjoy MBI's book.

Keith stared at the message. What final copy? What edited and deleted pages?

He turned to Sundstrom. "Where did you say Daniel Skinner sent *The Christian Doctrine* to be published?"

"To Daniel Elsevier, in Amsterdam, but it was too outside mainstream Christian thought to be published."

"And Elsevier never did."

Sundstrom responded: "Never, especially after Sir Joseph Williamson, who was responsible for licensing all publications in England, threatened Skinner with a lawsuit if it was published."

Keith tapped his pencil lightly on the desk. "So what did Skinner do?"

"He traveled to the Netherlands to talk Elsevier into changing his mind, but he refused. Elsevier even wrote to Skinner's father telling him that he would never 'think of such a horror of printing the defense of so wicked and abominable a cause . . . that he would never print a book so detested by all honest people.'"

Keith was totally engrossed: "So the young Skinner gave up?"

Sundstrom shook his head. "No. During his stay in the Netherlands he continued to look for other publishing companies. Remember, by the late 1500s Amsterdam was already the leading publishing center in Europe."

Keith reread the book's note and outlined his thoughts: "And one of them was the publishing firm of Milton's rabbi, Menasseh Ben Israel!"

Sundstrom was surprised. "Ben Israel had a publishing firm?"

"In Amsterdam, called the Printing House of Menasseh Ben Israel. In fact, on January 1, 1627 it was the first Amsterdam firm to publish a book in Hebrew."

Sundstrom sat back and listened, enjoying the lecture.

"And because of that, Amsterdam and "Amsterdam type" became the standard for Hebrew typography and the center of Hebrew publishing throughout the world for the next 200 years."

Sundstrom looked admiringly at his colleague. "So that's where this note comes in."

"Yes. Skinner must have explained to the Ben Israel firm the rejection by Elsevier and the threats by Williamson, and asked if the firm would make the *De Doctrina* suitable for publication. Because of Ben Israel's prior relationship to Milton, the firm must have agreed to help, but that to pass the censor it would need significant editing."

Sundstrom thought through Keith's logic. "But the Ben Israel group must have advised Skinner to see a magistrate in London about his personal liability, given Williamson's threatened lawsuit. Skinner must have agreed."

Keith nodded. "So the deed was done. According to this note, the offending pages were removed, major editing was completed and then the new *Christian Doctrine* was sent back to Skinner along with this copy of Menasseh's book as a gift."

Sundstrom made a few notes on a pad. "That explains the question our group couldn't answer. The handwriting analysis revealed that the first fourteen chapters were scribed by Skinner. What we couldn't figure was how Skinner would dare rewrite what the great Milton wrote. Now I realize he didn't, he merely neatly recopied the rough draft containing all the edits and deletions that the Ben Israel firm had made."

Keith responded. "That explains why the first part of the work appears 'finished,' because that was the part that needed to be rewritten, the part that defined Milton's concepts of God and Christ and Christianity. It was also the chapters filled with Milton's most heterodox thoughts whereas the second deals with prayer. One's individual prayer is not controversial, but the representation of basic theology can be roundly criticized, so the deletions and major rewrites only had to be done to the first part of the book The second part, copied by Picard, was filled with edits, corrections, and marginal notes, but nothing to suggest heresy, so it remained exactly as received."

Keith nodded. "And Skinner then brought the purged *De Doctrina* back to Elsevier to be published, Milton's watered-down *Doctrina*."

Sundstrom agreed. "But Elsevier was still not interested in becoming involved with controversy, and that's when Elsevier returned the *De Doctrina* to Skinner's father. He didn't trust sending it to the son."

"But at least we see why it took so long for Elsevier to return the papers to Skinner's father. It wasn't the cold winter that prevented the ship from returning *De Doctrina* over the winter, as scholars have thought, it was that Skinner had given them to the Ben Israel firm."

Keith paused while he put his thoughts into perspective. "But what did Skinner's father do with the book?"

"He sent it to Williamson, the censor, to keep his son out of trouble."

Keith completed the logical exercise. "And Williamson buried it, never to be published and, he assumed, never to be read again. But why was it buried under a pile of papers regarding the Popish Plot?"

They looked at each other thinking the same thing. *Was this coincidence?*

Sundstrom broke their thinking. "I'm not an expert on Williamson. Let's check him out."

They went online. What they found nearly floored them.

Williamson was arrested for being implicated in the Popish plots, but was released that day by the order of the king!

They looked at each other. *Williamson was involved in the Popish Plot?* Things quickly began to come together.

Keith scrolled down the screen. "Williamson was like the head of our FBI, he was Chief of Security, and made a fortune while he was at it. He became obsessed with anyone plotting against the king, and during the Restoration, England was rife with intrigue, especially the rumor that Charles II and the King of France plotted to make England Catholic again. And one of Williamson's obsessions was preventing *The Christian Doctrine*, or anything written by Milton that was religious or political in nature, from being published."

Keith recalled the two books displayed at the New York Public Library that had been banned by the orders of Charles the Second. "After all, Williamson served at the pleasure of King Charles, and the King had already banned Milton's political papers from being published in 1660."

Sundstrom followed. "But when Williamson brought Skinner in and read him the riot act, telling him that if *De Doctrina* was published he would have him tried and thrown in jail, what do you think Skinner did?"

Keith answered. "Skinner told him he had hired a magistrate to defend him, Sir Edmund Godfrey, who would help him publish the book."

Sundstrom chimed in. "So that's the tie in with the Popish Plot. Williamson must have hired some Catholic army officers who were beholding to him to get the *De Doctrina* back from Godfrey."

Keith interjected. "But he never had the book. So when Godfrey resisted, they killed him and tried to make it look like suicide. It was only later that Elsevier returned the purged *De Christina* to Skinner's father, and by the time Skinner senior sent it on to Williamson, the murder was a fait accompli."

"Do you think the king knew about the murder?"

"He certainly knew that Williamson was involved in stopping the publication of *The Christian Doctrine*."

"So the king was involved from the beginning?"

Keith sat back. "That would certainly explain why the king never took the Popish Plot seriously. He knew all along what really happened to Godfrey."

Sundstrom let out a slight whistle. "Well now. For God and Country. No wonder someone doesn't want this to get out. This is super scandal."

Keith was surprised at Sundstrom's remark. For God and Country? Isn't that what Bartholomew declared was the reason for the conspiracy. Was preventing the Manuscript from being published all to protect the church and king from the people learning the truth? Cover up!

Keith sat back pensively for several moments before speaking privately to the administrator.

"I think I will buy the Ben Israel book that's for sale."

While the purchase was being finalized, Keith asked, "When Leeds received this book from the Reich estate, was there anything else that came with it? A package of papers, perhaps?"

The administrator thought for a moment. "No, everything was extensively catalogued. If you didn't find it catalogued, then it's not part of the collection that we received."

Keith received the package, checked the time, and walked over to Sundstrom. "We better get out of here."

*

Shortly after, a tall, older gentleman with a full head of white hair and his younger associate were escorted into the room housing the Reich collection in the rare book section of Brotherton Library at Leeds University. The administrator recognized him immediately.

"Professor, a pleasure to see you. Unfortunately, the edition of *Mikveh Yisra'el* that you were interested in was purchased only a few minutes ago. I'm so sorry."

CHAPTER 65

Leeds, UK, 3:25 PM, June 10, 12 days

Keith and Sundstrom returned to the car with a great deal to think about.

"But what about the Manuscript? You've only told me about *De Doctrina*."

Keith looked at his friend. "While Milton was dictating *De Doctrina* could he also have been dictating the Manuscript?"

Sundstrom shook his head. "At the same time? How? Milton was in the midst of writing *Paradise Lost* while he was composing *De Doctrina*. To write a third manuscript at the same time would have been impossible, even for a blind Milton."

Keith came to an abrupt stop. "Unless?"

Sundstrom looked at his colleague. "Unless what?"

"Unless we've been wrong from the beginning."

"I'm listening."

Keith's eyes widened and a broad smile appeared. "Unless the Manuscript was part of the *De Doctrina*!"

"Sorry, old chap, don't think I'm following."

"The missing pages."

"Meaning?"

"Remember what the inscription said. 'Final copy of *De Doctrina Christiana* as requested and under separate cover return of edited and deleted pages; enjoy MBI's book.' Skinner received not only the 'religiously correct' version, but also the removed pages of the *De Doctrina*."

Sundstrom's smile broadened. "So that's what this conspiracy is about."

Keith leaned back. "Yes, those excised pages, those containing the most dangerous of Milton's thoughts, that is what comprises the Milton Manuscript!"

Sundstrom spoke softly, "And what we now have, what the world now knows as *De Doctrina* is Milton's original sans the objections."

"You mean the *De Doctrina* sans the Milton Manuscript."

"And that's what this Stigmata has dedicated themselves to preventing from being found? For what? What significance could Milton's attacks on Christianity have today?"

Sundstrom looked at his colleague. "Well, maybe the soul is making a comeback."

They reached the car and Sundstrom started the engine.

"I once told you that the best moment in a teacher's life is when his student becomes the teacher. You are giving me my best moments."

Keith placed his hand on Sundstrom's shoulder. "Thanks for your help."

Sundstrom pulled out and began the drive back to the airport.

"So some day you'll have to tell me about that book, *Mikveh Yisra'el*."

They drove the remainder of the trip in silence. When they reached the airport, Sundstrom parked in front of the sign for DEPARTING FLIGHTS to let his passenger out.

Keith looked at his mentor. "Why don't you read it for yourself."

He handed the package to Sundstrom. "It's for you."

Sundstrom was genuinely moved. "For me?"

"For being such a good friend and teacher."

Sundstrom was almost brought to tears. He spoke in a quiet raspy whisper. "Thank you. You've made me very happy."

As Keith exited the car, Sundstrom called out.

"So where are the missing pages?"

"I'm about to find out."

"In the States?"

"I'm betting on it."

"Good. Because I'll be attending the Tanzer Lecture at Harvard and we're all counting on you having the answers. That means you've got twelve days. Perhaps then we'll get together with my son. I'll read the book you bought me and give it to him as a gift. Maybe he'll see his old father's not such a bad chap after all."

"I'll second that. And once this mess is cleared up, I'm going to ask a very special woman to marry me – and if she says yes, I'd like you to be my best man."

Sundstrom looked at his friend. "I'd like that. I'd like that very much."

*

Sundstrom took his time driving home. He had never felt so complete, both personally and professionally. The day had been so special, and he looked forward to being part of one of the great discoveries in literature. When he reached Oxford, it was already evening. He parked the car, picked up his new gift, and walked to his apartment. As he opened the door and turned on the light, he was met by two visitors. Sundstrom was taken by surprise. He looked at the older one. "What are you doing here?"

"Why, Foster, I simply wanted to see your recent purchase. I'm sure it's most interesting. But I'm afraid you've become too involved with seeking the Manuscript."

Sundstrom turned to face the other visitor, the one with red hair. "So, it's you again. Haven't you caused enough damage?"

The corners of Abaddon's mouth widened into a diabolical smile as he stared at Sundstrom. Then, without warning, he rushed at Sundstrom and crashed his fists over his head, the rings on his fingers being forced into the professor's cranium. Sundstrom fell to the ground, covering his head, the blood already seeping onto his hands.

"What are you doing? Please, don't . . . not today . . . it's been such a wonderful . . ."

Not another word was spoken – there never would be. Foster Sundstrom was found the next morning, severely beaten. The coroner would note that he had nails through his hands and ankles, branded into his cheeks were the letters *S* and *L*, and a scribbled note: *Stigmata*.

BOOK VIII

CHAPTER 66

"I haven't seen you two in days. I figured you gave up." Janeway gave Kate and Jeff a big smile.

"Not at all. We've been reading up on Milton. I think we're ready for your graduate program."

"You could spend your time with a lot worse. When you have a chance, you should read our latest newsletter. Without Keith we decided to go to a monthly two-sided, one-page format. Actually, it was a combination of no Keith and no money. But we unexpectedly received a major gift of over three million dollars and we are already looking for a new editor. The new funds will also enable us to return to our old eight-pager. I'd be glad to put you on the mailing list."

They sat down and began their readings with a much greater understanding.

By lunchtime, Jeff's eyes were closing. He slid a final article in front of Kate with a note: *You read this. I'm tired and hungry.*

Kate smiled and wrote back. *So am I. I'll read it if you take me to lunch!*

*

The sky was clear, the sun bright, and the temperature rising as they stepped into a nearby luncheonette on 27th Street and ordered ice coffees and tuna salads.

Kate tapped her straw on the table and removed the paper. "I think we better focus on what we know."

"We know that Keith was an artist, that he had access to the Braniffs, that Joanne must have told him they were not catalogued, that he disappeared while the originals were at his home, that the copies had the same mark as his 1674 edition of *Paradise Lost*, and in his letter to Joanne he said he got into some trouble. Now where does that leave us?"

Kate looked at Jeff. "Keith was the forger?"

"It sure seems that way."

Kate shook her head as if bewildered. "But why?"

Jeff turned his palms up. "Depends on what kind of trouble. Money's a good start. If he knew Braniff's story and he had the drawings, three million dollars is pretty tempting."

Kate thought for a moment. "I don't see money as an issue. I mean, here's a guy donating these rare books to the library, that's not someone who needs money." She lowered her voice. "You know what I think? Keith was afraid of something."

Jeff added. "Then why copy the Braniffs?"

Kate persevered. "Call it women's intuition, but even if he copied the drawings, why leave Joanne? They were best friends – and beginning to realize it was more than that. No, something else had to be involved. We're missing something."

Jeff looked at her. "What if Keith was forced to copy the Braniffs?"

"Blackmailed?"

"Maybe, and he was forced to give the copies to whoever was blackmailing him."

Jeff gently pursed his lips and continued. "It's like our psych guys say, but this time instead of wanting to be caught, he wanted the blackmailers caught. As soon as the forgeries were recognized, he knew there would be an investigation."

"And that's why he left his calling card?"

Jeff paid for lunch. "But one the blackmailers would never see."

"But a thorough investigation would."

*

They walked back to the Society Library. From a stack of newsletters, Jeff took two copies, brought it back to the table and handed one to Kate.

"This must be Janeway's revised one-page format. Hot off the press."

"He said they're hiring a new editor."

They perused the newsletter until Kate poked her elbow into his arm. "Take a look at this."

"Something interesting?"

"Mostly society news bits, but there are two "Letters to the Editor." One is from a member unhappy with the Society's cutback, but the other one discusses a Milton sonnet. Tell me what you think?"

Jeff read softly.

When I consider how my life is spent,
Ere half my days in this dark world and wide,
And that one talent which is death to hide
Lodged with me useless, through my soul more bent
To serve therewith my maker

Jeff stopped, confused. "Have I read this before? Was this in first-year English lit?"

Kate looked at him. "We've read it before, but not in class. It was in Keith's letter to Joanne."

She took the copy of the letter out of her briefcase and handed it to him.

When I consider how my life is spent,
Ere half my days in this dark world and wide,

"So Keith was quoting Milton in his letter. Who wrote this?"

Kate replied. "A Mr. S. Hartlib."

CHAPTER 67

New York, June 13, 9 days

Janeway looked through his files. "We just received this fellow's Letter to the Editor and thought it most insightful, so we printed it. Let me take a look. *When I consider how my light is spent, Ere half my days in this dark world and wide . . .* Sure, Milton is discussing his blindness to the Lord. It's Sonnet Nineteen, one of his most famous."

Jeff looked at the newsletter again. "But that's not what it says. It says how my *life* is spent."

Janeway took another look. "You're right. My mind automatically says 'light.' That's the correct word. This fellow miswrote the word. Must have been a simple mistake. We haven't even sent the newsletters out yet. I'll correct it. I don't even know who he is."

Jeff looked at Kate suspiciously while Janeway moved his fingers through the files. "He's got to be here, somewhere. Ah, here it is. Mr. S. Hartlib, 128 Bennett Avenue, Cambridge, Mass. There's no phone listed."

Jeff and Kate returned to the library.

Kate spoke softly. "The same mistake twice? Is the letter to the editor and Keith's note to Joanne coincidence or is something else going on?"

Jeff hesitated, as if trying to recall something. "S. Hartlib, why do I know that name?"

Kate was surprised. "You've heard of an S. Hartlib?"

"A something Hartlib, but where? I just saw it." Jeff thought for several moments then snapped his finger, drawing further looks from the other readers. Without a word, he walked from the room and ten minutes later returned with Janeway carrying a book. Janeway placed the book on the table and left.

"Take good care of it."

Jeff sat next to Kate. Carefully he opened the cover of the 1674 edition to look at the inside facing.

"That's funny, I could have sworn I saw something." He studied the page carefully.

"There it is." On the lower corner of the inside cover, next to the binding, written in light pencil, was "From The Samuel Hartlib Collection, Univ. of Sheffield," and next to it was a small pencil drawing of a key with the words: *Palpable obscure.*

Kate whispered. "You're becoming a sleuth!"

"Becoming?!"

Kate smiled. "Who's Samuel Hartlib?"

"Better ask Janeway."

Janeway was busy at his desk when they approached.

"That's correct, Keith purchased this book when he was at Sheffield. It was part of the Samuel Hartlib Collection housed there. It was the last volume of *Paradise Lost* that he purchased, and his favorite."

"But S. Hartlib was the name of the fellow who wrote the editorial."

Janeway stopped for a moment. "That must be a coincidence. The Samuel Hartlib Collection is named after a seventeenth-century educator. It contains a large amount of his correspondence with people throughout the world."

"And what about the key?"

"What key?"

Jeff explained. "Someone drew what looks like a key next to Hartlib's name with the words *palpable obscure.*"

Janeway was perplexed. "I think you better show me what you're talking about?"

Niles walked with them into the library and scanned the title page. "I've never seen this."

Jeff thought for a moment. "Why would this book be different from the others?"

"I'm not sure." Janeway spoke to the librarian and together they left the room, returning with the other first editions of early volumes.

Janeway sat down and examined the other editions. "There's no writing in these. Keith must have drawn it."

Jeff sat back in his chair in thought for several moments.

"Why? What's different about this edition?"

"It's the last edition published while Milton was alive. He died on November 8, 1674, less than four months after this came into print."

"What happened then?"

Janeway let out a small smile. "Actually, by 1688 there was a change in political attitudes, and Milton was openly hailed as a hero in the struggle for liberty. Within thirty years the poem was proclaimed England's national epic. Time and most people had forgiven Milton for his religious and political views." Janeway paused, turned aside and quietly added, "But not everyone."

Jeff looked at him inquisitively. "What do you mean?"

Janeway didn't realize that he had been heard. "Oh, just that some people have never forgiven Milton for the sins he committed."

Kate looked at Jeff for a moment, thinking how odd a statement that was.

"After all these years?"

Janeway looked at them, but chose not to answer.

"It seems to me," Jeff stated as he changed the subject, "that Keith thought something must be unusual about this edition. Of the hundreds of copies that he looked at, you say he bought three, and of those, this was his favorite."

Kate added, "And he drew a key next to it. Why?"

Janeway had no answer.

Jeff, almost by habit, gently guided his fingers over the outer and inner sides of the 1674 cover, as if able to see with his fingers.

"Mr. Janeway, do you mind if I examine this book more closely? I'll take a picture, but no flash. I think we'll find something."

CHAPTER 68

New York, June 14, 8 days

"I found something." Jeff showed the digitized images to Kate and Janeway. "When I gently moved my fingers over the cover, I felt something unusual. It's similar to feeling a pulse or differentiating a normal lymph node from an enlarged one. Under magnification I observed that the binding had been tampered with. When we focus on the edge of the binding it appears as if there's a space within it, like a pocket. Perhaps we can take another look at the 1674 edition."

Janeway retrieved the edition from the storage room.

"Mr. Janeway, I need to go inside the binding. I should be able to without disturbing anything."

Janeway looked at Jeff. "You want to do surgery on such a valuable possession?"

Jeff answered. "I think there's something in it."

Janeway picked up the book and looked at it from several angles. "What are you going to do?"

He handed the book back to Jeff who began his probing. "Don't worry, I won't disturb your manuscript."

Janeway abruptly turned his head toward Jeff. "The what?"

"The book. I won't harm the book."

Janeway hesitated, then a thin smile. "Oh, sure, go ahead, but you better have malpractice insurance."

Jeff took out a small periosteal elevator from his briefcase, a surgical instrument used to reflect the thin vascular tissue that covers bone. It had a pencil shaped stainless steel handle about six inches long. One end was scooped out to a narrow spoon that ended in a point, and the other had a thin, flat, rounded ending, designed to lift thin tissue without tearing it.

Janeway's anxiety was couched in a joke. "I hope you're not going to use the pointed end."

Jeff carefully placed the blunted end in the area suggested by his digital image. Gently he slid the flat end of the elevator under the edge of the binding, and slowly peeled back what looked like an outer covering.

"The outer binding seems a little frayed at its edges, as if someone had already worked on it. It seems like the two pieces are held by a slight adhesive, similar to Sticky Notes."

Jeff gently separated the outer portion about halfway down before it was bound tightly again, revealing that it was the outer cover of a pouch or envelope."

"There's nothing here. Whatever was here was removed."

Kate was disappointed. "But what about the key? Does it mean that Keith found whatever he was looking for?"

Janeway's face turned pale. He almost fell backward, grabbed for a chair, and slowly sat down. "Is this possible?"

Jeff looked at him closely. "Are you OK, Mr. Janeway?"

Janeway drew a long breath. His head was down and his body slumped. Kate gave Janeway a cup of water to drink, and Jeff had Janeway put his head down between his knees.

Janeway mumbled. "He found it."

Jeff and Kate looked at each other in bewilderment.

"What is it?"

Janeway shifted his weight. "I can't believe it. Keith must have found it!"

Jeff had no idea what Janeway was talking about. He looked at Kate. "Found what?"

Janeway mumbled again. "The Manuscript. He found the Manuscript."

Slowly, Janeway braced his hands on the arms of the chair and rose to his feet and looked at the two of them.

"Who are you?"

Jeff and Kate were trying to understand Janeway's reaction.

Finally Kate answered. "I work for Pierre et Fils here in New York."

"Pierre et Fils?" Janeway was trying to put it all together. "Why are you here?"

"We're examining an art forgery of the artist Braniff. On the back of the forged art was a symbol like the one that opens the 1674 edition and several lines from *Paradise Lost*. We're following up on that, that's all."

"You what?" For an instant Kate saw Janeway's eyes filled with horror. Slowly he walked away.

"Are you sure you're OK?"

Janeway never turned back.

CHAPTER 69

New York, June 14, 8 days

What happened?

"Classic stress."

Kate couldn't understand. "But what could have set it off?"

"Selye first described it as 'flight or fright,' and this was fright."

"Of what?" They had no answer.

Suddenly, Kate looked up. "Maybe that's what he was saying. Did you hear him? Something about a manuscript, 'he found the manuscript.'"

Jeff looked at her. "What manuscript?"

For a moment they had no answer, until, like a chanted Greek chorus, "Keith's Manuscript."

Jeff reached for the last Journal and read from Keith's editorial. "Perhaps, someday, a Milton Manuscript will be found that will help us understand the mysteries that lie within Paradise."

He went up to the front desk. "Do you know anything about a Milton Manuscript?"

The administrator answered. "Yes. That was our past editor's thesis. I can get a copy for you, if you'd like."

They looked at each other. "Keith again?"

The administrator retrieved Keith's thesis and they began reading.

"So Keith not only postulated that there was a manuscript, but he wanted to find it."

Kate answered softly. "Yes. But why in the book with Samuel Hartlib's name in it?"

"He must have recognized the name. Janeway said he was an educator who corresponded with everyone. Let me check it out."

Jeff slipped into a chair behind one of the computers. After several minutes he walked over to the books lining the room. It was fifteen minutes before Jeff asked Kate to read the screen.

"This fellow Hartlib corresponded with the most brilliant people in the world, at least the Western Hemisphere. But until the 1930s, his correspondence was lost. The whole collection was given to the University at Sheffield."

Kate smiled. "Remember the note that Joanne had saved. It mentioned Sheffield. That's what Keith was doing in Sheffield."

They read the online information:

Samuel Hartlib, 1600–1662, wished to record all human knowledge and make it universally available for the education of all mankind, making information more available at a time when most knowledge was not categorized or standardized.

Kate looked up. "Hartlib was the Google of his age. But what's the connection to Milton?"

"I'll show you." Jeff opened the book he had brought back from the shelf. "This is Milton's treatise *Of Education*. Look at the preface. Milton addressed it to a London gentleman by the name of Samuel Hartlib. Milton was part of Hartlib's circle."

Kate seemed confused. "But why look for the Manuscript when it was already found?"

"What do you mean?"

Kate opened Keith's thesis to the section on Conspiracy Theory. "Keith wrote that several scholars may have had knowledge of the manuscript, but they were prevented from revealing the contents."

"But why?"

Kate continued reading. "To defend it as the supreme epic of the English nation and all Christendom."

"Protect it from what?"

Kate continued reading. "From those who attempt to discredit it with false accusations."

"So, if the Milton Manuscript refutes the greatness of England and its church, then there are those who apparently will go to extreme measures to prevent it from being revealed."

Kate thought for a moment. "Perhaps that's what Janeway meant when he said that some people have never forgiven Milton for the sins he committed."

Jeff stood up. "So Keith became a victim of his own discovery. Maybe that's why Keith disappeared. Someone was after the Manuscript and Keith had to get away."

"But why was Janeway so reactive when he learned about Keith's discovery? You would think he would be pleased. Sounds like the most important find since Milton died."

Jeff shrugged. "I'm not sure, but something scared him."

"What do we really know about Janeway?" Kate walked out of the library, and returned with a pamphlet, *The International Milton Society: What and Who We Are*. She turned to the bios on staff members.

"Jeff, look at this: Janeway traces his family back hundreds of years. He must be from one of the oldest families in England."

> Executive Director: Niles Prendle Janeway. Mr. Janeway was born in Cornwall, on August 7, 1951, the son of Charles Ladmor Janeway, the former Executive Director of the Society, and grandson of James Taylor Janeway, the previous Executive Director. He completed his schooling at Devonport and proceeded to Cambridge. Mr. Janeway traces his parentage to the famous William Prynne, the English parliamentarian and son of Thomas Prynne by Marie Sherston, who was born at Swainswick near Bath in 1600 and died in 1669.

"Now, Prynne I've heard of." Kate quickly clicked on the link to Prynne.

"Prynne was not only a brilliant lawyer, but an angry rebel whose pen condemned anything he disliked. Initially he had views similar to Milton. He was an outspoken Puritan critic of Church excesses and the Court of Charles I, especially after Charles married a Catholic Princess. But his attacks on church policies and of the immorality of the Court of Charles I were so radical that in 1633 he was arrested, tried, convicted of sedition, and sentenced to imprisonment, a £10,000 fine, and the removal of part of his ears. That gives you an idea of who William Prynne was."

Jeff listened intently. "Sounds like he was more radical than Milton."

Kate responded. "And sure made everything more personal. If you crossed paths with Prynne's extreme positions, you better be prepared to deal with a man who either loves you or hates you. This says that when Milton wrote essays advocating more liberal divorce laws, Prynne was furious."

"So," Jeff added, "Prynne and Milton found themselves on opposite sides of the issue."

Kate continued to read. "And it became personal. When Cromwell appointed Milton as an official state translator, part of Milton's duties were to investigate subversive material. On June 25, 1650, Milton was ordered to search Prynne's rooms for evidence of treason. Nothing was found, but you can imagine Prynne's reaction to Milton's invasion of his privacy. After that the poison grew. Following the English Civil War, when Milton supported Cromwell and the Puritans, Prynne turned against Cromwell. When Milton defended the execution of Charles I, Prynne went ballistic and never forgave Milton for coming to the defense of regicide. Prynne was even expelled from Parliament and, in 1650, imprisoned for another three years by the Puritans. And when the Puritan Revolution failed and Prynne backed the Restoration of Charles II, it was Prynne who argued for the most severe anti-Puritan measures against the supporters of the regicide. It was Prynne who demanded that Milton not be pardoned from those who were to be executed because of their involvement with the death of Charles I, and it was Prynne who led the attack against the readmittance of Jews to England."

Jeff started to appreciate the whole picture. "So Prynne hated a lot of people."

CHAPTER 70

New York, June 14, 8 days

They needed a break and went across the street for a coffee and bagel.

"You know," Jeff said, "according to Keith's thesis, he postulates that there's a secret society formed to defend against Milton's heretical writings, who pass their objectives down from generation to generation. What if there really was such a group? And what if such a group continues to defend against those writings, especially the revelation of the Milton Manuscript?"

Kate sipped her coffee. "So?"

Jeff continued, "Well, who would have been the original person to demand such revenge?"

"Prynne?"

"It's just a stab, and I may be skipping some steps, but let's assume it really was passed down from Prynne or his descendants who wanted to preserve his heritage. Who in this generation is part of Prynne's lineage?"

Kate put her cup down. "Janeway?"

"Wouldn't that explain Janeway's reaction when he learned that the Manuscript was found? He kept saying 'Keith found it.' And it would certainly explain his saying that some people never forgave Milton, even 350 years later."

Kate thought for a moment. "Prynne will surely never forget."

Jeff looked at Kate questioningly. "What do you mean?"

"According to his bio, even when in prison he continued writing his vicious assaults against the government. He was tried a second time and in 1637 was sentenced along with two other radicals. The rest of his ears were removed with a hot iron, and his nose was slit."

Jeff leaned back in his chair. "And no anesthesia? No wonder he never forgot or forgave."

Kate continued, "I was thinking more about the branding."

Jeff shot her a glance. "What branding?"

"It's what they did to Prynne. They branded his cheeks with the letters *S* and *L*, *seditious libeller*."

Suddenly Jeff rose and cut her off. "Let's go."

He threw a ten-dollar bill on the table and taking Kate by the arm rushed out the door.

Kate tried to keep up. "Where are we going?"

"Back to the Society office."

"Why?

"Because I examined a body at the ME's office that was identified as a professor of Milton Studies. His cheeks were branded with the letters *S* and *L*!"

*

"Where's Janeway?"

The administrator looked up from her work. "He left a few minutes ago."

"Any idea where he went?"

"He didn't say."

Kate looked at Jeff. "I think we should meet this fellow Hartlib, he's our only clue."

"Then give me one minute."

Jeff walked into the library while the administrator spoke to Kate.

"You were asking about the Milton Manuscript. There's a note about it in this month's newsletter." She handed several sheets to Kate who put it into her handbag.

Jeff reappeared carrying a large envelope.

"What's that?"

"The cup of water you gave Janeway. Another DNA sample to get to the lab, then we'll visit Hartlib, maybe he'll have some answers."

*

New York, June 14, 8 days

The call from New York across the Atlantic was made at 9:30 AM from a cell phone.

"We've got a problem."

"You were instructed never to call this number."

"I had no choice. I believe he's found the Manuscript."

"I thought you took care of that!"

"I thought so also."

"Are you sure?"

"If he hasn't found it yet, then he's getting close."

"So you know where he is"

"I have a good idea where he might be."

"Then the problem must be eliminated."

"Yes, sir."

"Before anything gets out."

Yes, sir, I'm already on it . . . There's one other thing."

"And what is that?"

"The art that was sold was a forgery. It's already being investigated. It will not be long before it will be traced. He's made us vulnerable."

Silence was on the other end of the phone . . . and then a dial tone.

BOOK IX

CHAPTER 71

Cambridge, MA, June 14, 8 days

Jeff pulled off the Turnpike exit to Cambridge shortly after 2:00 PM and found a parking spot on Bennett Avenue halfway down the block from the house. Number 128 Bennett, in a different era, had been an elegant townhouse that over the years had been converted into several apartments. It was located in a modest but neat neighborhood, composed of row houses that had been renovated. They walked up the steps of the building and opened the door to the small vestibule where they found Hartlib's name listed next to the buzzer for 3C. Kate pressed the button and waited. It gave no answer. She repeated pressing but still no results. Finally she tried the superintendent's buzzer and crossed her fingers. A response came from the intercom.

"Yes. May I help you?"

Kate answered. "We're looking for one of your tenants."

As they waited, a man in a sport jacket with a full beard, cane and a Boston Red Sox hat opened the inner door and walked down the front steps, excusing himself after almost colliding with Kate. A moment later a slender young man with jet black hair appeared. He spoke in a clear British accent, but with his darker skin was more likely to have come from Mumbai than London. Jeff figured he was a graduate student at Harvard or MIT and helped earn his way through school caring for the building.

"We're looking for an S. Hartlib."

"Sure, one of our new tenants. Great guy." The super pointed to his left. "You just missed him. That's Sam walking down the block now. Everyone seems to be looking for him today. I told the other fellow the same thing."

"What other fellow?" Jeff asked.

The super looked down the block. "The one standing next to the white BMW across the street. He was asking for Sam. I'd say he's been waiting bout half an hour."

Jeff looked at the BMW. "Did he know what Sam looked like?"

"No. He asked me how he could recognize him and I told him that Sam usually wears a sport jacket, got a full beard, uses a cane, and has a Boston Red Sox cap."

Kate and Jeff looked at each other. "Any idea where he's going?"

"Probably for coffee on Mount Auburn Street."

Kate and Jeff started to follow when they noticed the man by the BMW disappeared from view.

"That's weird. He ducked behind the car as Sam walked by. I thought he wanted to see him."

Jeff watched as the person reappeared. "Looks like he wants to see Sam but doesn't want Sam to see him."

Kate pointed to the figure across the street. "But he's following him. Who is this other guy?"

Jeff kept his eyes on the figures in front. "Can't tell. The cars are in the way."

Hartlib walked with a limp, and every few minutes would glance behind him, as if checking to see if anyone was following. The man on the other side of the street was keeping low, as if trying to stay hidden alongside the row of parked cars; whenever Hartlib would turn, he would crouch down.

When Hartlib reached the corner of Mount Auburn Street he stopped, letting the traffic go by. At the same time the man from the BMW continued walking on the opposite side until he reached Mount Auburn.

Kate looked at Jeff. "What's he doing?"

"Keeping his eye on Hartlib."

When Hartlib began to cross the street the fellow from the BMW took a last look, then turned and walked back toward his car. By the time Kate and Jeff reached the corner, the BMW stopped briefly at the intersection and then turned, drove past Hartlib and continued on.

Jeff turned to Kate. "Now, did you see who that was?"

"But why?"

The driver was Niles Janeway.

CHAPTER 72

Cambridge, MA, June 14, 8 days

They followed Hartlib across Mount Auburn and watched him disappear into one of the storefront cafés.

"What was Janeway doing here?"

Jeff brushed back the hair from his forehead. "I guess he wanted to see Hartlib."

"But why? He didn't even know him."

"Maybe he does." He looked at Kate. "But let's find out."

"You're sure about this?"

Jeff smiled. "Hey, I know that sonnet cold. You're going to be impressed."

Kate answered quietly, "I bet."

They looked through the café's window. "There he is."

*

At four in the afternoon the Brewers Cup was empty. It was a dimly lit café with a dozen or so wooden tables with polished tops stained dark brown, the kind of place that students might go to hang out. Keith was standing at the bar against the far wall, pouring a cup of coffee from one of the several coffee urns carrying signs naming the variety of coffee beans. He was speaking to a young woman behind the bar, in front of a mirrored wall that held a sign that read "WiFi connected" when they entered.

Keith saw them through the mirror as they approached. "Mr. Hartlib?"

Keith turned, looking suspiciously at the visitors. "Do I know you?"

"Actually, no. My name is Jeff Moss and this is Roberta Stiles."

Kate shot a look at Jeff, but he continued speaking.

"The super of your building mentioned you might be coming here. We read your response to Milton's sonnet in the Society Newsletter and thought you might be able to discuss your ideas with us."

"Are you members of the Society?"

"No, but we have a great interest in Milton."

Keith looked at them warily, not certain how to respond.

Jeff recognized his concerns. "We were impressed with your analysis and had been discussing this poem among ourselves. We were hoping you could help us. Could we buy you a coffee?"

Keith looked out at the street and then back at his two visitors. "Sure"

While Keith walked to one of the tables, the young lady instructed the others to take a paper cup and pour their own coffee. Milk and sugar with wooden stirring sticks were on a cabinet nearby. Jeff gave her a ten-dollar bill, received his change, and they sat on the cane chairs at Keith's table near the rear.

Jeff began. "Mr. Hartlib, I was interested in your interpretation of Sonnet Nineteen. Most believe that Milton was speaking about his eyesight."

Hartlib spoke in a slow, scholarly manner. "Yes, Milton's vision had been deteriorating, probably from a form of glaucoma. In spite of being advised to reduce his workload, he continued reading and writing late into the night, until, by the early 1650s, he was only able to differentiate between light and dark."

Jeff responded. "So the sonnet speaks of his blindness?"

Hartlib nodded. "That is the classical interpretation. Listen to the opening lines:

> *When I consider how my light is spent*
> *Ere half my days in this dark world and wide,*
> *And that one talent which is death to hide*
> *Lodg'd with me useless,*

"Milton feels that his talent for writing, his only profession, is now useless due to his blindness."

Jeff waited for Hartlib to finish and then added. "But then Milton questions his God."

Jeff quoted the next lines:

> *though my soul more bent*
> *To serve therewith my Maker, and present*
> *My true account, lest he returning chide,*
> *"Doth God exact day-labour, light denied?"*
> *I fondly ask.*

Hartlib appeared impressed. "Correct. Feel the rhythm. And when God asks for the final accounting as to what Milton has done with his life, the poet asks *was it not God who is preventing Milton from carrying out God's work?"*

Hartlib took another sip from his cup. "Then what, Mr. Moss?"

Jeff recited the next lines:

> *But Patience, to prevent*
> *That murmur, soon replies: "God doth not need*
> *Either man's work or his own gifts."*

Hartlib followed up: "Yes, Mr. Moss, patience prevents Milton from releasing his anger. So what does he do?"

Jeff completed the poem:

> *who best Bear his mild yoke, they serve him best. His state*
> *Is kingly; thousands at his bidding speed*
> *And post o'er land and ocean without rest:*
> *They also serve who only stand and wait.*

Like a teacher, Hartlib continued:

"Exactly, Mr. Moss. *They also serve who only stand and wait.* Milton realizes that God does not need anything from man except to bear whatever yoke God gives us. You get an A." Hartlib paused for a moment. "So you now have all the answers, is there anything else you wish to know?"

Jeff braced himself for a reaction. "How would you respond to someone who quoted the opening line as: *When I consider how my life is spent?*"

Kate tried to hide her surprise at Jeff's aggressiveness. Hartlib paused for a moment and looked more closely at both his visitors. "I believe that Milton would want his readers to consider their lives when they are reading the poem."

"So you believe that he was writing to each of us?"

Hartlib responded warily. "I believe that great literature must be meaningful to every generation, each interpreting the words to their own situation."

Jeff hesitated, "Then, sir, in your case, though you are not physically blind, why would the world be dark to you?"

Hartlib tensed, not saying a word, but one could see the temporal arteries pulsing as his face reddened. When there was no response, Jeff continued.

"And the line that reads: *and that one talent which is death to hide Lodged with me useless, through my soul more bent.* I'd rather not define talent as an aptitude but rather as a metaphor from the Book of Matthew, citing Jesus's parable of the talents? Isn't that when the servant buried the money that his master had entrusted to him and was cast out into the night?"

Jeff continued, "Have you buried something entrusted to you and, as a result, been cast out into the night? Are you a wanderer?"

It hit a raw nerve that flashed across Keith's face like a bolt of lightning, the masseters tightened forcing the teeth to clench, the pupils dilating. As if cognizant of his reaction, Keith tried to relax, but it was too late. Kate had seen it. It almost frightened her and instinctively she shifted backward in her seat. Keith looked at Jeff, as if reevaluating with whom he was dealing, or perhaps, dueling.

Jeff wouldn't stop. "And when Milton writes *'they also serve who only stand and wait,'* does it really mean that God simply wants each of us to bear our yoke, or did Milton mean that we should be proactive and forgery ahead?"

Keith looked at him inquisitively. "You mean forge ahead."

"I'm sorry?"

Keith repeated the correction. "Forge ahead. You said 'forgery.'"

Jeff answered cautiously. "Yes, thank you for correcting me. Forge ahead."

For a long moment, they stared into each other's eyes, as if engaging in silent battle. Not a sound was heard in the empty space. Kate watched, as if observing two fighters sparring, testing each other in the opening rounds.

Suddenly Keith rose from the table and walked out the door. Kate watched as Jeff followed him out.

"Hartlib, your keys!" Keith felt his pockets and turned around as Jeff tossed them.

Keith caught them. "Not mine." He threw them back at Jeff and walked away.

"Mr. Hartlib, once last thing." Keith kept walking. "Do you know a Niles Janeway?"

Keith stopped, turned, and defiantly strode back, his eyes fixed on Jeff. Jeff readied himself for an attack.

When Keith reached him he spoke with forceful quietude.

"Mr. Moss. Don't come looking for me again, ever."

Kate was at the doorway. As Keith walked away, Jeff followed him with his eyes, his muscles tensed. Kate said nothing. She just looked at Jeff, who like an exhausted fighter, watched his prey leave the field of battle. Finally she spoke. "What was that all about?"

"I'm not sure . . . yet."

Jeff went back inside and sat down for a moment, finishing his coffee. Finally, he threw their two cups into the garbage, but carefully picked up the third cup and placed it in a clean takeout bag.

"I think we've found more than what a poem means."

CHAPTER 73

New York, June 15, 7 days

Jeff replayed the message from the ME's office. It was Tom. A 9:00 PM opening came up for the DNA analysis.

Jeff texted back. "I'll be there, with a guest."

*

ME's Office, 10:00 PM, June 15, 7 days

Kate followed Jeff's procedure as he scrubbed.

"When did you find the coffee cup?" Tom was already in the lab setting up.

"Yesterday." Jeff knew he was bending the rules. "I'm sorry that I couldn't give you any notice on this. If you don't have the time, we can do it later."

"And I see you want an analysis on that cup I kept from the Jessup fellow. What happened?"

"I'm not sure, but it may be related to the death of the professor you worked on."

"We'll enter it into the National Missing Persons DNA Database and see if there's a match."

Jeff turned to Kate. "The major problem with DNA evidence is contamination."

"Isn't that what happened at the O.J. Simpson trial?"

Tom answered. "You got it. The collection analysis of the DNA was so poorly carried out that the evidence wasn't admitted."

"I hate to ask, I mean I know what it is, but what is DNA?"

Tom and Jeff looked at each other, as if to say "you take the ball."

Tom started. "Deoxyribonucleic acid is a complex molecule that's found in almost every one of the more than seventy million cells of the human body including hair, skin, saliva, and blood. It was discovered with some brilliant sleuthing by Watson and Crick in 1953 and it won them the Nobel Prize."

Jeff continued, "Watson and Crick determined that DNA is made of building blocks called nucleotides, each made of one of four types of bases, arranged as a double helix. They can extend out billions of building blocks long, but the bases are always paired: A for Adenosine is always matched with a T for Thymine, and C for Cytosine is always matched with a G for Guanine."

Jeff picked up a pencil and drew the configuration for Kate. "This is what it looks like."

$$A - T$$
$$C - G$$

"These pairs can be repeated billions of times, and with so many possible combinations and permutations, no two people will be the same."

Kate was listening closely. "So, from any part of the body you can get all the genetic information to identify that person."

Jeff nodded. "Correct." He pointed to a picture on the wall. "That's the double helix.

Tom was standing in front of an oven-like machine. "This is a thermal cycler. It heats to a temperature high enough to break apart those A–T, C–G connections and they go back to being single strands. Watch."

Jeff handed Tom the envelope containing the small specimen of blood he brought back from Hong Kong. He removed the contents and placed it inside the thermal cycler as if putting it into a microwave oven.

Jeff continued, "Then we simply isolate the parts of these long sequences that are usually unique to an individual, take pictures, store them, and log into them when we wish to see if another matches it."

"Except," Kate added, "we need a suspect to compare it to. Too bad we don't collect DNA samples at birth. Then we could identify everyone."

Jeff smiled. "So much for privacy."

CHAPTER 74

423 W. 78th Street, 11:00 AM, June 16, 6 days

"Good to see you again, Sam."

Steve Reich welcomed his visitor. "You wanted to speak to me?"

"I checked out the collection at Leeds. I found Ben Israel's book *Mikveh Yisra'el*, but I believe there was another part of that package that they didn't have and I was wondering if it might still be here?"

"What is it?"

"A manuscript of about 200 pages."

"Is there a name?"

"The Milton Manuscript."

Reich thought for a moment. "Well, we've got a lot of texts filling these bookcases. Shall we get started?"

Each took a side. It took an hour to go through everything.

"It's not here."

Keith was disappointed. He had really thought he had it figured out.

"There's one other possibility, the basement."

They walked down the stairs to where the electrical, furnace, and hot water heater were located.

Steve turned on the light and walked over to a corner where a large trunk was placed.

"Sorry for the debris. I don't get down here often, but I remember my mother mentioning there were some things that father didn't want to be sent out. If it's here it would be in this."

Steve opened the trunk revealing a number of dust-covered books, papers, and old family photographs. Together they moved the trunk closer to the light, and began to sift through the contents.

"I don't see it, unless it's in here." Steve reached down and picked up a seventeenth-century carved Westmoreland bible writing box made out of oak. It was about a foot long, two-feet wide and maybe one and a half feet deep. "Whatever it is we better take it upstairs."

Reich carried it up to the living room and placed it on one of the tables. When he opened it, he found a large brown envelope.

"Sam, you check it out. Maybe it's what you're looking for."

Keith sat down at the desk and opened the envelope, gently removing its contents. His heart raced as he read the cover page.

"The Milton Manuscript as received from Daniel Skinner. J. Williamson, 1677."

Reich was fascinated as Keith read the opening pages.

"Steve, Milton scholars have been looking for this for a very long time!"

"Then take good care of it. It's yours."

*

W. 78th Street, noon, June 16, 6 days

The cell phone rang as he walked back to his car carrying a large white Bloomingdale's bag with the treasure in hand. A reflexive shudder ran through him. Who knew his cell? Had he left something at Reich's home? As he checked the caller ID, a smile relaxed his concerned face: he recognized the UK number.

"Sundstrom, where've you been? I haven't heard from you since Leeds. You're not going to believe what I'm carrying."

There was no response. "Sundstrom, you there?"

"Keith Jessup?" Fright replaced the smile. He hadn't been called that in months.

The female voice continued, "Keith, this is Deputy Chief Constance Bathgate in Oxford."

He was confused. "Chief Bathgate? How did you get this number?"

"It was in Professor Sundstrom's mobile. Dr. Jessup, I'm afraid we have to talk."

CHAPTER 75

New York, June 21, 1 day

"We found a match!"

DeLordet and Kate looked up as if a hurricane had just blown into the room.

"Docteur, why don't you sit down – it's been a long day and I see you have some exciting news."

Jeff realized he had failed to relate the most important part of his discovery.

"We matched the DNA from the cup of water at the Milton Society with the DNA from the blood of the Hong Kong Buddha. It was Janeway's! Niles Janeway was in Hong Kong. He was the one who sold the Hong Kong drawing!"

DeLordet put his hands together, trying to fully digest the information.

"How did Janeway get the drawings? I thought Jessup did the forgeries."

"We believe he blackmailed Keith into giving them to him."

DeLordet leaned forward. "And Janeway assumed he was getting the originals?"

Kate nodded. "And that explains why Keith left his calling card on the back of the drawings."

DeLordet agreed. "Very interesting, *mes amis*. Our friend, Monsieur Keith, is most clever. He knew that Janeway would sell the forgeries and wanted him caught."

"I doubt that he knew Janeway was involved, but he knew that once the double cross was realized, his life was worth nothing."

DeLordet smiled, "And that explains why he had to leave Joanne."

Kate added, "To make sure that he was the target, not her."

"Except she became a target," Jeff added.

DeLordet nodded in understanding, "To get to him . . . So where is he?"

The silence was broken by Jeff's cell ringing. He spoke to the caller for several minutes then turned to DeLordet.

"That was Tom Davis. Keith Jessup is alive and well in Boston!"

They were incredulous.

Jeff continued, "Keith Jessup lives in Cambridge."

DeLordet, shook his head slowly, as if overwhelmed with information. "And, how do you know this?'

"Because Dr. Keith Jessup now calls himself Mr. Samuel Hartlib."

Kate's face showed surprise. "What!"

Jeff reviewed his phone call. "The DNA from Hartlib's coffee cup matched with Keith's salivary sample at the ME's office."

"What made you suspect Hartlib? I mean the way you substituted 'forgery' for forge. That was pure genius."

"That was pure accident. Saying forgery was a real Freudian slip, but he had quite a reaction."

Kate smiled. "But why throw him your keys? You knew they weren't this."

Jeff quickly answered, "When I saw how he reacted to the word 'forgery,' I wondered if he could have been involved. Did you notice how he caught the keys with his right hand – the hand a lefty ballplayer catches with. When he saw they weren't his, he threw them back at me – using his dominant hand, his left."

DeLordet quickly responded. "Like the artist who drew the Braniffs."

"Exactly!"

"And that explains his reaction when you asked if he knew Janeway. It was fear. He realized that somebody was getting close to finding his real identity."

DeLordet sat back in his chair. "So he had it all planned. Quite a story. I'd like to meet this Monsieur Keith Jessup. *Viva chevalerie!*"

Jeff took a piece of paper from his file. "Remember that Sheffield note that Joanne found. Now I understand what it means."

He handed it to Kate.

TO: Keith Jessup.

You had been advised not to pursue the Manuscript for health reasons. We hope your trip to Sheffield was for other purposes. That was a great deal of money you spent on an old edition of *Paradise Lost*. We certainly hope it was worth it.

She looked at him. "So there really was a conspiracy."

Jeff walked over to the window and looked out. "*Is* a conspiracy – and that means we have a problem. When Janeway saw Hartlib, he realized it was Keith. That means he identified the target. When Janeway left us at the Milton Society, he knew that Keith had the Manuscript."

DeLordet cut in, "But what if he doesn't disclose its contents?"

Kate explained, "It's too late for that. We told Janeway that the Braniffs were forgeries. That means Keith double-crossed him. These people are murderers."

"But what if he can't find Keith?" DeLordet asked.

"Oh, he'll find him. Read this:" Kate took out the copy of the monthly Milton Society Bulletin that Janeway's assistant had handed her.

THE TANZER FOUNDATION AND HARVARD COLLEGE
are pleased to present
DR. KEITH JESSUP
June 22, 8:00 PM.
Speaking on "Secrets of The Milton Manuscript"

DeLordet looked up. "*Mon Dieu.* That's tomorrow!"

Kate paused. "Harvard expects someone to be speaking."

DeLordet looked at Jeff. "Will he show up?"

"Knowing what we know about Keith, he'll show up." Jeff paused for a moment. "And so will his enemies. We have to warn him as quickly as we can."

DeLordet sounded concerned. "Well, *docteur.* What shall we do?"

CHAPTER 76

New York, June 21, 1 day

They divided the mission. DeLordet contacted Teng in Hong Kong, discussed his belief that the Braniff was a forgery, and arranged for it to be withdrawn from the auction. No reason would be given and Pierre's involvement would not be mentioned. An hour later he called Paz in Zurich and related the same information. To both dealers DeLordet expressed the hope that if the perpetrators were caught, sufficient funds might still be available to reimburse any losses. Teng and Paz appreciated the courtesy and agreed to confidentiality.

Jeff called Joanne and related the recent events and explained the plan. Joanne mentioned that Detective Tom DeMarco of the Boston Police Department was a friend of the family's and had arranged to keep her under surveillance.

"Kate's driving to Boston and will meet you at your home tomorrow around noon. Make sure DeMarco knows you and Kate are going to Harvard for the lecture in the evening. Ask him to meet me at 128 Bennett in Cambridge at 2:00 PM. I'll be wearing a blue Mets hat."

"Do you really think it's him?"

"The labs says it is. Now you tell us."

CHAPTER 77

Cambridge, MA, June 22, 7 hours

Keith walked to the closet of his small apartment. He had grown tired of staying a step ahead of Stigmata, constantly checking to see who was following him. From the top shelf he brought down an old metal case. Sadly, he noticed areas of rust eroding their way into the once polished steel surface and thought, *nothing lasts forever.* Carefully he carried the case to the corner of the room and placed it on the desk. The old case contained the only remaining personal documents that his father had left behind: discharge papers from the army, personal medical records, an old GI insurance policy, a letter of dismissal from the tire plant. He realized it was all that remained of a father he was still trying to please.

I wish you could be here. I know we could have worked this out. I'm tired of the anger. I think you would be proud of me tonight. I know Mom will be.

Keith looked older. The last few months seemed to have caused a change, the pressure had gotten to him, the fatigue of constant vigilance settling in. He closed the case and placed it back onto the top shelf of his closet. Next to it was the carved oak bible box. He carried it down, rested it on the desk and looked at it for a long moment. With a deep breath and deeper sigh he opened it and removed its contents, as if the pages inside were more precious than diamonds. The papers were yellowed, with some areas completely browned. *Nothing lasts forever.* On some of the pages the edges were torn – but overall they had weathered the 350 years as well as could be expected. *So this is what Livingston had spent his life seeking. Finally, we'll understand why Milton wrote his poem. Finally we'll understand what he wanted man to know: how God justifies His ways.*

The knock on the door interrupted his thoughts.

"Anand?

Keith returned the pages to the envelope and placed it into the box on his desk. He walked to the door and opened it, expecting the young superintendent. "Come in."

Niles Janeway entered the room.

"Hello, Samuel Hartlib."

Keith was taken by surprise. "Niles? What are you doing here?"

"Came to see how you were making out. We had no idea what happened to you."

"How did you know where to find me?"

"Oh, you know, word gets around. The Milton family is such a small group."

Keith eyed him suspiciously.

Janeway continued, "Why don't we sit down."

Janeway sat in one of the two chairs in the apartment and gestured for Keith to sit in the other.

"I like your new look. Your beard makes you appear more scholarly. Starting to get some gray in it, I see."

When there was no response, Janeway continued.

"So you will be speaking this evening?"

"Yes."

"On the Manuscript?"

Keith was trying to connect the dots. Something was wrong. "That's correct."

"So you found it?"

"I have."

"And you are going to reveal its contents?"

"I am. Did you come to hear the lecture?"

Janeway let a half smile appear. "Actually, I came for the lecture."

"I think you'll be quite surprised."

Suddenly, Janeway stood up. "I'm afraid you'll be the one surprised. There will be no lecture."

"What do you mean?"

"I can't let you disclose what the Manuscript says."

"And why is that?"

Janeway walked over to the apartment door and opened it. A man with red hair and scarred skin entered the room. Keith recognized the grotesque face: it was beginning to make sense.

Janeway turned back to Keith. "Give us the Manuscript."

"Niles, it was you? All this time you've been part of it?"

Janeway smiled, "Longer than you realize."

"Stigmata?"

"Yes, Stigmata. We've watched you since you chose to expand your thesis. Anything that touches on the Manuscript comes to our attention. How do you think you had a job waiting for you at the Milton Society? We needed you positioned to keep our eye on you."

"So that's what happened."

"We warned you, but you refused to listen. Now it's time to put this chapter to rest."

"As you did with Reynolds and Livingston?"

"I didn't want that. We begged them to stop their search but they refused."

Keith clenched his hands around the chair's arms. "But Sundstrom. Why? He had nothing to do with this?"

"An unfortunate accident." He turned to the red-haired man. "Some people get a little too eager."

Abaddon chuckled, revealing the toothless smile that Keith knew all too well.

Janeway continued, "It's time for you to decide: either give me the Manuscript or we will take it from you – your choice."

"Because you're afraid of what the Manuscript says."

"You know better than I."

"You have no idea what's in it?"

"You're the only one who's read it; our knowledge is simply passed by word of mouth from generation to generation."

"You mean you've murdered without knowing why?"

"We do as we were taught. It's what keeps the world orderly. Change is limited. Life remains predictable."

"No, Niles, the only part that remains predictable is your fear."

"Of what?"

"The truth. Milton's truth."

"And what is that?"

"To seek a faith far worthier than what the Church had offered, one that leads to real salvation."

Janeway raised his voice. "That is not the truth."

"That's Milton's truth."

Janeway was becoming agitated. "Lies."

"The Manuscript proves it."

Janeway banged his fist hard against the desk, causing the lamp to fall on the floor, shattering the bulb with a loud noise.

"That's why it can't be revealed."

Janeway's knees began to move, back and forth, as if each had their own pendular path.

Keith looked at him, not with fear but with pity.

"All Milton tried to answer is what every human asks every day – to understand the ways of God. Why the weak are weak and the strong are strong. Why some wax rich and others lack. Why some are healthy and others lie ill. Don't you want to know what is going to happen to you because of what you've done?"

The knees stopped swinging. Janeway sat silently for several moments, as if in deep thought.

Keith continued, "You're only denying the world from knowing the truth: That's what I'm to disclose tonight."

Once again the knees began their cycle. Janeway lowered his eyes to the floor.

Keith continued, "Don't you know when this all began?"

Janeway looked up and Keith continued.

"From the roots of your family tree, the hateful mind of a tormented, crippled, angry man who detested Milton and almost everyone associated with him. William Prynne, a man who hated Catholics, then Anglicans, then Puritans, and then Jews, who wore a mask of shame, the *S* and *L* that you burn into your victims cheeks, the same as was burned into him."

The knees stopped. "I never did that to anyone."

Keith glanced at Abaddon. "But others have and all because William Prynne wanted revenge against one of the most brilliant, honest, and courageous men that England ever produced. Why, Niles? Why are you part of this?"

Janeway jumped to his feet. "That's enough! Where is it?"

Keith pointed to the oak box on his desk.

Janeway raised his voice. "I'll burn it."

"Because you're afraid to let Christians decide for themselves whether Milton's views were based on logic or heresy? The truth will always come out. Welcome to the twenty-first century, where people can think for themselves. Perhaps we'll be better Christians for it. Milton thought so."

Janeway sat back, deep in thought. Keith could see he was trying to decide what to do. Finally he stammered: "If you give me that manuscript I can save your life. You can even go ahead with tonight's lecture, but you will have no proof to your testimony. No one will take you seriously."

Keith realized he was running out of options.

"I can't do that."

Abaddon put his hand under his jacket and pulled out a revolver.

"Let me kill 'im, Niles!"

Keith saw Abaddon's finger fluttering on the trigger.

"Let me kill 'im!"

Janeway stood pensively for what seemed forever. "No, Abaddon, I can't. Let's go."

"I ain't goin nowhere till I do what I shoulda done before."

"Abaddon, he's right. We've been led blindly. Let's go. It's over."

Suddenly there was a loud knock on the door. "Samuel Hartlib! Police, open the door!"

"Abaddon, let's get out of here."

The knock was louder. "Police. Open the door!"

"I'll get out, but Uncle's not going to want him to leave this room."

Abaddon pointed his revolver at Keith.

"Abaddon, don't." Janeway threw himself at the red-haired man, but it was too late, the shot was fired. Janeway held on to the bigger man, looking up into his eyes.

"Abaddon, why? Your own brother?"

"Not anymore." Abaddon moved back, letting Janeway fall to the floor. The door was thrown open, surprising Abaddon and forcing him against the wall, his revolver falling to the floor.

Jeff and Detective Tom DeMarco raced in. "What's going on?"

DeMarco was a big tough Italian, on the force for eighteen years, but Abaddon threw Jeff aside and ran right through the Detective as he raced out of the room and down the hall.

Jeff looked at Keith "You OK?"

"Yeah, fine. Your timing couldn't have been better."

"Stop that fellow."

DeMarco went after Abaddon while Keith rushed to Janeway's side, cradling his head in his hands. "Niles, I'm so sorry."

Niles spoke as if the energy of life was leaving him. "I couldn't do it. I knew you were right, but I was the last in line. There's no one after me."

Niles coughed up blood that oozed out of the corner of his mouth. "I had a duty." Niles tried taking a breath and Keith heard the gurgling rales. "Do me one favor?"

"Yes, Niles."

"Tell them, tonight. Tell them the truth."

Jeff knelt down besides Janeway, feeling for a pulse, and shook his head.

Keith laid Janeway's head down on the floor for the last time.

"I will."

*

Keith washed the blood from his hands, lifted the oak box from the desk and began to walk out.

Jeff observed, not saying a word.

"I have to go somewhere, but I owe you one." Keith smiled. "And the next time we have coffee, I'll do the buying, but no poetry."

Before he closed the door, he gave Jeff a last glance. "Thanks."

BOOK X

CHAPTER 78

Cambridge, MA, June 22, 5 hours

Keith needed to be alone and recess what had just occurred. If the lecture was to be delivered in just a few hours, he had to understand the rest of the story. His mind was still swirling when he entered Robinson Hall which housed Harvard's Department of History. As he had hoped, the building was almost empty, a transition between the end of the spring semester and the start of the summer session. He walked down the long, darkened corridor to a water fountain and took a long drink before entering one of the empty classrooms. His hands were still trembling as he managed to open the old oak box. He took a deep breath, focused on the task before him, and began to review its contents in silence. He had promised Sundstrom he'd have all the answers, but one question remained: What happened to the Manuscript from the moment Skinner received it from Ben Israel's Publishing House?

Keith read through the notes that Cyril Reich had written, until he reached the information he was seeking:

"It appears that when Sir Joseph Williamson, responsible for licensing publications in England, reviewed the revised *De Doctrina* sent to him by Skinner's father, he found that Milton's most heretical thoughts had been removed. Williamson threatened the young Skinner to hand over the deleted papers or face arrest. Skinner had no choice. He returned that portion of the *De Doctrina* to Williamson who retained it in his private papers. In 1701, Williamson's estate bequeathed his personal library to Queen's College in Oxford, including a manuscript of approximately 200 pages left in a beautifully carved oak bible box. It remained undisturbed for many years.

"Who was responsible for removing it from Oxford, and how it was sold into private hands from seller to buyer until it reached me, I never determined. Williamson's vast library of letters, dispatches, and memoranda are now all part of England's state papers, except for the one noted Manuscript written by John Milton. And as for King Charles II, the edict to prevent all of Milton's treasonous and blasphemous writings from being published has never been abrogated – it remains intact today."

Keith picked up the original receipt: For the payment of The Milton Manuscript to Daniel Skinner. Five Pounds.

Keith smiled. Skinner never did make his fortune.

BOOK XI

CHAPTER 79

Cambridge, MA, 7:00 PM, June 22, 1 hour

The sun had not yet set in Cambridge as Keith drove along Memorial Drive. Only the sounds of geese could be heard trumpeting overhead on their way to cooler climes. The countryside was filled with color, and the heat announced summer's official arrival. *Funny,* he thought, *it all began at the Spring Equinox and ends on the Summer Solstice.* A lot had transpired, from the sun being flat to the earth's surface to the moment when the sun is highest in the sky. Life does seem to have its balance. He recalled how the Druid's celebrated the day as the "wedding of Heaven and Earth." *No wonder a bride hopes for a June wedding.*

To Keith, it was the longest day of his life, which meant its night would be the shortest. As he looked out he couldn't help but notice how peaceful the landscape was beside the gentle flow of the Charles River. He wondered if someday he would enjoy such peace.

*

Harvard's Lowell Lecture Hall was filled to an overflow capacity. Those attending felt this lecture would be different. The prestige of the Tanzer suggested that this time the contents of the Milton Manuscript would at last be revealed.

Scholars and students, laymen and press were present. Justifying the ways of God to man was not limited to high scholarship. Harvard's TV cameras were awaiting the start, a big scoop for WHRB, the Harvard TV station and the student writers of *The Crimson,* Harvard's newspaper.

The stage was empty as the 350 attendees took their seats. Word had already leaked out describing what the speaker had gone through. Janeway's murder had been broadcast and the internet was rife with facts and speculation. A fugitive was still at large and security was heavy. Interviews with professors who shared their views on the validity of a Milton Manuscript filled the dead time until the start of the program, and Keith's disappearance and the odds of his presence was the topic of the hour. Regardless, the audience that filled Lowell Hall had been anticipating his appearance for weeks.

*

The oversized custodian wearing light gray work clothes and a black ski cap pulled over his ears hauled the heavy rubber trash can up the basement steps and into the entering lobby in the rear of the hall, his mop and broom sticking out above its rim. Jeff Moss and Detective Tom DeMarco were stationed at the entrance along with several patrolmen from the Boston Police Department as the attendees stepped through the security check. Jeff threw a quick glance as the worker moved the rubber container toward the foot of the stairs that led to the balcony, momentarily thinking how unusual for someone to wear a ski cap on such a hot and humid evening. The custodian, an ID with picture clipped to his shirt pocket, bent down to pick up a paper cup and threw it into the trash, keeping his face away from the officers as he hauled the container up the stairs. When he reached the upper level, he glanced to the front of the hall, a big toothless smile on his face.

CHAPTER 80

The Tanzer Lecture, 8:00 PM

The tower clock struck eight bells and the Hall had an anticipatory silence. Two officers from the Cambridge Sheriff's Department escorted the speaker through the rear entrance. Jeff and DeMarco had tried to dissuade him from giving the lecture, but he refused, saying he was tired of running. There had to be an end.

Keith approached the dais, carrying a wooden box under his arm. He stood tall as he looked out at his audience. For those close enough, the face was more traveled than a man befitting his age. How old was he? Thirty? forty? fifty? His appearance was that of a scholar that had no time for mirrors, at least external ones. He wore a green wool sport jacket with leather elbow patches, light brown slacks that could have used another press, and a faded brown tie. His full head of hair, perhaps grayed by turmoil, needed a cut, his blue eyes no longer as soft as they once were.

He placed the box down on the wooden stand and looked out at the expectant crowd. He took a deep breath, not from fear but accomplishment, and a subtle smile appeared as he thought of his professors. All that he had found, he would dedicate to them. He was certain they would be listening. As he surveyed the room not a whisper was heard. He knew that those standing in the aisles were plain clothes police, and he was advised of the heavy security assigned to the entrances. He gave a silent nod of recognition as Jeff and DeMarco entered from the lobby, eyes searching for something untoward, and yet, Keith felt no fear, as if there was no fear left to express. His eyes darted back and forth across the hall. Stigmata was here. He knew it. He could feel it. *Satan always brought the aura of death with him. But where?*

He began.

"We've been taught that John Milton's *Paradise Lost* is the greatest poetic achievement in the English language, not only the supreme epic of the English nation but in all of Christendom. We've been taught that Milton's poem defends the glory of Christianity and the victory of the Christian God, his Son Jesus, and the Holy Spirit over Satan and his forces of evil. Well, we've been taught wrongly."

The murmurs that arose were ones of scholarly bewilderment.

"Wrong because there are those, perhaps even amongst us, who have prevented the truth from being told – whatever the cost – even if that cost was life itself."

*

Abaddon rolled the rubber waste container into the small projection room on the rear balcony overlooking the hall and locked the door. He removed the mop and broom and lay them on the floor along the back wall. With care he lifted a long narrow box marked "mops," placed it on the table, opened it, and withdrew a Winchester Model 70 bolt action rifle. As he began its assembly, he heard the speaker continue.

*

"The Milton Manuscript has been found, thanks to the heroic work of Professors Thornton Livingston and Foster Sundstrom, who gave their lives to seek the truth. And what does it contain?" Keith paused as he surveyed the silenced audience. "The most heterodox of Milton's theological thoughts, consisting of the redacted material from the first fourteen chapters, the first 196 pages of the original *Christian Doctrine*.

"And those thoughts, heretical to some, was enough to cause a 350-year conspiracy that prevented its presentation to the Christian world, one that caused the deaths of brilliant scholars."

A hushed murmur generated through the room.

*

Abaddon worked quickly, attaching the forged chrome molybdenum steel barrel to the stock and placed it on the bipod mounting studs to accommodate the long range telescopic site.

*

"John Milton wrote *Paradise Lost* to justify the ways of God to man, not to defend the glory of Christianity nor the victory of the Christian Lord. Milton simply wished to understand why things happen. Do not lose sight of the message for the messenger.

"How, therefore, does Milton justify the ways of God? How does he understand the why? How are we to understand the context within which events unfold?"

*

Abaddon tightened the last of the gun site set screws and placed a single live round of Rem Core-lokt factory ammo into the chamber. He smiled as he remembered the first rule he had learned when his uncle had taken him to the shooting range. *Never point a gun at anything you do not intend to shoot.* He would be certain to heed that warning as he positioned the rifle's muzzle through the room's projector opening, aiming it at the stage, its target clearly encircled through the gun site.

As Abaddon took aim a momentary flash of light reflected off the polished surface of the gun's barrel. From the dais, Keith caught sight of it and looked up. There it was, the red hair and maniacal grin of the assassin. Jeff and DeMarco also saw the flash and instinctively rushed to the rear of the auditorium and up the stairway.

Abaddon had his scope set directly at Keith's heart as Jeff and DeMarco reached the upper landing and tried to open the locked door.

Abaddon laughed. "You're too late."

DeMarco threw his weight against the door, forcing the door open, but the shell had already been sent toward its target. The audience gasped as Keith crumbled to the floor. Abaddon tried to reload a second round, but DeMarco threw a punishing tackle into Abaddon's gut, throwing him against the wall and causing the rifle to fall. The big man threw DeMarco off and started to stand up when Jeff grabbed the rifle and brought it crashing down on Abaddon's head. Abaddon, like a wild bull, shook it off and raged at Jeff, forcing him against the wall, throwing open the door and rushing outside. DeMarco followed and tackled Abaddon around the legs, sending them tumbling down the stairs. Abaddon managed to get to his feet and struggled toward the exit as DeMarco yelled, "Stop him." As Abaddon reached the outer door he was confronted by several patrolmen and after a brief scuffle was placed in handcuffs.

DeMarco followed. "Get him out of here."

Jeff looked down at the podium, seeing Keith lying motionless on the floor. He raced down the stairs, trying to avoid the crush of panic. By the time he reached the podium, Keith was surrounded by police and paramedics.

"I'm a physician."

Jeff knelt down and felt for a pulse. "I need some cold water."

He placed a compress on his forehead and Keith opened his eyes. "You OK?"

"Yeah, guess so. A little dizzy." He withdrew his arm from under his jacket – his hand dripping with blood.

"You've been hit."

Jeff took a look at Keith's arm. The bleeding had oozed through his shirt and against his tweed jacket.

The paramedics opened their emergency kit and Jeff put on latex gloves and tried to determine the source of the bleeding.

"A flesh wound. You're lucky."

Keith smiled. "Actually, I was more chicken then lucky. I saw the barrel coming out and I tried to get out of the way. Just wasn't fast enough."

"Let's get you to a hospital."

Keith shook his head. "No. Patch me up. We've been waiting too long for this lecture. If I stop now, Stigmata wins."

Jeff helped Keith onto a chair and removed his jacket and shirt.

"Did you get him?"

"Yeah. He's in custody."

He wiped the area clean, applied an antiseptic and bandaged the wound. "This should do for a while. I think you should relax for a few minutes before you start."

Jeff reached into his jacket pocket and withdrew an envelope. "By the way, a well-dressed English gentleman, sitting in the rear, wanted to be certain you receive this. He said you would be most interested in its contents."

Keith reached for the envelope, almost by habit expecting another threatening letter. Instead he found the imprint of Twinings and Whitcomb and a receipt for the sum of five million pounds Sterling deposited into the account of Keith Jessup at Barclays Bank, with a short note:

> Professor Livingston wanted this delivered to you with thanks for completing his work. Now he can be at peace.
>   Colin Cuttermill

*

The FBI and Cambridge police began their questioning in the Robert W. Healy Public Safety Building at 125 Sixth Street.

"Please state your name."

There was no response.

"Sir, I am asking you your name."

Abaddon looked at them for an instant, then lowered his head in silence, a defeated man.

"It will be easier if you cooperate."

Nothing. The FBI agents looked at each other.

"Did you know a Professor James Bartholomew?"

Abaddon raised his head and looked into the eyes of the detective who asked, but remained silent.

The detective walked out of the room and returned several minutes later with a tall, willowy woman about fifty, with dark hair cut just above the collar of her clean constabulary uniform.

"Abaddon?"

She pulled up a chair and looked at the seated figure before her.

"Abaddon, I'm Deputy Chief Constable Constance Bathgate from the Thames Valley Force."

The big redheaded man looked up, and after a moment of trying to collect his thoughts whispered to the woman in front of him: "Why you ere?"

"To speak to you. Professor Bartholomew told me everything."

Abaddon studied her face. "No way. We swore. E wouln't tell no one."

"Because it's over."

"Whad ya mean?"

"There's nothing to pass down. The world is already learning what the Manuscript has to say. He's telling them now."

"Cuz I failed."

She nodded. "Because there's no one left. Your brother is dead. There are no offspring, no one to pass it on to. It's all in this note. It's over."

Abaddon looked at the note. "Can't be. I need to speak to uncle. Gotta warn im."

The Deputy Chief Inspector looked at him. "That won't be possible. Your uncle suffered a massive stroke just before I left. He died yesterday. The last thing he said was, 'It's over.'"

Abaddon looked at the Deputy Chief Constable and dropped his head. "Uncle dead? Then what's to appen to me?"

The agent approached Abaddon. "Abaddon Janeway, you're under arrest for murder."

BOOK XII

CHAPTER 81

The Tanzer Lecture, 9:00 PM

The scholars resumed their seats in Lowell Hall and Keith walked onto the stage, a jacket hiding his bandages. The audience rose in applause.

"I believe we left off, before the interruption, as I was about to justify the ways of God. I guess we saw the emotions that such a question raises."

Keith smiled and the audience laughed hesitantly, easing the tensions in both.

"Milton's search to justify God's ways was based on his vast knowledge of theology, philosophy, and metaphysics, as then known to the Western World. And so where did Milton go to justify God's ways? Back to the original Book, back to the Hebrew Bible. As he did with his views on Divorce, Milton returns to God's original Testament, where we find that *Paradise Lost was written to explore,* as he writes in *The Christian Doctrine,* the same question that Moses asked in Exodus 33, verse 13: *Now, therefore, I pray Thee, if I have found grace in Thy sight, show me now Thy ways, that I may know thee, to the end that I may find grace in Thy sight. And what was* God's answer to Moses on Mount Sinai?: *All that you will know of me is found in the thirteen attributes of mercy.*"

Keith paused for a moment. "Mercy, as explained to Moses, that is Milton's fundamental appreciation of God's ways, but a mercy defined by God. Milton's Manuscript teaches that if you are to justify God's ways you must understand them. That is what the thirteen attributes do."

The silence of the hall was broken by the monotonic sounds in a minor key, as Keith began chanting the Thirteen Attributes in Hebrew, using the original mystical cantillations that the high priest of Israel intoned as he stood before the Holy Ark of Solomon's Temple, 1,000 years before Christ. A melody that remains today, as it was then, for the millions of Jews throughout the world.

"Lord, Lord, God of *Rahum v'hanun erech apayim v'rav hesed ve'emet; notzer hesed la'alafim noseh avon va'fesha v'chata'ah v'nakeh.*"

Keith looked out at his audience: "What is their meaning?"

"The first Lord means I am the merciful God *before* a man commits a sin, and the second Lord means I am the same merciful God *after* man has sinned. If change is to occur it must be in the heart of the sinner, not in God.

"God of *Rahum*, the all-mighty lord of the Universe, full of loving sympathy for the failings and miseries of human frailty;

V'hanun – God is gracious, for once man has made his choice, God will console the afflicted and raise the oppressed. Do not put your faith in man, for his compassion is temporary, only God's is permanent.

Erech apayim – God is slow to anger, hesitant to punish the sinner, giving him the opportunity to change his ways.

Rav hesed – God's mercy goes well beyond what man deserves.

Ve'emet – And truth. God speaks the truth, but always in love.

Noseh hesed la'alafim. God's mercy extends to the thousandth generation, rewarding the good deeds of our forefathers to their infinite descendants.

Noseh avon, va'fesha, v'chata'ah – God understands man's weaknesses and through belief in Him one's sins can be forgiven and the soul returned to its original purity."

Keith looked out at his audience, as if understanding their thoughts.

"You ask how can Milton believe that a God who is all merciful can allow such destruction on His earth? The answer lies in Milton's overarching belief that God placed man on this earth along with certain natural laws, most significant of which is man's freedom of will, and God's power cannot, or will not, interfere with such laws. There are no exceptions. Earthquakes, tornadoes, volcanoes, floods – they must all occur as programmed, regardless of the consequences. And what of the soldier returning from war who shoots innocent civilians because he has the need to kill? Milton answers that God cannot interfere. Free will, the ability to choose between good and evil, must remain supreme. It is the same free will that Adam and Eve had when they ate from the Tree of Knowledge of Good and Evil. Does not Milton write in Book 5, lines 234 to 237, that Adam controls his own behavior?

"Milton realized that God's goodness cannot and must not destroy His justice. The unrepentant must suffer the consequences of their misdeeds. Mercy without Law is anarchy. As he writes:

> *Self-tempted, self-deprav'd: Man falls deceiv'd*
> *By the other first: Man therefore shall find grace,*
> *The other none: in Mercy and Justice both,*
> *Through Hea"n and Earth, so shall my glorie excel,*
> *But Mercy first and last shall brightest shine."*

Keith checked his watch. He was tired and a weakness overcame him. He drank from the bottle of spring water on the podium.

"I'm afraid I've kept you too long this evening. Perhaps we have time for a question or two."

A young man seated in the middle of the hall stood up and a hand microphone was brought to him.

"Dr. Jessup. Thank you so much for your presentation. I'm a first-year graduate student in Milton studies here at Harvard. You just quoted *Paradise Lost*, which I believe came from Book 3, line 130: *But Mercy first and last shall brightest shine*. If it's true that Milton finds the secret of God's Ways to be in the God of Mercy in the Old Testament, why were Adam and Eve forced to leave Paradise?"

Keith nodded approvingly.

"In other words, what you are asking is if the Old Testament teaches that God is so merciful, where is the mercy? That is, to go from a life of being served in Paradise to a life of service – is that mercy? That's an excellent question Mr. . . . I'm sorry, I didn't get your name?"

"Richard, Richard Sundstrom."

It came at him like a bolt of lightning. *Was this possible?* He looked carefully at the young man. He was short and slightly portly, but wore the most amiable smile.

"Any relationship to Professor Foster Sundstrom?"

"Foster Sundstrom is my father."

It took a moment for Keith to gather himself.

"Richard, let me answer you this way. I see you are using a Mac to take notes. Notice the logo that Steve Jobs created to identify his company – an apple. Where did that apple came from? From some tree in some ordinary apple orchard? Perhaps that's what Jobs may have told others, but I'd rather believe that he picked that apple from Milton's Garden in Paradise. And what of the apple? Surely it is not a whole apple; on the contrary, he took a bite out of it. Now why would Jobs select for his logo an apple with a bite in it? To make it appetizing? I don't think so. Rather, Jobs understood what Milton understood, that only through questioning the norm, that only by rising above the accepted, yes, by only challenging God himself, could man master the unknown. And how did Steve Jobs challenge God? By transgressing the only law that God gave to Adam and Eve – by taking a bite from the fruit of His forbidden Tree and becoming free to choose. In other words, Steve Jobs, like our first parents, understood that only by going beyond limitations can you create a new world.

"Milton's Manuscript teaches us that mercy does not mean avoiding the law. The law must be upheld, what else binds society? But if, as Moses and Milton say, God's ways are merciful then perhaps we must shift paradigms to find that mercy. What if God's mercy was for man to leave the Garden? The great rabbis teach that creation was never completed; rather, God challenged man to find the means to complete it. That, Richard, is God's mercy. What seems like punishment was truly a blessing. That is why Milton ends the poem as he does, with the Archangel Michael walking Adam and Eve out of Paradise. As Milton wrote:

> *Some natural tears they dropped, but wiped them soon,*
> *The world was all before them, where to choose*
> *Their place of ret, and Providence their guide.*
> *They, hand in hand, with wandering steps and slow,*
> *Through Eden took their solitary way.*

"That is how Paradise Lost so clearly, so triumphantly, justifies God's way – for Milton's God trumpets his call from the highest mountains: 'I offer you the world – now go out and make something of it!'"

*

As the audience rose in tribute, Keith extended his hands in thanks. His eyes drifted to a group standing together in the rear of the room: Joanne, Jeff, Kate, DeLordet, Rabbis Lecht and Shenken, Steve Reich, and Mr. Cuttermill. He took a step back, clasped his hands again and walked hesitantly to a chair. He was exhausted. The loss of blood and the physical and mental stress in delivering the lecture used up the last of his energy. Jeff made his way to the stage, and saw the pallor of the skin and the weakness in his gait and rushed to help. "Let's get him to a hospital."

"Jeff, the wooden box."

Jeff looked at Keith and smiled. "I'll keep it safe for you."

Two emergency medical personnel helped Keith onto a stretcher and escorted him through the rear entrance of the hall. As they moved toward the waiting ambulance, Keith looked up into the evening sky, the bright stars phasing in and out of focus. Joanne was waiting as he went by. He heard his name, "Keith!" It had been a long time. He tried to move his head toward the sound of her voice, tears filling his eyes. She walked along at his side and knelt down, kissed his cheek, and whispered into his ear. The ambulance doors closed and Keith drifted into a deep sleep – after Forgiveness . . . Paradise regained.

THE END

AUTHOR'S NOTE

Milton's relationship to Judaism and the Hebraic tradition has interested literary critics over the centuries. Though some sources are objective in their opinions, many are affected by author bias against Jews. Most recently, three books whose authors have credentials in both English Literature and Rabbinic writings have delved into the relationship of Milton and the Jews. Jason Rosenblatt's *Torah and Law in Paradise Lost* (1994) discusses Milton's depth of knowledge of Jewish divorce laws as taken from Deuteronomy in the Five Books of Moses. Golda Werman, in *Milton and Midrash* (1995) discusses the possible relationship between *Paradise Lost* and Milton's use of Midrashic sources, offering a line-by-line comparison between the poem and one particular rabbinic source. Professor Jeffrey Shoulson's brilliant analysis in *Milton and the Rabbis* (2001) discusses possible reasons for critical efforts to identify Milton's reliance on Hebraic and Jewish sources. It was Shoulson who argued, through his knowledge of both Rabbinic and English Literature, that without a "smoking gun" that can directly link Milton's writings to Hebraic sources, no such confirmation could be concluded.

The Milton Manuscript, in novel form, provides that "smoking gun." Based largely on Milton's *De Doctrina Christiana*, we follow Milton's own beliefs, his search for a basic Christianity, void of church hierarchy, and the poet's individual interpretation of the Bible from the original source – in Hebrew. Whether it be his views on marriage and divorce, the defense of regicide, the rejection of the Trinity, and multiple other criticisms of Church doctrine, Milton's belief in God turns to the origins of Christianity itself, origins that closely bridge the transition between Judaism and its offspring.

This book is based on historical fact and evidence as I have determined. The conclusions drawn are mine alone. Only Milton's Manuscript remains in need of final confirmation.

*

ACKNOWLEDGEMENTS

There are a number of people to thank for making this work possible. In terms of scholarship, I must thank JEFFREY SHOULSON, Chair of Judaic Studies and Professor of English at the University of Connecticut, and GORDON CAMPBELL, Professor of Renaissance Studies at the University of Leicester, for their insights. I also wish to thank DAVID REDDEN, Worldwide Chairman of Books & Manuscripts at Sotheby's, who gave freely of his time discussing the world of art. I thank SUSAN KAUFMAN for reading the early drafts.

SCHOLARLY BIOGRAPHIES
OF JOHN MILTON

Barbara K. Lewalski. *The Life of John Milton: A Critical Biography*, 2002.

Gordon Campbell, Thomas N. Corns. *John Milton: Life, Work, and Thought*, 2008.

THE MYSTERY OF THE MILTON MANUSCRIPT *by* BARRY M. LIBIN

A Guide for Reading Groups

OUTLINE FOR STUDY AND DISCUSSION

A. English History 1500–1700, and Its Relationship to John Milton and *Paradise Lost*
    - The influence of Luther and Calvin, and the Protestant Reformation
    - The relationship between Henry VIII, the Catholic Church, and Anglicanism
    - The relationship of Cromwell and the Puritan Revolution
    - Regicide: Charles I, Charles II, and The Restoration
    - Roger Williams, Menasseh Ben Israel, and their role in Jewish and English History

B. The Life of John Milton
    - His relationship to Catholicism, Anglicanism, Puritanism, and Church Dogma
    - His belief in the Trinity, Marriage, and St. Paul
    - Milton's interpretation of Christianity and his relationship to Hebraic and Jewish thought
    - The influence of his blindness, his imprisonment, and being on the death list in relation to his poem(s)
    - His relationship with Edward Prynne

C. The Poem *Paradise Lost*
    - The role of God, His Son, Satan, and Adam and Eve
    - The political and social influences of *Paradise Lost*